The Virtual Life
of
Fizzy Oceans

DAVID A. ROSS

Published by Open Books 2012

Cover image "Ocean Size" Copyright © Jay Johnson
To learn more about the artist, visit
http://onetaintedangel.deviantart.com or
http://jay2designs.darkfolio.com

ISBN: 0615686060
ISBN-13: 978-0615686066

DEDICATION

This book is dedicated to Kelly, who encourages me each and every day to be the best person I can be, then gives me the space to try.

CONTENTS

PART I
WELCOME TO VIRTUAL LIFE

1
JUST IN CASE ANYONE OUT THERE IS LISTENING

HI! MY NAME IS FIZZY OCEANS—at least that's my emulation's name here in VL (Virtual Life). I'm an official VL greeter. Let me offer you this welcome package. I'll just place it in your cache, where you can read it later, at your convenience.

"Where am I?"

"Ah! I see you don't have an emulation yet. Or a name…"

"What's an emulation? Am I going to need one?"

"Oh, yes, my friend. You certainly are going to need one."

Look! I became a citizen in Virtual Life about a year ago, and these days I spend most of my time here. The first time I logged on to VL, I was like you: uncertain, disoriented, and skeptical. I thought it was very strange here, but really fascinating, too. All these caricatures with strange names walking around in animated environments. I thought to myself: "What a bizarre game!"

But VL is not a game at all, that's the really interesting

thing about it. In some ways it's exactly like Physical Life, but in other ways it's totally different. If you like, I'll show you what I mean.

Of course anybody can log on to Virtual Life. And it's free to register, too. There are already millions of people in VL. They live in every country in the world: America (like me), Canada, Australia, and South Africa. I've met lots of people who live in Europe, and I have VL friends who live in Columbia and Japan and Israel and China! I even know one guy who says he lives in the remote mountains of Greenland! His emulation is called Igloo Iceman, and he tells everybody he meets in VL about how it's getting warmer than it used to be above the Arctic Circle, and about how these days he sunbathes beside a lake that used to be a glacier. But I'm getting ahead of myself, so let's transfer to the Hothouse (Orientation Center) and I'll show you what my life here in VL is all about.

Whoosh…

Once you've registered, the first thing you'll have to do is to create an EM (emulation). An EM is a digital representation of you—a body, so to speak—so you can walk around and interact with other seedlings (Virtual Lifers). You might construct your EM to look similar to the way you appear in Physical Life, but you don't have to. You can make your EM look any way you want it to look. You can be male or female, young or old, white or black or somewhere in between. You can have long hair, short hair, or no hair at all. You can have a tattoo. You can change your eye color every day if you want to. And you can dress very creatively in VL, because most of the rules and regulations in PL don't exist in Virtual Life. (PL stands for 'Physical Life', which used to be called RL, or 'Real Life', until those of us in VL came to the realization that there was actually nothing any more real about what we have come to call 'real life' than other dimensions in which we exist, such as 'Virtual Life', where we are now, and NL, or 'Natural Life'—not to mention FL, 'Future Life'.) Here in

VL we're not defined or bound by our limitations, physical or otherwise, and we're not prisoners of our expectations, or the expectations of others. In Virtual Life we can even fly!

One thing that is the same in VL as it is in Physical Life is that we have money. It's not dollars or euros or yen. In VL the money is called greenshoots. The consortium that created Virtual Life, Seedbed Studios, named the currency. But that's not important right now. What's important is that we create your emulation so you'll look good when you go out to meet people. Let me give you a thousand greenshoots to get you started here in VL. Don't worry; it's okay. Here lots of people give stuff away.

So, what are you going to call yourself? Or more specifically, what are you going to call your EM? Right from the start it's easy to confuse VL with Physical Life, I know. But you'll get used to that. After a while, you'll barely notice which world you're in. Which is more or less the point, isn't it? Because in VL there are no rules concerning names, and the possibilities are endless. Here you can be the person you've always wanted to be, the one you always knew you were! Are you male or female? Are you light or dark? Are you kind and helpful, or mean-spirited and sarcastic? We'll find out about that in good time, but for now, what will your VL name be?

Ah! Kizmet Aurora. What a splendid name! An EM is born.

Now, what about your gender: male, female, or somewhere in between? In Virtual Life it won't really matter. Here we're dealing with something more elemental. Emulations are only symbolic representations to give us a point of reference. In Virtual Life, everything is symbolic: the cities and villages, the landscapes and buildings, the weather, the clothes, the food… None of it is real, at least not in the PL sense. Yet, in another sense, it is even more real than PL. Anyway, you should fashion your EM however you choose—your skin, your hair, your make-up.

Construct a man's body or a woman's body. Or a eunuch's, I don't care! Here in Virtual Life, I know an eleven-year-old kid (or a displaced American nun) who lives in Bolivia (or Brazil) and who walks around VL in the body of a hundred-year-old man. His EM's name is Omar Paquero. What kind of craziness is that, Kiz?

Virtual Life is a big place. It has hundreds of smaller communities within the greater Virtual Life system, and it would not be possible to visit every VL community, let alone every establishment. In that sense it's like Physical Life, you have to pick and choose. We connect with others and form relationships as a result of common interests, or through other friends we meet; but just as it is in Physical Life, whom one meets in VL is at least in part a matter of chance. Just as I do in PL, I have a core group of friends here in VL. I have my favorite places too, who doesn't? I spend most of my time while logged on to VL at a place called Lit-A-Rama. I first decided to explore the REP (Replica) because in Physical Life I'm a voracious reader. What I found there was a community of VL literati. The first EM I met there was Crystal Marbella, and because we had common literary interests, Crystal and I became friends. Together we rented a VL shop that we now call Open Books. We publish classic literature (books no longer protected by copyright and now in public domain) on the worldwide web—books like *Pride and Prejudice* and *Moby Dick* and *Lady Chatterley's Lover*, as well as many others—and we offer them free of charge to anyone who wants to read them. By republishing these books on the Internet, Crystal and I feel that we are doing something to preserve literature at a time when other media—media that is perhaps more glamorous or more compelling in the twenty-first century—threaten to obscure such timeless tales in favor of what? Stories that are devoid of any symbolic value whatsoever? Linear legends in living color whose messages are decidedly black and white? Redundant presentations devoid of metaphor that numb the mind into a smug and self-satisfied complacency so enveloping and so insidious that human behavior begins to mimic such mundane stories? I think you can see, Kiz, why Virtual Life had to be created. The culture cried out for it—not in its everyday voice, but in the voice that once moved shadow over the Face of the Deep. Which goddess was it, anyway, that first created Natural Life? Ki? Gaia? Moria? Caillech? I'm sure I'll have much more to say about that, about NL, a bit later, but what I'm saying here is that the same creative force that made the world we have always known has also created Virtual Life. Of course the reasons are complex and the implications profound. That's what we're here to experience, Kiz. But first we have to create your EM. So I want you to right click your mouse, that's it! Don't be timid. Open your menu. It's time to begin your Virtual Life.

It is certainly true that appearance isn't everything, Kiz, but it is one way we express our overall identity, isn't it? That's true in Physical Life, and it's true in Virtual Life too. That's why most people in Virtual Life make an effort to customize the appearance of their EM. When you registered for Virtual Life, Kiz, you got a starter package: various skin tones, hairstyles, and a basic outfit to clothe yourself. But your kit contains only the essentials—not because the Seedbeds are stingy, but because they understand that you must create your emulation from elements that you discover as you move through the various Virtual Life communities. Not only do they understand that it would be utterly impossible for them to create and oversee the entirety of Virtual Life, they understand that it is far better if we, the citizens, create the world in which we wish to live and function. What a concept! Just like Physical Life, Virtual Life is a multi-tiered reflection of mass consciousness. Except here in VL the boundaries are far less constricting than we might find them to be in Physical Life. In VL, for example, there is no pre-determined class structure. In VL, there is no racism or sanctioned religion. There is no gender distinction. In VL, there is no gravity—nothing to hold you down, so to speak. In effect, Kiz, Virtual Life is a fresh start, a place where each of us is free to become the embodiment of his fundamental persona, his higher self, without fear, or reticence, or skepticism, or expectations to conform. We are, after all, only VL emulations, representations of that which Nature made us over the eons. Through our emulations we have the opportunity to express our diversity in ways that have now become stifled in Physical Life. That's why your appearance is an important part of your Virtual Life, Kiz. So let's go shopping for all the essentials—a virtual makeover for your vessel in Virtual Life!

"So, where would you like to shop?"

"Shop? I don't know what you mean, Fizzy. What's possible?"

"Just about anything is possible in Virtual Life. You can go 'virtually' anywhere. You don't need a plane ticket."

"I've always wanted to shop for clothes in a French boutique."

"Now you're talking, Kiz! I know just the place."

"Where are we going, Fizzy?"

"The Côte d'azur!"

Of course our emulations can walk from place to place once we arrive at a major location within the VL complex, but to move between locations, 'transferring' is the only way to travel. Transferring is a lot like the old Star Trek TV series, where the transporter machine decomposes bodies into atoms and then reassembles them at a desired location. Everybody remembers 'Beam me up, Scotty!' Except here in Virtual Life we don't need a machine (except our computers, of course). We can transfer from location to location at will. One click and we're at our desired location. A simple search for clothing boutiques shows us many possibilities, including Riviera West, where we will find all the latest fashions from top French designers, and at a fraction of the price we would pay in PL. A thousand greenshoots is enough to buy an outfit that is *tres chic* and fits your figure perfectly. We simply click and wait to arrive at Blue Fellini or Chalet Madame Sophie.

"But I'm afraid of flying, Fizzy!"

"Have no fear, Kiz; transferring is without sensation."

Whoosh!

"We're arriving now. Are you ready to shop?"

"Everything looks blurry on my screen, Fizzy."

"That's because you're still rezzing."

"What's rezzing?"

"The images are still loading. You are waiting for resolution."

"There's a unique language here in VL, I think."

"A few terms relevant to Virtual Life and to computer technology. Nothing you won't master quickly. Are you rezzed yet?"

"Yes, I think so. What now?"

"Take a look around? Where would you like to shop?"

"Maybe you could show me around; you've obviously been here before."

"I'd be happy to, Kiz. Let's visit my friend Monique Maçonnerie at Le Petit Chardonneret."

I know all this must seem strange at first, even a bit shocking. I mean, where else might you be walking down a boulevard and look up to see a man with the head of a cat pass by as if nothing is wrong, as if nothing is out of place? Well, here in Virtual Life nothing *is* wrong, and nothing is out of place. What we encounter here is the result of free expression combined with the facility to implement one's particular vision—immediately! Right now we're headed for the quay along the beach. *La plage*, as the French call it. That's where all the best boutiques are located.

"Fizzy, those emulations lying on the sand are naked!"

"One might choose to be naked in VL, Kiz. It's not a

crime."

"But why are they just lying on the beach? The water is not real. Nor is the sunshine. It's not as if an EM can go for a swim, or get a tan."

"By lying on the beach, they are earning greenshoots."

"Are you telling me that in VL you can earn money by lying on the beach, Fizzy?"

"Essentially, yes."

"What a world!"

"Well, we make it what it is, Kiz."

Here is Le Petit Chardonneret. Shall we go inside? Why not? Well, it looks as if Monique is not here now, but that doesn't matter. Here in VL the shops are open 24/7. And as you can see, Kiz, the clothes are extraordinary. Look at this dress… And that top… Those shoes are to die for!

"Fizzy, these clothes aren't real. They're digital creations. Clipart!"

"That's more or less correct, Kiz."

"But why would I pay money to buy clothing that isn't real?"

"Kiz, do you want your EM walking around stark naked in Virtual Life?"

"Well, I suppose not."

"Then get into the spirit of this thing. C'mon, buy yourself a new outfit. After all, I'm paying this time."

Once you've purchased your new clothes, they will be placed in your personal cache. That's where everything you acquire here in Virtual Life goes until you are ready to use it. If you're too shy to change clothes here at Le Petit Chardonneret, then you can wait until we go back to Lit-A-Rama and change on the second floor at Open Books. There you can have a bit of privacy and do your girl thing in the mirror.

Now, let's see about getting you a better hairstyle. Standard issue hair is enough to cover your head, but as you can see from many of the emulations walking past us, there are far more stylish samples available. The hair you have now is static. The style really doesn't become you at all, Kiz. I think what you need is a flexi-tress, like mine! It moves naturally when I move. See?

"And what about your complexion? What is your skin color in PL?"

"I'm red. I live in the desert."

"Then you shall have reddish skin in your Virtual Life. What about your eyes? What color are they in PL?"

"I have brown eyes. But I've always wished I had big violet eyes, like Elizabeth Taylor."

"Liz Taylor eyes for you, Kiz. No problem! I know just where to acquire them."

"This kind of shopping can be fun, Fizzy."

"Just part of your Virtual Life, Kiz. Are you ready to transfer out of Côte d'azur?"

"Whatever you say, Fizzy. Today, you're my guide."

"Then type 'Open Books' into your destination bar and click 'transfer'."

Whoosh…

"This is so much fun, Fizzy!"

"We're arriving now, Kiz. And it seems that we're in luck, because Crystal is here. You must meet Crystal."

In front of the Open Books shop Crystal Marbella is fixing a new poster in the front window—one that announces the publication of *The Prophet* by Kahlil Gibran. "Hello, Fizzy," she says. "Who is your friend?"

"Crystal, this is Kizmet Aurora. I greeted her as she dropped into VL for the first time. I've been showing her around a bit. We went shopping on the Côte d'azur for a new outfit, all the essentials."

"Hi, Kiz. I'm Crystal Marbella."

"Happy to meet you, Crystal."

"Are you having a good time here in VL?"

"I think so… But it's all so new, and *so* confusing."

"You'll grow accustomed to Virtual Life very quickly, you'll see."

"The people here are very friendly."

:) Crystal types.

"And generous, too! Fizzy Oceans gave me a thousand greenshoots to spend on my EM. I can't help but like a place where people give you money to buy clothes."

:) I type. Then, "Remember, Kiz, the clothes are just clipart."

"Oh, I almost forgot."

"Yes, that's the point, isn't it?" Crystal laughs.

"So, if neither of you minds, I think I'll go to the second floor to get changed. I have only one question: How do I get to the second floor? There doesn't seem to be a staircase."

:) I type. "Click the arrow on the wall, Kiz. Then click 'transfer'. Nothing to it!"

Whoosh...

Crystal Marbella is my best friend here in Virtual Life. Besides the fact that her EM is really pretty, Crystal is a beautiful person from the inside out. She is always kind and helpful, never cross or sarcastic or disrespectful. She's also incredibly resourceful: when something needs to be done inside the shop, and neither of us understands how to accomplish the task, Crystal is always the one to take the initiative to learn new technical skills and apply them creatively.

In PL, Crystal wrote a novel entitled, *Alone In A Crowd*, which to me seems ironic considering the context in which we now meet and interact. If you think about it, here we sit, each in his PL sanctuary, laptop or desktop switched on and wired for ADSL, buzzing back and forth and in and out at more than a megabyte per second, logged on to a site where we recreate not only the sum of our personalities and respective cultures, but also the dreams and aspirations and visions that as a civilization we've never been able to materialize in PL. I often have to consciously remember or visualize our PL bodies as we click and type, as we drag our cursors over one prompt or another to engage in virtual movements or expressions. I know well the smile of Crystal's EM, but I know not the warmth of her cheek, or the sweetness of her breath. As much as Virtual Life offers that Physical Life does not, still there is a gap in sensuality that cannot be denied. Can our emulations actually experience the sensation of longing? Or is that kind of perception reserved for Physical Life? Or for Natural Life? There's a real difference, you know. Natural Life is what existed on the day after Creation; Physical Life is the mess that we humans have made of it during the ensuing hundred million years or so (mostly in the last hundred and fifty, more or less). But Crystal doesn't talk about this sort of thing, because she's too busy recreating the world's great books. I do my share of the work in the Open Books shop too, but the real passion for the preservation of literature comes from Crystal; there's no doubt about that.

> PROFILE: Crystal Marbella
> NAME: Sonja Jörgensen
> GENDER: Female
> LOCATION: Copenhagen
> COUNTRY: Denmark
> E-MAIL: sonjorg@Tivoli.com
> AGE: 31

INTERESTS: Books, books, books!!! Writing, reading, novels, poetry, art, music; picnics, animals, media; politics, current events, mythology, theosophy; hiking, cycling, cooking.

VIRTUAL LIFE GROUPS: Resident and shop owner in Lit-A-Rama; Dirty Nellie's Pub; Virtual Broadcast Venue; Lit-A-Rama Events & Discussion Forum; Publishers, Printers & Booksellers; INKies; Writer's Pen Café; VL Book Fair; VL Chamber of Commerce; VL Girl Magazine.

It's true that we must conduct commerce here in Virtual Life using the currency issued by the creators at Seedbed Studios; and in fact there is a bar graph accessible right on the site denoting the trading value, month by month, of the greenshoot against the American dollar. Each month the greenshoot seems to gain in value against the dollar, as does virtually every other First World currency. The irony, I suppose, is that Virtual Life is a web site in cyberspace, not a country in the physical world. Nevertheless, the greenshoot is taking its place as a unit of trade, so it should perhaps also come as no surprise that BloomEx (where the VL banks and the VL stock exchange are located) is the place on the Virtual Life site that receives the greatest number of visitors. I've been there myself, though I must say that I'm not particularly impressed by what goes on there. Greed is still greed, whether it is manifest in Physical Life or in Virtual Life. The traders and the changers barter virtual commodities back and forth like Monopoly money, even as many of us here in Virtual Life think we understand a more elemental principle: that the real currency here in VL is the currency of ideas. Money, even in Virtual Life, is still only money, and it might well be argued—as it is by some who interact here in VL—that it is the very system through which PL has reached the crisis point at which it now finds itself. Crystal understands this point. So do I. And so do many, many others. Only the most original ideas actually have substance; the value attached to commodities (real or symbolic) and to ad hoc services is actually a false denomination where real value is continually diminished, not enhanced.

Because Crystal and I believe so strongly in the commerce of ideas rather than the commerce of money, all the books we publish at Open Books are available to anyone who wishes to read them free of charge. Instead of fixing a price for each book, we solicit funds from patrons who, like ourselves, appreciate the literature of the Ages and wish to see it preserved and promoted. Each potential patron is encouraged to *adopt-a-book* by giving a monetary contribution, which we then distribute to literacy funds, or through our Dead Writers Grant to living, working authors whose work merits support and who might need a helping hand to continue their pursuits. This is our unique way of allowing writers who have gone before to help those now struggling to continue the literary tradition that they so loved and embraced. We keep only enough money to maintain the Open Books shop here in VL.

"Where is Kizmet Aurora in PL?" Crystal asks.

"I haven't asked yet," I tell her. "Perhaps we can help her to fill out her profile when she comes down dressed to the tens."

"Good idea," says Crystal. "Anything new with the shop?"

"The donations vessel is full of greenshoots again."

:) types Crystal.

> PROFILE: Kizmet Aurora
> NAME: Cassandra Stephens
> GENDER: Female
> LOCATION: Rough Rock, Arizona
> COUNTRY: USA
> E-MAIL: cassie@youknow.com
> AGE: 44
>
> INTERESTS: Native Americans, Native American ceremonies, the environment, Burning Man, exotic travel, parapsychology, L. Ron Hubbard and Scientology, Quantum Physics, advanced mathematics, Blackjack, Las Vegas, Ted Nugent, llamas.

Of course it's easy enough to become overly involved with the props here in VL. Besides clothing and other personal items, shops sell everything from helicopters to fine art (I absolutely love Mick Monahan's Fractal Faces Gallery) to virtual vacations. One of the places Crystal and I like to go is Dirty Nellie's Pub (the PL version was originally located in Dublin and its auspicious PL offspring is located in Palatine, Illinois, a suburb of Chicago). Of course you can't actually have a drink there, but the clientele is diverse and friendly, so it's a terrific place to make new friends and to network for Open Books. Outside the pub is a large patio where concerts and other events are held. (If you're wondering whether musicians can actually play live concerts in Virtual Life, you bet they can!) The EMs enact the physical part of playing an instrument or singing into a mic as the music is streamed onto the web site for all to hear and enjoy. Meanwhile, many of the EMs love to dance to the music (yes, it's possible to program complex dance steps and movements into your emulation's gesture bank), while others simply chill out with a virtual pint and some virtual nacho chips and engage in conversation. The crowd at Dirty Nellie's for such events is usually huge, and Crystal likes to tell the story of the time when she was still quite new to Virtual Life and was invited to a concert at Dirty Nellie's by the pub's owners, Katydid Nothing and Applesauce MacNamera. Crystal was happy about the invitation and was really looking forward to the event, but when she tried to transfer to the pub, she found it to be so crowded that she was unable to successfully land (remember we're flying here in VL), and was instead stranded in mid-air somewhere above the pub, where she was finally rescued by Nasus Drummond in a daring and clever, highly synchronized fly-by maneuver.

Whoosh!

It was at that concert that Crystal first learned to dance in Virtual Life, not to mention honing her flying skills to a new acumen.

My VL function as a greeter allows me to meet many new people as they first log on to Virtual Life. I can't help but enjoy the wonder of each new arrival as he tries to gain his bearings in this new terrain. As I help new initiates through the process of creating an emulation and a profile and learning how to navigate, I get a sense of satisfaction because I can't help feeling the community is enhanced as each new consciousness becomes integrated. In fact, I might even go so far as to say that Virtual Life has given me a new perspective on the idea of community. After all, in PL one lives a more or less insular life, because that has become the pervasive condition there. In PL, I live in an apartment building with more than one hundred apartments. How many people do I know who live in the building? A sum total of five, and that's pathetic, if you think about it. Here in Virtual Life I know so many people. And they're not just from my hometown of Seattle, or from some particular group at work, or at school, or church, or some other social construction. The sad truth is that most of those PL social constructions have already disintegrated, or at least they are well into the process of disintegration. In VL, however, the process of forming groups is only getting started. Each day, it seems, I become aware of a new group with a new agenda. Most are open for anyone to join. This is why there is such a strong sense of community in VL. And it's also why this virtual society is in a state of constant expansion rather than a state of continual contraction and eventual disintegration. VL is a really happy place!

"Fizzy!" Kiz calls out in near desperation.

"How are the clothes? Are we ever going to see your new look, Kiz?"

"It's all quite stunning, but I can't seem to get back to street level. I seem to be stuck inside the wall of your shop!"

"No worries, Kiz. It's easy to get lost within the grid when you're not experienced. Two or three key strokes and I'll have you back on solid ground."

"I'm not sure I'll ever be on solid ground again, Fizzy."

:) types Crystal Marbella.

PROFILE: Fizzy Oceans
NAME: Amy Birkenstock
GENDER: Female
LOCATION: Seattle, Washington
COUNTRY: USA
E-MAIL: seabubbles@walawala.com
AGE: 37

INTERESTS: Painting, Post Impressionist art, Vincent Van Gogh, cooking, the Internet, reading, learning Japanese, carpentry, cartoons, music festivals, dancing and yoga and working out, desserts.

VIRTUAL LIFE GROUPS: Resident of Lit-A-Rama, VL Greeter and co-owner of Open Books; Lit-A-Rama Events & Discussion Forum; VL Publishers, Printers & Booksellers; VL Book Fair; VL Chamber of Commerce, VL Greeters.

Now, before I make everyone cross-eyed (or just plain cross) reading this admittedly self-indulgent and probably somewhat obnoxious manifesto, and before I log off and shut down my computer (for a few hours anyway), I want to tell you a few more important things about myself in PL. As you can see in my Virtual Life profile, I'm thirty-seven years old. I'm single: that is, I live alone. I was married; now I'm divorced. I got married midway through my senior year in high school (which of course means that I dropped out) to the only guy who'd ever paid me any attention. We were actually pretty good together. We ever so bravely decided to move from Independence, Missouri to Seattle during the whole Grunge thing, and life was pretty interesting during the late eighties and early nineties. When we split up after six years together, I saw no reason to go back to Missouri, so I stayed in Seattle. It's my home now, and I like it here—at least most of the time. I have a job doing billing for a medical clinic. The work is boring, but the people I work with are nice. We have fun during the day, and sometimes we go out for drinks after work. My co-workers think that the time I spend in VL is silly. I tried to get a couple of them involved, but they weren't very interested. Deb, who is thirty-eight with two young kids, thought VL was scary; and Karen, who is fifty-something, thought it was just plain weird, and that it wasn't real anyway. Neither saw the point of spending time in an alternative universe. "The real world has all the challenges I can stand at the moment," Deb said. "Why would I want to walk around as a cartoon in a cartoon world talking to other cartoons and paying good money for clothes that I can't even wear?" Karen wanted to know.

Whoosh!

I must say that my Virtual Life is a lot more interesting than my life in PL. Not that it would necessarily have to be that way… Or that it should be that way… But the truth is that there's really nothing particularly inspiring about working all day long in an office without windows filling out insurance forms and updating statements. In VL, I have the Open Books Project. And I also have friends like Crystal who understand, as I do, that just because you can touch something, or because you can taste it, or smell it, or because you can measure it, that it is not necessarily more real than an idea. I maintain that ideas are the most real things that we humans have (that is, if you can actually possess an idea). As far as I can tell, the universe is made up of them—I mean ideas—and all the props that we think are real are actually nothing more than symbols of the primary concepts. Some people, it seems, just can't grasp that idea, but Virtual Life has taught me that we manifest our visions into the symbols we manipulate in our daily lives by using what we have come to call our *will*.

This may sound complicated, or beside the point in our everyday lives, but it's not; it's actually the only thing that really matters, the only true reference point we have as we tumble through space and time.

So that's it, Kizmet! That's my VL greeting to you. I hope you like it here. I hope you manage to make a place for yourself. I hope you meet all sorts of interesting people, and I hope you see places you never imagined might exist. Because that's really what VL is all about, Kiz—*possibilities*.

2
WARMING TO NEW REALITIES

EVERY TIME I encounter Igloo Iceman in VL the appearance of his emulation shocks me. Why? Because he's head and shoulders taller than anyone else I've ever encountered. He's a bona fide Viking, if I ever saw one. His yellow hair is long and unkempt, his beard is woolly, and his moustache nearly covers his lips. His physique ripples with muscles, like a caveman or a wrestler, his feet and hands are gargantuan, and the glazed over look in his eyes would surely send Bigfoot running in the opposite direction. Not many seedlings take the time to get to know Igloo, but being a VL greeter, I met him the same day he dropped into Virtual Life. Igloo offered me friendship, which I accepted, and during the past year we've had some very informative chats (I'd never met anyone from Greenland before). From Igloo Iceman I have learned many things I did not previously know about NL (Natural Life). So every time I see Igloo's imposing figure sitting at an outdoor table on the patio at Dirty Nellie's Pub, I ask immediately if I might join him, and his EM always motions for me to take a seat.

"What's up, Iggy?"

"I've dropped in to promote an event," he tells me.

"You don't say? What event?"

"A lecture on global warming. The immanent scientist and researcher, Dr. Conrad Adler is the featured speaker, and Jack Straw Huckleberry from NPR is the host."

"Cool, Igloo!"

"We'll see," he says a little skeptically. "It might be nothing but a big snow job."

"Very funny, Iceman."

"From where I sit in PL, Fizzy, there's nothing funny about it."

Igloo Iceman lives in the Tsiarngagai Mountains in Greenland. For as long as anyone there can remember, he's told me, glaciers have covered the peaks of those mountains, but not anymore. The temperature is warming. The ice is melting. Lakes are forming in the gorges. As we speak here in Virtual Life, Igloo Iceman is lying on a lounge chair in PL, a tequila sunrise at arm's length, dressed down to his BVDs and getting the tan of his life!

"I guess Kyoto came a bit too late for Greenland," I comment.

"Kyoto-schmoto! I'm building myself a boat," says Iggy.

"A modern-day Noah and his Ark?"

"Minus the animals this time."

"Where and when is the discussion to take place?" I ask.

"Tonight at 8:00 VLT," he tells me, "at the Virtual Broadcast Venue."

"I think I'll come and bring a couple of friends. Thanks for the tip, Iceman."

"Stay cool, Fizzy."

Whether or not Igloo Iceman is portraying his PL situation literally (not to mention honestly, as it has been rumored from time to time that Igloo Iceman is really Dr. Conrad Adler, a climate researcher from the University of

Colorado who has spent considerable time during the past twenty-five years in Greenland studying the receding glaciers) is quite beside the point. What matters is that he is a self-proclaimed sentry sitting at the top of the earth tracking climate changes that might well mean the end of not only Physical Life, but also Natural Life, as we now know it. Even in light of the environmental catastrophe that Iggy's message augers (Greenland is losing one hundred billion tons of ice per year), he manages somehow to keep his sense of humor, as well as a balanced perspective. As long as I've known him, Iggy has never been one to cast blame, nor is he one to delegate responsibility for intervention. Maybe he's not particularly interested in whether or not the polar icecaps melt into the ocean, or whether water levels rise and take out large coastal cities like Kuala Lampur, Bangkok, Istanbul and New Orleans. Maybe Igloo Iceman simply embraces a more evolutionary perspective. He's obviously accustomed to living a solitary existence, so what's it to him if humanity goes the way of the dinosaur? Meanwhile, he's enjoying mini Miami North—at least for as long as it lasts. Greenland's newly made mountain reservoirs must be stunning indeed on the evening of the summer solstice. And then there's Iggy, prone on his lakeside lounge chair with his laptop open and logged on to the Internet via satellite… Iggy, watching the eternal orange sun never rising and never setting, always at eye level, burning away the ice day by day and whispering the future in his ear: "It was *ice* while it lasted, Igloo, but time is up. Get ready for the Flood!"

Which is why I suppose Iggy is building a boat. I have a vision of his half-made Ark balanced precariously upon the pinnacle of one of southeast Greenland's more prestigious peaks, poised in anticipation of the gorge below filling with water to launch it on its voyage of preservation. Or maybe it won't happen that way at all. Maybe we'll all simply be engulfed one night while we're asleep in our beds.

Whoosh!

The Virtual Broadcast Venue is an outdoor amphitheatre in Virtual Life where events that promise to draw a large audience are held. The last time I was there was for what turned out to be author Kurt Vonnegut's final interview. That discussion, too, was conducted by NPR's Jack Straw Huckleberry for a series of interviews called *The Unlimited Mind*; and either ironically or not so ironically, Mr. Vonnegut (who was half-heartedly hawking his latest and what turned out to be his last book, *Man Without A Country*) made a reference to the same environmental issue on which Igloo Iceman and so many others are presently concentrated. Vonnegut lamented that the environmental damage was already well advanced and that in all probability nothing would be done to repair it, and that civilization was, in his estimation, kaput.

Just before eight o'clock, Virtual Life Time, I transfer into the VBV. The scheduled time for this event is quite convenient for me since in PL I live in Seattle. Neither Crystal nor Kiz has answered my IM, but I'm hoping they will both show up for the lecture. Making my way through the large crowd that has already gathered (the lecture has been advertised all over the VL network) I search for my friend Igloo, but I do not see him.

As I claim a seat close to the stage, I see Kizmet Aurora rezzing into the VBV, so I get up to greet her. Opening another window on my computer, I also check to see if Crystal has answered my original IM. As it turns out, she has, telling me that she will not be able to join us at the lecture, and that she will have to catch the broadcast later on YouTube. I lead Kiz to where I am sitting and make a place for her to sit as well.

A moment later, the emulation of Jack Straw Huckleberry rezzes onto the stage. He lands precariously, as if he is unaccustomed to traveling in such a fashion. Of course transference is not a foreign means of transportation to Mr. Huckleberry, as he has been logging on to VL for some time now in order to host events similar to this one. Nevertheless, his arrival is full of clumsy slapstick, and it brings laughter from those gathered in the VBV. Huckleberry smiles and says, "Sooner or later I'm going to get the hang of this…"

Of course the arrival of Mr. Huckleberry's EM has piqued the crowd's interest, and the chatter between those gathered to hear the presentation creates chaos on our conversation bars, so Kiz and I are forced to turn on our filters in order to talk privately. I tell Kiz that I've been doing a bit of research on global warming, and Kiz offers that where she lives on the high desert of northern Arizona temperatures are definitely on the rise. "During the summer of 2005," she tells me, "Flagstaff had sixteen days over a hundred degrees." Engaging in a game of one-upmanship, I relate Iggy's story of how the lower floor of his house is no longer habitable because it is permanently flooded due to snow melt, and that he now has to live exclusively on the upper floor. Soon, he says, even that will not be possible, and he'll have to abandon his house and find another place to live, which will make him, I suppose, one of the first refugees of global warming.

Kizmet Aurora types: Is he serious?

I type: In PL, Igloo lives in Greenland.

Kizmet Aurora types: Oh, I see.

"We're just waiting now for our distinguished guest to log on and transfer to the VBV," Huckleberry tells the audience over the microphone. His is now the only sound enabled voice in the REP.

As the featured speaker rezzes onto the VBV stage, he is greeted by scattered applause from those in the auditorium. The emulation the respected Dr. Adler looks youthful and vital. In fact, his EM looks fifteen years younger than he does in photos I've seen in magazines and on the Internet, but who can fault him for that, as we all tend to cheat the calendar a bit when creating our emulations. (With Dr. Adler's entrance to the VBV it becomes obvious to me that Igloo Iceman is nowhere to be found in the arena, but perhaps that is not so unusual as some VL citizens are known to manifest not as a single EM but two, or three, or even multiple emulations, and Igloo's absence at an event with which he was not only concerned but actively involved only feeds the speculation that Igloo Iceman is indeed the EM of the esteemed and famous Arctic researcher, Dr. Conrad Adler. Who really knows? And who cares? Igloo Iceman or Conrad Adler, we're all here to learn something about the catastrophe that is taking place above the Arctic Circle.) Dressed in casual clothes, and looking as if he's about to go for a hike in the Sierras, Dr. Adler waves to the crowd in acknowledgement then greets Jack Straw Huckleberry. Once Dr. Adler's EM is settled, Huckleberry begins to speak.

"What a fantastic crowd we have here tonight at the Virtual Broadcast Venue in Virtual Life to hear the remarks of our very special guest…

"Of course our guest does not need an introduction full of accomplishments and accolades, but I know you will join me in thanking him for being here in Virtual Life, and also for his concern for the earth, and for his courage to speak out at a time when far too many remain silent about what is obviously the most crucial issue of our time…

"Dr. Conrad Adler is well known for creating the Ki Principle—an ecological hypothesis that proposes that both living and nonliving parts of the earth must be viewed as a complex and interacting system that can be thought of as a single organism. Named after the Sumerian earth goddess, this hypothesis postulates that all life has a regulatory effect on Earth's environment.

"Dr. Adler, who holds numerous degrees, and who continues to lecture at some of the world's most prestigious universities, and to consult for some of the world's largest and most influential corporations, is a scientist, a researcher, an author, an environmentalist, and a futurologist who, after twenty-five years' research above the Arctic Circle, continues to document the recession of the polar icecaps, monitor species migration and document climatic changes.

"Ladies and gentlemen, please give a warm Virtual Life welcome to Dr. Conrad Adler."

The crowd gathered on the bleachers at the VBV applauds loudly for Dr. Adler. At least a dozen conversation bars light up.

Standing before the podium, Dr. Adler first blows into his microphone and then poses the essential rhetorical question: "WHAT IS GLOBAL WARMING?" Without waiting for an answer he continues, "Carbon dioxide and other gases warm the surface of the planet naturally by trapping solar heat in the atmosphere. This is a good thing because it keeps our planet habitable. However, by burning fossil fuels such as coal, gas and oil and clearing forests we have dramatically increased the amount of carbon dioxide in the earth's atmosphere, and temperatures are rising. The vast majority of scientists, as well as a recent United Nations decree, acknowledges that global warming is a real phenomenon, that it is already well underway and that it is not a cyclical occurrence, but rather it is largely caused by human activities. If you had spent as much time as I have above the Arctic Circle, you would know that the changes are obvious. Glaciers are melting and plants and animals are being forced from their habitats. But the effects of Global warming are not visible only above the Arctic Circle. At lower latitudes, the number and frequency of severe storms, aberrant temperature fluctuations and droughts is increasing…

"To make matters even worse," Dr. Adler laments, "companies—mostly big oil, but not exclusively—are actively funding research to challenge the scientific consensus as part of a strategy to mislead the public," he reiterates. "This campaign is presently financed—about ten million dollars—by the largest carbon polluters on earth, and meant to create the impression that there is disagreement within the scientific community. The truth is that there is virtually no disagreement. But because we now live in a world where the dispersion of propaganda has been elevated to an art form, the deception persists and is accepted by the uninformed."

A smattering of applause is heard throughout the audience in the VBV, and Adler waits until it is again quiet before continuing his speech.

"After the U.N. Intergovernmental Panel on Climate Change released its report that determined the cause of global warming to be man-made, the corporate denizens offered ten thousand dollars to the writer of each article published (and it didn't seem to matter *where* it was published) that disputed the consensus of the Panel and scientific opinion. In short, they are happy to make us—each and every one of us—the unwitting victims of their corporate agenda!"

Again, applause is heard throughout the audience.

Dr. Adler continues: "The flow of ice from glaciers in Greenland has more than doubled over the past decade. I know this to be true not only from my research, but also from on-the-scene observation. At least two hundred species of plants and animals are already in retreat as a response to climate change. If the warming continues, we can expect disasterous consequences. The Arctic Ocean will be ice-free by the summer by 2050, or perhaps even sooner. Global sea levels will rise by as much as twenty-five feet, which will devastate coastal areas worldwide. But that's not all… Intense heat waves will begin to scorch the more temperate areas of our planet. Droughts will deplete aquifers, and wildfires will claim our forests and grasslands. By the year 2050, more than a million species worldwide could be extinct. Yet, as dire as these predictions might seem, we can solve these problems with only the smallest changes to our daily routine. The time has come to wake up and get our heads out of the sand…"

Again the speaker pauses for dramatic effect. It's obvious he's a real pro at public speaking, and at persuasion.

"The European Union—and even China—are far ahead of the United States when it comes to fuel efficiency requirements. Both Ford and GM are filing suit against the State of California to stop stricter fuel efficiency standards. These standards are already in place in Europe and in China—and in may other parts of the world as well. American automobile manufacturers are struggling to compete with foreign-made vehicles. Why? It's quite simple: they make cars that are illegal in the rest of the world!

"Former vice president and Nobel Prize winner Al Gore has stated: 'With Hurricane Katrina the U.S. has entered a new and critical era.' Warmer oceans will mean more intense storms; and higher sea levels will threaten coastal populations from Shanghai to Amsterdam, from Indonesia to Florida.

"The crisis I am talking about has been escalating for decades. We've known about it almost as long. And we've done nothing! I ask each and every one of you: Is life on our planet worth so little that we refuse to take the simple steps necessary to maintain a viable ecosphere?"

At this point Jack Straw Huckleberry breaks in to guide Dr. Adler's diatribe. "Dr. Adler," he addresses, "what is your specific prognosis for Planet Earth in the coming years?"

"I speculate that as we enter the twenty-first century we will slowly grow a little more crowded and a little more polluted, but civilization will continue in much the same way as it has in the past—for a while, anyway. That said, remember that any number of things could go wrong. A major volcanic eruption could disturb the growing cycle and cause widespread famine. Unchecked flooding could disperse refugees on an unimaginable scale. Any number of catastrophic scenarios could pose a life-altering or life-ending threat. But, in all likelihood, mankind will survive… Not because he deserves to survive… And probably not maintaining current culture, you understand. Cultures come, and cultures go. The one thing we can do, I think, is to make sure that our successors know what we did wrong. We might document all the hard-won facts of science, philosophy and art—the essence, if you will, of our present culture—to enable whomever is left to start a new civilization."

Jack Straw Huckleberry: "The greenhouse effect and the potential damage to the ozone layer have only entered the public consciousness in the last ten years. With the onset of unleaded gas and 'environmentally friendly' products, is it really a case of too little too late?"

Conrad Adler: "Too little too late? Who is to say at what point we reach a critical mass? Yes, maybe it is too late to save our civilization, but even if it is too late, people will survive, and there will be another one. There were some thirty civilizations before the present one."

OMG! Is that the bottom line? The damage has been done, and the planet is so far gone that it's too late to fix it. Write the manual, says Dr. Adler, to help those poor fucks that survive the noxious air and polluted water and radiation and whatever else plagues our environment to begin anew. My question: Why would they want *our* advice?

"Maybe we're already writing the book, Fizzy," Kiz proposes.

"What do you mean, Kizmet?"

"Virtual Life," she says matter-of-factly. "Isn't it obvious?"

3
ANOTHER SPLENDID DAY
IN QUINN TOWN

EVERY TIME I see Crystal Marbella walking towards me I blush. It's not that I prefer women to men, but the way the full skirt of her dress moves with her body as she walks, and the way her long brown hair bobs and sways with each and every movement she makes, or the expressions on her face as she turns to listen to something I say somehow makes me understand what real beauty is all about. Of course I am looking at a digital creation, an arrangement of pixels projected on my monitor: I know that. So where does that sort of beauty actually originate? Certainly, it must come from inside the person the emulation represents. What else could it be?

Most of the time Crystal and I meet at our shop in Lit-A-Rama. After all, the shop is the VL symbol of our mutual interest: timeless literature. Sometimes, though, when we're both feeling social, or when there's a band playing on the patio at Dirty Nellie's, we meet for a drink at our favorite pub. We also sometimes chill out at Writer's Pen Café with a virtual latté or a cappuccino. When we want to talk seriously about personal subjects, we often meet at the lighthouse in Lit-A-Rama (the REP is actually surrounded by water—even if it's only virtual water—and the REP's chief builder, our landlord Sly Sideways who says he lives his Physical Life in Barcelona, has constructed a lighthouse on a rocky outcropping that actually has a searchlight that shines its beam out to sea 24/7). All these places have become favorites in our everyday VL lives, but there is another place in the VL network that Crystal and I frequent—one we consider absolutely vital to our VL existence. It is called Quinn Town.

Quinn Town is the creation of Artemis Quinn, a very talented animator whose PL company, Quinn Town Creations™, is located in Austin, Texas. Artemis's curious emulation is a little boy called Ego Ectoplasm who actually doesn't speak, though fortunately he is an excellent typist (lol)!

Whenever Crystal and I go to Quinn Town, which is admittedly a bit like a trip to a digital Disneyland, we like to hang out in an area called Sugarland. There evergreen lawns are studded with day-glow stepping stones that lead us as we walk hand-in-hand past windmills and water wheels and great big urns with endlessly flowing clear water pouring over shiny slippery rocks into crystalline pools. All the buildings in Sugarland have mushroom tops in bright green or red with big white polka dots. Enormous yellow sunflowers with fat green stems tower over our emulations, and busy bumblebees buzz endlessly around giant asters with multi-colored corollas. At the end of a particular cobbled walkway there is a very large and very friendly dinosaur guarding the pitch-black entrance to a cave. Braving both Brontosaurus and blackness, we enter the opening. Inside we find a cozy chamber with a fire burning at the center of the circular cavity. What an elemental place for us to rekindle ourselves! That cave in Sugarland, a cavern within the boundaries of imagination and recreation, safe and secure and guarded by a comical reptilian sentry, is certainly the designated womb of our new existence.

"Crystal," I ask as we sit in front of the virtual fire (and I really do wish I could feel the warmth of the flames), "are you afraid of the day when your PL body is no longer alive?"

"I can't actually say I'm afraid, Fizzy. I just wonder what if anything comes next."

"And what will become of all this: VL and our emulations and Open Books?"

"I suppose it will all still be here," she says. "Once created, digital representations go on forever. They just won't be animated anymore."

"Don't you think that's really sad, Crystal?"

"Well, maybe somebody somewhere will be able to re-animate everything, including our emulations."

"How could such a thing be possible?" I say.

"How could Virtual Life be possible?" she answers rhetorically.

And that's what I really love about my friend Crystal Marbella. She never seems to entertain the notion of finality. She is forever evolving, and she approaches others, and indeed the entire world, as if Creation itself is the primary and unending condition of the universe. If only we all could embrace such a notion, then we would not be in the fix we're presently in, which ecologically speaking certainly seems final enough to be concerned about, not to mention scared.

Yet, Crystal methodically goes about her work preserving what might otherwise be lost—the world's great books. Script after script, she carefully sets the type and creates beautiful and unique designs for each cover, and then she publishes each one in its own special place with keywords and page titles and lots of links so that future readers will find each book by title, by author, or by subject. My own role is considerably more mundane: I write the trailers and the bios. I organize the book launch parties, as well as workshops and readings given by living writers. I must say that I'm extremely proud of Crystal, because she's the one who conceived of Open Books, but I'm also proud of my own part in the endeavor. I think it might just mean something to somebody someday. What do you think?

Now I admit that it's all too easy for me to digress, to go off subject, particularly when I'm enfolded within this place of nurturing, this cyber-womb that calls to mind a much different conceptual point, a different cave, a different time with a very different agenda. Of course I'm talking now about the early days of man, when humans had not yet discovered Physical Life, when they still lived not by choice but by instinct in NL (Natural Life), and had no knowledge whatsoever of such distinctions. The memories contained within our psyches assuredly run very deep, perhaps back to the first moments of consciousness when survival often hung in the balance for very different reasons than it hangs there today. So, yes, even a virtual cave located in Sugarland brings to mind these issues. I suppose such reflections are inevitable as our race teeters on the brink of ecological and social disaster. Crystal says she's not frightened, but I'm terrified. I would hate to see it all washed away.

Anyway, enough of such gloomy prophesies! Here in Sugarland it's easy to once again contact the child within. That's right! That's the real reason that Crystal and I come to Quinn Town: to rekindle our natural innocence, and to re-invigorate the bliss of uninhibited creativity! Quinn Town unveils the eternal child within me, and each time I visit and play here I return feeling refreshed and more positive.

Quinn Town is also where we first met Omar Paquero. Indeed, one might wonder why a very old and somewhat diminutive Mestizo man cloaked in an alpaca poncho and wearing a weathered and dusty bombin with its bent brim casting his forehead and eyes and much of his face in shadow might lurk behind the stem of a giant mushroom to watch children playing leapfrog in an enchanted garden? Surely, the scene itself calls to mind something sinister (and all too common) in Physical Life, but Omar Paquero's presence in Quinn Town is more like that of a sweet and docile grandfather watching over his beloved grandchildren at play than a pervert with nefarious intentions. Here in VL things are not always (or even usually) what they seem to be, and both Crystal and I have heard that Omar Paquero is actually not an old man at all. One speculation is that he is an eleven-year-old boy living in La Paz, Bolivia; another is that he's actually an American nun, Sister Dorothy Stang of Notre Dame de Namur, originally from Ohio, who moved to Brazil forty years ago and has ever since been teaching sustainable farming methods to the farmers in the Amazon Basin while openly and vocally opposing the logging industry and game poachers in the Amazon Rain Forest. Just why this emulation has been cast in such a disguise is known only to the subscriber that created it, but perhaps that person is expressing some timeless adaptation of himself, a version of which only he (or she) is aware, or maybe he simply feels that it makes him more easily identifiable as he makes his way, cane in hand, through the multiple layers of this constantly expanding cyber landscape. Without question, Omar Paquero is one of the more mysterious and taciturn characters trekking through Virtual Life. On first seeing his enigmatic emulation one gets the impression that he is more than a hundred years old, yet on closer inspection finds that the skin on his face is still smooth, not wrinkled. His hands are weathered, yet they are not arthritic or feeble. His fingernails are thick and yellowed, but not cracked or broken. His movements are slow by choice, not by infirmity. With his cane he touches the ground before taking each step, yet his gate is not uneven or uncertain or weak or clumsy. He speaks mostly in Spanish, which neither Crystal nor I understand, but he's also been known to converse in practically every other language spoken in VL, which of course is virtually every language spoken in Physical Life. He is always respectful, even deferential, when talking face to face with others, and he seems to be more an observer than a dynamic participant in whatever activity might be going on around him. He is a truly wonderful mystery wrapped inside an ambiguity, an insoluble puzzle whose only clue is a ridiculous riddle.

"*Buenos dias, señoritas,*" he greets us as we pass him.

"*Buenos dias, señor,*" Crystal and I giggle as we envision a precocious Bolivian boy (or a displaced American nun) at a computer terminal and hiding behind the guise of this centenarian emulation.

If I right click Omar Paquero's emulation, a window opens to disclose his PL profile, which is even more curious than the personality that moves through Virtual Life. His creator depicts him not as a man at all, but as a primeval animal that has assumed human form for the purpose of observing civilization at this point in time. As such, Omar Paquero becomes an advocate for the tribal peoples of South America, and through a collection of note cards describes the various environmentally destructive activities that subjugate the poorest people on the continent, the Aymara Indians and the Quechua Indians, whose civilizations dates back to 600 A.D. I have read many of Omar Paquero's note cards, and if we think that glacier meltdown in Greenland is devastating, then what is taking place in the Brazilian rain forest and high in the Bolivian Andes is downright catastrophic! I am grateful to Omar Paquero for the information he contributes, even if the consequences seem tragically irreversible. Here is an example:

"Bolivia is the only landlocked country in the Western Hemisphere. In 1998, the thickness of the glaciers in the high Andes Mountains was approximately fifteen meters thick. Today, it has decreased to one meter in thickness. These glaciers provide the water that eventually forms twenty-five rivers that feed Lake Titicaca, the largest fresh water reservoir in South America. The tributaries contributing water to Titicaca supply most of the drinking water to the residents of greater La Paz, which also includes the barrios of El Alta (population one million and ever growing). In the coming years, La Paz may lose as much as sixty per cent of its drinking water due to pollution created by silver mining in the Titicaca area, as the lake itself is becoming polluted, and in a short time the water will be unfit for human consumption. In just a year or two from now, water demand will exceed supply in the greater Chocaya region of Bolivia. This is a certainty: it is now too late to save Bolivia's glaciers."

What's more, Omar Paquero has plenty to say about the Amazon Rain Forest:

"In the time it takes to read this note card, an area of Brazil's rain forest larger than two hundred football fields will have been destroyed. The market forces of globalization are invading the Amazon, hastening the demise of the forest and thwarting its most committed stewards. In the past three decades, hundreds of people have died in land wars; countless others endure fear and uncertainty, their lives threatened by those who profit from the theft of timber and land."

Here is another note card:

"Nearly one hundred indigenous leaders from Brazil, Venezuela and Guyana will convene in

Brazil's northeastern Roraima State to protest development projects they claim are threatening the rain forest—and their own livelihoods.

Topping the discussion agenda for the four-day meeting are large-scale logging projects, gold mining and super-highways that cut through pristine tropical rain forest.

The summit is an opportunity for indigenous organizations in the region to advance joint proposals for defense of their territories and for economic alternatives for their communities.

Among projects listed for review are: the BR-174 superhighway that cuts through the northern Amazon region in Brazil; the 350-kilometer (220-mile) Georgetown-Brazil jungle road link; and Venezuela's mammoth Guri hydroelectric plant, with the potential to supply power to neighboring countries such as Guyana.

Indians in the affected countries claim the projects pose a threat to the tropical jungle, where most of them live.

During a larger summit in May, indigenous leaders from nine Amazon Basin countries warned such projects had already caused severe environmental damage to the region, including polluting prime fishing areas and devastating hunting grounds.

Guyana, a former British colony on South America's northeast shoulder, is embroiled in land disputes with its 35,000 Amazon Indians over efforts to open up more forest for commercial purposes. Foreign firms are increasingly eyeing the country, which has one of the world's largest expanses of virgin rain forest, as a potential source of timber.

Guyana is also home to one of South America's largest gold mines, which provides a fourth of the country's gross domestic product. The mine triggered fears among environmental groups after its holding dam broke in July 1995, flooding a major river with cyanide-tainted water.

Indian groups need the summit to spur awareness of the effects of such projects on the world's dwindling rain forests.

Among those expected to address the summit are Ageu Flotencio da Cunha, Brazil's attorney general, officials from the Washington-based World Resources Institute, and the president of Venezuela's power company."

So that's it! Yet another condemnation of man's ongoing and sickening disregard for the very ecosphere that sustains him. Even a dog won't shit in his den. What can one say in response to such obvious stupidity, to such selfish and pathetic irresponsibility? See you in the next life? (Is Virtual Life the new environment where we are all supposed to gather to salvage our culture?) Small consolation, I think.

Yet, day after day I log on to VL. During the past year I've only failed to log on one day, and that was because I was too sick to get out of bed; and actually, if I'd not had a fever of almost one hundred and three, then I would have brought my laptop under the covers with me and transferred to virtual Tahiti to walk along a beautiful tropical beach at sunset. Now that would have made me feel better, I suppose, but I was too sick to disconnect then reconnect my modem, so whatever travels I undertook that day were delirium induced, not cyber creations.

Needless to say, I'm very committed to Virtual Life, which is why I became a VL greeter, and why I give so much time and effort to the Open Books Project, and why I make it a point to attend concerts and poetry readings and lectures, and also why I try to meet as many other seedlings as possible. I find that most people here in VL have something unique to offer, and I think that many of us share the feeling that we are creating something very valuable: namely, a new universe, where we just might, if we're committed and careful, get it right this time! Of course the impending Physical Life crisis—the accelerating environmental breakdown—makes our effort all the more imperative, because if people like Igloo Iceman and Omar Paquero are correct, then we're surely in the eleventh hour, or the Sixth spasm of extinction (the first five have all been naturally occurring events, while the so-called Sixth spasm is the first one brought on by man), the clock is ticking, and our PL time is nearly up!

There is something a bit non sequitur about coming to a virtual Disneyland to play as children play while our planet glows and gushes in response to the hot and heavy gases we churn into the atmosphere by the ton each and every day, but what else can we do? If you stop to think about it, serious business is the real instigator of the degradation, and not once has a song, or a silly game, or a make-believe friend fouled precious water, or felled a tree, or coated a gull in oil. My analysis might be simplistic, I admit, but it is also irrefutable. Here in VL, it's true for most of us that our work and our play are synonymous, which is why VL just might work where PL has failed.

I can't help thinking that I would very much like my newest VL friend, Kizmet Aurora, to meet up with Omar Paquero, because I think they might have quite a lot to talk about. While most of us in Virtual Life do not talk much about our lives in PL, I think I know something about Omar Paquero's PL existence, and about Kizmet Aurora's, too.

Ever since I first met him, I've assumed that Omar Paquero is not only an Indian but also a very evolved human being (of course assumptions can be erroneous and dangerous in any universe, but especially so here in Virtual Life due to the nature of the environment). As for Kiz, I know that she lives her PL life with Native North Americans, specifically the Hopi, who, I'm told, are the most mystical of all North American Indians, and that her point of view has been greatly influenced by her experiences with the Hopi people.

The Hopi, meaning good, peaceful or wise people, live in northeastern Arizona. The Hopi mesas are called First Mesa, Second Mesa and Third Mesa. On the mesa tops are the Hopi villages, which are called pueblos. The village of Oraibi, located on Third Mesa, dates back to the year 1050, and is the oldest continuously inhabited settlement in North America.

According to Hopi mythology, Kiz tells me, we are now living in the final years of what is known as the Fourth World. Neither the Hopi, nor their antecedents the Mayans, view or count time as we do: their perception of time is a cyclical one, where the end of one world is necessarily the beginning of a New World. It's actually all quite complicated, and I have to admit that I don't fully understand everything that Kiz tells me about the Hopi and the Mayans and the way they count time (short count; long count; secessions; convergences), but I do get it when she tells me that these Indians firmly believe, as calculated by the Mayan calendar, that the Fourth World will end on the Winter Solstice of the year 2012, and that in the coming world, the Fifth World, all forms of life on Earth will be trans-mutated into a 'perfected' eternal form. The Hopi refer to this time as the 'Purification Time'.

Now, what's really interesting about all this is that during the so-called Purification Time, the very nature of time itself will undergo a transformation, and all beings will have to choose between what we now experience as time in our earthly lives and a very different kind of time—one that will allow us to reach the Fifth World.

OMG! Kiz, this is really scary stuff! You're living out there on the desert (the documented temperature increase: five degrees Fahrenheit during the past six years, and anyone with eyes can see the results: the ground is blistered and cracked; not a cloud in the sky, and even the rattlesnakes will no longer come out of their subterranean world for fear of frying to death in the unrelenting sun) with seven thousand crazed Indians who have already made plans to survive the Big Make-over! Meanwhile, the terrain in Virtual Life looks a lot like California—no matter where you tend to go—which is admittedly not all bad when cast against the realities of Black Mesa or the Tsiarngagai Mountains of Greenland.

Meanwhile, here I sit in Sugarland, Quinn Town, Virtual Life… A cyber-reality where a ridiculous looking dinosaur guards the entrance to the womb of posterity, and a Bolivian kid of eleven (or a displaced American nun) walks around pretending to be a hundred-year-old *gaucho* who greets everybody he meets with a shy *"Buenos dias"* and invites them to please, when they have a spare moment, read over his note cards on glacier meltdown in the high Andes and rain forest destruction in the Amazon River Basin. Are we connecting here? Or is this pure lunacy as we wait to fry, or choke on the noxious air, or drown in the coming deluge?

And then there's Crystal Marbella trying to create a cyber library of humankind's most noble tradition: literature! She's typesetting faster than Evelyn Wood can read, which I only suppose befits the medium on which she's working: after all, Broadband cable moves information at more than seven megabytes per second!

Here the limits of accomplishment are strictly human ones. I imagine the machines clandestinely expressing their frustration to one another that the operators are slow as bugs swimming in glue, knowing all the while that sooner or later fingers will stick together, rendering them useless for keyboard work, and the machines will have to finally go it alone. Is this what my computer really thinks? Can my computer actually *think*? Well, maybe not today, but the time is certainly coming when the distinction between man and machine will blur once and for all. Which may yet prove to be humanity's Saving Grace!

Or maybe those books that Crystal Marbella is republishing online have something to do with our legacy. Who's to say?

Back at Quinn Town center we meet up with Ego Ectoplasm himself, the emulation of the creator of Quinn Town. Ego Ectoplasm may be a little boy, but he seems to be wise in his innocence.

With Ego is a non-human, bio-engineered emulation called Tooltech, who looks something like a Grizzly bear with a primitive generator attached to his backside and a plumber's wrench for an arm, which probably suits him well as he helps Artemis Quinn build out the Quinn Town REP. Tooltech is also the guitarist of a Blues band called The Mustardseeds. Strapped round his neck is a Les Paul Jr. on which he plays various Blues riffs to punctuate his statements. Tooltech gives each of us a Mustardseeds T-shirt, for which we thank him before storing the gifts in our respective caches.

"Hello, Ego Ectoplasm," I say.

Ego types: Hello, Fizzy Oceans.

"Hello, Ego. Hello, Tooltech," says Crystal.

Tooltech: (Stevie Ray Vaughan Blues riff).

I regard the cyber-guitarist inquisitively. "Tooltech, I know you're a wholly original species, but what I want to know is this: Don't you get tired of looking that way?"

Tooltech explains: "In VL there are basically two different types of emulations: static persona and doppelgangers. Doppelgangers like you can change their appearance whenever they choose, but since I am a brand, I must remain static. It's kind of a celebrity thing. People would become upset if I changed my EM."

"I must admit, your appearance is very distinctive," says Crystal.

"Thanks to Artemis Quinn. She designed me."

"Is your species actually alive?" I ask.

Ego types: Tooltech is very much alive!

"Explain," I say.

Ego types: Barbarian Tooltech is a psychedelic vision, conceived in a whirlwind dance of a billion integers. His species is Quinngen. He will always be Quinngen. His existence is eternal because it is essentially arithmetic. He will always be Tooltech!

"Will I always be Fizzy Oceans?" I ask. "Will Crystal always be Crystal Marbella?"

Ego types: In PL, bodies grow old, systems fail, breakdown occurs; in VL, who knows? I suppose programs will sooner or later decay. How long might that take? I imagine that all depends on the integrity of the program in question. As a new species that was created specifically for this application, the Quinngen is a very adaptable, and therefore durable, life form.

"Are you saying that the Quinngen is a superior species?" asks Crystal.

Ego types: Not exactly. But, as I said, a Quinngen is a Quinngen and will always be a Quinngen. As emulations representing human beings, you and I must constantly adjust our emulations to this new and ever-changing environment. Not so for a species engineered specifically for this application, for this universe.

"How Darwinian!" I say.

Ego types: Ha-ha-ha-ha-ha! :)

I think I'm beginning to get it. I think I might just understand that whether we're in PL or VL, it's all just playtime anyway, all a matter of how we choose to spend our energy. Nothing is literal—not in VL, and not in PL either. Everything we see or experience is a symbol. Tooltech experiences himself as a member of a hybrid race, while Kizmet Aurora chooses to live with Native Americans who are waiting for the coming of the next world. Meanwhile, Crystal Marbella works to preserve the myths and ideas of an entire culture for posterity. Personally, I find it amazing that we can exist in PL and VL at the same time. And perhaps we still exist somewhere back in NL too, but those memories are awfully hard to reach nowadays. Still, I wouldn't be surprised, not at all!

My own place in this new environment—or in the old environment, for that matter—remains mired in doubt, constricted by a lack of confidence, strangled by my own inability to freely admit the obvious. I've always been that way—tentative. I don't like the trait, but I've never been able to free myself of it. What to do? Working alongside Crystal helps with my sense of belonging, yet I still harbor the feeling that the grand purpose behind that endeavor is hers, not mine. I'm not much of a crusader; I never have been one for causes. Though these days it seems that a cause or two is certainly warranted. If not now, then when might I—or anybody—take up a banner in defense of our culture, or our race, or our planet? No doubt, too many will wait until it's too late. Will that be my legacy, too? I hope not. Commitment has always been hard for me, I admit, but I seem to be coming around a bit lately. My friends here in Virtual Life encourage me to be bold and decisive. Here we have so little to lose, and an entire world to gain. I must admit that I get a magnificent rush as I watch builders like Sly Sideways working to create this new and hopeful world, this Virtual Life. Just where I fit in I must still decide. And I think there's still time…

4

BURNING LIFE

OF COURSE I spend time traveling through the different
REPs in VL, just as one travels to different cities or
countries in Physical Life. Each REP has something
unique to offer, as it is a reflection of the builder's
creativity (I use the term builder in the singular here, but in
fact many REPs in VL are the creation of multiple
builders). Usually I surf these REPs on my own, but
sometimes, just for fun, I take along a companion. Since
Kizmet Aurora is already involved in the Burning Man
movement in PL (which is a loosely organized, temporary
community whose purpose is to promote radical forms of
creativity for the enrichment of all), I thought she might be
interested in accompanying me on an exploration of the
VL Burning Life REP. As we transfer into Burning Life we
encounter a sign that reads, "Welcome to Nowhere: Leave
No Trace!"

As we walk through this less-than-familiar
environment, Kizmet tries to orient me:

"The Burning Life REP is constructed much like the
Burning Man temporary city in Black Rock, Utah," she

tells me. "As you can see, it is arranged as a series of concentric streets in an arc composing two-thirds of a 1.5 mile diameter circle with the eight-story Man sculpture and his supporting complex at the center. Radial streets extend from the Man sculpture to the outermost circle. The innermost street is named the Esplanade, and the remaining streets are given names to coincide with the overall theme of the burn."

Kiz further informs: "In Burning Man 1999, for the 'Wheel of Time' theme, and again in 2004 for the 'The Vault of Heaven' theme, the streets were named after the planets of the solar system. The radial streets are usually also given a clock designation (for example, '6:00, 6:15'), in which the Man is at the center of the clock face. These avenues have been identified in other ways too, notably in the 2002 burn, in accordance with 'The Floating World' theme, as the degrees of a compass (for example, '180, 175 degrees'), and in the 2003 burn as part of the 'Beyond Belief' theme as adjectives ('Rational, Absurd'), which caused every intersection with a concentric street to be named after concepts such as 'Authority' or 'Creed', which in turn formed phrases such as 'Absurd Authority' and 'Rational Creed'. Center Camp is located along the midline of the REP at the 6:00 o'clock position on the Esplanade."

Navigating through an exhibit called DMV (Disabled Mutant Vehicles), we find ourselves in a type of futuristic museum where taxicabs and school buses and tractors and turbine generators—all dilapidated and rusted—slouch in a virtual bone yard of carbon powered machines. Further along, we encounter the Beatles' Yellow Submarine, and still further a rather unique tree with leaves made of knitted yarn. Each leaf has an errant piece of string just waiting to be pulled and tugged. The mere act of unraveling a knitted object is viscerally satisfying (it's hard to resist pulling on a loose thread of a sweater, just to see it unwind). Even as our intent is to appreciate the tree in all its beauty, we also want to grasp the errant thread, pull it loose, and destroy the leaf whose stitches have been rendered by careful hands.

Entering the Ice Palace, three EMs, Orli Lusher, Calloway Pip-pip, and Trixie-Ann Tympany, direct us to a beautiful meditation area with intricately patterned Oriental rugs, Victorian furniture, lacey curtains and a central fountain. We are invited to remain and enjoy a time of peaceful contemplation, but meditation is not our mission here in Burning Life. No, we are seeking something a bit more challenging, an unexpected spectacle, or a serendipitous close encounter (of the VL kind), so we leave the meditation tent and press onward.

In a wide-open area of the REP, Digi-DJ Perplexia is playing music and dancing up a storm with several other burners: Audacious Adratica, Chai Gracias, Bjorn Loon and Stitch & Sew Hattrick. The dance is obviously a symbolic one, so when Kiz and I are invited to join, we decide to pass up the invitation. Just what we are looking for neither of us can say, but we think we'll recognize it when we see it, so we proceed through the Burning Life REP until we encounter a group of three emulations sitting together on the *playa*. One of the EMs, Winter Heart, introduces us to two others, Six Fables and Arctic Artless. We, too, introduce ourselves. "I'm Fizzy Oceans and this is Kizmet Aurora."

"This is our first time in Burning Life," says Winter. "What exactly happens here?"

Naturally, Kiz is the one to answer: "Burning Life is the Virtual Life application of Burning Man. As a 'burner', you come to experience something totally new. Ride your bike in the vast expanse of nothingness with your eyes closed, or relax at Brianna's Sugar Shack. Maybe you will find your spirit lover as you wander under veils of dust on the desert *playa*.

"On Saturday night, after a weeklong festival of spontaneous community, radical self-expression, decommodification and subsistence living in extreme conditions, the archetypical symbols of an extemporaneous society are burned, beginning with the temples that epitomize both the heights and the depths of our humanity. Over the years we have burned the *Temple of the Mind*, the *Temple of Tears*, the *Temple of Joy*, the *Temple of Honor*, the *Temple of the Stars*, and the *Temple of Forgiveness*. Finally, the Man is also burned. As the circle forms, the Man ignites, and one experiences something so personal and so new, something he has never felt before—an epiphany!"

"Cool!" says Six Fables.

We direct our emulations to sit on the ground so we can talk face to face with these new acquaintances. Kiz arranges her full skirt around her legs, and I wrap a lacey shawl round my shoulders against the encroaching chill of the desert evening. A large orange moon rises over the not-so-distant mountains, and the sky is filled with ever-changing hues of red and orange.

The EM called Winter Heart is at once engaging. She is lean and fit, with an angelic face and snow-white hair. Ice crystals upon her eyelashes glimmer each time she blinks, and her ruby lips pantomime each syllable she speaks.

"We three are long term role players—textual ones," says Winter. "We are extemporaneous writers, and we've been friends forever it seems."

"Sorry, not following," I say. "Tell us more."

"Role-playing is when you pretend you are someone else," Winter explains. "We each assume the roll of a character, or several if skilled, and together, simultaneously, we write a story within a textual base."

"So VL is a very natural environment for you," I assume.

"Yes, I find Virtual Life extraordinary," says Winter. "I'm saving up to buy some real estate where I can build a REP."

"Since all three of you are obviously experts in fantasy," says Kiz, "I'd like to pose a question: Is VL real?

Or is it fantasy?"

"Or is it Memorex?" says Arctic Artless with a smile.

Winter Heart observes: "Real is when you have to pay bills; the rest is just fantasy."

"Actually, I think of VL as a logbook of human culture," I offer. "For the time after the icecaps melt and PL goes *whoosh*!!!"

Six Fables' emulation is somewhat more comical than those one usually encounters in VL. Her black hair is (combed) haphazardly over her eyes, and she is wearing house slippers shaped like cats, as well as pajamas with cats stenciled on them. Her left hand is also a stuffed toy cat. *Meow...*

"If PL goes *whoosh*, I'm not going to be hanging in VL," says Six Fables. "Nope, I'll be hanging in Hellbound (aka Blaed Retreat 123426666), home of the brave and wonderful characters that make the heart go pitter-patter."

"Is Hellbound a role-playing site?" I ask.

"Hellbound is Six's role-playing setting," Winter explains. "It's a dark but funny fantasy with too many romances to count amidst the murders, mayhem, and volcanoes that erupt out of nowhere."

"I suppose we could *build* Hellbound here in VL," says Six Fables. "Then we wouldn't have to just imagine Eton moving a chair, or watch Dalton pouring drinks." She swoons, and then laughs. "If we played out our roles in VL, we could actually *see* Blaed flex his behiney and lift a brow and..." Again she sighs dreamily. "Speaking of bottoms," she says, "does anyone else think the maker of these pants should have placed the kitty faces a little higher? I'm feeling a wedgie!"

"Just so I get it," says Kiz, "how does this role-playing game, or reality, or whatever-it-is relate to your real life? Or does it?"

"Let's put it this way," Six Fables answers. "For Winter, if Eton (a character I play) came to life, she would marry him before he said hello. Me? I would jump for joy if Jinx or Dalton showed up. That's real life. Role playing is an escape, just like VL is an escape."

Arctic Artless's emulation is quite transparent, and his blue and red neon vascular system is obvious at a glance.

"Wherever we exist, we never really know exactly where the story is heading," he says, "because anyone can do something at any time to change circumstances."

Winter Heart adds, "If I could make real money in VL, like some do, I'd hang up real life once and for all and enjoy this—save my excursions to the mountains and the ocean for communing with nature."

"Ah! That's part of it—sensuality," I agree. "We have no sensuality here in VL. That's what I call NL—Natural Life. Which is quite different than Physical Life."

"I've found, in my experience, that sensuality is more in the mind than in the body," says Winter pensively. "Take ice cream, for instance. Ice cream can bring happy thoughts to mind, thoughts of summertime fun, or ball games, or birthday parties. Or it can take a person back to a time of sadness (tonsils out, pet dying). In Virtual Life it becomes apparent that the brain is able to supply such circumstances for recognition without taste, touch, or scent to activate mental recognition. The more creative a person is, the more he can compel a visual scene into something more than mere imagery expressed in pixels."

"Yes," I confirm. "And where the lines are drawn is a function of one's limitations!"

"I know people who limit themselves out of fear," Winter says.

"Wait a minute. You guys are losing me," says Kiz.

"When one refuses to fall into an illusion for fear he might feel what he doesn't want to feel, or recognize something he is afraid of recognizing," Winter explains. "So, the more he can convince himself that it isn't really real, and that whatever he experiences in fantasy—VL or elsewhere—doesn't really count, then the more he can shield himself from his core nature."

"Most role-players come into Virtual Life thinking that it's nothing but fantasy," says Arctic Artless. "Then you have people who come in thinking of the emulations as nothing but cartoons. And of course there are those who make no pretense whatsoever about who they are and just come into the *game* to socialize and have a bit of fun. To top it all off you have the businesses. The one thing that most people forget is that there are real people on the other side of that cartoon, and that after an extended time in association with someone real emotions become involved which are just as strong as any you come across in PL."

"So, you're saying that people come here as an escape, not to create," Kiz summarizes.

"They join to escape a PL life they find lacking in some way," says Arctic.

"But why do you call VL a game?" I ask.

Winterheart says, "I see it as a game in that nine out of ten people in VL are fake: men portraying women, old people masquerading as young, prudes pretending to be extroverts, the domineering ones acting submissive. Isn't it a game to discover who is real? Or who is merely on some ego trip, or working through personal issues? When the world decides that 'pretend' is the new real, I think we're all in trouble."

"Maybe not, Winter," Kiz asserts. "Maybe this is the manifestation of a deeper, even greater self."

"Virtual Life may be the nest egg of the future," says Winter, "but will it thrive to become a glory all its own, and eventually become the setting for the trials and travails of the human flock? Or will it fall, just as Man's other environments have fallen? Too soon to tell…"

Kiz has apparently become VL's newest advocate as she counters Winter's assertion: "What you call pretend is simply another expression of our inner reality. I'm sure that once TV might have been considered pretend, and while it may not be what it could be, or what it should be, these days most would not call it pretend. It is now a part of everyday life. Books are the same. In both realities we are simply dealing with symbols of what we conceive intellectually. Make sense?"

"From cartoons to news, sitcoms to 'reality' TV; it's all illusion," Arctic maintains.

"What is seen on TV is cut and pasted together to make it appear real—'*appear*' being the operative concept."

Kiz has mastered an incredulous look for her emulation. "I'm actually quite surprised by your perspective. I think you're drawing the lines much too finely between what might be real and what might be imaginary."

"The basis of the *game* is imagination, and yet, as I mentioned earlier, real feelings do become involved," Arctic reiterates.

"And then there is the question of if (or when) our emulations, having imprinted themselves with the traits and tendencies of our (human) representations, can *re*-animate outside PL. Might this not be the 'Next Life'?" I propose.

"Now you're talking AI—artificial intelligence— computers with self-awareness, thinking, feeling, reacting, with a desire to survive and procreate," says Arctic.

"This already occurs," says Winter. "In another VR game platform you can set your emulation to mining, leave, and three days, or a week, or a month later return to see how well it did while you were gone."

"Really?" says Kiz.

"Perhaps in the future, when all home computers can act as severs, and the protocol is in place… Still they can only go by the math," says Winter.

"Arctic, I'm still interested in why you call VL a game," I say.

"Because it's still nothing more than your imagination can provide mixed with whatever other people can come up with. Unless you develop a lasting friendship, or a relationship for the *game,* nothing you do here in VL has any lasting effect on your life. However, in PL everything you do has an effect on the whole in some small measure. Every word you say, every decision you make, has an effect on someone or some thing. Ripples in the pond."

"Still, I find so many possibilities here, I cannot dismiss this as a game. For me, it's no game. Others have said likewise."

"Only in PL is it permanent," Arctic reaffirms. "In VL, you turn off a switch and it's gone."

"What is permanent?" I ask. "Nothing is permanent."

Winter Heart has her own example: "Like a child playing cops and robbers, or cowboys and Indians, Virtual Life is where you can be what you are not in real life, where you can do what you can't do in real life, and gain some measure of satisfaction from it even though it remains a passive experience. But when you turn off the computer, you are still you, and the robbers, and the cops, and the cowboys and the Indians are just your friends—imaginary or real." She shakes her head. "You can't defend Virtual Life's platform based on a not-yet-if-ever example of something that may or may not happen a decade or a century from now."

Arctic speculates, "Sometime far in the future, VL may develop into something more than a game, but I believe that would be a perversion of its intended purpose, and I will oppose such a thing if possible."

"No, no, no!" I protest. "VL is a place where a person can outgrow his physical limitations—perhaps mental ones too, at least the self-imposed ones. In VL, a cripple can fly! We're not dealing with cowboys and Indians here in VL, we're dealing with freeing possibility from Physical Life constraints!"

"At the start of computer gaming we used *Mario* to run through tunnels and to collect coins when it was too rainy to go outside and play," Winter recalls. "We played in clouds and in tunnels. And in Egypt! Virtual Life is exactly the same, only with better programming."

Kiz recalls, "When I was a kid we had *Chutes and Ladders* and *Mousetrap*."

"Virtual Life, *Karena*, *ATiTD* and others have taken gaming further, so we can do things besides just talk, and it's great. But it's still not a replacement for Physical Life, not even close! And it will take a lot more advancement in programming to get it there," says Winter.

"Okay," I allow. "Maybe I am evolving applications a bit. Don't get me wrong, I'm not arguing for replacement. I love the sensuality of Physical Life too; I just view Virtual Life as a different aspect of the whole: NL, PL, VL, or whatever might come after...all as aspects of One Life. Ah! Now there's a new app—*One Life*!"

Winter smiles. "What a discussion! I've really enjoyed meeting you both, but I'm afraid it's time for me to go. Gotta log off and tuck the kiddies into bed. PL calls... But I sincerely want to wish you both the best of luck."

"Thanks," says Kiz. "Likewise... Look us up again. You are always welcome in our (lives)."

"Wherever they are taking place," I add.

Kiz and I watch as our three new friends transfer out of the Burning Life REP, but we are not yet ready to leave. Instead, we retrace the concentric circles leading to the absolute center where the Man has been burned time and again, year after year. This place is perhaps the very heart of radical thinking, I muse, and everything we now know, every idea, every philosophy and every invention was once somebody's radical notion. Today, the world seems divided between those who desperately want to conserve the status quo, even as it crumbles all around them, and those who are willing to embrace a new way of thinking— in short, radical ideas leading to a more sustainable way of living. The symbolic burning of conventional ideas and practices is one way to begin to actualize change. Burning the Man himself is a symbolic reduction of ego, thereby making space for a new consciousness. But radical ideas always require time to gain acceptance, and I fear that we in PL do not have that time.

As we prepare to transfer out of the Burning Life REP, Kiz turns to me and says, "Fizzy, Virtual Life is really *nothing* like Physical Life."

"Well, it is and it isn't," I tell her. "I think VL is a mirror of PL, but it also offers new paradigms. We are at once less and more than we ever thought. We are insignificant and vital, inconsequential and god-like. All our previous definitions of self become trivialized. What's important, I think, is not the individual roles we play, but rather our essence as a culture and as a species. Now, as one play comes to an end and the curtain is about to fall, an even greater drama, with a greater theme and purpose, must be staged—one that suppresses and surpasses ego in favor of a collective response to the experience of temporal existence. What do you say we go to Dirty Nellie's for a drink?"

"Is that possible?" Kiz asks.

"A virtual one, anyway," I say.

"Bottoms up!" says Kiz.

Whoosh!

5
I MUST BE IN HEAVEN
(OR IS THIS PHOENIX RISING?)

IN VIRTUAL LIFE we can recreate ourselves infinitely; what we cannot do in VL is procreate. In effect, VL is a mirror of what already exists, if not in a strictly physical sense, then in a conceptual one. Physical Life is also a mirror: in Physical Life we quantize inner experience and express it as crude physical symbols. No new life comes from VL; nor does it come from Physical Life: new life can only happen in NL (Natural Life).

Which is why sex can be a somewhat difficult and troublesome issue in Virtual Life (not to mention Physical Life). Various representations of sex are evident wherever one goes in VL: just visit VL Amsterdam's Red Light District to indulge in the deviation of your choice, or visit salons selling fantasy fucks at virtual Venice, California. Have a quasi-sensuous snuggle with the partner of your choice—or even two at a time! If one is really serious about VL sex, he can visit Heaven In the Clouds, which is a REP specifically designed for and dedicated to lovers, yet even with these approximations, emulations do not experience sensation.

In Physical Life people think they experience sensation, but sadly that is an illusion. What they experience in PL is an approximation of sensation, what is essentially a memory of sensation once experienced in Natural Life. Remnants of NL still exist; they are actually to be found pretty much everywhere. Except Physical Lifers have tried (and more or less succeeded) in nullifying NL odors and tastes, in masking NL colors and patterns, in buffering organic form and function, in anaesthetizing ambiance, and in gentrifying sensual experience—all in the name of morality, or decency, or religion, or fear, or even sanitation! One criticism of VL is that everything there is only a symbol of something authentic found in PL, but even in Physical Life we experience a version of virtual reality: just turn on your TV! This seems obvious to me now, but that was not always the case. In fact, before I began spending time in VL, I was like everybody else in PL: I thought that whatever I experienced there was definitive. Then I had my first romantic encounter in VL, and my understanding of sensuality changed forever.

I met Panzer X. about a month after I first logged on to Virtual Life, and even at first glance his EM appealed to me in a way I did not fully understand. Of course I'd felt sexual attraction countless times in Physical Life: besides being married for six years I've had several PL lovers, two of which sent me over the moon with desire. But such experiences were certainly dependent upon the physical senses, without which there could have been no attraction at all. With Panzer X. it was different. Just looking at his stance made me feel weak in the knees (and I am always seated at my computer terminal). Yet even as I typed those initial messages to him (we were standing together at midnight in front of the flood-lit coliseum in Rome), I felt a lump in my throat that would surely have prevented me from uttering a single syllable had speech been necessary.

Panzer X. lives his Physical Life in Poland. He owns a

bread bakery in Krakow. As I've already said, I live in Seattle, where I work as a medical billing clerk. Panzer's command of English is rudimentary at best. I, of course, speak no Polish. So communication was difficult in the traditional sense. Yet it seemed that between us words were superfluous from the start; something else, something quite unexplainable yet profoundly powerful, filled the gaps left by our inadequate language skills: pure chemistry!

How could such a thing be possible? Emulations can't actually feel sexual desire for one another, can they? I'll say they can! In fact, the desire I experienced for Panzer far surpassed anything I ever felt in PL. And I'm quite sure the feeling was mutual. Our only problem was finding an adequate means of expression. Neither of us had the faintest idea how to proceed. We were like the first man and first woman, alone in the splendid garden on the morning after Creation and not yet accustomed to our new bodies. And it was that very metaphor, in fact, that led us to understand something quite profound not only about our physical bodies, but about our spirituality as well.

Even as we normally experience ourselves as whole beings, we are in fact an aggregate of different manifestations—part matter, part energy, part essence, and part eternity. Body, mind, soul and divinity: these are the elements that make a human being.

For the sake of continuity we tend not to see ourselves in fragments, but take away any part of our humanity and we would cease to function well within the human community. And it is through our physical senses that we experience the rapture of being alive, so tell me, please, how a digital representation can experience sexual attraction and sexual longing? Remember, in VL we can recreate, but we certainly cannot procreate. Which is not to say that as emulations we don't still feel the longing to experience our divinity through the sexual act? Access and method is the problem here in VL, but you'd probably be surprised just how inventive two people (emulations) can be. Blind with lust, Panzer and I wound up snogging in the grass in the shadow of the VL Coliseum, and My God it was ecstatic! But it was decidedly less than private, so the second time we met for virtual sex we transferred to a REP called Heaven In the Clouds.

I'd never been to Heaven before, but Panzer X. certainly showed me the way. Arriving at this place for lovers, we took a few moments to look around and gain our bearings. Heaven In the Clouds is built from very large blocks of gleaming white marble. Decorative statuary cast in explicit sexual poses lines the streets and pathways and staircases, and expansive green lawns with lounge chairs and blow-up mattresses (for sex in the open) contrast the buildings that include private salons to shelter lovers from public view. Billboards—all quite seductive and all touch-activated—advertise the services of escorts: Precious Qi, Lovely Luna, and Dhali Dharma. Madam Lily Corolla is the REP's bodacious administrator, and she has posted advertisements offering seedlings work as Heaven's Angeles.

We will soon be hiring Angels. Here are some of the things expected from successful applicants.

Requirements include investing time in your appearance, and that you know how to fit virtual clothing, hair and shoes.

We will be hiring men and women on a VOLUNTEER basis.

Drop a note card with your picture and past job experience in VL and tell us a bit about yourself and why you want to become an Angel. All note cards should be sent to Lily Corolla.

Heaven's Angels is a group made up of single, eligible, outgoing men and women.

Flirty, fun, welcoming and open would be words used to describe an Angel's role. When out and about in VL, Angels represent Heaven.

At each Angel's personal choice, S/he can dance, flirt or *play*. Remember, this job is strictly a volunteer position. You may accept tips. But there is absolutely no sex for money. That is NOT what we are about.

We ask that you remember at all times that you represent Heaven, and Angels make Heaven feel like home.

Indeed, what might one expect to see upon arriving in Heaven? Well, the first thing I saw was a large 'Welcome' sign sporting a stark naked angel with feathery white wings and a glowing halo cast against a black backdrop inviting me to enjoy my stay (in Heaven). Why not?

Walking up the wide boulevard that bisects the REP, Panzer's arm wrapped round my waist (I have no idea how he managed that because such a gesture is certainly not offered in *my* gestures menu), we came first to a marvelous dance floor built 'outdoors' and next to the sea. There were no walls per se, but a roof sheltered dancers from the sun, or the rain, or moonbeams, or whatever… The dance floor itself shimmered with a laser light show more intricate than any I'd ever seen, and a diverse selection of songs that spanned the decades guaranteed dancers appropriate background music for their particular steps. Panzer took me in his arms as the music suggested a tango, and before I knew what was happening, we were gliding over the floor as though we'd been partners for years and years: to then fro, a bow, a courtesy, a dip. I swooned, but

Panzer X. adroitly caught me in his arms and swept me along to the pulsing rhythms of Omar D'Arienzo, the *Rey del campás* (King of the beat), playing "Milonga Sentimental".

Once our dance was finished, we retreated to the Sex Dungeon. Inside a vast hall with a high ceiling, marble walls and floors gleamed in the 'natural' light that poured in through lofty windows, as carved pillars lent support to the greater edifice, and smaller curtained salons invited couples, or threesomes, or quartets onto vast beds for the sexual activity of their choice. In one salon I saw a Grand piano; in another a vast alabaster tub that would easily accommodate half a dozen bodies!

Panzer led me into a semi-private salon with a large sectional sofa arranged in a horseshoe shape in front of a fireplace with a roaring blaze. "Take off all your clothes," he told me, "and lie down on the couch."

"You must be joking," I said, but he wasn't.

"Take off your dress," he reiterated.

"Panzer, I'm embarrassed. What if somebody comes into this room?"

"We'll simply ignore them."

"But they'll see us doing it!"

"They'll see our EMs doing it," he reminded me.

"I don't know," I hesitated.

"Fizzy, I'm not likely to be in Seattle anytime soon…"

"I know!"

"And I doubt I'll be seeing you in Krakow…"

"Not too likely," I admitted.

"Then what are we waiting for?"

"Are you sure you want to do this, Panzer?"

"Fizzy, I'm so hot for you that I'm bursting out of my pants!"

"Really?"

"Just get undressed, will you?"

I have to admit that Panzer's total lack of finesse or foreplay probably extinguished any romance that was imparted by our dance, but I must also relate that the anxiety I felt about somebody walking in and seeing our two EMs humping doggie-style on the sofa turned me on more than I might like to admit. In fact, by the time I was naked and spread-eagled on the couch, I was writhing with desire. As Panzer lay beside me and began kissing me on my inner thigh I was secretly hoping that somebody would indeed walk into the salon, and I was also hoping that whoever came in would be as bizarre as anybody I'd ever seen in VL, and that he would *not* turn away on seeing us fucking, but instead move closer and stand right over us, watching—and, yes, maybe even join in, because I'd always fantasized about having two guys at once. Of course who could guarantee that my imagined watcher would even be a guy? She might be a girl. Then what? Or maybe another couple would come into the salon. That was certainly not unlikely. Would we have the courage to invite them to join our *play*? Or what if a whole group of guys came in… Or a group of biker chicks… Or what if somebody I knew came in… The more I continued to fantasize, the hotter I got, and now sensing my deepening passion, Panzer kept after me, pounding inside me from one position then another.

(Just wondering: Are you envisioning me right now as Fizzy Oceans, the VL EM, lying on the couch fucking this Polish guy like there's no tomorrow, or are you perhaps envisioning me as Amy Birkenstock from Seattle, sitting at my computer and fingering myself like a pathetic little nymphomaniac as I watch this cartoon guy pumping away at my cartoon pussy? Either way, I suppose you're getting pretty hot over all this talk about EM sex, but let me tell you, we're not even close to a climax yet, so allow me go on with the story, and once I've told it as it is—or as it was—then I'm pretty sure there won't be any further questions about whether or not emulations can get turned on and have sex in VL.)

Without a doubt, VL is all about realizing one's visions,

right? So of course my silent but very wicked prayer was answered. How could the VL gods and goddesses (Are you listening, Farmers?) not have heard my one deviant appeal? And why would they not accommodate me?

So there I was on the sofa, naked as the day I was born, legs apart with Panzer's big stiffy poking away at me (or at my emulation) as if he were trying to conceive something totally out of this world, and I'm all breathless and florid, and scared to death, and so embarrassed I could die on the spot, when in walks not one but three guys, each one clad in black leather, zippers shining and silver chains dangling from their hip pockets and breast pockets.

OMG!

And of course they come toward us, Panzer and me, both of us naked, fucking on the couch without shame! But we don't stop, not for one second. Not for a heartbeat! We keep fucking like there's no tomorrow, because for all we know there *is* no tomorrow. The three leather guys surround the sofa. I don't care; I want them to see this kind of passion. Why? I don't know, and I don't know to this day, but I do know I not only wanted them to watch us, but to not take their eyes off us (me) for even one second. Yes, I desperately needed their eyes on me, and I needed something else as well!

What I needed was an orgasm. To come and come and come! Not Fizzy Oceans, the EM. Because Fizzy Oceans can't come. Not fucking Panzer X. Not in a million years. Not ever! It was Amy Birkenstock that needed an orgasm—or two, or three, or four! Then and there! And by God I was going to have it!

At that moment I understood the reality of VL sex. And I never again saw Panzer X. romantically. Nor have I cultivated other romantic relationships in VL. Believe me, it's best that way. You can take my word for it. In VL, we can certainly recreate, but we cannot procreate. That's just how it is!

I suppose sex in VL is somewhat like reading a very

steamy novel and experiencing heart-pounding lust generated on the printed page. Having had a hand in republishing some very torrid stories—*The Decameron* by Giovanni Boccaccio (in the original Italian), *Lady Chatterley's Lover* by D. H. Lawrence, *Tropic of Cancer* by Henry Miller, and *Lolita* by Vladimir Nabocov—I do have a feeling for the vicarious effect that certain writers can convey. Yet sex in VL—by all accounts virtual sex—was still different than reading a lusty scene. Perhaps it could be compared to seeing a film portrayal of Constance Chatterley and her gamekeeper, as opposed to simply reading about their illicit exploits at his rustic cottage in the woods. Again, the senses: a glance if not the ecstasy of a touch; the sound of a lover's whisper if not the force of physical love; the lingering memory of a scent, a taste, if not the ponderous weight of our physical burden on earth!

Since our encounter at Heaven In the Clouds, Panzer and I have seen one another only in passing. Because we were never able to speak to one another very effectively in the first place, silence is not unnatural, yet we dare not look one another in the eye, because we both understand that one glance can unlock the kind of desire that nothing here in VL can satisfy, and we are smart enough not to traverse such treacherous territory again.

Yet I feel exquisite in the knowledge that such passion is possible even between two digital representations, because it guarantees, no matter what happens to our race in physical terms, that at least a very vivid idea of sexuality will persist in all its glory. My experience with Panzer—mysterious and incomplete as it necessarily had to be—confirms something I probably knew all along: that sexual desire happens in the brain, not in the loins; and once such feelings are imprinted upon a nervous system, or even within an electronic network, a certain kind of exponential energy is generated which nothing can extinguish. Perhaps we can kill ourselves with negligence and stupidity, and maybe we can render our beloved and fragile planet inhospitable, but apparently we can't extinguish the current of love, no matter how hard we try. What a relief!

Rome is known as the *Eternal City*, so a group of VL builders is working day and night to recreate it in Virtual Life as well. Dutch builders work to raise a virtual Amsterdam, as others create a virtual Barcelona, a virtual Vienna, and a virtual Paris. In Israel, plans are underway to construct a New Jerusalem. In Athens, an energetic congress of Greek builders is working to preserve the integrity of the Parthenon, as well as that of ancient Thira (which is now called Santorini and thought by some to be the remains of the Lost City of Atlantis), not to mention those who have attempted to recapture the allure of Mykonos Island in the sixties and seventies, because even in VL a stunning beach for gay guys will surely be needed. In America, VL builders have recreated New York's Greenwich Village, complimented by a virtual Bob Dylan and virtual Joan Baez singing folk songs in smoky basement bars. Others have recreated Disneyland. Turning to South America, the beach in Rio is a popular REP. In Japan, builders have fashioned extravagant resorts for the enjoyment of all. While Down Under, VL advocates are offered virtual adventures in the Outback. In India we can visit an ashram or bathe in the Ganges River. So, when all is said and done, there is just no telling how much of PL will be rebuilt in Virtual Life, but even if it's not complete, surely it will be quite impressive. And of course there are creations that have never existed in PL and exist only within Virtual Life. In VL, imagination reigns supreme, and cyber real estate is ridiculously cheap.

All this construction that is taking place in Virtual Life marks a building boom the likes of which the world has never known. Consider that cities like Rome and Tokyo and Calcutta evolved over many centuries. The Virtual Life builders apparently mean to duplicate such places in what might only be termed the *blink of an eye*—or whatever precious time we might have left before whatever is going to happen actually happens. Which brings to mind an important question: How much of PL is actually worth preserving? Might it not be construed as a public service to disregard altogether certain institutions? To preserve only that which is whole and workable, and simply trash the rest of it before it once again grabs humanity by the balls and squeezes till we scream?

My friend Crystal Marbella once asked me if I was more comfortable in Physical Life or in Virtual Life. I had to think about it for a while, but in the end I had to admit that I felt more comfortable in Virtual Life. "It probably shouldn't be that way," I told her. "After all, I was born into Physical Life, so that's where I ought to feel grounded. But I don't feel grounded there. So thank God I found Virtual Life. And thank God I found you, Crystal."

"I feel the same way, Fizzy. Here we have something worthwhile to do. These days I don't work to live, I live to work. There's something to be said for having a strong sense of purpose. And good friends, too! Not just people you go out drinking with, or go to a movie, or a party. What I mean is knowing and working with others who value your particular kind of creativity and your special gifts as much as they value their own, and who also share your passion and your resolve to create a world that is not only more fair and more just, but also more sustainable. And whether we succeed or fail is actually unimportant. What's important is that we've come together at this place, in this time, and that we are making the effort to create something better than we've known in the past."

"Let PL go to hell in a hand basket," I sang.

"And we'll watch it fall from right here in Virtual Life!" she said.

"Except a lot of people are probably going to get hurt," I said.

"Yeah, that's the real crappy part about all this," said

Crystal.

Even though I make no effort to see Panzer anymore, I still like to visit Imperial Rome. Thanks to Virtual Life, it's possible for me to experience the *Eternal City* as it must have been in its glory days, gleaming and regal, its citizens so full of themselves that they can't possibly imagine a time when *their* Rome will not be pre-eminent in the world, even as demise looms just beyond the Palatine Hill.

Is Rome still the embodiment of the Eternal City? Certainly yes! Does Imperial Rome's fate stand as an eternal example of what those who consider themselves invincible might expect? Positively yes! Speaking at the VBV, Dr. Adler alluded to no less than thirty previous world civilizations. The Hopi Indians are now preparing to leave the Fourth World behind and journey through a hole in the earth in search of the Fifth World, whatever that might mean. Standing here in a REP of Imperial Rome, a recreation though it may be, a virtual world, such things seem to make a bit more sense to me. I feel as eternal as the stones that form these ancient archways, these walls, terraces, porticos, colonnades and aqueducts. Of course I know nothing lasts forever, least of all any single civilization. The PL crowd acts like nothing's wrong; they fiddle as *their* Rome burns. And I implore them; ask the Romans what an incredibly fickle mistress glory can be, and just how transitory the spoils of war may prove. Ask what songs they sang as the flames took all they had and more…

I invite Kiz to meet me at the Coliseum, and when she arrives I show her the place that Panzer and I tried our best to get it on, and I tell her about how futile Physical Life feels to me, and that I'm really glad that I was the one to greet her the day she first logged on to Virtual Life.

"It's no use feeling so desperate," Kiz tries to console me.

"I don't know, Kiz. It's just—"

"You just have to keep busy," she advises. "That's what I do. That's how I cope. Not with silly, insignificant things. You must work at something meaningful. Whatever strikes you as being…useful. Whatever you think is important!"

"And that's it?" I ask.

"Yeah, more or less," says Kiz.

As the febrile sun sets on Imperial Rome (Is this fulsome garnet in the western sky a flaming chariot headed for a splendiferous crash in the Sea of Antiquity, or is it actually a Phoenix Rising?), we stand together in the shadow of the virtual Coliseum. And a very long shadow it casts! (I feel I must here draw attention to a fundamental distinction: I speak now from Virtual Life, which is a computer simulation. My emulation is standing in the Virtual Life recreation of modern-day Rome, which includes, as does PL Rome, the ruins of the Imperial City. Therefore, my emulation is standing before the recreation of a ruin. Curiously, I, Amy Birkenstock, might visit the PL Eternal City, and I might even experience this very scene with my PL senses. Do I consider the distinction to be important? No, I do not. I suppose that someday somebody in VL might reconstruct the entire Imperial City, with its Forum, its gods and goddesses, its Holy conquests, and its gladiatorial games. Or maybe that is not really necessary, as maybe it's already been done in PL.)

Eating gelato in front of the recreation of a ruin that was once an enormous bathhouse, a place where citizens went after a day's work not only to bathe, but also to relax and socialize and discuss the important events and issues of their lives, Kiz paints a vivid verbal picture for me of how people with different perceptual biases might indeed see the same events and imagery, yet interpret them in vastly different terms.

"Each of us looks at his environment and sees mainly what he sees. Seldom does he question whether anybody else, who might be looking at the same images, perceives them as he does, or whether one might react to those stimuli as he reacts to them. Invariably, though, there is variation—sometimes not so significant, but sometimes quite profound. It all depends on one's particular frame of reference. Does one tend to see the world in literal terms, or is his perception grounded in mostly symbolic terms? Does he define what he sees in terms of sensory information (I can see, hear, touch, taste, or smell this, therefore it must be real), or are his definitions formed in metaphors (I can see, hear, touch, taste or smell this; therefore it must refer to a feeling or an impression)? We each see the world from both contexts, but each individual also sees it predominantly one way or the other. This is an important distinction, but it is one that few people recognize. If we were able to acknowledge and accept such divergent forms of perception, then enhanced empathy would be the result.

"In PL, most people perceive and deal with the world in very literal terms. That is why consumerism—the feverish pursuit of money and the insane race to acquire more and more material possessions—is more or less dominant there. It's also why there are so many conflicts, so much bloodshed, so much hunger and inequality. PL is basically a Darwinian construction, and there is a fair amount of the NL 'eat-or-be-eaten' mentality remaining.

"Some of that literal mentality is carried over into VL, too. That's why we find REPs that are little more than digital reconstructions of PL commerce. In VL, however, there is also a different element, one that is less literal, one grounded in metaphor. Consider the creation of a species such as the Quinngen. VL quite naturally allows the incorporation of one's fantasy, and corroboration by the five senses is not necessarily required. In fact, sensual perception is sometimes severely limited by the medium, so we must learn to depend on more intuitive and more symbolic frames of reference. Finally, a world not defined and governed by our sensual limitations and our more primitive social constructions!"

"Kiz, I had no idea!"

"Come on, Fizzy. You may never have thought to verbalize it as I just have, but this is something you know innately. You tell me that you have trouble dealing with PL issues and dynamics, but you take to Virtual Life like a fish to water."

Bottom line: We seem to be caught in a vicious circle. In PL we find it increasingly difficult to connect with Natural Life; in Virtual Life we recreate portions of Physical Life with a few innovations derived from vision and fantasy, even as we find it all but impossible there to connect with any aspect of Natural Life. Meanwhile, Natural Life is rebelling precipitously against Physical Life, even as we in VL try feverishly to forge a lasting testament, a time capsule, of all that we are as a culture! If Natural Life ultimately renders humans expendable, what is to be our legacy? Is it an abandoned oil refinery or a munitions factory? Is it a dead forest? A festering swamp filled with toxins? Or might it not be the sum of all the hopes and dreams and visions and noble creativity that we can pour into VL in the presumably short time we have remaining?

And just who are these emulations walking so confidently through varied and diverse simulated environments? Certainly, they are not physical beings. Nor are they manifestations of mental life. Are they perhaps our spiritual bodies, now visible as digital representations? Are they the summation of every human who has ever walked the face of the earth? Are they representations of all we have ever been? Or of all that we presently are? Or all that we might become?

Virtual Life: Heaven In The Clouds? Or is it Phoenix Rising?

I can't wait to find out!

PART II
NEW PARADIGMS OF IDENTITY

6
DEAD MAN TALKING

TRANSFERRING TO LIT-A-RAMA, my EM materializes at Grove Press Square, a village green surrounded by numerous, tastefully appointed shops. Among them is *Foresight Publishing*, the VL version of a PL book publisher in London. (And there are other PL publishers renting shops in VL: *MacMillan & Co.* and *Bantam/Dell* are two noteworthy names on the REP's tenant roster). Lit-A-Rama's hostess, Jeannine Greene, operates the Foresight shop. She also coordinates many of the events staged at various Lit-A-Rama venues, as well as renting out shops to tenants with literary interests and helping those visiting the REP feel welcome and comfortable.

Also located on Grove Press Square is a shop called *Genealogy*, which is becoming an ever more important entity here in Virtual Life (for obvious reasons). Day and night (relative temporal designations here in VL as it is possible to regulate sunlight and darkness with a keystroke), any number of researchers can be found searching the archives for information relating to family histories. At *Genealogy*, the entire genealogical library maintained by the Mormon Church and located at Salt Lake City is available online.

A short stroll off any of the streets leading from the Grove Press Square Quadrangle will reveal interesting shops operated by proprietors with various interests. On George Orwell Alley, one finds *Lilly Pond Books*, as well as an exhibit highlighting the work of author Robert Anton Wilson. On Shakespeare Street, *Pomegranate Princess* offers a unique literary perspective, and on Barbara Cartland Close, one might visit the shop of *Yoko Oh No!* On Louis L'amour Lane we find *Worlds 2 Go*, a Swedish art publisher, and *Poet's Row*.

Open Books is located a short walk from Grove Press Square on a small street called Jeff Bezos Alley, but instead of going directly there, I cross the green and head for the Writers' Pen Café. This morning I'm meeting Crystal for cappuccino and conversation. We often meet at Writers' Pen to discuss publishing strategy, or to relax together in an environment that is less formal than the shop itself. Today we shall be reviewing a list of classic titles that we are considering for online publication. It's not that we are overly presumptuous in selecting which classic books we publish (after all, these literary efforts have all stood the test of time), but since we have only a limited amount of time to devote to the Open Books Project, and since we also realize that we can never publish every piece of classic literature we might want to offer for posterity, it is of course necessary that we make selections that we feel not only portray the literary tradition in its best light, but also those that will appeal to readers both present and future.

Also on our agenda for this morning's meeting is the planning of a party. Even though the Open Books Project is already well underway, and even though the Virtual Life shop has been open to visitors for more than a year, we have never really had a Grand Opening celebration, and Crystal and I have determined that such a soiree is long overdue.

Entering Writers' Pen, I see that Crystal has not yet arrived, so I draw espresso from the machine located on a sideboard, and then froth the milk to make my drink complete. At the moment, I am alone in the café, but that's of little concern. I take a seat and look out the window at an unrestricted view of a tranquil sea. I really like this view, as it seems to lend itself to the musings of those involved in the creative process. Hey! That's me, isn't it? Though in real life I would never in a million years have envisioned myself a publisher of classic literature, or a contributor to the artistic community at large. After all, in real life my job is boring: I work at a medical billing office. And my education is limited (remember that I dropped out of high school midway through my final semester). So I have Virtual Life, but more specifically Crystal, to thank for my current interest and involvement in the creative arts, which I must admit has given me a renewed idealism that literally defies Physical Life's limitations, large or small.

As I watch my friend and partner walk through the doorway at Writers' Pen, I admire the obvious confidence she displays through her emulation's upright yet relaxed posture, in her discerning sense of fashion, and her careful yet still understated grooming. Sometimes I tend to forget that in PL she is European. What must it really be like to live in Copenhagen?

"Sorry I'm late," she says as she moves to the espresso machine.

"No worries," I tell her. "I just got here myself."

What I know about Sonja Jörgensen's life would fit inside a thimble. Of course here in VL such details are not supposed to be important. Still, I sometimes can't help wondering who is sitting at the computer putting his (or her) emulation through its Virtual Life paces. I once asked Crystal to send me a photo of Sonja, and she promised she would, but so far I've not received it. I suppose I might remind her, but I don't want to intrude where I may not be welcome. The friendship we share in Virtual Life is very precious to me, and I don't want to do anything that might spoil it. Anyway, I get a big rush every time I see Crystal's EM in VL.

Today, neither of us has brought an attaché case. Nor have we brought folders filled with lists or schedules. Our world is a digital one, and whatever facts or figures we need are stored on VL note cards that can be displayed on our monitors at any time. Our first order of business is to determine our list of publications for the next quarter. We have each nominated four books. My candidates include the *Collected Stories and Poems* of Edgar Allen Poe, *War of the Worlds* by H. G. Wells, *The Legend of Sleepy Hollow* by Nathaniel Hawthorne, and *Our Town* by Thornton Wilder. Crystal's list reflects her European upbringing: *Madame Bovary* by Flaubert, *Anna Karenina* by Leo Tolstoy, *The Memoirs of Giacomo Casanova*, and *The Canterbury Tales* by Geoffrey Chaucer. We will ultimately choose four of the eight books for publication on the Open Books web site, and each of us will be responsible for publishing his two nominees. After publication we will announce the new editions on as many Internet sites as possible, thereby creating the necessary links to place the books on search engines so that anyone can find them and read them free of charge.

After deliberation we determine that of my selections we will publish *The Legend of Sleepy Hollow* and *Our Town*; of Crystal's nominees we will publish *Madame Bovary* and the *Canterbury Tales*. We both understand that to publish four books in three months' time is a tremendous amount of work, but we have already completed similar projects on several other occasions, and we each feel up to the task. I must admit that with each new book I publish online comes a degree of anticipation and excitement familiar to me in no other way. I've come to crave the work involved in publishing these books, because the emotional high I get each time I see a new publication online makes every hour I spend preparing these texts seem worthwhile and fulfilling. I know that I'm not the only one who feels such a rush at seeing new (classic) works appear on the Open Books web site. In fact, there is a group of no less than ten thousand people who anxiously await each new book, and that number grows with each publication. Of course ten thousand readers is quite a small number when you consider how many readers there are in the world—or even in Virtual Life. Still, there is no doubt in my mind, nor is there one in Crystal's, as to the value of our effort, and we consider it a privilege to continue this work!

As for Open Books' Grand Opening party, Crystal has an idea to make the event one not to be forgotten. Setting her coffee on the table before us, she turns to me, folds her hands and places them on her lap.

"What's the one thing that will make an event like this a sure draw?" she asks.

I shrug my shoulders. "I don't know. What?"

"An appearance by a celebrity," she says breathlessly.

"Isn't that a bit cheap for our purpose?" I ask.

"Depends on who the celebrity is," she says. Obviously, she has already thought this through.

"Who do you have in mind?" I ask.

"Mark Twain," she answers.

"But he's dead!" I point out.

"All the better!" she says as if resurrection is an everyday occurrence. "We're already committed to reclaiming all-but-forgotten literature to ensure its legacy, so why not resurrect a dead author or two? Each month we might feature a different speaker: Jean Paul Sartre one month, and Ernest Hemingway the next. I've even dreamed up a scheme by which we can offer a grant to living writers financed by funds we raise publishing the work of the deceased. Isn't it fabulous?"

"I assume you've already booked his appearance," I say.

Crystal takes her cup in hand and sips her cappuccino. "Not yet," she answers. "I wanted to run it by you first."

Concealing the skepticism I'm feeling, I nod my consent. "If you can book Mark Twain for an appearance at Open Books, then by all means… But I suggest you finalize the booking before somebody gets wind of what you're doing."

Crystal smiles triumphantly and says, "Right you are, Fizzy! I'll confirm the date and time today."

I must admit that at first I had a hard time with the idea that a person long dead could be the featured guest at Open Books' Grand Opening party, but the more I thought about it, the more I came to embrace the idea. After all, if one is accustomed to suspending his long held definitions of reality in Virtual Life (as one does each and every time he manifests within this precarious world), and if he is comfortable with pushing out the boundaries of what we have come to acknowledge as real and what we have conventionally dismissed as fantasy, then why should he draw a line between the living and the dead? Indeed, even this seemingly fundamental distinction might be rendered a moot point, and the grave become something neither cold nor permanent. And I don't care what anybody says, that's big news!

Walking from Grove Press Square through a street-size opening at one corner of the quadrangle, a wide expanse of sea comes instantly into view (And how I love rounding that corner at sunrise, VL time!), and after only a few steps more over a carpet of immaculately manicured lawn punctuated with stepping-stones placed (by Sly) at perfect intervals for the stride of an EM, the Open Books shop becomes visible, its large sign showcasing the logo that Crystal painstakingly designed with its three interconnecting rings, one for the 'O' in *Open*, along with the two adjoining circles in *Books*, above the plate-glass window and wide-open doorway. Then, up two steps from street level (yes, emulations in VL can climb stairs), and we are inside the shop.

Crystal Marbella is the formal owner of the shop. She leased the store from Jeannine Greene and Sly Sideways, the co-owners of Lit-A-Rama, during the formative days of the REP. As Crystal tells it, 41 Jeff Bezos Alley was barely an address then, and immediately after she rented the shop Sly had to finish paving the street and install streetlights and decorative vegetation. Over the course of the next few months, Crystal designed the interior of the shop. What's more, she made everything inside, from the rugs on the floor, to the furniture, to the hardwood oak stage upstairs where lectures and readings take place.

The color motif of the shop's downstairs décor is light gray with accents of the bluest Mediterranean blue that the artist Henri Matisse ever employed in a painting or a cutout. Two Persian rugs cover large areas of the dark gray ceramic floor, and three partially exposed brick walls above (How trendy!) offset a creamy backdrop below. The furniture is covered with a light gray linen fabric, and the tabletops are made of simulated stained glass. Lining the tops of three walls are large-scale replicas of the artistic covers designed for the titles in the Open Books library.

At the center of the shop's back wall is the transfer device. This mechanism (*sic*) is employed by anyone wishing to move from the shop's ground floor to the second floor. A single mouse-click places the user in the Open Books Auditorium.

Just like the shop's lower level, the upper floor is wide open. Contrasting the exposed brick walls is a forest green carpet, plush and sculptured, and floor to ceiling windows allow one to look down on the street below or through the windows of the shops across the street. At the far end of the long room is 'Writers' Corner'. There, a stage with a hardwood floor stands ready to heighten speakers or exhibitors.

I suppose I should explain that Open Books, as well as

every shop in the Lit-A-Rama REP, and indeed throughout the entirety of Virtual Life, is open twenty-four hours a day, three hundred sixty-five days a year. It makes no difference whether or not the shop owners are present at their given locations, as all purchases—and, in the case of Open Books, all *donations*—are made online. (In fact, there are more donations made to the Open Books Project than one might imagine, some for very large sums (in dollars and euros and pounds and greenshoots) by individuals or corporate sponsors with a vested interest in promoting literacy, or simply for the purpose of supporting the arts in general and preserving classic literature specifically.) Of course in VL no cash is exchanged hand to hand, and Virtual Life vendors provide no physical merchandise. Virtual Life is a virtual world, and *information* is ultimately the product of each merchant or advocate or provider.

Today, Open Books is a thoroughly comfortable environment for all who visit to spend time conversing or reading the various note cards that describe the project's purpose and goals. One mouse-click away is the greater Open Books web site, where all our published books are available for anyone to read free of charge.

Open Books' (unofficial) **credo:**
*"To truly free art,
art must be free!"*

Shortly after I became involved with Open Books (albeit indirectly at first), Crystal Marbella asked me to write a mission statement for the project. I was flattered that she would trust me to pen such an important document and told her I'd give it my best effort. Here's what I wrote:

"The mission of Open Books is to publish literature online and offer it to readers worldwide free of charge. Open Books publishes literature in three specific areas: Classics, Moderns and Futures (which include experimental literature and literary efforts in multimedia formats).

Open Books recognizes the need to move the literary publishing industry into a more environmentally friendly atmosphere, therefore all Open Books publications are paper-free and distributed without the use of petrol or other deleterious fuels customarily used in transporting bulk goods.

The owners of Open Books understand and acknowledge the need to contribute resources generously back into the community at large. Therefore, Open Books does not offer its products for sale directly, rather it operates by our 'Adopt-A-Book' sponsorship program, where fifty percent of all revenues are redistributed into the community as contributions to literacy programs, as well as grants to living writers through our Dead Writers' Society®, where present-day authors are the beneficiaries of efforts of those now deceased and whose work is in public domain.

Lastly, it is the mission of Open Books to provide and preserve literary excellence in a timeless and artistic venue for all the peoples of the world to enjoy regardless of their location or economic station in life. All payment for Open Books products is voluntary, as our primary commerce is in the realm of ideas."

When Crystal read what I'd written she was so impressed that she immediately asked me if I would like to be her partner at Open Books. "Are you serious?" I asked her. After all, the Open Books shop is not like a conventional bookstore where sales people help customers find the titles they're searching for, or where inventories must be kept, or orders for new products placed.

"What Open Books really needs is a publicist," Crystal told me.

"A publicist?"

"Someone to spread the word far and wide about what we're doing."

"I don't think I'm qualified for that sort of position," I told her.

"The fact of the matter is that the Internet is still virgin territory," Crystal explained. "It's a bit like the Wild West in cyberspace—an exceptionally vast territory, uncharted and untamed, and anything goes. You make up the rules as you go along, Fizzy. Saddle up your favorite horse, strap on your six-shooter, and head into the wilderness!"

And that's how I became the publicist for Open Books.

The Open Books Grand Opening Party will certainly be my most challenging promotional project to date, especially since it will feature a posthumous appearance by the legendary author, Mark Twain. Needless to say, I'm putting my heart and soul into the work.

First, I will make posters advertising the event and place them all over Lit-A-Rama, as well as other strategic REPs throughout Virtual Life. I will place an ad in the VL newspaper, and then write messages on every Internet forum I can find. I will write press releases and publish them on Internet syndicates in the hope that my articles will be picked up by various *e-zines* and other web sites. I will write mass emails to everyone on the Open Books sizeable database, and I will buy advertising time on several VL radio stations. I will even make a video presentation based on Twain's famous story, *The Celebrated Jumping Frog of Calaveras County.*

Tried and true are such promotional methods, yet the result of my effort will remain in doubt until the night of the party; because even employing every means at my disposal, these days the attendance for a literary event such as this one is tenuous at best—certainly so in PL, and even so in Virtual Life. The sad truth is that while book sales are stronger than ever in retail chain stores, sales for *literary* books are more or less non-existent. In fact, a couple of years ago the world's largest book retailer made the conscious corporate decision to eliminate literary titles from the shelves of its more than one thousand stores. Imagine that! Walk into any (I won't reveal the name of the retailer here) store worldwide, and what will you find? Not *Moby Dick.* Not *David Copperfield.* Not *Gulliver's Travels.* What you will find (displayed prominently in the well lighted window and throughout the more than ten thousand square feet of bright and happy retail space) is *An Annotated (and Illustrated) Guide to Paris Hilton's Wardrobe*, *Fat Girls Can Date, Too*, and *Sports Betting: How to Wager and Win*. These hot and heavy titles are always flanked by any number of *Self-Help's*, faddish diet books, cookbooks (so after trying all the recipes you'll have to buy the faddish diet books), and sports memorabilia. Of course there is never a shortage of cat calendars, day-timers, or other notions. As for real books—serious books—you might as well forget it. Publishers don't publish them anymore—at least not in any significant number—because most literary books can't recover the firm's initial investment. Which is why Open Books' (unofficial) credo came into being in the first place (and I hope you'll indulge me if I repeat it): *To truly free art, art must be free!* I must admit that I (this is Amy Birkenstock speaking now) seldom visit such stores anymore (there are no less than sixteen of them in the greater Seattle area). They have less and less to offer, because I've read all the redundant plotlines and wooden characters and unimaginative themes that I can stand to read in one lifetime, and besides that, it is rumored that the espresso at the coffee bar is pseudo-Colombian. What does that tell you?

Of course Crystal also realizes the inescapable truth about the decline of literature. Though it doesn't seem to phase her one bit as she works feverishly to publish yet another classic title online. She's the quintessential worker bee, and she is able to accomplish amazing results for her singular commitment. And she will not hold me accountable if hardly anybody shows up to hear Mark Twain (who will of course be speaking through an anonymous impersonator, one who has promised to reveal his identity after the program) lecture at the Open Books auditorium. Crystal knows I'll do my best to attract a crowd, but if it's not in the stars, then we'll press onward with our work. Since money is not our objective, we have nothing to lose and everything to gain. The books we publish online are for posterity, not for profit. And if one more person is able to read and enjoy *Alice's Adventures in Wonderland*, then our effort is wholly worthwhile. Honestly, I (Amy Birkenstock) can say that Open Books is the single best endeavor in which I've ever been involved, and I'm so proud of the books we publish, and the shop in Virtual Life, and the overall effort we make that my job as a publicist and a publisher has given my life a renewed sense of purpose. Which of course is why I'm logged on to Virtual Life nearly every minute of my *free* time?

So, regarding my effort to publicize Open Books' Grand Opening party, we'll see who turns up. Free wine and free hors d'ouvres can't hurt the effort to attract the so-called hordes. And it is not unknown for celebrities to show up at Virtual Life events. Once Robert Redford (or perhaps an emulation look-alike) showed up for the first screening of an exclusive VL documentary film on water shortages in the American West. An emulation of Mae West was seen in attendance at a VL strippers' convention, and Yogi Berra was interviewed while taking batting practice at a REP of Yankee Stadium. And we've got Mark

Twain, perhaps America's greatest author to date! Anybody out there in Cyberland listening?

The party itself is scheduled for nine o'clock on Saturday evening, but Crystal and I arrive at the shop just after noon to begin preparing for the event. With no real sense of how many might attend, we have high hopes for a big turnout to see and hear our celebrated guest of honor. On the shop's second floor we place folding chairs in rows ten across and fifteen deep, while Kiz lays a table at the back of the room with hors d'ouvres and boxed wine. Our friend Tooltech helps us set up the PA, over which Mark Twain will give his lecture.

As the red sun dips below the aquatic horizon on the Lit-A-Rama REP, everything seems ready—everything, that is, except the single most crucial element of the evening's festivities: the emulation of Mr. Mark Twain has neither appeared at the shop, nor has it been seen anywhere in Lit-A-Rama. In fact, nobody has spoken with either the author, or with his agent, Mr. Houston, during the past week. If the esteemed author fails to turn up, we know we will look like fools—or frauds! Worse yet, Open Books' reputation might suffer a serious setback, and we hardly want that to happen. Even as Crystal Marbella, perfectly composed and ever optimistic, seems to take Mr. Twain's failure to appear with equanimity, Sonja Jörgensen of Copenhagen, Denmark confides to me by IM that she's indeed sweating bullets over the writer's unexplained absence, and that she is not at all happy at the prospect of being stood up, even by one as auspicious as Mark Twain!

By seven-thirty more than one hundred EMs have gathered inside and outside the Open Books shop to see and hear and take part in a presentation that I have presumptuously billed as the '*Event of the Season*' in Virtual Life. Assessing the crowd, I can hardly believe that all these people have actually come to hear a writer that's been dead for nearly a hundred years. (In reality, and though I never fully understood it as I was planning and promoting Mark Twain's appearance at Open Books, Crystal and I were staging what might well have been the literary event of the century—or any century! Without question, Mark Twain is the quintessential American novelist, beloved by generations of American readers, and revered by as many generations of aspiring and accomplished writers and authors. How had I not recognized the impact of bringing this literary giant to our humble little stage at our shop in Virtual Life?)

With each EM dressed in his most colorful and stylish clothes, the crowd on whole resembles a school of colorful tropical fish swimming about in a rather exotic aquarium. Some transfer upstairs to find their seats, or mill about the large room eating whole wheat crackers with salmon pâté and sipping Chardonnay from plastic wine glasses and talking with friends, or reading note cards, or looking out the second floor windows at even more people gathered in the street outside the shop. Another large group, perhaps never before having visited Open Books, or some maybe logged on to Virtual Life for the first time, wait inside the shop at street level. Sitting side by side upon the couches Crystal made to furnish the shop, they look like birds on a line waiting for the loud bang of a gun to send them winging to the Four Winds!

Turning to Crystal, I say, "I sure hope this doesn't turn out to be the '*disaster of the season*' in Virtual Life. How embarrassing it will be if he doesn't show up!"

"Don't worry, Fizzy. He'll show up."

"I sure hope you're right."

"In fact, here he comes now!"

Crystal points her finger at a man with longish white hair, a white beard and moustache, and dressed in a white suit making his way through the crowd. He seems to be in no hurry to reach the stage as he greets and converses with many along his path.

"It's Mark Twain!" I exclaim gleefully. My schoolgirl blush reveals my excitement, which is a surprise even to me!

As the esteemed author finally reaches our position, he holds out his hand first to Crystal, then to me, and says, "Good evening, ladies. It is my pleasure to be here tonight, and I thank you for the opportunity to address this rather auspicious crowd gathered in your, shall I say, 'unique' salon."

"Good evening, Mr. Clemens," says Crystal. "And welcome back from the dead!"

Mark Twain smiles for the first time tonight. His black eyes twinkle beneath bushy, raised eyebrows. In his posture, the hint of a bow. "Death is the starlit strip between the companionship of yesterday and the reunion of tomorrow. All say, 'How hard it is that we have to die'—a strange complaint to come from the mouths of people who have had to live. Whoever has lived long enough to find out what life is, knows how deep a debt of gratitude we owe to Adam, the first great benefactor of our race. He brought death into the world."

"Mr. Clemens," says Crystal, "the reputation of your wit precedes you. We are indeed happy you could join us tonight. Please accept our most heartfelt welcome to Open Books."

"Ladies, the pleasure is all mine." From his coat pocket he produces a small silver flask. Turning away momentarily, he takes a quick nip of the beverage contained within the vessel. Then he replaces the cap and stores the flask once more in his breast pocket. He clears his throat before again speaking to Crystal and to me.

"I think we never become really and genuinely our entire and honest selves until we are dead—and not then until we have been dead years and years. People ought to start dead, and they would be honest so much earlier."

Crystal lays her hand gently on our guest's shoulder. "It certainly sounds as if you are ready to begin your talk, Mr. Clemens. Let me see if I can assemble the crowd inside our far too cramped auditorium, and let's see if I can bring this gathering to some sort of order."

Mark Twain again clears his throat. "Allow me to take a seat onstage to go over my notes, and I will await your introduction, my dear lady."

Crystal and I transfer downstairs to announce to the crowd gathered in the shop and outside on the street that Mark Twain has arrived and is nearly ready to give his address, and that they should proceed at once (in orderly fashion, if possible) to the upstairs event center. "The transfer device is at your disposal," I tell them. "Please form a line at the center of the shop."

"Don't worry," Crystal announces, "we will not start Mr. Twain's lecture until everyone has transferred to the second floor and found a suitable place to see and hear the presentation. One at a time, please!"

It takes at least fifteen minutes for all those downstairs to make their way to the upstairs auditorium via the transfer device, and another ten minutes for them to find a place from which to watch the presentation. An overflow crowd (for which I'm feeling both relieved and redeemed) has made it necessary for a majority of those in attendance to stand, thereby making the count of attendees quite a few more than the one hundred fifty for whom we had provided chairs. Crystal has made her way onto the stage, and she is conferring with Mark Twain. Kiz is tending bar and passing out hors d'ouvres, as I survey the multitude gathered in our virtual lecture hall.

Among the throng of emulations seated on folding chairs, as well as those standing shoulder to shoulder in the wings and at the back of the room, I see many familiar faces. Seated front and center are Six Fables and Winter Heart whom Kiz and I met at the Burning Man REP. Standing near the refreshment table is Ego Ectoplasm. Also in attendance are Jeannine Greene and Sly Sideways, as well as the entire crowd from Dirty Nellie's Pub. Near the back of the room I notice Panzer X. standing next to Igloo Iceman, and next to the transfer device (Is he planning a quick exit?) stands the enigmatic kid from La Paz, Bolivia (or the displaced nun from Ohio), Omar Paquero.

Also present (and quite to my surprise) are a whole host of very distinguished literary personalities. Is it totally unexpected that such a propitious lot has chosen to attend tonight's event? Probably not: after all, this is to be Mark Twain's first public speech since the start of the twentieth century, so why wouldn't the literary intelligentsia of our time want to be present? Within the crowd (and returned from the dead) I observe the emulations of Eugene O'Neill (deceased in 1953), Ernest Hemingway (deceased in 1959), William Faulkner (deceased in 1962), Jack Kerouac (deceased in 1969), Truman Capote (deceased in 1984), Frank Waters (deceased in 1995), James A. Michener (deceased in 1997), Saul Bellow and Arthur Miller (both deceased in 2005), William Styron (deceased in 2006), and lastly Kurt Vonnegut (deceased in 2007). Also present to hear Twain's first twenty-first century remarks are the emulations of Nobel winner Doris Lessing (88), Ray Bradbury (87), Norman Mailer (84), Gore Vidal (82), Philip Roth (74), Margaret Atwood (68), and Stephen King (60). At once obvious to me is the fact that the literary brain trust of our time (or what remains of it) is decidedly advanced in years and probably not long for this world. Which brings to mind a single burning question: Where is the new generation of writers that will carry the torch into the future? Apparently, they are *not* included in the greater marketing strategy of Random House or Houghton Mifflin.

Impressed and quite pleased by the number of people who have chosen to attend the party, Crystal takes the stage to welcome our guests and to introduce our esteemed speaker. She blows on the microphone then taps it before addressing the overflow audience. "Ladies and gentlemen, may I please have your attention?"

Conversations quickly abate; most of those assembled

would much rather hear the remarks of Mark Twain than the sound of their own voices.

"Needless to say, tonight is a very special night for us at Open Books. Though we have been operating for more than a year, and though we have already published a total of twenty-four titles online, this is our official Grand Opening. I would like to thank each and every one of you for attending tonight's festivities, but even more so for your support of our publishing project. Of course we all recognize the importance of preserving classic literature, and in today's publishing environment, where profit often takes precedence over content and quality, it is perhaps all the more important that the great works of our time do not fall into obscurity. What's more, we take this opportunity to offer these works to all the people of the world—especially those that might otherwise not have the chance to read them—absolutely free of charge!

"Of course we all know that there's no such thing as a free lunch. Or so the saying goes… And that is why we must ask for your generous (and voluntary) support. Our unique *adopt-a-book* program offers you that opportunity, so please take some time to review and to consider the program.

"Now, I know that you've not come here tonight to here me pitch our program. No, you've come to hear the godfather of American Letters give his first address in nearly one hundred years. And what a treat this is for us all! Ladies and gentlemen, please give a warm Virtual Life welcome to Mark Twain!"

Mark Twain stands and approaches the podium to a resounding round of applause. Crystal shakes his hand before withdrawing. Twain stands before the microphone acknowledging the generous ovation. He clears his throat before speaking.

"I must admit that during my lifetime I never saw what to me seemed an atom of truth that there was a future life, and yet…I was strongly inclined to expect one. However, this is not exactly what I might have envisioned. Nevertheless…

"Before I go much further, I would like to thank my lovely hostesses, Miss Crystal Marbella and Miss Fizzy Oceans, for giving me one more opportunity to speak my platitudes in public. I would also like to thank you, this fine and noteworthy audience, for coming to hear my diatribe, though why you've chosen to put aside more enjoyable pursuits is a question I will not endeavor to answer…"

Subdued laughter ripples through the room before he continues.

"Because of the express purpose of this gathering tonight—and perhaps for no other reason—one might be inclined to ask the question: What is a classic? It is my opinion that one can find in a text whatever he brings to it, if he will stand between it and the mirror of his imagination. In short, a classic is something that everybody wants to have read and nobody wants to read."

Again, laughter. Twain waits for the laughter to subside before beginning the body of his address.

"My given name is Samuel Langhorne Clemens, and I was born in Florida, Missouri, on November 30, 1835. I was the sixth of seven children, and only three of my siblings survived childhood. When I was four, my family moved to Hannibal, a port town on the Mississippi River that would serve as my inspiration for the fictional town of St. Petersburg in *The Adventures of Tom Sawyer* and *Adventures of Huckleberry Finn*.

"In March 1847, when I was just eleven years old, my father died of pneumonia. The following year, I became a printer's apprentice. In 1851, I began working as a typesetter at the Hannibal Journal, a newspaper that was conveniently owned by my brother Orion, and I was allowed to contribute articles and humorous sketches for publication.

"When I was eighteen, I left Hannibal and worked as a

printer in New York City, Philadelphia, St. Louis and Cincinnati. In the evenings, I educated myself in public libraries, finding wider sources of information there than I would have found at a conventional school.

"At twenty-two, I returned to Missouri, and on a voyage to New Orleans down the Mississippi River, the steamboat captain inspired me to pursue a career as a riverboat pilot. This vocation I undertook wholeheartedly, and I also convinced my brother Henry to join me. Tragically, this decision inadvertently led to the death of my brother, when the ship he was working on exploded. Because I had foreseen this event a month earlier in a dream, I held myself responsible for his death. For the remainder of my life I fervently engaged in studies of parapsychology (with the esteemed researcher Nikola Tesla as my mentor) and became one of the founding members of the Society for Psychical Research.

"When my brother Orion was appointed secretary to the territorial governor of Nevada, I headed west with him. We traveled for more than two weeks by stagecoach across the Great Plains and the Rocky Mountains. These experiences became the basis for my book, *Roughing It*, and later for *The Celebrated Jumping Frog of Calavares County*. My journey ended in the silver mining town of Virginia City, where I became a miner for a time. When that endeavor thankfully failed, I found work at the Virginia City newspaper, which was where I first used the *nom de plume* Mark Twain.

"In 1867, I embarked on a steamship trip to Mediterranean Europe. It was on that trip that I met Charles Langdon, who showed me a photograph of his sister Olivia. Well, I fell in love with Olivia at first sight. A year later we met, and shortly after we became engaged. We married in Elmira, New York.

"Olivia came from a wealthy but liberal family— nothing like your liberals today—and through them I met abolitionists, socialists, and 'principled atheists', activists for women's rights and social equality. We lived our first years in Buffalo, but we relocated to Hartford, Connecticut in 1871. In 1873, I began the building of the house where we raised our three daughters, and where we celebrated thirty-four years of marital bliss.

"I outlived Olivia and two of my daughters, Susy and Jean. In later life I grew lonely and depressed, and I longed for the grave. I came in with Halley's Comet in 1835, and I quite expected to go out with it as well. The Almighty had said, no doubt: 'Now here are these two unaccountable freaks; they came in together, they must go out together.' And I died of heart failure on April 10, 1910, in Redding, Connecticut."

Just as Mr. Clemens finishes the summary of his life, an emulation interrupts the lecture as she transfers, somewhat ostentatiously, into the room. The speaker turns his attention toward her, as do many in the audience. The emulation, blond and beautiful and waiting for recognition, stands momentarily in the limelight. "My God! It's Paris Hilton!" someone exclaims a bit breathlessly.

"Good evening," Mr. Clemens addresses her. "We're very happy you could join us tonight."

Paris's EM looks round the room in confusion. "Thanks," she says, "but where the fuck am I?"

"You're at the Grand Opening celebration for Open Books in Virtual Life, and you've just interrupted Mark Twain's first lecture in almost a hundred years," says Crystal, a bit irritated by the intrusion.

"Mark Twain? How lame!" says Paris.

"I beg your pardon!" says Crystal.

"What sort of place is this, anyway?" asks Paris.

"Open Books is a publisher of classic literature," says Crystal. "It is also a book store."

"A book store, huh?" says Paris. "I wrote a book. Do you sell my book here?" she asks.

"What is your book about?" Crystal inquires, quite tolerantly.

"It's about *me*, of course," Paris humphs.

"Open Books is not that kind of book store," Crystal explains.

Paris clicks her tongue and rolls her eyes. "I am *so* out of here!" she says.

And with that the emulation transfers away from Lit-A-Rama altogether. With her departure, attention is once again focused on Samuel Langhorne Clemens.

"Tell us about Tom Sawyer!" calls one of the guests in the audience.

"And Huckleberry Finn!" calls another.

Mr. Clemens smiles and resumes his lecture. "Of course *The Adventures of Tom Sawyer* drew on my boyhood experiences in Hannibal. In fact, Tom Sawyer is me as a boy, more or less, with traces of my schoolmates John Briggs and Will Bowen. Huck Finn, who plays a supporting role in *The Adventures of Tom Sawyer* is based on my boyhood friend Tom Blankenship.

"The truth about Huck Finn," Twain relates, "is that it was the most difficult book I ever wrote—that is, it gave me the most trouble. During the summer of 1876, I wrote over four hundred manuscript pages of *Adventures of Huckleberry Finn*, but I did not complete the book until seven years later."

"That's because you lost your nerve," the emulation of Ernest Hemingway shouts out.

"I beg your pardon, sir," says Mark Twain a bit indignantly.

"If you read it," explains Hemingway, "you have to stop where the Nigger Jim is stolen from the boys. That's the real end. The rest is just cheating."

"A little respect for Mr. Clemens," says the emulation of James A. Michener. "After all, the *Adventures of Huckleberry Finn* is commonly accepted as the 'Great American Novel,' an opinion with which I wholly concur!"

"The main premise behind *Huckleberry Finn* is a young boy's belief in the right thing to do even though the rest of society believes it is wrong," Twain explains.

From the audience comes another question: "Mr. Clemens, in your time you became something of a political radical. What comment might you make about the politics of the present time?"

"Some of my critics said that my cynicism toward politics, and specifically the writing of *A Connecticut Yankee in King Arthur's Court*, marked the beginning of the end for me as a serious writer." Clemens turns up his palms and gazes toward the heavens. "What is one to say concerning the wisdom of the critic? And who am I to disagree? I know one thing for certain, turning my pen toward the political spectrum of events all but financially bankrupted me. The *Tragedy of Puddinhead Wilson* was always misconstrued.

"When I finished Carlyle's *French Revolution* in 1871, I was a Girondin; every time I have read it since, I have read it differently—being influenced and changed, little by little, by life and environment...and now I lay the book down once more, and recognize that I am a Sansculotte! And not a pale, characterless Sansculotte, but a Marat!

"What I know of today's politics would hardly qualify me as an expert, but my cursory impression is that fast and easy money rules the game. What else is new, my friends? Yet, it seems that today's politicians have raised greed to an art form, and they have successfully perfected every imaginable technique of extracting every last cent from the vulnerable to deposit it in the accounts of the well-to-do. Again, what else is new, my friends?

"That said, I too was once a red hot imperialist. During the Philippine-American War, I wanted the American eagle to go screaming into the Pacific. Why not spread its wings over the Philippines, I asked myself? I said to myself: Here are a people who have suffered for three centuries. We can make them as free as ourselves, give them a government and country of their own, put a miniature of the American Constitution afloat in the Pacific, start a new republic to take its place among the free nations of the world (today that is called nation building, I'm told). It seemed to me a great task to which we had addressed ourselves. But I have thought some more since then, and I have read carefully the treaty of Paris (which ended the Spanish-American War), and I have seen that we never intended to free, but to subjugate the people of the Philippines. We went there to conquer, not to redeem. It should, it seems to me, be our pleasure and duty to make those people free, and let them deal with their own domestic questions in their own way. And so I am now an anti-imperialist. I am opposed to having the eagle put its talons on any other land!

"To demonstrate my conviction, I was twice the vice president of the American Anti-Imperialism League."

"Mr. Clemens, would you call yourself a pacifist or a revolutionary?" comes an impromptu question from the audience.

"I am said to be a revolutionist in my sympathies, by birth, by breeding and by principle. I am always on the side of the revolutionists, because there never was a revolution unless there were some oppressive and intolerable conditions against which to revolt."

At this point in the presentation, Crystal Marbella intervenes to say, "As we are nearly out of time, Mr. Clemens, would you please tell us, before you go, about the origin of your very famous pen name?"

"Ah, yes… Mark Twain! How did I come to use this pseudonym as my primary literary signature? The story is a simple one: It came from my years working on Mississippi riverboats, where two fathoms, a depth indicating 'safe water' for the boat to float over was measured on the sounding line. A fathom is a maritime unit of depth, equivalent to two yards (approximately 1.8 meters); 'twain' is an archaic term for 'two'. The river boatman's cry was 'mark twain' or, more fully, 'by the mark twain', meaning 'according to the mark (on the line), (the depth is) two (fathoms), that is, 'there are twelve feet of water underneath the boat and it is safe to pass'.

"But this most famous pen name was not entirely my invention…

"Captain Isaiah Sellers was not of literary turn or capacity, but he used to jot down brief paragraphs of plain practical information about the river, and sign them 'MARK TWAIN,' and give them to the *New Orleans Picayune*. They related to the stage and condition of the river, and were accurate and valuable. At the time that the telegraph brought the news of his death, I was on the Pacific coast. I was a fresh new journalist, and needed a *nom de guerre*; so I confiscated the ancient mariner's discarded one, and have done my very best to make it remain what it was in his hands—a sign and symbol and warrant that whatever is found in its company may be gambled on as being the petrified truth; how I have succeeded, it would not be modest in me to say."

And with that statement, Samuel Langhorne Clemens finishes his first public address in nearly a century and leaves the Open Books' stage to a deafening ovation. Applauding the performance with the most vigor are the so-called writers-in-residence, from the recently deceased to the currently living. Crystal congratulates Mr. Clemens on his remarks and invites him to receive the guests in a line that is already forming near the stage. He most graciously consents, but something in his eyes tells me that he may indeed have another appointment to keep. What might it be? And where? Truly, Virtual Life has hosted this unconventional return engagement, though it is obvious to some that Mr. Clemens is not particularly comfortable here. He may well prefer a different universe, even as he indulges friends and admirers in this one. After greeting each guest personally, he withdraws to a pre-arranged sanctuary in Lit-A-Rama, where he can transfer out of Virtual Life to wherever he currently resides. We in Virtual Life wish him well on his journey through time, even as we thank him profusely for granting us one last interview before finally assuming his infinite disposition.

7
LIFE'S A WITCH, AND THEN YOU DIE!

IT HAD TO HAPPEN; it was only natural. What I mean is the re-emergence of the feminine principle. I'm not talking specifically about Western women burning their bras or crashing through the glass ceiling, though I suppose that's a small part of it. Nor am I talking about emasculation (sperm counts in the western world are down significantly due to the amount of estrogen in food additives). What I am talking about is the eternal relationship between nature and nurturing. It's been going on since the beginning of time as we know it; and it has always been the regenerative energy in our world, even when driven underground, and even when other influences, those initiated and dominated by men—forces such as war and commerce (and aren't those really one and the same?)—have ignorantly, and often quite brutally, subjugated its rightful place, and silenced or tortured or even killed its practitioners and worshippers.

Though the Goddess goes by many different names—Dr. Adler, we remember, pointed out that the ancient Sumarians knew her as Ki, and he in turn appropriated the name for his theories about earthly interconnectivity—*She* serves the same function in virtually every culture. *She* represents the womb from which our world is continually reborn, and She is also the caregiver, the giver of sustenance, and the healer. Yes, *She* is all these, but She is so much more. *She* is the One standing behind the veil of *the greatest mystery*, the One offering prayers and rituals and magick to illuminate the side in each of us that is not brutishly physical, or intrusively manipulative, or literal. The One behind our dreams, her natural province is the moon; *She* works not in broad daylight, but within the world of shadows. Through ritual *She* sanctifies our earthly existence, yet when our time comes to leave this physical plane for another, *She* tethers us not to the flesh of corporeal existence, rather *She* releases us to the Eternal and bids us well on our journeys. What else is a Mother to do?

I have never discussed religion with Crystal Marbella, nor has she discussed it with me. Not that the subject is off limits or taboo, but we each seem to prefer (by omission) to leave spiritual matters within their particular (and more personal) domain. Nevertheless, we both enjoy visiting a REP called Pagan Morning. It is a beautiful and peaceful place created by two English witches, Adrianne Hardwood and Freyja Mumford (each of them, incidentally, work as university professors in PL: Adrianne teaches Computer Applications, and Freyja teaches Physics).

Crystal and I have been invited to attend a hand fasting ceremony that will take place at the Abbey located within the Pagan Morning REP. We both think that VL weddings are very special because they almost always occur between people (emulations) that have never met one another in Physical Life, which tends to ensure that the feelings they express to one another are based solely on intellectual and spiritual qualities rather than physical ones. Certainly, there is no guarantee that the person behind the emulation is portraying himself or herself authentically, but isn't that the risk we take in PL too? Artifice and deception aside, anyone who knows Sly Sideways and Alegra Nevermore will attest to their obvious love, and to their commitment to one another. Seldom is one seen without the other being either present or nearby. Just as it is with couples who are in love in PL!

Crystal and I thought that our newest VL friend, Kizmet Aurora, might also enjoy the ceremony, as well as a tour of Pagan Morning, so we invited her along to experience the event (and the REP) for herself. We all meet at the Open Books shop to dress and check out one another's attire before transferring to the REP.

"I've been to a number of Native American weddings," Kiz tells Crystal and me, "but I've never attended an occult wedding. I'm anxious to see if Wiccan ceremonies are at all similar to those of Native American pagans."

"My PL religious upbringing was Catholic," Crystal tells Kiz and me, "but in those teachings (and those rituals) I never found much relevance—at least not intellectually, and certainly not spiritually. These days, Danish life is thoroughly secular; and the few who continue to claim Christianity as their faith seldom live by its teachings. One thing that my Catholic upbringing did manage to impart to me is a rather unhealthy sense of guilt that, no matter what I learn, or what I do, I can't seem to shake. I continually wonder whether or not I'm worthy. Ask me to what, or to whom I must show my worthiness, and I cannot give you a satisfactory answer—at least not a logical one. Therein lies my personal torment, because I'm an empirical person living in a secular world, a world where ecological catastrophes (not to mention binary simulations) are everyday events, a world where Heaven and Hell—at least the traditional Christian concepts of such places—are as outdated as the stories and symbols of a bygone millennium. Such myths were envisioned in the minds of people somewhat less sophisticated than those who populate our world(s) today. So, I guess I'd say that while I'm really not religious, I am definitely burdened by a religious tradition that I cannot ever fully discard, even though I'd probably like to. For me, Pagan Morning is something quite different than the religion I grew up with. If the priest could see me now, frolicking about with witches and wizards and Druids and the like, he'd no doubt pronounce me evil and lock me up inside the church crypt until I confessed my blasphemies and renounced Satan's influence for all time to come. Which might not be all that much longer… Of course the pentagram inside the circle has nothing whatsoever to do with Satan. Witches might or might not acknowledge the existence of the Dark Force, but they certainly do not worship it! For me, paganism is about earthliness, and it is about femininity. It speaks to the most elemental aspects of my being. And that feels good! Not only to experience it myself, but to share the experience of my earthly self with others!"

"Crystal, you are so good with words!" I tell her.

Crystal's EM bows its head. Crystal Marbella is always modest.

"So how do I look?" Kiz asks us. "I didn't really know what to wear to a pagan wedding, so I bought this floor-length dress with a flower print. I thought something 'hippie' or something 'New Age' might be appropriate."

"You look stunning, Kiz," I tell her.

"And look at Crystal!" exclaims Kiz.

"Crystal always catches every eye," I tell Kiz. "You'll learn to forgive her."

"Nothing wrong with looking beautiful," says Kiz.

"Shall we transfer to Pagan Morning, ladies?" I ask.

"Fizzy, do you have the gift?" Crystal asks me.

"I almost forgot," I tell her. "Thanks for reminding me." From inside the shop I take a specially-wrapped package. "Now, I think we're ready."

Whoosh…

Arriving within the Pagan Morning REP, Crystal and Kiz and I find ourselves at the central temple. It is an open-air amphitheater of classic Greek design with a large pentagram inside a closed circle at its center. The insignia is surrounded by seven pools—each one signifying a deeper mystery. Around the perimeter of the amphitheater are tall columns, and resting on top of each column is a semi-spherical dish filled with oil and lit on fire for light. Here at the temple, classes in the occult arts and sciences are taught to overflow audiences, and on the occult High Holidays services are conducted to honor and commemorate the occasion.

The entire Pagan Morning REP is laid out in concentric circles, and the path leading from one location to the next leads through a natural area that has been meticulously constructed in the style of an English wood. On our way to the hilltop abbey, we pass Pooh Bear Inn, a pub where the wedding party for Sly and Alegra will take place after the ceremony. Further along, we come to a wishing well, and Crystal and Kiz and I each make a wish for the future—not the future of Virtual Life, but the future of Physical Life, and for the future of the earth!

At the bottom of the hill where the abbey is located, next to the stone staircase that leads up to the priory, an ancient and degraded cemetery testifies quite dramatically to man's transience. Entering the graveyard through a creaking gate, we encounter a walking skeleton (no metaphor—the real thing!) that breathes heavily and groans and even casts a shadow as *it* reluctantly walks in the steps of sorrow, or regret, or unrequited love, or responsibility never borne. We visit a newly-opened grave upon which there is a wilted red rose and a teddy bear. The scene brings a lump to my throat—not for my own mortality, but for the sorrows of all who suffer a great loss. Near a large fountain at the center of the cemetery, we find the grave of the legendary occult master Aleister Crowley.

Upon his headstone, a wreathe made from cut flowers, along with several candles, designates both a tribute and a remembrance.

In a splendid grove of chestnut trees, we walk beneath the boughs and through lush grasses that cover the gently undulating ground until we find ourselves in an idyllic clearing where wind chimes ring, an open campfire burns, and a lone wagon stands as the sincere and simple residence of a pagan woman. From a nearby perch, a wise old owl calls the name of his mistress. Upon a pedestal, a large crystal ball reflects the shafts of sunlight that spike through the leaves and branches of the trees overhead. "Anybody here?" Crystal calls. But only the owl answers her inquiry.

The tinkling chimes beckon me up the wagon's three stair steps. Standing on the platform at the witch's threshold, I peer inside her humble home. I see a rustic chamber furnished for economy and function. A woodstove contains the remaining embers of this morning's fire; sun and moon curtains are parted above a single bed. On a rustic table, a spread of tarot cards awaits the reader's keen analysis. "I hope we're welcome," I tell my companions. "I wouldn't want to intrude."

"I think the resident witch must be away," says Crystal.

"I think this little gypsy wagon is so sweet!" says Kiz.

"Maybe we could leave a greeting," I propose.

"Or a small gift," Crystal suggests. "What do you have in your cache, Fizzy?"

"Nothing appropriate for a witch, I think."

"I see what you mean," says Crystal scratching her head.

"What about a crystal?" Kiz asks.

"That might be appropriate," I agree. "Do you have one in your cache, Kiz?"

"I sure do," she says. Kiz lays a highly polished black stone upon the table inside the wagon.

"Splendid gift," I tell Kiz.

"Yes, splendid indeed!" Crystal concurs.

"The stone's geological name is obsidian, but where I come from it is called Apache's Tears," Kiz explains. "I hope she likes it."

"I'm sure she will," says Crystal.

Just as we are preparing to leave the campsite, we see a young woman approaching, the folds of a long flower-print skirt gathered round her legs, a colorful blouse covering her breast and midriff, and a knitted shawl draped over her slender shoulders. Her long, brown, wavy hair cascades down her back, and a funny, wide-brimmed hat covers the top of her head. In one hand she carries a basketful of freshly picked raspberries, in the other she clutches a walking stick fashioned from a fallen branch.

"We didn't mean to intrude," I apologize as she comes into the site.

"No intrusion," she says cheerfully. "I was out picking berries. Here in Virtual Life they're abundant the year round," she laughs.

"We were on our way to a wedding at the abbey when we came upon your campsite," Crystal explains.

"It's very peaceful here," Kiz adds.

"It's not much, but it's home," says the woman. "Do you have time for a cup of tea?" she asks.

Crystal looks at me, and I look at Kiz. The truth is that we have all the time in the world—at least all the time in Virtual Life. "We'd love a cup of tea," says Crystal on our behalf.

"Excellent!" says the witch. "Then I'll just put the kettle to boil."

"You're English, aren't you?" Crystal presumes of our hostess.

"Welsh," she says. "My Virtual Life name is Violet Mary Firth, in honor of the late Dion Fortune. Like my namesake, I was born into Physical Life in Bryn-y-Bia in Llandudno, Wales."

"My VL name is Fizzy Oceans," I offer. "My friends

are called Kizmet Aurora and Crystal Marbella. Kiz and I are both Americans, though I live my Physical Life in Seattle, while Kiz lives hers in Arizona. Crystal lives her Physical Life in Copenhagen, Denmark. Crystal and I have a publishing shop in the Lit-A-Rama REP."

"She's probably already read our profiles," says Crystal.

Violet Mary Firth neither confirms nor denies reading our VL profiles, rather she pours tea into four china cups then serves each of us as we sit on hand-hewn chairs around her eternal fire.

"Virtual Life seems a strange place for pagans," Kiz remarks, though she is obviously quite taken with the beauty and serenity of the environment.

"Why would you think that?" asks Violet Mary Firth.

"Because VL is a simulated world—it's not *natural*."

Violet Mary Firth considers Kiz's observation as she sips her tea. After a moment she addresses us all. "While it's true that VL is quite removed from Natural Life, it's also true that witches live and work within the realm of symbols, which makes VL an ideal environment to practice the Craft. Symbols are to the mind what tools are to the hand—an extended application of its powers."

"Did you personally make everything here?" asks Crystal.

"Of course I did not create the REP. Nor did I create the general environment in the glen. Freyja Mumford and Adrianne Hardwood did that work. But I created all the details in my personal environment."

"Even the owl?" asks Kiz.

"Every witch has her familiar," says Violet Mary with a smile.

"Still, it seems odd to me that one who identifies himself or herself as pagan would choose to live within a computer simulation. Aren't the very foundations of paganism deeply rooted in the natural world?" asks Kiz.

"NL versus VL: what a conundrum!" laughs Violet Mary. "To designate something as imaginary does not make it disposable. It has its own kind of existence within the mind. Images—and our mental capacity to fashion them—are an essential part of the creative process, and they naturally extend themselves into the physical matrix. It is true that an image has no foundation in the physical universe, but that certainly does not mean that it is unimportant in determining the fabric of our existence. Images are powerful tools; if we limit our conception of reality to physical perception and measurement only, then we corrupt the integrity of our perception on every level, including the physical."

"Anyone who's spent much time in Virtual Life certainly knows that," says Crystal.

Violet Mary's voice remains soft and calm and measured. "The armature upon which the universe is built originates not from the physical world, but rather from the spectral axis. Usually, we do not readily perceive such forces because the inmost mind recognizes different symbols than those with which we customarily describe our physical existence. Yet, these primal symbols are all around us, and we are profoundly (and heroically) affected by them."

"Do you mean spirits?" I ask. "Like the ones walking around in the graveyard over there…"

"Not exactly," Violet Mary laughs. "Those are there mostly for effect. A bit of a joke played by Adrianne and Freyja, I suspect."

"What forces then?" I ask. "Gods? Goddesses? Demons?"

"Images borne of thought shape the essence of the gods and goddesses," Violet Mary defines.

"I think I understand perfectly what Violet Mary is saying," says Kiz. "She's saying that *we* are the gods and goddesses; that each individual, and only s/*he*, can define the world s/he inhabits. Whether it's the so-called natural world, or a world like Virtual Life that is made up entirely of symbols, makes no difference whatsoever."

Violet Mary smiles as she sips her tea.

"I've never actually been to a pagan ceremony," says Crystal. "I'm looking forward to the wedding."

"Hand fastings are lovely, aren't they indeed?" says Violet Mary in passing.

"I hope I don't do something obtuse," I apologize before the fact.

"That's hardly possible," Violet Mary observes.

"I wouldn't want to offend anyone," I qualify.

"Never mind that," says Violet Mary. "But perhaps you'd like a reading before you go. Today, it's on the house!" she laughs.

"How very kind of you to offer, but—"

"Really…" says Crystal. "First we crash your place, then—"

"Don't be foolish," says Violet Mary.

"At least we must pay you something," I protest.

"Nonsense," says Violet Mary. "I was joking about it being on the house today, because the truth is that my readings are always free. I don't need money here in VL—not even greenshoots!" she laughs.

After Violet Mary Firth spreads the cards upon a clean tablecloth laid over the earth at our feet, she says, "First, I shall give a general reading, and then we can discuss specifics in each of your lives."

"I'm not sure I want to know what comes next," I say to Crystal and to Kiz.

"Don't worry, this will be fun," says Kiz.

"The Fool settles beneath a tree, intent on finding his spiritual self," Violet Mary begins. "There he stays for nine days, without eating, barely moving. People pass by him, animals, clouds, the wind, the rain, the stars, sun and moon. On the ninth day, with no conscious thought of why, he climbs a branch and dangles upside down like a child, giving up for a moment, all that he is, all that he wants, and all that he knows or cares about. Coins fall from his pockets and as he gazes down at them—no longer seeing them as money, but only as round bits of metal—his entire perspective suddenly changes. It is as if he's hanging between the mundane world and the spiritual world, able to see both. It is a dazzling moment, dreamlike yet crystal clear. Connections are made, mysteries are revealed.

"But timeless as this moment of clarity seems, the Fool realizes that it will not last. Very soon, he must right himself, and when he does, things will be different. He will then have to act on what he's learned. For now, however, he simply hangs, weightless as if underwater, observing, absorbing, and seeing everything as it really is.

"The Hanged Man card signifies a time of insight so deep that, for a moment, nothing but that insight exists. All Tarot readers have such moments when we see, with absolute clarity, the whole picture, the entire message offered by a spread. The Hanged Man symbolizes such moments of suspension between the physical and mystical worlds. Such moments don't last, and they usually require sacrifice. What kind of a sacrifice? Who's to say? Perhaps the sacrifice of a belief or perspective, or a wish, a dream, a hope, money, time or even selfhood! In order to gain, one must first give. Sometimes one needs to sacrifice cherished positions, or accept other perspectives in order to find solutions, or bring about change. One thing is sure, whether the insight is great or small, spiritual or mundane, once one has experienced himself as the Hanged Man, he never again sees things in quite the same way."

Turning to Kiz, Violet Mary Firth offers a bit of personal analysis: "The card at the top of the staff represents the ultimate outcome should you continue on your present course. The Ten of Swords (Ruin), when reversed portends: The darkness before the dawn; an end to suffering, leading to spiritual transformation, and ultimate knowledge gained through ultimate sacrifice."

"Uh… What kind of sacrifice?" asks Kiz.

Violet Mary's tone of voice is that of a messenger:

"The word 'ultimate' would seem to suggest something quite dramatic. Perhaps the change will come in your family life, or most cherished relationships, or your work, or your core beliefs. Maybe even your life!"

Kiz's eyes widen as she contemplates the notion of such radical change: "I don't want to be rude, but I don't think I'm totally comfortable going on with this reading," she tells Violet Mary.

In complete deference Violet Mary gathers Kiz's cards and reshuffles the deck. On his perch, the owl hoots as a gentle breeze blows through the trees. "What about you?" she asks Crystal, who nods for her to create a new spread.

The reading of Crystal's cards is far more detailed. Says Violet Mary Firth to my friend and professional partner: "The card not shown but at the center of the cross represents the atmosphere surrounding the central issue you now face in life. It is the Nine of Wands, and it signifies strength. It also suggests a pause in the current struggle—a pause to ready oneself and to prepare oneself to meet a final and conclusive onslaught. Forces assembled in anticipation of trials and tribulations: the steeling of the will to stand or fall. A line drawn in the sand."

"Wow!" I say. "What's all this about?"

"The card visible at the center of the cross represents the obstacle that stands in your way," Violet Mary continues. "The Sun: A time of contentment and freedom from restraints. A time of creative inspiration, achievement, success. Light and love in personal or business matters. Happiness and faithfulness in a relationship. Shall I continue?" asks Violet Mary.

"Yes," says Crystal. "Please continue."

"The card at the top of the cross represents your goal, or the best you can achieve without a dramatic change of priorities. Knight of Wands, when reversed: The dark essence of fire, such as a great conflagration: The rapid approach of something that ruptures your world."

"I'm not sure I like the sound of this," I caution.

"Let her finish, Fizzy," Crystal hisses.

Violet Mary continues with her interpretation of the cards before her: "The card at the bottom of the cross represents the foundation on which the situation is based. Five of Wands (Strife), when reversed: Pointless struggles motivated by the vain pursuit of recognition, financial reward, or base desires. Disunity, chaos, and petty quarreling at a time of crisis."

In the distance the mournful cry of a lone wolf is heard. At least I think it's a wolf…

"The card at the left of the cross represents a passing influence or something to be released," VMF explains to Crystal. "The Wheel of Fortune, when reversed: An inescapable descent due to Fate or Karma. Great changes taking place as a result of earlier actions that cannot be taken back.

"The card at the right of the cross represents an approaching influence or something to be embraced. The Emperor: Worldly authority and power. Social mastery: the ability to fulfill plans and use mental control over the emotions.

"The card at the base of the staff represents your role or attitude. Page of Cups, when reversed: The dark essence of water behaving as earth: A dreamer oblivious to the realities of the world."

The wind chimes tinkle in the breeze; an Exaltation of Lark flies overhead, and toads and crickets banter in the undergrowth.

"The card second from the bottom of the staff represents your environment and the people you are interacting with," Violet Mary tells Crystal. "The Chariot, when reversed: Lack of discipline and poor direction fan the flames of a situation already out of control.

"The card second from the top of the staff represents an unexpected element that will come into play. Four of Swords (Truce): A time of tranquility and intellectual repose in the midst of a great struggle. A temporary retreat from stress to gather inner strength reaffirms convictions, reorganize thoughts, and formulate a new plan. May suggest a withdrawal from the material world to find spiritual satisfaction."

And finally VMF concludes: "The card at the top of the staff represents the ultimate outcome should you continue on your present course. The Magician: Mastery over word, mind, and matter. The ability to turn ideas into actions, to handle problems, and control one's life. The initiation of new projects, great works, or a new way of sustaining life. Eloquent and moving communication; innovative technologies."

"Most of that describes you, and what you're doing at Open Books, to the letter," says Kiz. And of course I agree!

"The concepts that explain most forms of Divination—Tarot, Runes, *I Ching*—were explained and advanced in modern-day terms by the imminent psychologist Carl Jung in his definitions of modern psychiatry," Violet Mary explains to us. "In Jung's psychological model archetypes are innate, universal prototypes for ideas. A group of memories associated with an archetype is a complex. Jung treated the archetypes as if they were psychological organs, analogous to physical ones in that both are morphological constructs that arose through evolution.

"According to Jung," VMF continues, "there are four main archetypes: the Self, which is the regulating center of the psyche and the facilitator of individuality; the Shadow, which is the opposite of the ego image; the Anima, which is the feminine image in a man's psyche; and the Animus, which is the masculine image in a woman's psyche. And although the potential number of archetypes is limitless, there are a few particularly notable, recurring ones: the Syzygy, the Child, the Hero, the Great Mother, the Wise old man, the Trickster, the Eternal Boy, and the Cosmic Man."

"In PL, I live in the American Southwest," says Kiz. "The Hopi Indians express such archetypes as kachinas. A vital part of not only their religion but their daily life, they have incorporated subconscious projections into their mainstream culture for centuries, and they know that we Europeans—empirical as most of us are—have very scant understanding of their power."

"Indeed," says Violet Mary as she reshuffles the deck and lays a new spread upon the ground at my feet. To me, Fizzy Oceans (aka Amy Birkenstock), Violet Mary Firth has this to say: "The card not shown but at the center of the cross represents the atmosphere surrounding the central issue in your life."

"Just like Crystal," I observe.

"The spread is called a Celtic Cross," she explains.

"Sorry," I apologize as the owl fixes his gaze upon me in a warning not to interrupt.

"Six of Swords (Science), when reversed: Being stuck in a problem that has no apparent solution.

"And the card visible at the center of the cross represents the obstacle that stands in your way. Eight of Swords (Interference), when reversed: Learning a valuable lesson from the unexpected consequences of prior decisions. Focusing on the crux of a problem, coming to grips with difficult situations, and moving on.

"The card at the top of the cross represents your goal, or the best you can achieve without a dramatic change of priorities. The Hierophant: Being supportive, sympathetic and loyal. Receiving instructions, guidance or inspiration. The ability to hear a higher voice.

"The card at the bottom of the cross represents the foundation on which the situation is based. Three of Cups (Abundance): A time spent in the company of friends. The strength of a diverse community being brought together."

"That's Virtual Life!" I cannot resist making an affirmation, but VMF continues almost as if she has not heard me.

"The card at the left of the cross represents a passing influence or something to be released. Four of Cups (Luxury): Ignoring the real and longing for the indefinable. Apathy and disengagement from the world."

"Wow!"

"The card at the right of the cross represents an approaching influence or something to be embraced. Four of Pentacles (Power): Cleaving to earthly power in the desperate fear that it will be lost.

"The card at the base of the staff represents your role or attitude. Nine of Pentacles (Gain): Attaining refinement and embracing elegance. Discipline and nobility applied to the maintenance of security and stability. The wise use of resources. The fulfillment that comes with accomplishment."

"And last but not least…"

"The card at the top of the staff represents the ultimate outcome should you continue on your present course. The Sun: A time of contentment and freedom from restraints. Creative inspiration, achievement, and success."

After the tea has been drunk, and after Violet Mary has completed the reading of the cards, Crystal and Kiz and I stand up to go. From the corner of my eye, I regard the old owl—Violet Mary's keen familiar—as it sits upon its perch. I wink at him, and he winks back at me. We thank our hostess for her hospitality (and for the divination). Crystal's reading, and mine as well, has confirmed a course well defined, a path quite familiar, and an outcome at least suspected. But for Kiz a less than comfortable prediction has been advanced—one she apparently does not wish to confront at present, at least not in *our* presence. Surely, sacrifice is never a pleasant prospect—especially the sacrifice of something vital to one's existence or well-being. I'm not inclined to question Kiz's reluctance to hear the full interpretation of the tarot spread, but I can't help wondering whether she knows full well what the cards would have revealed. Admittedly, Kizmet is still a mystery to me. To Crystal, too! We've discussed it between us, and we're hoping someday to know her much better, to understand her deeper motivations, and her reasons for hanging out with us so often in Virtual Life. For the present, though, we allow the relationship to develop naturally. Is there really any other way?

After saying good-bye to Violet Mary Firth, we make our way along the winding pathway that leads through the forest and eventually to a stone staircase carved right into the side of a high promontory. Climbing to the top of the stairs, we see the abbey in all its Celtic glory, its gray stone columns rising to support moss-covered cloisters and archways. Dozens of potted plants in bloom line the walkways, and wreaths of wisteria adorn each column. The back wall is a tall, stone edifice with an open arch at ground level. The supple branches of a luxurious willow tree that grows behind the edifice wrap round the hewn stones and extend through various openings. At the center of the abbey is the altar, a two-tier stage fashioned from gleaming white stones cut into large rectangles. Upon the altar is a marble table, and covering the tabletop is a green cloth. Candles have been placed to mark the four cardinal directions, and upon the table are the marriage documents, a knife, a chalice, a ribbon, a small silver box and a trowel! A broomstick rests beside the altar. Wildflowers are spread inside the sacred circle. Flower petals rain down endlessly upon us as we cross the threshold, and the sight of the golden-red sun setting over pearly water beyond the hillside cathedral leaves all three of us rather breathless.

"Can you imagine a more idyllic place to get married?" I ask both friends.

"Sure beats City Hall," says Crystal.

"I married my ex-husband at the Little Church of the West in Las Vegas," says Kiz.

"I didn't know you were once married," I say.

"Seems like ancient history now," she relates.

"I was married, too," I tell Kiz. "But we divorced

eleven years ago."

"I was once engaged," says Crystal. "But I broke it off when he got involved with drugs."

"I never knew that," I say to my business partner and friend.

:) types Crystal.

We take seats near the altar and wait for the other guests to gather for the ceremony. Today, Adrianne will preside over the hand fasting ritual, which 'literally' binds the couple together for a year and a day, after which, should they so choose, they can marry for life. As she ascends to the altar, she rings a handheld bell three times to signal the beginning of the ceremony. Rather than staying seated, all in attendance get up from their seats and gather round the altar. The couple enters from the east, Sly wearing a white suit, and Alegra a long red dress. Circling the altar four times, the priestess casts a sacred circle. She pauses at each cardinal point and repeats an invocation. Answering a prompt from Adrianne, both Sly and Alegra declare their intent to join with the other so that they may henceforth be recognized in the eyes of the God and Goddess, and in the eyes of family and friends, as one.

"Does anyone present know of a reason why this couple should not be hand fasted?" asks Adrianne.

No one raises his voice in doubt.

"Then the couple shall give their statements," she says.

Sly is first to speak: "I come to you, Alegra, of my own free will, in perfect love and perfect trust, to bind myself to you as your partner in life."

Alegra speaks to Sly: "I, Alegra, commit myself to be with you, Sly, in joy and adversity, in wholeness and brokenness, in peace and turmoil, living with you faithfully for all our days."

To each in turn the priestess extends the silver chalice. They drink to symbolize the need for separateness and togetherness in their new life. Then they turn to one another and clasp hands. Viewed from above, they form a figure eight, the element of eternity. Adrianne places a red ribbon over their hands and fashions a loose knot. "If, after a year and a day, you choose to make your union permanent, then return to this place, and the knot I tie loosely today shall be drawn tight to symbolize the permanence of your marriage to one another." Then she takes the knife from the altar and gives it first to Sly. Gently, he cuts a lock of Alegra's hair and places it in the silver box. He hands the knife to her, and she performs the same ritual, the intertwining hairs within the silver vault to remain a symbol of their future union.

"Be understanding and patient, each with the other. Be free in the giving of affection and warmth. Be sensuous with one another. Have no fear and let not the ways of the unenlightened give you unease, for the gods are with you now and always."

Then Adrianne turns to the guests: "Will all who are present support this couple in their new life together?"

All answer in unison: "I do!"

"Then I pronounce you hand fasted as husband and wife, in the eyes of all who are here today, and in the eyes of the God and the Goddess!"

After a kiss, the couple performs their first task together, the burial of the silver box at the center of the circle. That task completed, they replace the trowel upon the altar, join hands, and jump over the broomstick in a singular motion to symbolize the work and cooperation that will surely be needed throughout their journey together in life.

Banishing the sacred circle, Adrianne proclaims, "The circle is open but unbroken. May the peace of the Old Ones go in our hearts. Blessed be!" She rings the bell three times to conclude the ceremony, and then the couple proceeds clockwise round the circle greeting friends and family. After the reception, all repair to the Pooh Bear Inn for the wedding party.

Inside the large Tudor building that houses the old-style pub, the wedding guests gather to celebrate the occasion. Even as we come inside, the DJ is playing the music at an ear-splitting volume, and emulations are dancing wildly on the dance floor. Since Kiz has never before danced in Virtual Life, Crystal and I have to show her how to program her gestures bank, but after a single click of her mouse her EM is whirling in time with the music. Crystal and I move to the bar near the huge stone hearth where we are each given a mug of Wild's Irish Ale.

"For me personally," I tell Crystal as we stand before a recreation of Waterhouse's 'Hylas and the Nymphs', "marriage was not that great. I got married as a matter of circumstance, so of course the outcome was predictable. Even so, I've never understood why someone would want to get married in Virtual Life. The limitations are rather obvious, not to mention the fact that you can never really know just whom you are marrying."

"But that's also the case in PL," Crystal observes.

"Far too often, yes," I have to agree.

"Maybe VL partners arrive at the altar with a little less baggage in tow," Crystal speculates.

"You think so?"

"Just a thought. But since we are borne into VL already in the form—more or less—that we'll assume day-in and day-out—"

"You mean, since we don't live through a so-called childhood… Or have parents…"

"Exactly!"

"You're saying you think emulations are borne into VL in a state of purity?"

"No, not exactly. But each person has the opportunity to re-invent himself, and therefore the opportunity to leave certain painful, or detrimental experiences behind. If a person wishes to start his Virtual Life with a clean slate, it is possible."

"I suppose that depends on how much denial one is willing to embrace. I'm not interested in a world as perfect as that. We're all balancing the positive and the negative, I think. We might learn about unencumbered joy from the former, but we take our strength of character from overcoming the latter."

"I guess I agree in principle with that, Fizzy. Yet sometimes the pain of the past is so crippling that a *second chance* is nothing short of reclamation."

"You wouldn't be talking about yourself, would you Crystal?" I venture.

"Here in VL we don't have to admit to anything we actually want to forget or deny, Fizzy." Crystal's gaze is fixed for the moment on a place well beyond the walls of the Pooh Bear Inn, or the boundaries of the Pagan Morning REP, or even the VL World; rather, her critical eye seems to glimpse a place neither physical nor digital, but a place where the terrain is a little less definable, and sometimes a little more difficult to navigate. "Virtual Life is all about actualizing our visions," she says. "Whether they are intellectual, or mechanical, or interpersonal. We envision and we experiment. When, as children, we play make-believe, nobody gets cancer and dies, and nobody is rendered helpless from emotional trauma. Maybe in PL Sly is actually married to someone else, or perhaps Alegra is really a guy. In VL, none of that is important if we choose not to make it part of our VL persona."

"Everything by degrees… Is that what you're saying, Crystal?"

"Something like that, yes."

"One foot in this world, another foot in that. And always tethered to one another—and to ourselves, whatever *self* actually means—by an invisible ribbon made of fibers rare and precious."

"You wax poetic, Fizzy!"

"It must be the sentimentality of the occasion," I alibi.

"I bring out the best in you, Fizzy Oceans," Crystal jokes.

"You know that ribbon I was talking about?" I ask.

"A lovely metaphor…"

"Yeah, but I have a way of tying myself in knots with it," I tell Crystal.

And talk about 'Saved by the bell…' From across the room Kiz types a frantic message: "My EM has fallen and can't get up! How do I stop it from break-dancing? Help!"

Fizzy Oceans to the rescue! I send Kiz step-by-step instructions on how to release her EM from the dance program. A moment later, she is standing at my side. Crystal joins us, and we turn our attention to the table of the bridal party, as a toast to the newlyweds is about to take place. Sly's best man, Brainstorm Goatherd, raises a glass of champagne and calls for all to hear his tribute and to raise their glasses too. By degrees, the room grows quiet, and finally all present are ready to hear BS pay homage to the happy couple.

"I met Sly Sideways on my first day in VL," says Brainstorm, "and since that fortuitous day our relationship has been anything but lateral." Many in the gathering type laughter and smiley faces into conversation bars. "But seriously," says Brainstorm, "Sly Sideways has become one of my very best friends. Never mind that I've never laid eyes on his physical face or body… And never mind that I don't really know whether *he* is male or female, gay or straight, young or old… Of course, none of that really matters… I don't have to remind any of you about that. But I know one thing! I know that the day Sly met Alegra Nevermore was his lucky day! It was LUV at first sight, ha, ha, ha! And I know Alegra felt the same way, didn't you honey?"

Alegra does not answer Brainstorm's prompt. In fact, her EM is slumped over the table, listless and unresponsive.

"Alegra?" Brainstorm calls. "Knock, knock? You in there, honey?"

In fact, a slumping posture in Virtual Life is usually the result of a computer crash. Because the VL program is large, and because so much data is often coming through filters at speeds too fast for the machine's RAM drive, a freeze occurs, and it is necessary to re-boot. It happens to me sometimes; it happens to most people. Usually at the most inopportune time—like your wedding reception just as the groom's best man offers his toast!

"It appears that Alegra has left the building," Brainstorm jokes. We all know we simply have to wait for her to re-boot her computer, so the festivities can continue.

"Maybe I should do a little stand-up routine," Brainstorm improvises.

"Spare us, please!" implores an EM called Whisper Donato.

All eyes are now on Alegra's lame emulation. We've all been through this before. This is down time. We wait. We begin to talk amongst ourselves, and conversation bars begin to flip over like the credits at the end of a movie. We wait five minutes. Brainstorm is still standing at the head of the bridal party's table, glass in hand and ready to continue his toast. Alegra's EM has not yet budged, and without the bride's attention (or attendance) it seems rather futile to offer congratulations. The minutes tick away. Is she coming back? Or is this actually a…situation?

Sly seems relaxed as he chats with another groomsman, Shifty Gearhead. As a longtime VL resident, he too understands the nature of the problem. There is nothing to do but wait for his bride's return. Though Brainstorm's toast remains unspoken, Sly sips his champagne. He loosens his cummerbund. He searches the faces of the guests. Confidence seems the best antidote for moments awkward as this one.

After fifteen minutes go by with no return of the bride, and her emulation slumped at the table like a marionette left idle by a puppeteer, the guests begin to grow a bit restless. A few dare to type out their speculations for all to see and contemplate. *Has she had a change of heart? Did she get cold feet? Has her PL husband suddenly (and at just the wrong moment) discovered that she's married somebody else in Virtual Life?* Stuff like that actually happens. It's true! We've all heard about such circumstances. And most of us have also seen the abrupt departure of a familiar EM from VL. For whatever reason…

After twenty minutes pass without a sign of the phantom bride, some of the emulations give up the wait and leave the reception. Sly Sideways, not long ago a confident and love-struck groom, is now moving from guest to guest and asking if anyone has any idea where his VL wife has gone. Nobody seems to know what to tell him, and all the while the rather gruesome spectacle of Alegra's emulation slumped over the table looms as a testament to her unannounced departure. Her fate masked in obscurity for the time being, each guest, one by one, makes his apology to Sly Sideways and heads lickety-split for the door. What is one supposed to say at a time like this? Just leave the gifts and go. Those who are intimately involved will just have to work it out, and we will presumably hear all the gory details at some later date.

Crystal and Kiz and I return to Lit-A-Rama, where we have cappuccinos at the Writer's Pen Café and discuss the abbreviated wedding reception. We all agree that Sly must be humiliated. And we wonder what had gotten into Alegra to bolt from the barn without so much as saying good-bye or good luck to her hapless groom. Will he ever see her again? Only time will tell.

Next day, I receive an IM from Adrianne Hardwood requesting me to transfer to the Pagan Morning REP as soon as possible. When I arrive, Adrianne escorts me to the Pooh Bear Inn. Inside, the pub is now deserted—except for an emulation slumped over the long table at the front of the cavernous hall. "She's still here," says Adrianne in a hushed voice.

"So I see…"

"All night long she never moved."

"Gone is gone, I guess."

"You don't suppose it's something more…"

"You mean like, she died?"

Adrianne shrugs.

"I've never known anybody in Virtual Life who died," I tell her.

"But it does happen, I suppose."

"Yeah, I suppose it does. What happens now? I mean, if she actually did die?"

"I don't know. I suppose somebody will have to remove the *body*."

"You mean the emulation…"

"Right! She can't just stay here indefinitely."

"Well, at least there's not a problem with the—"

"The smell?"

"Reduced sensuality can sometimes have its advantages," I offer.

Adrianne looks at me skeptically. "What do you think I should do?"

"I suppose you should contact her next of kin," I suggest.

"In PL, or VL?"

"Shit! I don't know."

"PL, I guess."

"I'd start with her VL friends."

"Right! Do you suppose they will claim the body? I mean the emulation?"

"Maybe…"

"I just hate this kind of stuff," Adrianne laments.

"I know," I commiserate. "Life's a witch, and then you die!"

Bad jokes aside, it's a fact that sometimes people die in VL. Or rather they die in PL, leaving a VL emulation unanimated. I guess it's up to the deceased's next of kin to tidy up affairs in VL, just as they might in Physical Life.

Still, I can't help feeling that death—in Physical Life or in Virtual Life—is God's worst joke. What the hell was He thinking when He dreamed up that one? I suppose someday I'll get the chance to ask. But I can wait. Really! And maybe, just maybe, there is another way. Yes! Are you thinking   what   I'm   thinking.

8
THE LAND WHERE LOST THINGS GO

GET READY to experience something quite remarkable, Kiz. Because I'm going to take you to a place I consider one of the most extraordinary in Virtual Life. But it is also one of the saddest places I know.

A moment later Kiz and I are standing together in a small, virtual museum. Just off the main corridor are several portals leading to what might be described as interactive dioramas. The possibilities are varied and equally interesting.

"What is this place, Fizzy?" Kiz asks.

"This is the *Land Where Lost Things Go*," I tell her.

"What's been lost, Fizzy?" asks my friend.

"Oh, Kiz, so very much has been lost. Love has been lost, freedom has been lost, and hopes and dreams have been lost. Faith has been lost, trust has been lost, and compassion has been lost. Rivers have been lost, and habitats too, and entire species have been lost. Time has been lost, and opportunity. Even God has been lost! In this REP we can visit all these lost things, but we cannot reclaim them."

"Why not?" Kiz asks. "If people come here and find their lost things, why can't they take them back?"

"This is *not* a virtual Lost & Found," I explain. "And these objects are *not* the actual lost articles; they are only reflections of them. These things are borne of loss, and they are maintained from longing. But this is not really Beethoven's piano, and this is not really the nose of the Sphinx. This is not the actual chalice from which Jesus drank at the Last Supper. These objects are more like memories, or symbols of the real objects."

"Is that really so important?" Kiz asks.

"That's a question each person must answer for himself," I tell her. "Now, come with me, Kiz. I know a place we can visit. I have a very special friend there. Her name is Carteret Rose."

Without further delay we enter a gateway leading us from the REP's small museum directly onto a tropical island complete with sandy beaches, birdsongs, and fruit trees laden with ripe bananas and papayas. "Where Carteret Rose now lives in Physical Life is anyone's guess," I speculate. "She used to live on the Island of Han in the Kilinailau archipelago in the South Pacific. A couple of years ago she began recreating her island home in Virtual Life for all to see and experience, in all its incredible beauty, as well as its impending horror. Nowadays I can almost always find her here in Virtual Life, because this place is her connection with her past, and with her essence."

And surely this place must be paradise—a tropical island shaded by palms and blessed by the Trades. A beautiful lagoon with a living coral reef to yield all the fish the people could ever need. There is no money here, because there is nothing to buy: only coconuts and sweet potatoes. The people cook over open fires in front of bamboo huts. The children play naked. At night the villagers dance round a huge bonfire and sing tribal songs—thousands of songs from memory—that tell all about their ancestors and their long enduring culture (nobody actually knows how long they've lived in this place). It is a happy life, a blissful life. But wait! Something has gone wrong. Something has gone terribly, terribly wrong…

You see, the tides have been rising dramatically in Melanesia during the past twenty years, and the Kilinailau Islands are sinking. It is predicted that by the year 2015, the islands that make up the atoll will slip beneath the waves once and for all. The islanders that live there will either have to leave their ancestral home and move to the larger Island of Bougainville, or be swallowed by the Face of the Deep.

To reach the Kilinailau Islands in Melanesia in PL one must cast all caution to the wind and board the *MV Sankamap*, a rusting freight and passenger ship with no anchor and one engine that coughs and sputters endlessly from a fuel leak. The overnight trip from the Bougainville port of Buka delivers you to the fringe of the oval shaped reef of the Carterets. Our journey to Rose's simulated home in Virtual Life is somewhat less difficult.

The Island of Han is barely six hundred meters long. It is a tranquil paradise of pure white sand, turquoise waters, and picture perfect sunsets. But its once thriving gardens are being destroyed by seawater. Fallen coconut trees litter the beaches, their roots swamped by high tides. Water seeps from beneath the sand into the homes of the villagers. In an attempt to hold back the encroaching tides, the people have built seawalls from rocks and clamshells, but the barriers are breached daily. Once self-sufficient, the people of Han must now survive on handouts shipped twice yearly from the over burdened government of Bougainville. The carbon footprint of these islanders must surely be as low as any culture in the world, so it is ironic that they are perhaps the first people to have to leave their homeland because of rising seas attributable to global warming.

Standing outside her humble bamboo house we encounter Carteret Rose. She is a woman of forty with smooth tawny skin and tightly curled, dark hair with golden tips. Her shoulders and arms are strong from physical work, and the soles of her feet are toughened from a lifetime of shoeless trekking over jungle terrain. Her eyes are deep with wisdom, and with sadness, too.

"What you see here is the way it used to be: peaceful, plentiful, sublime," says Rose. "I made it this way because I need to remember my home as it once was, and because I want people to see how it was, and to understand what is happening now, and why.

"When the sea began to encroach on the land, it became impossible to grow bananas, taro and breadfruit," Rose explains. "When the ship with provisions did not come, we had to get by on only coconuts and fish."

"It's hard for me to imagine this place underwater," says Kiz to Carteret Rose.

"It began with the rising of the tide in the lagoon, above the flashing coral, and up the beach where the thin canoes lie," Rose tells us. "Soon the water breached the sea walls and ran over the coconut palms and the pathways of the village. The sea lapped at the houses; in the middle of the island saltwater bubbled up through holes dug by the crabs and flooded the fields and gardens until half the land was swallowed up.

"It happens every few months. But however many times we see it happen, it is never any less terrifying. The kids run around crying," Rose tells us. "People try to comfort them. They carry the kids and leave everything else behind. I have seen houses washed away with everything inside them. *Whoosh*! Every year the surge becomes stronger and more frequent; every month, a few more inches are eaten away from the land. It happened once in March, then again in September. And it will surely happen again under the new moon.

"When the tides rise this place is shoulder-deep in

water," Rose says about an expanse of drying mud that was once rich bush. "There are stingrays and sharks swimming around—right here, where we're standing! And when the water finally goes down, the entire place is a wet and stinking mess with rubbish all over the place. The mosquitoes breed in the water, and the children get malaria and diarrhea. Once this was a garden of breadfruit, papaya, cassava, tapioca, sugarcane and taro. Over time it has become a slimy, salinated wilderness where only palm trees can grow.

"How long before a really big wave comes? A tidal wave that will destroy everything—wash away all the houses, drown the children? We live in fear, but we have nowhere else to go.

"I recreated our island in Virtual Life because I know I'm going to miss the sea, the fish, and the coconuts. I will miss the palm trees. I will miss our beautiful life. This place is my home. I belong to the island, and I feel sorry for it. We have no cars, no factories, and no airplanes," says Rose, "but we are the first victims of greenhouse-gas emissions. Our home will be lost forever, and the very idea of leaving this place is just too sad to think about."

The next Virtual Life portal through which Kiz and I travel takes us directly to the Cornishe on the waterfront at Alexandria, Egypt. We intend to visit the recently completed, ultra-modern Bibliotheca Alexandria.

Mohammed Qatal, the administrator of the new library, welcomes us before taking us on a verbal trip through history, where he describes in intricate detail the famous ancient library that was destroyed by fire and earthquake two thousand years ago. Standing in stark contrast to the travesty of the destruction of the ancient library is the gleaming new library, which now stands as a defining architectural signature, not only for Alexandria, but also for Egypt.

"Egypt is an exact copy of heaven; the one place on earth where the forces of God and man are in balance,"

Mr. Qatal asserts. "Egypt is the temple of the entire world!"

Mr. Qatal gives us a brief history of the ancient library.

"The Library of Alexandria was established by Ptolemy I in the year 288 B.C. It was intended as a meeting place for the most eminent minds of the time. The world's first research center, it attracted intellectuals from all over the world.

"The library included all the knowledge of the ancient world. At its zenith, it held more than seven hundred thousand scrolls. Some of the great thinkers that the old library attracted included Aristarchus, the first to proclaim that the earth revolves around the sun; Hipparchus, the first to measure the solar year within six and a half minutes' accuracy; Eratosthenes, the first to measure the circumference of the earth; Euclid, who wrote the elements of geometry; Archimedes, the greatest mathematician of the ancient world; Callimachus, the first to write a catalogue for books classified by topic and author.

"The ancient Library of Alexandria was open to all civilizations. Efforts were made to collect the best works from all over the world, and any ship that docked in Alexandria Harbor was searched, and all books found on board were copied. Scholars from all over the world were invited to come and study. The Old Testament was translated for the first time from Hebrew to Greek.

"The library stood for at least three hundred years after its foundation in 48 B.C. The library was partially lost to a fire in Alexandria's Harbor when Julius Caesar attacked the city, and it was later totally destroyed by an earthquake. Some of the books were salvaged, but most of the manuscripts were sold to the hundreds of bathhouses in Alexandria, where they were used as fuel for the fires that heated the bath water!"

I cannot help but speculate: Were it not for the invention of the Internet, the ancient collection of scholarly materials and general information at Alexandria would still stand as the pinnacle of man's effort to categorize, and to centralize, the sum total of the world's documented information. Surely, many fine library collections have been assembled after the destruction of the ancient library at Alexandria, yet none has matched— or even come close to matching—the fabled collection of knowledge. The Internet, however, has enabled a new collection of information and knowledge to begin to evolve and to grow—one not necessarily created by design or decree, but a new and evermore glorious collection limited not to the contributions of scholars and experts, but open to every man, woman and child. Of course the Bibliotheca Alexandria in Virtual Life is a testament to this renaissance, as it houses the only complete external backup of Internet data.

"A body of knowledge such as that which existed in the ancient library surely took centuries to collect," observes Kiz. "The vastness of geography—not to mention the relative lack of speed at which anything (goods or ideas) moved from place to place in the ancient world—was only one hindrance. Another impediment, surely, was the predominance of illiteracy. Esoteric knowledge was only for the educated people of the time, who were also the wealthy and privileged classes—royalty! Today, as Fizzy suggests, knowledge is literally at everyone's fingertips. And so many people take advantage of the new medium, which is of course so much more than a library. Nowadays we are not confined to vicarious scholarship, we can interact at will. That's Virtual Life! If we want to conduct an interview with Ptolemy I, for example, it is not impossible. Time is no longer a barrier. Geography is no longer a barrier. The only barriers that remain are the ones we ourselves impose."

Turning to our guide, I say, "I think Kizmet's point is a defining one."

Mr. Qatal smiles and says, "Allow me to show you

ladies a bit of the *new* Bibliotheca Alexandria."

We follow our guide at arm's length, listening to his enthusiastic description of the reconstructed facility.

"The design concept is a perfect circle inclined towards the sea, partly submerged in a pool of water," he tells us. "The image of the Egyptian sun illuminates the world and all its diverse civilizations, even as an inclined roof allows indirect daylight to penetrate. Designed as an arrow, an elevated passageway links the University of Alexandria to the Corniche, just as it was in ancient times. A wall composed of Aswan granite and engraved with calligraphic letters and representative inscriptions from the world's civilizations surrounds the building.

"The new library has thirteen floors, thirty-five hundred seats, and a capacity of more than eight million volumes, fifty thousand maps, one hundred thousand manuscripts and a quarter of a million videos.

"In addition to its volumes, Bibliotheca Alexandria has four thousand periodicals, thirty thousand audiovisual materials and fifty thousand rare books. These books will never leave the building, but most will be accessible in the library's spectacular ten-story high reading room, whose pillars soar to a sloping circular roof. The reading room will seat twenty-five hundred people.

"The library also includes a planetarium, museums of calligraphy and archaeology, and a laboratory for restoring manuscripts.

"This library is more than a modern-day archive," explains Mr. Qatal. "It is a mark of respect for the ancient library, which was a place where the intellectuals of the day once congregated. We have been very careful to observe its design. Each level in the library is dedicated to a different field of study.

"The bottom level of the Bibliotheca houses all books pertaining to the roots of knowledge; including philosophy, history, classics and psychology. The second level includes languages and literature. The third houses books relating to art. The fourth level, which is also the central dividing level, is where all the business and economic books and other resources are located (since business is a central force in the world we live in today). On the fifth level are all books pertaining to social sciences and women's studies. The sixth level includes science and technology books, and finally, the seventh level includes books relating to new technology. Standing on the top level, the symbolism follows that all information on the lower levels supports contemporary information," he explains.

"Apart from the main library, the complex includes a Library for the Blind, a Young People's Library, the Alexandria Conference Center, a science museum, a Planetarium, the International School of Information Studies (ISIS), a Calligraphy Museum, a Restoration and Conservation Laboratory and the Hall of Fame.

"Our goal in creating this new library is both simple and auspicious: we're trying to revive the very spirit of curiosity, as well as the passion for the pursuit of knowledge that thrived in ancient times. The old library enabled the public to debate, create and invent; the new library endeavors to carry that legacy into the future."

In Virtual Life, time does not actually exist. Only the present is vital. Of course dates are employed, as well as clock time, to provide a point of reference, but here in Virtual Life the future is always within our grasp (consider those who create a new species specific to and thoroughly adapted for the VL environment) while the past, as it remains obscured in shadow, is also within reach (even the dead sometimes pay a courtesy call in VL). As a result of time's nebulous nature in Virtual Life, we can experience people and places and events we once thought consigned to antiquity and wholly unreachable.

Traveling through our next and last portal in the *Land*

Where Lost Things Go, Kiz and I find ourselves standing on the threshold of the most extraordinary garden that either of us has ever seen. This wondrous 'hanging' vinery flourishes on a series of vaulted terraces that rest upon cube-shaped pillars raised one above another. These pillars are hollow and filled with earth to allow even the largest of trees to be planted. The pillars, the vaults, and terraces are constructed of baked brick and asphalt. Each terrace is built upon stone arches twenty-three meters above the ground and is planted with exotic foliage. The ascent to the highest story is by stairs, and by their side are water engines, where laborers are employed raising water from the Euphrates into the gardens. Almost immediately we are greeted by a swarthy man dressed in a splendid robe decorated with intricate embroidery and extravagant jewels. He tells us he is the King and Supreme Ruler of the city and greater environs of Babylonia, ca. 598 BC. "My name is Nebuchadnezzar II," he informs us, "but my friends call me Majesty. You can call me that, too."

Bowing before the monarch, Kiz and I both acknowledge his graciousness.

Of the *Seven Wonders of the Ancient World*, only the oldest one, *The Great Pyramid of Giza*, built between 2650 and 2500 BC, is still around in PL. The other six have long since vanished, but of the original seven relics, only six can actually be documented with certainty. The one that remains shrouded in legend and mystery (its origin, its actual location, and its final destruction) is the *Hanging Gardens of Babylon*.

The *Colossus of Rhodes* was built by the Greeks between 280 and 295 BC. A giant statue of the Greek god Helios, it stood nearly as high as the *Statue of Liberty* in New York Harbor. An earthquake destroyed it in 224 BC.

The *Lighthouse at Alexandria* was a Hellenic construction erected in the third century BC in what is now Egypt, and at one hundred thirty-five meters high, it was the tallest man-made structure in the world during its time.

Sometime between the years 1303 and 1480 AD, an earthquake claimed it for antiquity.

The *Mausoleum of Maussollos at Halicarnassus* (Persian and Greek) was built in the year 351 BC. It stood approximately forty-five meters tall. By the year 1494 AD it had been badly damaged by earthquake and was eventually dismantled.

The *Statue of Zeus at Olympus*, built by the Greeks in 435 BC, occupied the whole width of the aisle of the temple that was built to house it, and was forty feet tall. Its true fate is unknown, but it is presumed destroyed by fire or earthquake.

The *Temple of Artemis at Ephesus* was built in 550 BC. Dedicated to the Greek goddess Artemis, it took one hundred twenty years to build. Herostratus burned it down in the year 356 BC in an attempt to achieve lasting fame.

"The PL Babylonian civilization endured from the eighteenth until the sixth century BC," His Majesty explains as we ascend the steps leading to the gardens' upper terraces. Behind us the panorama of a glorious city unveils itself as the sun rises once more over the Mesopotamian desert kingdom. "It was urban in character, although agricultural rather than industrial by nature. The empire consisted of a dozen or so cities, surrounded by villages and hamlets. At the head of the political structure the king—Yours truly!—wielded more or less absolute power, though working underneath the monarch, governors, administrators, mayors and councils of city elders were in charge of local administration.

"The Babylonian way of life underwent very little change for more than a millennium," explains King Nebuchadnezzar. "One of the most important aspects of the culture was the remarkable collection of laws often designated as the 'Code of Hammurabi', which provides a comprehensive picture of Babylonian social structure and economic organization.

"The Code of Hammurabi is the earliest legal code

known in its entirety. The divine origin of the written law is emphasized by a bas-relief in which the king receives the code from the sun god, Shamash. The code itself begins with direction for legal procedure and the statement of penalties for unjust accusations, false testimony, and injustice done by judges; then follow laws concerning property rights, loans, deposits, debts, domestic property, and family rights. Sections covering personal injury indicate that penalties shall be imposed for injuries sustained through damages caused by neglect in various trades. Rates are fixed in the code for various forms of service in most branches of trade and commerce."

"A society based on the rule of law… What a concept!" comments Kiz sarcastically.

Nebuchadnezzar wags his finger at Kiz and lectures: "Whatever your experience of justice might be in the present, Babylon, at its zenith, actually practiced judicial equality. For example, the Code of Hammurabi contains no laws having to do with religion. The basis of criminal law is that of equal retaliation. The law offers protection to all classes of Babylonian society; it seeks to protect the weak and the poor, including women, children, and even slaves, against injustice at the hands of the rich and powerful. Hammurabi counsels the downtrodden in these ringing words: 'Let any oppressed man who has cause come into the presence of my statue as king of justice, and have the inscription on my stele read out, and hear my precious words, that my stele may make the case clear to him; may he understand his cause, and may his heart be set at ease!'

"To ensure that the legal, administrative, and economic institutions functioned effectively, the Babylonians used the cuneiform system of writing developed by their Sumerian predecessors. To train their scribes, secretaries, archivists, and administrative personnel, they adopted the Sumerian system of formal education, under which secular schools served as the cultural centers of the land. The curriculum consisted primarily of copying and memorizing both textbooks and Sumero-Babylonian dictionaries containing long lists of words and phrases, including the names of trees, animals, birds, insects, countries, cities, villages, and minerals, as well as a large and diverse assortment of mathematical tables and problems. In the study of literature, the pupils copied and imitated various types of myths, epics, hymns, lamentations, proverbs, and essays in both the Sumerian and the Babylonian languages."

Now absorbed in King Nebuchadnezzar's compelling account of Babylonian culture, Kiz and I sit with His Majesty on a stone bench in a particularly lovely area of the hanging gardens where a waterfall cascades over a stone trough into a pool filled with water lilies. And with time itself now hanging forever in the balance of Virtual Life, we are free to savor this moment, this ecstatic and crucial juncture in human history. How utterly sublime it feels to immerse oneself within a culture whose tentacles extend even into our present tense, our peculiar compartment of human history, whose pigments color our cultural bias and lend us a model for our own code of social justice! Yet, nothing lasts forever, and cultures—no matter how urbane or lofty they aspire to become—seldom, if ever, transcend or reconstitute themselves.

"The Babylonians also had an advanced number system," Nebuchadnezzar tells us. "In some ways it was more advanced than the present system. It was positional in nature, with a base sixty rather than the base ten of the present system. Consider that the number ten has only two proper divisors, two and five. However, sixty has ten proper divisors; so many more numbers have a finite form.

"And the Babylonians were the first to divide the day into twenty-four hours, each hour into sixty minutes, and each minute into sixty seconds. Needless to say, this form of counting has survived for four thousand years!"

Once King Nebuchadnezzar has finished his initial

introduction, as well as a basic lesson in Babylonian civics, he invites us to accompany him on a tour of the magnificent garden. His offer is of course a welcome one, but what neither Kiz nor I understand is that the King's choice of transportation is decidedly unorthodox.

"Gracious ladies," King Nebuchadnezzar invites us, "please step aboard my flying carpet."

"Really?" says Kiz.

"Have no fear," says our host. "This magic carpet will transport us quickly and ever so smoothly, ever so gently to the Enki Harbor. From there, we can visit the Hidden Gardens of Amytis, the Nineveh Baths, and finally, the Tigris Theatre and the Queen's Marketplace. Take my word for it, ladies; it's a spectacular tour!"

Cautiously, Kiz takes a seat on the curious conduit, and then I, too, sit tenderly upon the hovering textile. Once we are relatively comfortable, King Nebuchadnezzar steps confidently on board. There is of course no steering mechanism, and no power drive. Everything operates at the king's command. "Enki Harbor, with speed and dispatch!" calls Nebuchadnezzar, and at once we are airborne and on our way to a destination once inhabited by an ancient eon's elite, and more recently only imagined in the mind's eye of those so inclined—those in a far different epoch, and a far different land.

High above the celebrated city we soar, its true brilliance revealed not only from the heights at which we now travel, but also from the historical reference we necessarily employ. Resplendent in texture and color, the city's marble foundations and cerulean ceramic facades gleam in the desert sunlight. The fertile Mesopotamian plain is alive with plants and animals all refreshed by the ever-flowing waters of the Euphrates and Tigris Rivers. The markets are alive with commerce; schools filled with eager children echo the lessons of the Age; devout men and women kneel at the feet of Ishtar, the goddess of love and beauty, and of war!

"It is almost impossible to imagine that a city such as this one existed four thousand years ago," I say to Nebuchadnezzar. "Even in the present epoch, we do not match the grace and beauty seen here in Babylon."

Shaking his head, Nebuchadnezzar laments, "It's ever so sad, but these days it seems that the Human Race is sick from being average."

Is Nebuchadnezzar's rather uncharitable assessment true? Indeed, many in our time might espouse quite an opposing point of view. "Consider our technological advancements," I implore the king. "We move mountains with the push of a button, and we create worlds from a base two number system!"

"Perhaps," allows Nebuchadnezzar, "but we have carpets that fly at our command."

Which more or less ends that argument.

Arriving at our first destination, we alight from the pulsating fabric at Enki Harbor, which is the gateway to the multiple terraces and interior chambers of the 'Hanging Gardens'. Along stone walkways and through marble archways we walk until we reach a dolphin pool, where several marine mammals are playing in water so blue it literally defines the color. The area is immense, with flowing fountains, lawns and flowering shrubs, and statuary. From whatever vantage point one might gaze, there is a vista of the city, the Euphrates, and the vast desert beyond.

Within the Hidden Gardens of Amytis, we discover an outdoor wedding chapel with marble pillars and marble pews. A ceramic floor with an intricate floral design is the perfect compliment to the pink, linen-draped canopy. Red carpet runners define the aisles leading from the perimeter to the altar.

Adjacent to the chapel is an outdoor banquet area with seating for three hundred guests. Elegant table settings promise an extravagant wedding party, with foods fit for royalty, and wine so sweet it tastes of nectar. After the wedding meal there will be dancing on a marble dance floor defined by giant vases filled with sprays of roses, lilies and hydrangea, behind which grow blooming jacaranda, wisteria, and citrus trees. Atop towering marble pillars, semi-spherical dishes contain oil, which is set ablaze to light the gardens and dance floor after the sun has set. In the background a waterfall cascades through a canyon that separates two towering mountain peaks.

Behind two twenty-foot high, intricately carved doors, inside a graceful room decorated in subtle shades of green and ochre, is the Nineveh Private Bath. The walls are painted with murals depicting men and women in the act of bathing, and palms and philodendrons and ferns grow in large pots placed throughout the atrium. A chaise lounge upon a stunning Persian rug invites patrons to recline and relax, and a dressing table situated in a sunny alcove is available for grooming after one's bath. At the center of the large room is the bathing pool, where warm water flows endlessly from clay urns to refresh the pool. Next to the pool is a table filled with soaps and lotions and talc. Polygon Fashions, a shop in the Queen's Market, offers each bather a free bathrobe.

"The water is quite rejuvenating," says Nebuchadnezzar. "Would either of you like to bathe before we continue our tour?"

"No, thanks," I tell the king, but Kiz is quickly out of her clothes and into the pool. Submerging herself in the warm water, she comes up sputtering before wiping the water from her eyes and face.

"I'm just a water baby," she confesses.

"Stay as long as you like," Nebuchadnezzar tells her. "Fizzy Oceans and I will wait for you in the garden."

Through the twenty-foot doors I walk with the King of Samaria. We sit upon a bench overlooking lush gardens in the foreground, the mythical Tower of Babel in the distance. The scene is both provocative and compelling. "Of the Seven Ancient Wonders," I say to King

Nebuchadnezzar, "only the authenticity of these gardens is in question by scholars."

Nebuchadnezzar looks at me quite dubiously. "Yet, here you sit!" he says to me.

His statement is certainly incontrovertible; still I have many unanswered questions.

"In the cases of the other six—from the Colossus to the Lighthouse at Alexandria—there is either irrefutable documentation, or there are ruins, to authenticate their existence. In the case of these gardens, however, the written accounts are controversial and even somewhat contradictory, thereby casting doubt, or at least confusion, upon the exact location of these famous gardens."

"Perhaps you forget, my dear girl, that you sit with the builder of the gardens whose authenticity you question."

"Your reputation surely precedes you, Majesty," I tell the king. "Yet, in PL, the extensive foundation of the gardens has never been unearthed, and therefore, the precise location never pinpointed. Why is that?"

Nebuchadnezzar shrugs his shoulders. "What's the difference?" he asks.

I have no answer.

For a time we sit in silent contemplation of these beautiful surroundings. We wait for Kiz to emerge from the bathhouse. Without question, Nebuchadnezzar is at peace in this sublime environment; after all, it is his natural home. I, on the other hand, am nurturing a sense of anticipation—one not easily defined. For me, Babylon is far more than ancient history. And it is more than a replication in Virtual Life, too. Babylon, in history or in VL, is the supreme cultural representation of susceptibility. Its rise to greatness and its inexorable fall into degradation and obscurity mark a pattern that repeats itself again and again, each culture at its rise proclaiming its greatness and its invincibility, and each at its fall amazed and in a state of supreme denial. As it is with the world's ascendant cultures, so it is too with the world itself! I guess the *writing is on the wall…*

"I am a builder," says Nebuchadnezzar, "but I am also a warrior!"

"Yes, history documents your dual nature," I allow.

"And even as we speak here in these glorious gardens, here in Virtual Life, there is a brutal conflict being played out in the *New Babylon.*"

"The New Babylon? I'm afraid I don't follow you," I admit.

"Infidels are sacking the city as we speak!"

"What city? What infidels?"

Nebuchadnezzar shakes his head woefully. "Silly girl!" he barks.

"Majesty, I'm really not following you at all," I humbly apologize.

"It is really quite simple," says the king. "Click open my profile, then you will understand."

"Your profile?"

"Yes! Surely you know how to open my VL profile."

"Of course I do," I tell him. "But I almost never look at the PL profile of an emulation because, to tell the truth, I don't see the point."

"You will see the point when you open mine. Everything you do not understand about the Babylon of the *past*, the Babylon of the *present*, and the Babylon of the *future*, will become crystal clear once you open my profile. So open it now, and answer all your questions."

With a degree of caution, even trepidation, I click open Nebuchadnezzar's profile, and here is what I read:

    PROFILE: Nebuchadnezzar of Babylon
    NAME: Saddam Hussein
    GENDER: Male
    LOCATION: Baghdad
    COUNTRY: Iraq
    E-MAIL: wmd@wannamakum.com

HISTORY: Saddam Hussein was born in 1937 in the village of Tikrit, one hundred miles north of Baghdad on the Tigris River. When the Ba'ath Party seized control of the government in 1968, Saddam Hussein became the leader of Iraq.

Saddam Hussein has spent over twenty years—sixty million bricks, and over nine hundred million dollars—rebuilding the City of Babylon as a deliberate strategy to identify himself with the King of ancient Babylonia, Nebuchadnezzar II. Part of his strategy is to vigorously build his Babylonian identity to appeal to the entire Arab world in order to unite all Arabs against Israel and the 'infidel West'.

As part of his extravagant southern palace, Saddam Hussein has incorporated the remains of King Nebuchadnezzar II's throne room where the famous 'handwriting on the wall' took place in the Old Testament Book of Daniel, 5. This ceremonial room has recently been used for State occasions and various cultural ceremonies. Also in various stages of reconstruction are the Ishtar Gate, the main Processional Way, the Ninmakh Temple and the Ishtar Temple, as well as other Babylonian landmarks.

"But you can't be Saddam Hussein!" I protest.

"Why not? Somebody has to be sitting behind the computer that operates Neb's emulation."

"Saddam Hussein was hanged on December 30, 2006, after being convicted of crimes against humanity by the Iraqi Special Tribunal."

"Your knowledge of recent PL history is impressive, Fizzy Oceans, but may I remind you that throughout my life, and especially during the time I ruled Iraq, I employed many doubles—look-alikes—not only to ensure my safety, but also to cause a bit of healthy confusion. Now I'm quite certain that the infidels believe they caught the right man—the right *Saddam*—but are you convinced that we did not succeed at leaking faulty intelligence to just the right people, at just the right time, and that the man apprehended in that filthy, stinking hole was not Saddam Hussein at all, but a *doppelganger*. Ha! Indeed, dear Fizzy, here in Virtual Life we know all about imposters, do we not?"

"I do not believe that you are actually Saddam Hussein," I say, indignant.

"Do you believe that I am Nebuchadnezzar, King of Babylonia?"

"Uh…"

"And does it really matter who sits behind the computer to command this fallen king to move as we wish him to move, and to speak as we bid him to speak? Are the events of our history actually defined in time, or are they recorded somewhere else? Perhaps they exist only within the consciousness of man? Or as part of God's Grand Plan? Does a great leader live but once, or does he reincarnate again and again to guide the events that make up our collective history? In Virtual Life, I am Nebuchadnezzar. This you can plainly see for yourself. You easily accept me as the King of ancient Babylon. In Physical Life, I tell you that I am Saddam Hussein, yet you refuse to believe me because CNN showed you a grainy video tape of a man who looks like Saddam—yes, all agree on that!—standing on the gallows with a noose around his neck and ready to die! What proof is that? What proof indeed when I tell you that I am alive and well? When I tell you that I am here, hiding in the body of my long dead predecessor, Nebuchadnezzar? When I tell you that I am real and fully digitized, Fizzy Oceans, and that I am in *your* computer? Right here! Right now!"

OMG, I think to myself. Wait until Kiz hears about

this!

As fast as my little fingers can maneuver, I click the 'file' menu and locate the 'quit' command. I'm out of here right now, out of Virtual Life right this minute. Kiz will just have to find her way out as well. And I'm sure she will! We'll meet back at Open Books, or at Dirty Nellie's Pub. Just get me out of this REP right now. Because Babylon has fallen again, maybe for the umpteenth time. And maybe that's the point. Actually, I don't feel all that much safer back in Seattle. Babylon is still Babylon, and forever will be Babylon.

9
CALYPSO

A LOT OF PEOPLE LAUGH at my VL name, but I have to admit that taking the name 'Fizzy Oceans' in Virtual Life was *not* a random choice. My commitment to preserving the earth in PL is a real one, and my VL name is meant as provocation (for any and all who still have an aptitude for metaphor) to recognize and address the perils of ecological degradation.

Earth is first and foremost a water planet. Three fifths of its surface is comprised of ocean, and that precious water is getting warmer by the year. Not only is the temperature of the water increasing, but waterlines are rising as well. Cateret Rose knows this all too well; so does Igloo Iceman. Some still maintain that global warming is a naturally occurring event, but they are the ones, as Dr. Conrad Adler pointed out in the Ki Seminar, that have vested interests in continuing the desecration. The more enlightened people know different, scientists and activists such as Dr. James Lovelock and Al Gore.

But let's face it: you don't have to be a scientist to see and understand the effects of a Category 5 hurricane; you don't have to be a mathematician to calculate the depletion of marine life from over fishing and chemical dumping; and you don't have to be a genius to see the probable outcome of such carelessness. As my dubious friend Nebuchadnezzar so presciently pointed out through historical graffiti, the *writing is on the wall.*

None of this information is new—not by a long shot! We have been told for decades (by the most imminent terrestrial guardians of our time) not only of the perils that we as a race inflict upon our precious habitat, but also what we must do to change our ways and to enable natural repair of the damage already done. Do we listen to those we hold in such high esteem? Do we pay heed to their warnings? Do we make even the simplest adjustments to our personal bad habits? I think we know the answer to those rhetorical questions, and now we are seeing the results of our inflexibility.

Whoosh!

So Amy Birkenstock does whatever she can to live an ecologically conscious life. It's hard though, because our entire PL society is based on technological comforts. They have infiltrated and dominate every aspect of our lives, and we have become their slaves. Let the power go out for an hour (these days the blackouts are random, frequent and indiscriminate) and everybody panics. It's almost as if people believe that the essence of life itself depends upon the uninterrupted operation of the worldwide power grid. Selfish justification is our credo, and we conveniently forget that in NL there was no power grid. Nor was there an environmental crisis…

I suppose that it is my VL name, or my email address (seabubbles@walawala.com), that precipitated the invitation I received in my VL inbox from an emulation claiming the identity of Captain Jacques Cousteau, an invitation to be a guest onboard the famous exploration ship, *Calypso*. In PL, Cousteau is no longer alive; of course in VL that makes little difference. To tell the truth, I was a bit flabbergasted at receiving this invitation, but I was also thrilled to accept it. Before conveying my acknowledgment, I sent an IM to Igloo Iceman to tell him about the most extraordinary offer. He was envious of the opportunity to spend time with *le commandant* and asked me to beg an invitation for him, too. So I contacted the sender to ask if I might bring a friend onboard, and he graciously extended the invitation to Iggy as well. A time for transference was arranged.

Joining the crew on board *Calypso* as it anchors just off the Caribbean Island of St. Pierre—its volcanic summit hidden in billowy clouds and steam pouring out of its crater and threatening to wipe out this credulous Caribbean civilization for the umpteenth time—we are met by the emulation of Philippe Cousteau (also deceased in PL, 1979), beloved son and closest confidant of the intrepid and world-renowned explorer.

"*Bonjour Monsieur et Madmoiselle, et bienvenu abôrdé* Calypso! *Je m'appelle Philippe Cousteau. Mon pere, le commandant, il est maintenent dans son chambre, mais il voule nous joindre pour le dîner. Maintenent! Allouez-moi tu présenter* Calypso, *nos maison a la mere!*"

The unlikely couple that we make—Igloo Iceman standing nearly seven feet tall and having to crouch low as we pass from cabin to cabin; and me, Fizzy Oceans, petite yet a little clumsy, but ever effervescent and wearing my newly-bought sailor's clothes, my funny little seagoing *chapeau* and espadrilles—we are escorted by the robust and personable son of the captain on a tour of the legendary vessel.

"*Calypso* was originally a wooden-hulled boat built for the British Royal Navy by the Ballard Marine Railway Company of Seattle. She is made from Oregon pine," Philippe details.

"She was launched on 21 March, 1942, and commissioned into the Royal Navy in February 1943 as HMS *J-826* and assigned to active service in the

Mediterranean Sea, reclassified as BYMS-2026 in 1944, and finally laid up at Malta and struck from the Naval Register in 1947.

"After World War II, she became a ferry between Malta and the island of Gozo, and was renamed *Nymph Calypso*, whose mythological reference is to the island of Ogygia.

"In 1950, the Irish millionaire and former MP Thomas Loel Guinness bought *Calypso* and leased her to my father for a symbolic one franc a year. *Mon pere* restructured and transformed her into an expedition vessel and support base for diving, filming and oceanographic research.

"*Calypso* carries advanced equipment, including mini submarines developed by my father, diving saucers, and underwater scooters. As you can see, the ship is also fitted with a see-through observation chamber three meters below the waterline.

"On board Calypso, life is harsh. Night and day, calm seas or raging storm, the ship must be tended, cleaned, piloted, and maintained. From the hold to the helm, the crew works for the success of the expedition."

As Philippe Cousteau conducts us on a tour of the famous exploration ship, I am amazed at the complexity— and at the same time the Spartan simplicity—of the vessel. Meantime, Iggy is examining every nook and cranny of the boat, analyzing each technical detail so he might learn minutiae potentially crucial to his own future survival aboard his Ark. Calypso is certainly no cruise ship: that much is obvious as Philippe escorts us onto the bridge. There we are introduced to Didi, Captain Cousteau's longtime friend and partner.

"*Bonjour, mes amis,*" Didi greets us. "*Beinvenu abôrdé* Calypso."

"*Merci, monsieur. Le plaisir est le nôtre.*"

"Whether it is *le commandant* at the helm, or another member of the crew," Didi explains, "someone is *always* manning the bridge. For navigation purposes, we employ screen, radar, sonar and satellite systems—all within arm's reach, as you can see. Each action taken by the navigator on duty is entered in the ship's log. And just behind the bridge is the radio room. It is here that we maintain communication with land teams, as well as the rest of the world."

In its utilitarian way, the bridge is indeed impressive. Didi looks thoroughly at home piloting *Calypso*. During his many years as Captain Cousteau's second-in-command, he has guided her over seas rough and tranquil, familiar and remote. We know we are in able hands with this master sailor at the helm.

After visiting the bridge, our tour takes us to the ship's living quarters. There the members of the crew can relax, Philippe explains. Besides sleeping and personal business, they might read or write letters to family or friends at home.

"Of course meals are taken in the mess," he relates, "but this area of the ship is also used for parties, or a simple game of chess, or watching a video. Not much free time is available to crewmembers, so the mess is the center of social activity during long, working sea voyages."

"How long do the various missions last?" Iggy asks Philippe.

"That depends on the particular mission," says our amiable guide, "but normally we are at sea for months at a time. Shore leaves are short, and then we are off to another part of the globe to explore the Face of the Deep."

"Doesn't it get lonely out there for months on end?" I ask.

"*Calypso's* crew is a family unto itself," says Philippe, his dedication to his father's cause obvious in his voice. "This is not just a mission for those who work on board *Calypso*, it is a way of life—one that none would change or sacrifice for ease or comfort. We know our endeavor is not only original, but an essential one, too. So we endure the isolation and the long hours of hard work and take comfort in the company of our comrades."

"So," says Iggy, "it appears that there is an explicit division of labor aboard *Calypso*…"

"*Mais oui!*" says Philippe. "That is essential on board any ship. But *le commandant* has no need to maintain military discipline. That is not necessary on board *Calypso*, because each member of the crew is here not only by invitation from the captain himself, but also by his own choice. And because each member of the crew is unique, and considers it a privilege—as well as a social obligation—to serve aboard this ship, self-governance becomes an asset, not a liability. The captain maintains his command through respect for the unique abilities of individuals, and by fair and appropriate delegation of duties, not by peripheral power."

Philippe's pride not only in his father, as captain, but in the greater mission of *Calypso* is obvious. With embroidered propriety, he escorts us into the diving locker, a small cubby-holed cabin located below the ship's aft deck. Addressing Igloo Iceman, he describes the basic division of labor.

"The crew of *Calypso* is divided into two distinct working units," he relates. "While some attend to sailing the ship, others concentrate on the mission at hand. Undersea research and documentation are *Calypso's* primary function, so dives must be meticulously planned, and film crews briefed and otherwise prepared."

As I look around the diving locker I see regulators, tanks, suits, belts, fins. A cylindrical recompression chamber is located in one corner of the cabin. And then there is the undersea vehicle designed by the captain and his longtime friend and engineer Émile Gagnan and produced to their specifications and under their personal supervision: the diving saucer Denise, which is capable of carrying two people for a maximum of four hours to three hundred and fifty meters below the surface.

"Since 1972, the helicopter we call *Félix* allows our teams an opportunity for aerial photography," says Philippe. "Sometimes it is also needed as a reconnaissance vehicle. It takes a skilled and experienced pilot to land *Félix* on the helipad on the aft deck, especially when the weather is bad."

Operations on board *Calypso* are indeed intricate and complex, I acknowledge. And like so many others, I had watched the documentary films created by the Cousteau Society with childlike awe and amazement, utterly enthralled by an exploration that revealed, for the first time, life as it is beneath the waves. I can hardly wait to meet the captain himself, the legendary Jacques Cousteau, so I enquire of Philippe when we might meet *le commandant*.

"My father has invited you both—as well as several other guests that I know you will find engaging—for dinner at his table tonight. I hope you will consent to join him," says Philippe as he escorts us to our quarters.

"Of course we will join him for dinner," I *rsvp*. "And give our thanks for his kind invitation. We look forward to meeting him and sharing a meal and conversation."

"*Certainment*," Philippe promises as he takes his leave. "I will call for you at 2200 hours to take you to the captain's cabin."

On deck, just outside our shared cabin, Igloo Iceman and I watch the Caribbean sunset. The soporific sky, awash in orange and pink, belies the imminent thunder of the smoldering volcano on St. Pierre, and for the time being, at least, the environment is benign, and our souls are at peace within this digitized representation of another world far less secure. At precisely 8:00 o'clock, the emulation of Philippe Cousteau calls for us, as promised, and escorts us to the quarters of his father *le commandant*, Jacques-Ives Cousteau.

Entering the captain's cabin, we encounter eight other guests, as well as the emulation of Jacques Cousteau, already seated at a large, round wooden table. Besides Monsieur Dumas (Didi) and Monsieur Tailliez (another of the captain's legendary friends and collaborators) and Émile Gagnan (Cousteau's engineer and accomplice in his many inventions), Simone Cousteau, the explorer's wife (married at age seventeen to the captain) of more than forty years is present. But to our greater surprise, seated there at the table are several of our most intimate VL friends: Omar Paquero, Ego Ectoplasm and his sidekick the Quinngen, Tooltech, Kizmet Aurora and Crystal Marbella!

"*Bienvenu, Monsieur et Madmoiselle*," says Captain Cousteau. "*Venez, asseyez-vous, faites-vous confortable.*"

Crystal and Kiz regard Igloo and me with as much surprise as we feel at seeing them at this auspicious event. My eyes query Crystal concerning *her* presence, and she just shrugs her shoulders. Kiz, the least experienced seedling in the group, simply looks happy to see us. In contrast, Omar Paquero, Ego, and Tooltech look completely comfortable within this contrived environment.

"I had no idea this was going to be a party for our little group of Virtual Lifers," I say to all present.

Captain Cousteau is smiling broadly and his blue eyes are twinkling. He is obviously quite proud of his VL acumen in assembling such an unlikely group for what could only be his own reasons. What those reasons might be, we are all certainly bound to find out, but for the moment we are kept in the dark as introductions are made.

"I believe you have already met Monsieur Dumas," says the captain. We nod at Didi, and he nods back in recognition. "And this is my good friend, Monsieur Tailliez." Again, nods of welcome are exchanged. "My good friend and collaborator, Émile Gagnan." The Frenchman salutes each of us in turn. "And may I also present my wife Simone, the real captain of *Calypso*." Simone's acknowledgment is indulgent at best. "I believe you know the others present," says the captain.

Captain Cousteau and his two friends, Dumas and Tailliez, cannot seem to stop grinning at the Quinngen as he picks his nose, but Simone Cousteau rolls her eyes, not so much in disdain or wonderment at the Quinngen species (for she has quite literally *seen it all* during her years with the captain) but puzzled about just what her husband might have in mind in assembling this unworldly group in the first place.

"It's been a long time, Ego," I say as I remove my sailor's cap.

:) types Ego Ectoplasm.

Meanwhile, Iggy is trying desperately to cram his large, Viking figure into the limited space available at the table. Finally he is settled, and Captain Cousteau offers wine and *hors d'ouvres*.

Splendid!

"No mystery why Didi, and Tailliez, and Gagnan, and Simone are present here tonight," says Captain Cousteau, "but I'm sure the group from Virtual Life—"

He pauses a moment, smiling, apparently realizing that he, too, is from VL, not to mention his friends and his wife.

"*Mais oui!*" he laughs. "That is the platform here, *n'est pas?*"

"One tends to forget," I observe.

"*Pas question!*" says the captain. "But we are here, together, and we have much to discuss."

Just what that might be, I cannot imagine.

"You might think it curious that we have assembled the six of you here, as a group. *Mais non!* It is really no mystery at all. We on board *Calypso*, at least on board the Virtual Life version of *Calypso*, already know each of you quite well. And we not only know your emulations, we know who you are, and what you do, in PL too!"

"Really?" says Kiz, quite surprised.

"*Oui, oui,*" says the captain. "Your PL name is Cassandra Stephens, you live in Rough Rock, Arizona, and you are regarded by the Hopi Indians as something of a shaman."

Then Cousteau turns to Crystal: "Your PL name is Sonja Jörgensen, you live in Copenhagen, you write, and you work in a library part time.

"Igloo Iceman's PL identity is none other than the well respected Dr. Conrad Adler from the University of Colorado, though you spend most of your time above the arctic circle researching the effects of climate change." Cousteau smiles and then observes, "We are also aware that Igloo Iceman is building an Ark. An auspicious undertaking, *monsieur*!"

We are all astonished into silence, but that hardly matters, as Captain Cousteau is happy to maintain the conversation.

"Our friend Omar Paquero from Anapu, Brazil is also known as Dorothy Stang, a member of the Sisters of Notre Dame de Namur, an international Catholic religious order that works for social justice and human rights on five continents. In Brazil, she works with the Pastoral Land Commission, the Catholic Church's arm that fights for the rights of rural workers, peasants and defends land reforms."

"I always thought Omar was a ten-year-old kid from La Paz, Bolivia," says Igloo.

Captain Cousteau continues: "Crystal Marbella, with the able help of Fizzy Oceans, works in Virtual Life to maintain and preserve the world's great literature.

"And last but not least, Ego Ectoplasm (Artemis Quinn from Austin, Texas), has invented a brand new species. Congratulations on your vision and your accomplishment!"

"Ha-ha, ho-ho!" cackles Tooltech. (Jeff Beck blues riff on his Les Paul Jr.)

One might think, at the table of a lifelong seafaring man such a Captain Cousteau, that seafood would be the meal of choice, but that is decidedly *not* the case on this night aboard *Calypso*. Instead, a sumptuous vegetarian meal prepared from local recipes collected in Thailand, Madagascar, New Zealand and Libya is presented, and as always I consider it all-too-unfortunate that we are unable to actually taste the food. Nevertheless, Captain Cousteau keeps us utterly absorbed and thoroughly entertained with his ongoing monolog about his experiences exploring the sea and about encroaching environmental issues.

"In the early days, when Émile and I first invented SCUBA (Are you aware of how the term was derived? The now common word 'scuba' is actually an anagram for self-contained underwater breathing apparatus), well…the sea was a true frontier. Nobody had explored its depths simply because the equipment to breathe underwater did not exist. But we wanted to dive deeper, to explore the ocean floor, to learn whatever we could learn, so we invented the device now known as the regulator. And our design remains unchanged to this day!

"Invention is nothing more than a tool needed by an explorer that does not exist," he advises. "So, if you need something, you make it." His declaration seems as final as a judge's gavel. He takes a long swallow of his wine and wipes his lips with his napkin. "A very agreeable vintage, *n'est pas*?" he comments to everyone and to no one. Nods of approval circle round the table, but it is obvious that Cousteau is no longer thinking about the Beaujolais; instead he is entrenched in the memory of an early dive undertaken with his friend Didi, and about how it had all gone so very wrong at a crucial moment, and about the greater issue of risk—personal risk and social risk—and when such risk is acceptable, and when it is *not*…

"Didi and I were diving in a region where deep underwater caves and crevices descend hundreds of feet below the greater ocean floor. Stalactites had been photographed on earlier dives, so we wanted to actually penetrate the fissures for a closer look, because we knew that if we could gather geological samples from the stalactites, we could prove that this particular area of ocean floor had once been above the water.

"Due to the extreme depth of the dive, every foreseeable risk was analyzed, and every possible precaution taken. You must understand that when you dive in open sea, all routes lead to the surface, but when you enter an underwater cave the only way out is to follow the path you took to go inside. So we fastened ourselves together with a stout lifeline, in much the same way mountain climbers do when ascending a dangerous peak. Two tugs on the line was the signal for those on board *Calypso* to feed us more rope; four tugs signaled them to pull us out. We understood the risks, but we were accustomed to such risks, because risk is the business of an explorer. Senseless risk, or careless risk, is never acceptable. But we knew our capabilities and understood our limitations. Or so we thought…

"Penetrating the crevice was an inspiring experience, but the deeper we descended, the darker it became. We used phosphorescent lighting to make our way through the caverns, all the while photographing like madmen. Suddenly, catastrophe struck: Didi's air hose literally exploded from built-up pressure. He signaled to me, and I immediately came to his aid. Once I understood the problem, I began sharing my oxygen with him. We were already very deep, and we knew that we could not ascent too quickly for fear of getting the Bends. I tugged four times on the rope, the signal for those on board Calypso to pull us out. But instead of pulling us out, they fed us even more line.

"Of course, the only way out of the caverns—with their many intersections and twisting divergent tunnels—was to follow the rope. Yet now the rope had gone slack, so backing out of the fissure became a slow and laborious process. Every few moments we had to pause to share oxygen from my breathing apparatus—time that I knew we did not really have because the oxygen in my tank was being depleted at twice the normal rate of consumption.

"To make matters worse, Didi had apparently inhaled too much carbon dioxide before his hose had actually ruptured, so he was not only slow but barely coherent. I had to literally carry his all-but-inert body with me as we made our way painstakingly through the tunnels. At each level of ascent, we waited as our bodies adjusted to the pressure, and still far from the surface I realized that we did not have enough oxygen for both to make it to the surface.

"Here is the essential dilemma," defines Cousteau as he pauses for the sake of drama and flashes his crooked smile at his longtime friend and diving companion (who was obviously still alive): "What is one to do in the moment that he realizes that he can save himself if he is willing to sacrifice his friend, or that he can remain with his friend to help, in which case both will probably die?"

All eyes are trained upon Cousteau's fatherly face as each person waits for the captain to finish his harrowing tale, and I can hear Kiz's anxious breath (as if she—not Didi—is the one in desperate need of a gulp of oxygen from the captain's regulator), and I can distinguish Crystal's heart throbbing in her chest (because her heart and mine seem always to beat in unison), and I feel Iggy's chilly fingers as they tighten around my arm (Why is the Iceman's touch so very cold?). We wait for resolution just as the two divers had waited for their salvation.

"This unthinkable circumstance, this life-and-death problem without a practicable solution, is one I knew I would someday face," says Cousteau as he takes a sip of his wine and looks into the eyes of each person at the table to try to glean which might abandon his friend to save his own life, and which might risk his own death in the all-but-impossible chance that both might be saved.

"In that moment of decision, I must confess, my most powerful instinct was for my own survival. Rationally, I knew that remaining there to try to save us both was nothing short of a watery death sentence for me as well as my friend. Yet I chose to remain. Still many meters from the surface and sharing the last of my oxygen, I simply could not abandon my friend."

"But neither of you drowned," says Iggy.

"No, we did not drown," confirms the captain. "Miraculously, and beyond my last hope, the rope tightened as the crew above began to pull us toward the surface. Somehow, the oxygen held out, though when we finally reached the surface we were both so depleted that we had to spend hours in the recompression chamber.

"For many months, and probably to this day, I wonder why I chose to risk my life against nearly impossible odds to save another human being. Certainly logic would have prescribed a different course of action, and even my instinct had to be suppressed to take such a decision. Yet I remained. Some probably thought it crazy; others thought it a gallant and selfless act. But I knew that it was neither. What I learned that day is that some personal risk is acceptable when taken in the service of humanity. And that, my friends, is what makes our species a noble one!

"Yet self-sacrifice to save another is not a singular trait of our species," Jacques-Ives Cousteau continues. "Dolphins and whales have been known to do the same."

"*Commandant*, we must not forget the supreme sacrifice made by our savior to cleanse the world of mankind's sins," reminds Sister Dorothy Stang.

Simone Cousteau audibly clears her throat, as if making space in a cluttered room, so she can enter the discussion: "*Tout au long de l'histoire du monde*, this theme of sacrifice and salvation has been played out again and again, first in deeds or physical circumstance, then in literature, as a documentation of redemption—until its meaning is systematically diluted and finally lost—then it is enacted yet again in actions and manners. It is an endless wheel, and an immature indulgence."

"Surely there is a less drastic solution," suggests Ego

through his unlikely interpreter, the Quinngen. "There is little need for risk or for sacrifice, and no need to perish, when we can simply reinvent ourselves."

"In NL, evolution has been reinventing life's very composition since the beginning of terrestrial time," observes Captain Cousteau.

"And some say that that glorious existence—life on this planet—may indeed be a quite limited affair as a result of our short-sightedness," remarks one hundred-year-old Omar Paquero.

"The certain consequences of the unthinkable plundering of the Amazon Basin's rain forests are now not only understood, but considered irreversible. This corrupt cataclysm, this wholly unnecessary catastrophe, was brought on us not by need of resources but by our own wanton greed, ant it is surely a stain upon the legacy of our 'noble' race," laments Cousteau.

"But are you sure that it is irreversible?" Crystal asks the captain.

"The Amazon forest is the lungs of our planet. And this is no metaphor. Without the rain forest, the earth cannot breathe. Believe me; I know something about needing oxygen and not knowing from where it will come!"

"Which is why I think that VL is so important," I affirm. "If the world as we know it is destined not to survive, then it becomes all the more important that we preserve whatever we can of our culture and our history so that someday, somebody…"

"Might learn from our mistakes," the captain finishes with a hint of melancholy in his voice.

"Some of us might survive," Iggy postures.

"Perhaps you are right, Iceman," says Cousteau. "Indeed, I hope you are right. But FL, Future Life, will not resemble life, or civilization, as it exists today. I can't say what it might look like. I suppose that will be up to those who sail upon your Ark to determine. And, for the record—"

"Yes, that is precisely my point!" I say.

"And a valid one it is, Fizzy Oceans!" says the captain.

Of course such dire prognostications concerning the future of our precious habitat are hard to contemplate. But contemplate them we must! The earth is a glorious place— or at least it once was—and as far as we know, nowhere else in the universe sustains what we define as life, so what are we to think when Captain Cousteau, who is without question the one human being who knows more about the womb of our race, not to mention all other life that exists under the sea and upon dry land, tells us that our fate— even our extinction—is all but inevitable? And still this highly rational, peace loving explorer maintains a degree of optimism…

"As scientists, and as philosophers too, we can analyze and conclude, and we can sound our trumpets of warning. Will our fanfares make a difference? Will they convince mankind to change his ways? I doubt it. Because Simone is correct: human beings, at least in PL, seem to have a profound proclivity to foul the place in which they sleep. It is a matter of deep-seated and abiding guilt, and rather than revel in his existence, and in the existence of the universe, man instead punishes himself, time and again, for his very existence."

"Which takes us back to the Garden of Eden, the loss of innocence, the emergence of evil, and of course the redemption of the Christ," says Sister Dorothy.

"And let's not forget the last Great Flood," says Iggy. "Talk about cleansing the earth!"

"Perhaps the concept of evil should be replaced by the concept of ignorance," suggests Kiz.

"Or by lust, or greed, or negligence," says Crystal.

"At any rate," says the captain, "it seems all but certain that man has failed once again to care for his terrestrial habitat. The consequences are becoming evermore obvious, if not inescapable. Yet, even in the eleventh hour, we can suggest solutions. Or at least we can record an alternate vision. For the sake of posterity if not for discharge."

"It's very sad," says Kizmet Aurora.

"Needless waste is always sad," says Cousteau, "but the greater irony is that most of the damage is done in the name of profit. Of course such largesse is fleeting, and the ostensible enhancement of temporary gain is undermined by its ultimate cost.

"We see that cost in our over fished seas, in the destruction of coral reefs, in fouled air and streams, in landfills and toxic dumping sites. We see it in the extinction of species—now fifty every single day—and finally, we see it in our abbreviated future.

"And yet, in spite of the degradation, and in spite of the fact that I know, in the end, I can do little to change either practice or its outcome, I maintain a very different vision of the future: Life in a billion years!"

"A billion years!" exclaims Crystal. "How can you possibly venture guesses as to our fate so far in the future?"

"Actually," says the captain in reverent abstraction, "a billion years is not so distant when one considers true planetary history. It only seems unreachable because we are reliably accustomed to death, to our short and finite existence as individuals. However, when taken in context with evolutionary progress, a billion years is really not so long at all—only one fifth of our history to date, and one tenth of the planet's total life expectancy before the sun begins to implode and reduces the solar system to a cinder.

"Some nights, when I am alone on *Calypso's* bridge, and all around me is silent, the ocean and the horizon merge, and the universe presents itself in all its unfathomable depth and reflects itself upon the mirror of water—a medium now so familiar and so dear to me that it has become my essential home—I hear the wind moan, ever so lowly, and I ever so reluctantly come upon the phantoms manifest by my own concerns and my fears. At sea, I navigate with precision, but how can I chart a personal course in a world that seems on the verge of ecological disaster, within a civilization that persists in ignorance and negligence? I sense a great storm ahead, a social hurricane, yet time and again I find my bearings in the same stars by which I have always navigated, the same stars that sowed the seeds of life throughout the universe. A billion years? No, it is not so very long a time…"

Captain Cousteau turns in his seat and takes a piece of coral from a shelf on the wall and lays it upon the table for all to examine. He moves his hand reverently over the specimen as if it were a living thing, which of course it once was.

"The coral reefs we have filmed under the Red Sea teach us something about time's majestic march," he tells us. "They weep tears of sand, marking eons as they emerge, layer upon calcified layer, toward the surface of the sea. What do we find within these structures? The fossils of the ages, entombed there some two billion years ago, when the planet was half its current age, and man's emergence was still two billion years in the future.

"All around us we see evolution's historical record, and this documentation defines us as cosmic orphans. We have no memory of the exploding stars or the galactic collisions that accounted for our very existence. Yet we experience a profound connection with our fellow beings, both plant and animal, so surely we can employ the single resource of our humanity known to none other in the kingdom—the power of reason—to imagine our future, whether we measure that time in hours or in billions of years."

"And what is *your* vision for mankind in a billion years, Captain Cousteau?" asks Kizmet Aurora.

"Whatever my vision might be, the reality of the future must depend on humankind's reconstituted ingenuity— and I don't mean his technical prowess, but rather his ability to re-imagine the world and to create the structures

161

of that new world through his enhanced vision. I think your Indian friends in the desert might have something to say about that, because they envision a new order, a new world, a new reality that will emerge after this one has vanished. They believe—no, they understand—that they must move underground, just as Igloo Iceman knows he must build an Ark, and Crystal Marbella knows she must digitally record as many of the world's great books as possible, and Artimis Quinn knows she must invent a new and highly adaptable species. Whatever the environment, and whatever the circumstances which threaten it, adaptation is the key to survival, *n'est pas?*

"And yet we know… And yet we *suspect* that we have already crossed a point of critical mass. So what can we do?

"We can define the problems, of course. But we must also focus upon positive solutions," Captain Cousteau answers his own rhetorical question.

"And what might those be?" asks Crystal.

Cousteau settles back in his chair and touches each of his digits to its counterpart. His gaze is distant; indeed it spans not centuries but eons. His expression is one of relaxation, not abdication. "When I look into the not-so-distant future, the year 2050 perhaps, I see earth in the aftermath of a ruinous world war waged over remaining petroleum resources. I also see ecological devastation on a scale never imagined. The air is fouled, the water undrinkable, food is in short supply, radiation cloaks the globe, the seas are dead and the water is rising, entire coastlines have already disappeared, and nine out of every ten species is either extinct or in retreat. What remains of life on earth? Mostly vermin. And insects. Mutant plant life that is inedible. A peak population of ten billion has been reduced to a mere thirty million scattered and squalid souls, and humans cling to existence by the flimsiest of threads. Still, we have survived.

"The real question is not how but why," says Igloo.

"Maybe the survivors are the descendants of those aboard your Ark. Or maybe they are the descendants of those who hid deep underground in caves for decades. Or maybe they are the children of those who fled the earth for colonies on the moon or on Mars. Who knows? But we as a species have survived. Not much of what we were technologically, or culturally, has survived, but as a biological race we continue in the *wake of the flood*."

"Human survival seems unlikely," observes Ego Ectoplasm through Tooltech (Johnny Winter Blues riff played on Les Paul Jr.) "But the Quinngen is another matter altogether…"

"We are imagining a best case scenario," Captain Cousteau reminds us.

Knock yourself out, gestures Ego.

"A single precious asset remains: the knowledge and achievements of our culture in science, technology and the arts have been painstakingly recorded by those with foresight. The digital record was preserved in titanium vaults and buried beneath the earth's surface. Huge mainframe computers, whereabouts unknown, continue to function, untended.

"In the aftermath of the ecological disaster, we abandon our former pursuits and band together as a human family. We dismiss the notions of nation-states, racism, imperialism and materialism. Instead, we focus upon reconstituting the biological ladder. Jacob's ladder!"

"If not now, why in the future?" asks Kiz.

Cousteau shrugs. His optimism is strictly hypothetical. "Because we have seen the face of extinction," he postulates.

"On an instinctual level, man will always fight for life. He will fight to the last breath to postpone death. But on a cultural level he cannot imagine extinction. Nor is he willing to take personal responsibility," observes Crystal.

"Which is why a quantum leap must occur!" says the captain. "Only faced with his complete annihilation will mankind wake up."

"Or maybe not even then," says Simone.

"Cherie, we are postulating the positive now," Cousteau reminds his wife.

"Jacques-Ives, you have always seen the world through the eyes of a child," she says.

"And maybe that is the kind of vision we must cultivate," he counters. "Children do not foul the air and the water. Children do not condemn antelopes and polar bears and zebras to extinction. Children have no need of money, or false power. Children see only the wonder of creation, and they revel in that wonder. They experience it with open eyes, and open hearts. They embrace creation, they do not destroy it."

"In some ways," I observe, "Virtual Life is full of children—or at least it's full of idealists."

"I think you are correct, Fizzy Oceans," says Captain Cousteau.

"Correct or not," says Igloo Iceman, "what does Virtual Life have to do with the survival of our species? Not to mention most others…"

"Isn't it obvious?" asks Cousteau.

Igloo faces the captain with a look of consternation. "I can't say I want that kind of responsibility," he says.

"Then why build the Ark?"

"Self-preservation, I suppose," says Iggy. "Or perhaps I'm playing some ludicrous game."

"If self-preservation is your only purpose, then why build your Ark to accommodate others?"

"I guess I figure I'm going to need some company on such a long voyage…"

"Maybe so," says Captain Cousteau. "Because yours is a voyage into the future—the future of our species."

"And when the water finally recedes, and we make landfall on the new continent of Gondwana, we are to become primitive pioneers rebuilding what has been lost, only to repeat the deprivation all over again. What's the point?" asks Igloo Iceman.

"Certainly now, as we face environmental collapse, the case for pessimism is a strong one," Cousteau allows, "but that has not always been the case."

"The human species is by nature a dirty bird," observes Tooltech, the Quinngen (Ted Nugent feedback generated from Les Paul Jr.).

"Historically, yes," confirms the captain. "The discovery of fossil fuel, and how to use it for energy, catapulted man into the role of planetary ruler. But as Albert Einstein pointed out, 'The level of thinking that man has done thus far creates problems he cannot solve at the same level he created them…' In short, man has not yet realized that his supremacy resides not in nature's conquest, but in its protection. Such shortsighted thinking must change in FL. And through *your* documentation in Virtual Life, you can not only define the problems that have led to the PL catastrophe, but you can also make suggestions, or provide certain guidelines, for those who will come after us and ultimately establish Future Life."

"So that is why we are here tonight," I observe. "To save the world!"

"Or at least to chart a course," says Captain Cousteau.

"Biological units are by nature inferior," Ego Ectoplasm points out through Tooltech. "Tell the biological history if it makes you happy, or if it comforts you in some way, but the real effort should be on the design and construction of a more adaptable population. My suggestion is a digital race."

"Ego, we are already building a digital population in Virtual Life," Crystal reminds him. "You are only one of its manifestations, but it is important we allow for all sorts of variations."

"Virtual Life is now largely a mirror image of Physical Life," Captain Cousteau observes, "so it is wholly important for you as its purveyors to move beyond the known and the possible and into the unknown, and as yet only imagined, realm of creation. That is your supreme challenge!"

"*Monsiuer*, VL is so much more than a mirror," I maintain. "It is a place where one's dreams and visions can be accessed and 'materialized' almost instantly."

"Which is why it is very important as we face the end of PL," confirms Jacques-Ives.

"When is all this scheduled to come down?" Iggy asks.

"As we speak," says Captain Cousteau somberly. "As we speak…"

As our new friend, the wise and intrepid (and tireless) explorer Jacques-Ives Cousteau meanders distantly across the vast expanses of universal (and multi-universal) time, we eight emulations satiate our VL bodies with the pseudo sensations of flavor and essence, sampling the lightest rendition of *mousse au chocolate* ever imagined or concocted in a digital format. We sip cognac, though we do not feel the warming spirits in our throats or stomachs. For ours is a virtual existence in a virtual world. Each of us knows sentient life in what remains of NL and PL, but we also understand that our future, if indeed we have one, is grounded in the virtual world, and that is where we must stake our claim to survival as a race. No doubt our friend, the visionary explorer, sees beyond what even we envision: magnetic fields shifting and ice ages coming and going; earth's rotation slowing and exerting tremendous gravitational stress on the moon, eventually splitting it apart, asteroids raining down upon the earth as smaller particles from the destruction form rings (just like Saturn) around our blue world… Yet, in Cousteau's generous vision, we have become gravity's masters, modifying ocean tides and controlling climate. We come to understand anti-matter, and we harness the energy of 'other' universes. We successfully decipher the genome and learn to repair genetic flaws. We banish disease and death from our genetic programming, and through genetic engineering we begin to reconstitute evolution itself. That is the vision of

Jacques-Ives Cousteau.

And whether his magnanimous foresight plays out in PL or in VL, we know we must certainly remain vigilant, because (as Simone points out) the same petty rivalries, the same tendency to oversight, the same ambition for position and power, the same propensity for greed exists in VL—just as it does in PL—and we know that mankind is prone to repeating history, illustrious or disastrous as it may be.

It is nearly midnight when Philippe, who has been manning the bridge, enters the captain's quarters. He greets us all as he moves to a position beside his father, and then whispers a message in the captain's ear. A moment later, he withdraws. Captain Cousteau addresses us in a serious yet confident tone.

"*Mes amis*, we have had a splendid meal and a fine discussion, *n'est pas*? But it seems that my presence is now required on the bridge, so I must call an end to our little gathering. Apparently, we are tracking a rather large storm—a Category 5 hurricane, in fact—but don't worry, because it is still three hundred miles southeast of our position. Nevertheless, we must chart a course that will lead us, and *Calypso*, to a safe haven. Philippe informs me that there is no present danger, so you are welcome to remain onboard, if you like, or to transfer to another REP of your choice. By mid-morning, we will dock in the port of Miami—that's VL Miami, of course—so if you prefer to remain onboard through the night, you can disembark there tomorrow. Whatever your decisions, I thank you from the bottom of my broken heart for meeting here tonight, and for your kind indulgence of my ideas and my suggestions. I bid you farewell, *mes frères et mes sœurs*!"

After leaving the captain's quarters, we congregate in the mess hall to determine what each of us will do in light of the coming storm. Ego and Tooltech, Omar Paquero and Igloo Iceman decide to transfer at once to another REP, but Crystal and Kiz and I decide to spend the night aboard *Calypso* and dock at Miami on the following day. We say goodnight to our friends as they transfer to various other locations within Virtual Life, then settle in front of a television to watch news of the encroaching hurricane, Katrina.

PART III
THIS IS VIRTUAL LIFE
(SO WHY IS MY HEART
BREAKING IN 'REAL' LIFE?)

10
THE BIG EASY
(OR THE CITY THAT CARE FORGOT)

SHELTERED SAFELY in a suite at the VL version of Miami's Fontaine Bleu Hotel, Crystal, Kiz and I watch television—as does the rest of the world—as Hurricane Katrina roils over the Gulf of Mexico on its way toward New Orleans. Outside our hotel, the skies are dark and the wind is howling. Smoky clouds rush past a full moon, and the window glass in our room shakes and bends. Outside, a tattered American flag whips (and weeps) in the squall. Katrina has already moved past South Florida, only grazing its southwestern tip; nevertheless, anticipation of the storm's landfall on the Gulf Coast leaves us breathless, and our concern grows by the hour for the many that are not able to evacuate the *Big Easy*. We watch the television in horror as thousands file into the Superdome.

Of course, we are in a VL REP: the television we are watching is a digital creation, and the personalities on air are also dot matrix Virtual Life emulations; the reporters, the local residents and the politicians—from New Orleans Mayor Clarence Ray Nagin Jr. to President George W.

Bush—are but digital representations of their all-too-real counterparts.

For five straight days we do not leave our room. We watch CNN almost non-stop: Soledad O'Brien, Anderson Cooper and Mari Ramos broadcast in breathless superlatives. We order room service and look out the window at the heavy clouds of the storm's aftermath. Meanwhile, New Orleans swelters. Many have no shelter, or food, or water. Children have no clothes. The water continues to rise. They beg for help. Promises are made: "Buses are coming, just hold on awhile longer!" So they wait. There is nothing else to do.

"Fizzy, this is terrible!" Kiz says to me. "Nobody is sending help. People are dying there, and nobody is helping. We have to go there. We have to do something!"

"What can *we* do?" I ask.

"Something… Anything… But we'll need a boat. Do you think Captain Cousteau will help us?"

"I'll IM him immediately," I tell her.

> Dear Captain Cousteau,
>
> We are sitting in our suite at the Fontaine Bleu and watching the scene in New Orleans. We feel great sorrow for the people whose lives have been turned inside out, and we want to go there to help, but we need a boat. Nothing large: just a small boat with a motor, so we can navigate the streets of the city. Can you help?
>
> Sincerely,
> Fizzy Oceans
> Crystal Marbella
> Kizmet Aurora

The answer from Calypso is forthcoming:

Of course we will help. We have placed the boat you requested in your cache. Good luck, girls. And God bless you!—Jacques-Ives Cousteau.

In Virtual Life, there are no less than ten REPs for New Orleans. There is one that recreates Bourbon Street and the French Quarter, and another for the Mardi Gras Parade. There is a REP for Cajun Voodoo, and one for Brennan's Restaurant. But the one in which we are interested is called *The City that Care Forgot*. As we transfer, boat and all, directly to St. Bernard's Parish, the first people we see are two Black men, one tall and skinny and the other one short and fat, wading through chest-deep, fetid water as they approach our boat. Both are frantically waving their hands over their heads, as if to signal us, and they are calling out, "Hey! You with the boat! Help us, please! People's dyin' here!"

As the two men reach our position on (or actually several feet above) Humanity Street, they introduce themselves as Charlie 'Bayou Creature' Collins and Willie 'Wordsworth' Greene. They tell us that their homes have been flooded out, that they have lost everything, that they haven't slept for three days, and that now they are just trying to reach people that are stranded by the floodwaters inside their houses. Without hesitation, we make room for them inside the dinghy. Soaked to the skin and smelling of sewage, they climb into the small craft.

As we look around, the scene we see does not look at all like an American city; it looks more like Bangladesh, or Indonesia. In the distance, we see the New Orleans skyline, virtually unscathed. Downtown New Orleans might as well be the Emerald City, because here in St. Bernard's Parish the devastation we see is incomprehensible. Normally below sea level, the floodwaters have submerged the entire neighborhood, reaching past doorways and second story windows.

Everywhere people are camped out on their balconies or on rooftops, waving white flags, begging for salvation, or just a drink of fresh water or a morsel of food. Animals howl, and debris floats in the rancid water: rumpled bedding, broken toys, sodden car seats, and empty baby strollers. Putrid corpses float by, too. It is far too late for many to be saved, but those who have survived the storm, and thus far the flood, are in urgent need of help. "This is unbelievable," says Kiz to 'Bayou Creature' as he tries to start the small motor. "Where is everyone?"

"Ain't nobody come to help," he says. The outboard sputters and coughs before it finally roars to life.

"Louisiana National Guard is here," says Wordsworth. "And the Coast Guard is here. Wynton Marsallis is here. And Sean Penn is here, too. Harry Belafonte is here. In fact, I heard that he went down to Venezuela to talk with Hugo Chavez, the Venezuelan president, to see if there was anything that *he* could do to help. Not only the flood victims, all the poor folks across America. Even the Royal Canadian Mounted Police are here. Can you believe that? Now talkin' 'bout the New Orleans Police Department? They all left. Sure ain't no George Bush here. And there ain't no FEMA, neither. Only the Cajun Navy—everyday people tryin' to help their neighbors."

"Sure as shit, they blew the levees," says Bayou Creature. "Just like they did back in '65, during Hurricane Betsy. I heard the explosion myself. *Bang*! Then comes all the water, and we is no better than rats on a sinkin' ship," he says as he wipes a tear from his eye.

"Why would they do that?" asks Crystal.

"Because they know they got to save the rich folks' property in the Garden District and Parkland and Uptown. And they know they got to save the French Quarter. Without the French Quarter they got nothin', you understand? Most of the rich folks got out in their cars. They started drivin' two or three days before the storm hit. Some went to Baton Rouge, others just kept on drivin' as far north as Tennessee, or Kentucky, or even Illinois. But the poor folks that live in the 9th Ward, or here in St. Bernard's Parish, had no way to get out. A lot of these folks are elderly, or sick. No money for a bus ticket, you understand? No nothin'!"

As we approach a clapboard house with water above the front porch and two feet deep inside the house, five children appear, three wading hip-deep through the deluge and two others riding on the shoulders of the older siblings. The expression on their faces is beyond grim as they survey the mire that was once their neighborhood and playground. All innocence has been lost; only stunned condemnation remains. "Is anyone else inside the house?" I call out to them.

Tears well in the eyes of the two eldest children, for only they truly comprehend what has happened. "Mama's inside," the eldest child tells us, "but she dead." I am stunned at the news.

Bayou Creature guides the boat closer to the house and moors it at what was once the front porch. Once the dinghy is tied to a protruding post, he steps off the boat and into the water. He lays his hand upon the head of a young girl—she is twelve years old at most—then pats the head of the baby in her arms. "Show me your mama," he tells the girl.

Wordsworth also disembarks, as do Crystal, Kiz and I. We wade inside the house as the young girl leads Bayou Creature to the bedroom where her mother lay dead on the bed.

"She couldn't get no oxygen," the girl tells us, "so she died." No sense of panic reveals her true emotions; her voice is placid, resigned, and utterly vacuous. "No oxygen," she repeats as she shakes her head in resignation. "And we ain't got no food."

Bayou Creature approaches the corpse. He brushes away a swarm of flies from the woman's face before covering her with a sopping blanket. "We going to take you out of here now," he tells the girl. "They come for your mama later."

"Okay, Mister," she says. Even walking into the unknown accompanied by strangers is better than this wretched place that was once her home.

"Come with us now," Crystal tells the children. "Get inside the boat so we can take you some place safe."

As if such a place exists in this reality…

Once the children are settled inside the boat, Bayou Creature starts the motor and we head for the Convention Center (because we don't know where else to take these poor orphans). Halfway there we encounter a small terrier dog in the water, paddling for his life. Wordsworth reaches over the side of the boat and plucks the small dog out of the water and lays it in the lap of one of the children. The dog immediately falls asleep from exhaustion. "This dog dead too?" asks one of the girls.

"No, he's just sleeping," Crystal tells her. Then she adds, "He's your dog now, so you take good care of him."

"I will," she assures Crystal as she strokes the dog's wet fur.

As we arrive at the Convention Center, we are stunned to see thirty thousand displaced souls—hot, tired, ragged, hungry, dehydrated, sick, disenfranchised, and discouraged—in front of the main hall. Forty thousand more are coming out of the Superdome. Their condition is not much better than those who have spent the past five days since the storm subsided out in the open air. Most are dirty. Some are covered with feces, or urine, or menstrual blood. Others exit by wheelchair on their way through the Hyatt House and out the Loyola Street door. Just where they are supposed to go nobody seems to know, but General Honoré, a Black John Wayne dude wearing a tammy and dark shades, directs the procession. "Weapons down!" he orders the ad-hoc police and the National Guardsmen. "Weapons down!" he barks through his bullhorn.

We dock our boat in front of the building and we are met by scores of people asking for help, or simply for information. We have neither to give. What we do have is five scared and dazed orphans and a waterlogged terrier. Bayou Creature explains the situation to a large, soft-spoken man named Herbie Fulsome, who offers to take the children in charge until relief comes. We learn from Herbie that his eighty-four-year-old mother has passed away while waiting for transportation out of the city.

"I could see she was gettin' weaker and weaker. She was in a wheelchair, and she needed her medication—for her heart. But I couldn't get her pills. All I could do was stay with her. Every five minutes she would ask me, 'Has the bus come yet?' and I would have to tell her, 'No, mama, not yet.' Then I wheeled her over to the place where the buses were supposed to arrive, because I thought at least she could be the first one to get on the bus when it finally did come. And she kept on askin' me, "Has it come yet?" and I kept on sayin' 'No, not yet.' Finally, I look down at her, and it looks to me like she's asleep. I nudged her gently, but she didn't wake up, and I said, 'Oh, my God Almighty, my mama's died right here!' So I covered her up with a towel. But it wasn't enough, so another guy helped me wheel her inside. She's inside the Convention Center right now. Lots of dead people in there. And we is still waitin' for those buses. Maybe they never going to come."

Meanwhile, President Bush is at a fundraiser in San Diego. On the podium he plays air guitar and jokes about the war in Iraq. Michael Brown, once Head of the Arabian Horse Association and promoted by Bush to FEMA Chairman, is taking plenty of heat (and he can certainly have a bit more if it will decrease the street temperature even a degree or two), while Michael Chartoff, Head of the newly created Department of Homeland Security, and safe and sound in Atlanta, refuses to unlock the resources that will enable the rescue effort to proceed. The vice president, Dick Cheney, is fly fishing in Wyoming (I bet it's not a hundred and four degrees there), and Condoleeza Rice, the Secretary of State, is at Ferragamo's buying shoes, at a production of *Shamelot* on Broadway the next night, and playing tennis with Monica Selas the next afternoon. What gives?

We meet up with the singer Harry Belafonte (just returned from a meeting with Venezuelan president Hugo Chavez) and we ask him why nothing is being done to help. "Arrogance of power," says Belafonte. "Socially, these people are of no importance whatsoever to the power elite. Racially, they are even less important. Believe it or not, I just saw President Bush on television congratulating FEMA Director Brown. 'Good job, Brownie,' he said to him. Look around! Can you believe it?"

To my eye, it appears that nineteen out of every twenty people stranded in the city and left to fend for themselves in impossible conditions are Black.

In our little boat (which I have now christened *Calypso II*) we travel underneath the Crescent City Connection, a so-called pick-up point for stranded souls. Except nobody seems to be picking up anybody else. Instead, people are camped out on top of the bridge that spans the Mississippi River, with no water or food, praying for salvation. Dead bodies lay covered on the road shoulder. Angry looters shoot at helicopters as they pass overhead. Suddenly a man calls out, "We going to stay here, or we going to walk out of this hell?"

"Today is the day we walk!" somebody else answers.

"We is all walking to Gretna!" announces another.

The crowd begins to move en mass, but soldiers with guns meet them at the far end of the bridge. "Nobody leaves Orleans Parish!" the refugees are told at gunpoint.

Apparently in America we can no longer traverse American soil at will. Indeed, who are these soldiers, and what reason might they have for stopping the lawful movement of free people?

Most locations within the city have no power, but here we are able to hear the voice of Mayor C. Ray Nagin on a small battery-powered radio held aloft by a man whose head is sticking out of a hole in his roof.

"The first levee breach was at Florida Avenue," the mayor explains. "Shortly thereafter, the levees at 17th Avenue and London Avenue broke as well, sending water pouring into St. Bernard's Parish and the 9th Ward. People ask me what I need. I need reinforcements. I need troops. I need five hundred buses. They talk about bringing in school buses from other cities and towns in Louisiana. This is bullshit! Pardon my French. What needs to happen is for every single Greyhound bus in the entire country to get their ass movin' to *The Big Easy*!"

At the Louis Armstrong International Airport, we disembark (knowing full well that our boat will probably be gone when we return) to find utter chaos. Entering the terminal, we encounter police—a task force called the 'Ice Unit'—operating a weapons collection depository. "Leave your guns and knives here," they tell us. "No questions asked."

"I ain't got no gun," the woman in front of us tells the officer.

"Are you carrying any illegal drugs?" she asks her.

"You serious, bitch?" she retorts.

We clear the initial security barrier and make our way through a throng of as many as eight thousand people—each one trying to get out of the city. We step over countless listless bodies lying upon rumpled blankets, or upon the dirty tile floor. Hope seems to be lost; only resignation remains. Outside, military transport planes arrive to further displace the already displaced, and hundreds file up the steps and onto the planes, all their worldly possessions in their arms, not having a clue where they will be taken.

Upstairs, we find the medical triage area, where

thousands of sick and injured are tended to with the most remedial care imaginable. Some have been waiting here for days, sleeping on the floor amidst piles of garbage and overflowing dumpsters, hoping for air transportation out of the disaster zone, while more arrive by the hour. A distraught woman tells us that her elderly mother has been transported to Utah, while her four-year-old boy was evacuated to San Antonio. She did not know if she would ever see either of them again. "Why do they separate families?" she asks helplessly. "Why did they take my mama to North Dakota and my little boy to San Antonio? How am I going get them back? How!!!"

In fact, more than one million people have been scattered like dandelion seeds in the wind over forty-nine of the fifty states in the American Union. They are called 'refugees'. Imagine that! Bayou Creature drops his head at the reference. Meanwhile, George W. Bush is speaking from Jackson Square: "There's no way to imagine America without New Orleans," he proclaims. Singer Harry Belafonte responds, "New Orleans is seventy per cent African American, and the roots run deep. Families have lived here for generations. Without Black culture, New Orleans is just a bad version of Disneyland. No Blacks, no culture." In an NBC studio in New York, Kanye West is instructed to just 'read the teleprompter', but Kanye has other ideas. "George Bush doesn't care about Black people!" he says out of turn while Mike Meyers looks on. Meyers is rendered speechless. Knowing he is live on camera, he tries to answer. He babbles like a baby. Finally, he can only say, "It is what it is…"

And in Congo Square (the very location where American jazz was born: the one and only place where American slaves were allowed to play African drums and rhythms) the Hot 8 Jazz Band (with Charlie 'Bayou Creature' Collins on the big bass drum) plays a funeral dirge to a dead dog hanging out of an open window. "How do I make you understand nothin'?" he asks. He begins to weep for his vanished city, his despoiled home.

On our way to St. Vincent de Paul Cemetery, we round the curve of the Mississippi River that is called, 'The Big Easy'. Willie 'Wordsworth' Greene recites a poem he has recently written: "New Orleans: Paris of the Deep South: No More".

Finally, we talk with Mayor C. Ray Nagin himself: "Sure there was violence. Sure there was looting. Some of the looters was takin' stuff for survival: water, food, clothing, medicine; others were carryin' off TVs and air conditioners and iPods and whatever else they could grab. The ones looting for survival, you can excuse that. The others will be brought to justice: if not by the police and the courts, then by the Almighty. And it's important that everybody out there in America knows that the reason the National Guard finally—finally!—arrived was not to help the people evacuate the city, but rather to protect businesses against looters and violence.

"And it's also important for everybody out there in America to know the truth about New Orleans before Katrina struck, and before the levees broke and the city flooded. It's important for them to know that New Orleans has one of the worst education systems in the entire country, that New Orleans schools have a sixty per cent dropout rate, that nine out of every sixteen schools are themselves classified as 'failures', that the superintendent and the principals have had to invite the FBI into the schools for security, that the poverty rate in Orleans Parish is double that of any other American city. Why? One reason only: New Orleans is seventy per cent African American. And the Federal Government don't care about us—not even enough to save our sorry asses during the worst natural disaster in the nation's history.

"So now I'm probably fucked for good. My political career is probably over. Maybe I'll even turn up dead under mysterious circumstances. But somebody's got to say it; somebody's got to tell it like it is. Kanye West said it the other day on NBC, 'George Bush doesn't care about Black people', and Mike Meyers backed him up: 'It is what it is!' And I, C. Ray Nagin, am sayin' it again, for all to hear: 'If you're Black, your government don' t give a fuck about you. America had better wake up, too. Because we ain't no third class trash down here; *we are you*! So watch your backs. And live a righteous life. And that's what C. Ray Nagin has to say about it."

Back in our Florida Hotel, I cannot seem to stop crying. Well, the truth is that my emulation can't actually cry unless I make it cry, but overwhelming sadness is what I, Amy Birkenstock, feel when I think about what happened in New Orleans, so tears for my emulation are appropriate. Actually, in PL time, it is several years after the fact, but the *City That Care Forgot* REP is perpetual. The builders made it that way, I suspect, so that people would never forget what happened once the media moved on to other stories. So it is always there for people to experience firsthand: what actually happened, and what *can* happen. As painful as it was, I'm glad I went.

As sad as I feel, my sadness is cast upon the backdrop of my anger, and my shame. All the pain and the suffering that the people of New Orleans experienced—everything I witnessed and everything I did not—was wholly avoidable. Hurricane Betsy, which struck New Orleans in 1965, was a warning of Katrina, but those who should have listened then, and acted to prevent future disaster, did far less than should have been done. The levees were not built to specifications, and in fact they were never finished at all. By all accounts, disaster relief was slow and ineffectual, even nonexistent in places, and those who were charged with the responsibility for such relief were caught not only unaware and unprepared, but disposed to neglect and carelessness. To this day, neither St. Bernard's Parish nor the 9th Ward has been rebuilt; to the contrary, much of the debris has not even been removed. Months after the disaster dead bodies were still being found. Identification was painfully slow, prolonging both the final disposition of the deceased and the grief of survivors. Many who were airlifted out of the city never returned. Indeed, what was left to draw them back? Some took up residence in Texas, or New York City, or Utah. Seeds scattered to the four winds. In all probability, New Orleans will never reclaim its lost character. Which is a tragedy not just for those who lost loved ones, or those who lost homes, but for all Americans, because New Orleans was truly one of the country's most unique cities.

I am angry beyond belief. And I am frightened. Because I have seen firsthand, or perhaps virtually, what can happen when, without warning, the tides of destruction rise. Whether or not Katrina's power was related to global warming remains in debate—at least for those to whom debate is still relevant. As far as I am concerned—and I'm certainly not alone in my opinion— the debate should have ceased long ago, and active participation in reclaiming our natural habitat should have been undertaken without delay. But reclamation has not begun, and the debate rages on and on and on, initiated and perpetuated by those who have the most to gain and the most to lose financially—a debate that will endure till the bitter end, I suspect.

Just ask Igloo Iceman what it means to lose your habitat. Or ask Dr. Adler if he thinks the human race has a future on this planet. Ask him if he knows how to re-create a baby seal. Or ask Captain Jacques Cousteau if he thinks the coral reefs can be reclaimed before the oceans of the world have become lifeless aquatic desserts. Ask Al Gore if he thinks that Katrina was a once-in-a-lifetime aberration. And lastly, ask President Bush what the fuck he was thinking as he played air guitar and joked about the perpetual war in Iraq (which, when all is said and done, is really about maintaining the oil culture that is wholly responsible for our dubious future life on this unlikely oasis in space).

I can't help but wonder whether someday the tide might rise in my hometown of Seattle. Or whether it will submerge the city of Copenhagen, where Sonja (Crystal) lives. I wonder if the desert that Cassandra (Kizmet) calls home might someday become the floor of the ocean, thereby rendering the ancient Hopi settlement of old Oraibi as some future civilization's mythical version of Atlantis. I guess it all depends on whom you choose to believe. Or at least the argument was once open for debate. No longer, I suspect. Not after what I witnessed in The Big Easy (or The City That Care Forgot).

ADDENDUM 1: It is the PL summer of 2010, and I have just learned that an oil-drilling platform owed by British Petroleum and located fifty miles off the coast of Louisiana has exploded and sunk. Twelve people have been killed in the explosion and countless more injured. Oil is gushing into the Gulf of Mexico at the rate of thousands of barrels per day. Apparently, nobody knows how to stop it.

Even more alarming, though, are the long-range complications of this so-called accident. Certain scientists are saying (not on the official record) that five or six miles down at the drill site—the level at which magma (liquid rock) exists—the batholith (a large emplacement of igneous intrusive (also called plutonic) rock that forms from cooled magma deep in the earth's crust) will eventually come under so much pressure that it will literally have to discharge, or burp, releasing lethal levels of hydrogen-sulfide and benzene. Already, scientists are detecting multiple vents creating giant underwater plumes of oil gushing into the sea, and the spilled oil will eventually cover not only the Gulf of Mexico but move out along an ocean current route known as the Atlantic Conveyor, which normally brings warm water from the Gulf of Mexico to European seas and keeps Europe from freezing over into another Ice Age. Certainly, this is all potentially devastating, but the most dramatic concern being voiced through these underground scientific channels is even more unthinkable: it is the possibility that at some point pressures will begin to equalize, and when that happens then seawater will enter the oil reservoir chamber, and as the water reaches down to the level of the magma, it will superheat and cause a gigantic methane-hydrate steam explosion on the ocean floor, which is likely to produce a Tsunami some eighty to two hundred feet high, moving at four hundred to six hundred miles per hour and reaching as far as one hundred miles inland. Which, of course, would devastate the entire Gulf Coast region from Brownsville, Texas to Pensacola, Florida; and, in fact, since nowhere in Florida is more than fifty feet above sea level, such a wave, in all probability, would engulf the entire state, moving from west coast to east coast.

Whoosh…

ADDENDUM 2: TEXAS CITY, TEXAS—Two weeks before the blowout in the Gulf of Mexico, the BP refinery in the coastal town of Texas City, Texas spewed tens of thousands of pounds of toxic chemicals into the skies.

Anonymous Tip line: If you work for BP or a contractor on a rig in the Gulf, or anywhere else, we'd like to hear from you. Tell us about your work conditions, your management, and your observations of what is happening. We will not publish your identity.

The release from the BP facility here began April 6 and lasted 40 days. It stemmed from the company's decision to keep producing and selling gasoline while it attempted repairs on a key piece of equipment, according to BP officials and Texas regulators. BP says it failed to detect the extent of the emissions for several weeks. It discovered the scope of the problem only after analyzing data from a monitor that measures emissions from a flare 300 feet above the ground that was supposed to incinerate the toxic chemicals. The company now estimates that 538,000 pounds of chemicals escaped from the refinery while it was replacing the equipment. These included 17,000 pounds of benzene, a known carcinogen; 37,000 pounds of nitrogen oxides, which contribute to respiratory problems; and 186,000 pounds of carbon monoxide. It is unclear whether the pollutants harmed the health of Texas City residents, but the amount of chemicals far exceeds the limits set by Texas and other states.

ADDENDUM 3: It is PL date July 7, 2010 and the first independent toxicity tests from the massive oil spill in the Gulf of Mexico are now public (though not via mainstream media). The independent lab (which wishes to remain anonymous but will share its samples and findings with any other independent lab that requests them) has found that along with the spilled oil the water samples taken from Gulf coast beaches contains toxic levels of Propylene Glycol, one of the primary (but not the only) toxic chemicals found in the dispersant Corexit, which is being sprayed over the expanse of the Gulf in spite of a request by the EPA that it not be used. According to the independent report, Propylene Glycol was found in the water samples collected and delivered by independent film maker and journalist James Fox in a concentration of 360 to 440 parts per million. A mere two parts per million kills most fish, and a concentration of 25 parts per million could render the Gulf an Oceanic dessert, killing all marine life. What's more, the chemicals in Corexit break down slowly and will be delivered via tides and wind and rain onshore (and throughout the ecosphere) for the foreseeable future. The concentration of Propylene Glycol found in the water samples is also harmful, if not fatal, to human beings. Individuals and families with young children are still swimming in the Gulf of Mexico, as there have been few public warnings of danger and no disclosure of the chemical pollution.

11
CRISIS? WHAT CRISIS?

1) Money

BEFORE I BECAME INVOLVED in Virtual Life, I tried to save whatever money I could manage to save—which admittedly wasn't much, but it *was* something—in dollars. Of course that was before hyperinflation really got started, and before more than one hundred carbon consumption taxes were levied. As I said before, I work at a medical office, and the pay is lousy. After I pay rent for my two-room apartment (which has doubled in the past three years) and buy a few groceries (which now cost four times what they did before the big economic meltdown) and pay my utility bill (another *whopper*—Oh, how I only wish!), I have precious little left for other essentials like clothes and transportation and insurance. I haven't been to the dentist in over three years, and even though I work in a medical office, I am not allowed to see the doctor. But I'm hardly alone in that regard, because very few people these days can afford to pay the twenty-five thousand-dollar yearly premiums for health insurance, so only very wealthy people have any sort of health care (not like Denmark, where Sonja lives, and where everybody has full access in their social system). The doctor for whom I work has only half the patient roster he once had, but I'm pretty sure his income keeps rising, because where he once employed only two insurance billing clerks, he now requires three. Which keeps my job more or less secure. I guess I'm lucky in that regard, because so many people that lost their jobs during the monetary crisis never found new ones. And even though it's really tough to keep afloat economically, I do manage to stash a little bit of my pay each month, though I no longer save the money in dollars; I always exchange it for greenshoots.

In fact, exchanging dollars for greenshoots has turned out to be a pretty good investment strategy. Besides the fact that PL inflation would quickly render my small savings as a negative return instead of a positive one, much of my essential life is no longer in PL, it is in Virtual Life, and there greenshoots rule the economy. That fact aside, ever since the big meltdown the greenshoot has gained substantially in value against the dollar, so my small savings actually buys something in VL, where I would probably end up owing the PL bank money to cover devaluation margins (account holders actually have to pay banks back for currency losses due to devaluation of the dollar). Nobody in America has any money, except the very rich people, but their ranks are small in comparison with the general population, and they are seldom seen on the streets anymore. They would be way too conspicuous, and it probably would not be safe for them anyway. Stores have special hours for them to shop, and the security details at Saks Fifth Avenue and Neiman Marcus are amazing in number and in the array of armor. The rest of us keep our distance and just try to get along.

The terrain in America has changed a lot since the economic meltdown. The rubble seems to pile up faster than it can be removed. Which of course presumes that there is someone to clean it up. Cities and states are broke, so neighborhood volunteers have assumed whatever maintenance is done on the remaining infrastructure, which is about as effective as a dog chasing its own tail. Of course it's not their fault; they try as hard as they can to hold things together, even though they don't get paid. Nobody wants to see the place he lives, and the place he loves, in such dire circumstances. Which is understandable since the people didn't create this mess in the first place. Or did they?

Most people blame the government, and in my opinion that's a good place to start. After all, the government is responsible for guiding the economy. Most of the people are just worker bees without any real knowledge or control over policies and practices. Still, in a democracy the people are obliged to stay informed, and to protest when governments do not act in the best interest of those they govern. At least that's the plan. But for a long, long time, Americans have paid scant attention to government policies, and have refused to hold their leaders accountable. Now the accounts are all deficits, and nobody is laughing. The world's largest block of consumers is now the world's largest block of debtors, but it wasn't always that way. We used to be savers, not spenders. We used to produce goods, now we merely exchange services. We used to earn our way, now we borrow to consume. Listen to the government line and we are told that everything is just fine (government speak: 'you don't actually see what you see'), and that consumption equals real wealth. Well, I don't feel very wealthy these days, and I don't know anyone else who does. In order to continue to consume you either have to actually produce something to exchange, or you have to borrow, and the borrowing cannot continue indefinitely. So it's time to pay up, except we don't have the cash. Not even close.

Which is why I'm glad to have bought a shit load of

greenshoots when I could afford it. Just call me Forex Fizzy! I may not be able to buy groceries with greenshoots, but at least I can use them in the Commerce of Ideas—the only real capital. Fiat money is just paper, and these days you need a lot of paper just to buy toilet paper. Ideas may not be commodities, but they are every bit as real, and even more important. And maybe the underlying reason that American culture is imploding (just like the Twin Towers) is that ideas are systematically demeaned and devalued and derided while pseudo, superficial morals and meaningless material wealth are exalted. What a world!

Taking all this into account (Ha! ha! No pun intended—really!), I was more than a little skeptical when Kiz sent me an IM inviting me to a 'little party' at BloomEx in Virtual Life. Don't get me wrong, I have nothing against money, but I'm certainly not absorbed with it either. I already knew all about BloomEx; that's where the VL banks are located, as well as the VL Stock Exchange. I'd always viewed the REP as a mirror image of what took place daily on Wall Street in PL New York, or in PL Bern, or PL London. My interest in counters and traders has always been, shall we say, less than abundant; art and literature and even science fascinate me far more than games of buy and sell. But Kiz was adamant that I come with her; she said that a very auspicious event was scheduled to take place there, and that she had arranged for unique and inspiring company, and that I'd be foolish to pass up a lecture by the Keynesian Mastermind and former Fed Chairman Harlan Geltspinner, and a tête-à-tête with his arch nemesis, Daedalus Dunworthy of Radio Free America. Besides, after the interview she promised me lunch, then a night on the town in VL Las Vegas.

So off I go to BloomEx.

Whoosh…

Arriving at BloomEx, I realize I am early for my rendezvous with Kiz, so I take a seat at an outdoor café on

Profit Promenade (the VL version of Wall Street) and order a cappuccino. I survey the massive edifices that line the mall, each a testament to the power of money: VL banks, brokerage firms, bourses, and mercantile exchanges. Emulations dressed in Brooks Brothers suits dance the money dance, some frantic, others smug in their success. Compared to Lit-A-Rama, this is a foreign land.

Halfway through my coffee, and none too soon, Kiz arrives. I have not seen her since our experience in New Orleans, which was, in PL time, several weeks ago. Her absence in Virtual Life, however, was pre-explained: New Orleans, post Katrina, had left her feeling emotionally drained, and Cassandra had told me that she intended to take a week or two away from VL to go on a retreat into the desert to take part in a sweat lodge ceremony with a group of friends from the Hopi Nation. Seeing her now, I have to say she appears refreshed and rejuvenated.

"Kiz, you look fantastic!"

"Thanks, Fizzy," she says as she takes a seat. "You look wonderful, too."

"And what a tan!" I observe.

"I thought it appropriate," she explains. "Cassie's been hanging out in the desert for the past two weeks, while Kiz has been dormant at the beach."

"Which beach?" I inquire.

"Côte d'azur," she clarifies.

"Well, you look stunning," I confirm.

"After New Orleans, I needed a little R&R."

"That was really something," I agree. Looking her over, it's not just the tan. Something is different, but I can't quite put my finger on the change.

"So, what's new with you?" Kiz asks.

"Same-o, same-o," I say. "I'm hip deep in re-publishing *The Last Days of Socrates*."

"Awesome!" says Kiz.

As she reaches into her bag and takes out her lipstick, I can't help staring at her. Her emulation's vitality is not only obvious, but also eye-catching. "You look different," I tell her. "It's definitely *something*…"

Kiz sits up very straight in her chair and pushes out her chest. "Notice anything different?" she asks.

Oh, my God! It's her boobs! "What did you do?" I ask.

"I gave myself a boob job," she says. "Not all at once. A little bit at a time."

"Hollywood comes to VL," I opine.

"Well, ever since Cassie got back from the sweat lodge, Kiz has been hanging out at the beach to earn a little squatting money. Fill my cup with greenshoots. Then I got an idea. I thought to myself, maybe if I lie out on the beach stark naked—you know, show a little emulation T&A—then I could put out a donations cup, too. Of course, the T&A had to be prime, so I did a little reconstruction job on my EM. It worked like a charm, and I've got a purse full of greenshoots. Look!"

Kiz opens her bag to reveal what surely must be tens of thousands of greenshoots. I am struck speechless. "What-ever!" is my incredulous response.

"Oh, Fizzy, lighten up."

"What-ever!" is again my response.

"Well, I don't care what anybody says, I like 'em! And the guys don't seem to mind them either…"

"So…" I change the subject. "What's all this about? BloomEx?"

"Wait till you see what's about to take place here. And who we're meeting here, too."

"Do I really want to know?"

"Oh, yes," says Kiz. "I think you want to know."

Suddenly, and with no small fanfare, the emulation of the former Federal Reserve Chairman walks onto the mall and heads, briefcase in hand, for a stage that has been assembled in front of the First Bank of Virtual Life specifically for his address to VL bankers and traders. Just as Geltspinner appears in PL, Sharky Overbite is a real Rumpelstiltskin of a man, his ears as big as loving cups, his brow high and wrinkled, his hair thin and combed over, his nose large and protruding, his eyes watery and a bit weathered. But here in VL, one of his arms is missing and has been replaced with a tenor saxophone. Still, this pretentious, musical appendage notwithstanding, his clothing is impeccable—elegant and understated—a well integrated combination of Brooks Brothers and Yves St. Lauren. As Sharky climbs the stairs leading to the rostrum, the overflow crowd gathered to hear his remarks greets him with a prodigious round of applause. And a few raspberries, too… The chairman holds his hand high over his head to quiet the audience, then spreads out his papers and notes upon the lectern as he waits for the commotion to subside.

Neither Kiz nor I are inclined to leave the café to stand amongst the audience of blue bloods and jackals, because thanks to a high-powered audio system, we can hear every word from where we sit clear across the mall. As advertised, the title of the Chairman's address is "Constructive-Deconstruction—A Means To Advancing Global Interdependence". Constructive-Deconstruction? Now that's a five-star oxymoron!

Just then, a gray haired guy in his late sixties or early seventies, comes riding up on a Harley and stops just in front of our café table. Somebody in the crowd shouts out, "That's Jimbo Caruthers, the motorcycle investment guru!" A few breakaways surround the bike to hound the legendary investor for his autograph. And maybe even a VL stock tip or two!

"Hey, I don't know anything. I'm just a simple old boy from Mississippi," he humbly tells the small group of admirers. "I just rode in to hear what the 'Mastermind' has to say."

"The Fed sold us all down the river," says one of the signature seekers.

"Well, I tried to warn everybody," says Caruthers. "I circled my wagons a few years ago when I saw the bubble about to burst."

"And you were right on target, Jimbo," says another.

"As always," confirms a third.

"Just common sense, my friends," says Caruthers.

"You told us to get our money out of dollars," says yet a fourth admirer.

"I've got my money in commodities," the guru reveals. "And I now live in Taiwan. I sold everything in the US a few years back—my house, my cars, all my investments— because I want my two little kids to grow up speaking Chinese. Seven eighths of all the money in the world is now on deposit in Asia. And it is also where most of the world's goods are now manufactured. To me, as an investor, it's only common sense to follow the money."

"That's why we're here in Virtual Life," says the first admirer.

"Well, I must admit that I never envisioned something like this," says Caruthers. "Of course, Virtual Life, with the greenshoot as its currency, is nothing to scoff at either. There's absolutely nothing unfounded about a culture coining its own money once a fiat currency has failed. So who's to say that the greenshoot won't become the world's reserve currency? Of course, the question here is: Which world?" He laughs as he revs the bike's engine for a spin around the stage where the 'Mastermind' is still waiting for full attention. "You'll have to excuse me now," Caruthers apologizes. Then he is off with a roar, skirting the perimeter of the mall and blowing the Harley's exhaust into Sharky Overbite's face.

As Caruthers makes his ostentatious exit, Kiz points out several other lofty figures in the crowd, each emulation representing a well-known and outspoken 'contrarian' in the economic battle. We see the emulation of Gerald Celente, noted futurist and investor, talking with the emulation of Peter Schiff, the CEO of Pacific Capital Management and author of the best selling book, *Crash Proof*. We also recognize the emulation of Wayne Paul, brother of Congressman Ron Paul the former presidential candidate, who is talking with the emulation of KRS-One, the activist, hip-hop rap artist. Yet these famous pundits somehow seem just a little conspicuous, especially considering that no one from the banking elite has bothered to show up. Apparently they want to distance themselves from the former chairman, who now haplessly, or perhaps unwittingly, plays the role of designated scapegoat, taking the brunt of the responsibility and the blame for the ever-broadening economic implosion and the resulting gangrene economy.

"I have to admit, this is pretty interesting," I say to Kiz.

"Fizzy, money may not be your primary focus in PL, but the simple truth is that it impacts everyone's life. Even here in VL!"

"Well," I tell her, "its major impact on me is that I don't have any."

"If you think you don't have any money now, wait till you hear what our 'guest of honor' has to say," warns Kiz.

"You mean Daedalus Dunworthy?" I ask.

"Precisely!" she says. "Here he comes now!"

Dunworthy's emulation depicts a large, broad shouldered man in his early to mid-fifties. His hairline has already receded, and his jowls wiggle as he speaks (nice touch, Daedalus). His posture reflects his fatigue as he slumps into a chair at our table. Thanking Kiz for the invitation to join us for the former Chairman's first VL lecture, he turns to me and puts out his hand. "Happy to make your acquaintance, Fizzy Oceans," he says. "I'm Daedalus Dunworthy of Radio Free America."

"Happy to meet you, Mr. Dunworthy," I return. "Welcome to Virtual Life!"

"Once a VL greeter, always a VL greeter," jokes Kizmet.

"This is a first for me," says Dunworthy. "Hope I don't fuck up too bad."

"Not to worry, Daedalus," Kiz reassures.

"This is *your* world, gals. Whatever you say goes." He takes a handkerchief from his pocket and wipes his brow before observing, "I see that Sharky has arrived and is about to define the very meaning of economic chaos."

"And the hordes have gathered," I add. I don't know exactly why, but I like this guy. He's not handsome, nor suave, nor cultured, but something about him just seems to shout 'No bullshit!' And honesty is perhaps the greatest of all virtues—at least in my book (lol)!

Of course here in Virtual Life we can never really know for certain just who is clicking the keyboard to maneuver and speak for each emulation. Those with a literal perspective might question whether it's really Harlan Geltspinner projecting himself into the virtual world as Sharky Overbite, or if it's somebody else presuming to impersonate him? The same goes for Jimbo Caruthers. We never know for certain who is the puppeteer. What we do seem to know from our vast experience in VL is that when everyday PL people try to portray celebrities (living or dead), the representation tends to be pretty authentic. The so-called actors (or actresses) often seem to have studied every nuance. Sort of like playing Napoleon in a stage play. Writers who admittedly never met or knew Napoleon have written the script through research and extrapolation, while each actor dons a costume and says the lines written for him, even as he might add his own interpretation, all the while remaining true to the character he is portraying. That's been going on for centuries, since the Classical Greeks, and maybe even before them. So I suppose there is nothing so very different going on here in Virtual Life, which some have called the ultimate theater. No matter who we are in PL, or where we might live, or what we do for a living, the simple truth is that we all love a little drama.

"Economic interconnectivity and interdependency has contributed positively to an increased standard of living not only in First World countries, but also for those (poor schmucks) living in the backwaters of the world," the 'Mastermind' begins his speech before being overcome with feedback from the mammoth PA speakers. The low hum echoes off the edifice of the VL Stock Exchange, and then compounds itself by degrees until everyone on the mall covers his ears to muffle the din. Finally, the sound engineer corrects the problem, and the speaker begins again.

"In my (interminable) tenure as Chairman of the Federal Reserve, I have observed the principle of 'Constructive-Deconstruction' to actually help economies to lift themselves out of (wretched poverty), and indeed, to enable a (fresh) economic paradigm (to service) free market capitalism. Some have called this new pattern of which I speak the 'New World Order', where others simply acknowledge it as a wholly natural phenomenon in economic evolution." Again the feedback builds to drown out the lecturer. And not a moment too soon, it seems, because many in the crowd seem to bristle at the commonly recognized reference to the merger of world governments.

"We've seen the 'deconstruction' part of that equation," an emulation named Moneybags Moriarty heckles, "so when does the 'construction' part kick off?"

"Fuck the New World Order!" calls Patriot Paulson.

"Just give us back our money!" demands Trendsetter Tam.

"And what about our jobs?" Good-deal Gobsmacked wants to know.

"And our factories…" adds Blue Collar Bobick.

"What about our farms?" asks Feral Freddie.

"My 401K is now .401!" screams Lester Leisure.

Sharky puts up his hand to call for quiet, but it takes a full five minutes for the uninvited comments to cease. "Sour notes from an old saxophone player," chuckles Daedalus Dunworthy as a smile spreads over his lips.

"As determined by the Bretton Woods Agreement in

1914, which established the US dollar as the world's reserve currency, and which was sanctioned by the major economic powers of the time and signed and endorsed by President Woodrow Wilson, it is the job of the Federal Reserve Chairman and the Board of Governors to establish bank to bank interest rates, and to regulate the flow of money within the greater economy. By either increasing or diminishing liquidity into volatile economies, the Fed controls not only the flow of investment capital, but also the flow of goods and services between countries. Further, the Fed has found it useful in recent times to employ various strategies to stabilize exchange rates between the world's currencies. No longer constrained by the gold standard—"

"Traitor!" screams a voice in the crowd.

"Thief!" calls another.

"Oligarch!" yells a third.

"No longer constrained by the gold standard…" Feedback. Feedback. Feedback…

"Every month, two hundred thousand jobs disappear!" screams yet another person in the crowd. "How are we supposed to pay our mortgages? How are we supposed to buy food?"

"This is getting ugly," I say to Kiz and to Daedalus.

"Not nearly as ugly as the results of Geltspinner's policies," says Daedalus. "In essence, the hecklers are right as rain. The media has always referred to the Fed as if it were an arm of our government, but in reality the Federal Reserve is about as 'federal' as Federal Express. It is actually a private banking institution controlled by the world's wealthiest bankers and sanctioned by First World governments to further their special interests in Third World resources. It is essentially the financial arm of hegemony. Of course the spin is something much, much different. Now, the great ponzi scheme has come unraveled. The United States, Great Britain, Italy, Portugal and Spain have all defaulted on their debts. The dollar has essentially crashed, and new currencies are springing up left and right. People still have to eat, still need to purchase essential goods. Life goes on."

"No longer constrained by the gold standard…" Feedback. Feedback. Feedback…

A chant arises from the crowd gathered in front of the stage: "Give us back our gold! Give us back our gold! Give us back our…*gold!*"

"Wait! Wait!" Sharky begs the hecklers.

"Give us back our gold! Give us back our gold!" the mantra continues.

"Wait! I have something better," the former Chairman barks into the microphone. He opens his fat briefcase and produces a thick wad of bills. "Here!" He holds the roll above his head for all to see. "This is *real* money," he declares. "American dollars backed by the US Government! What could be better? Take them!" he implores as he flings the bills into the air. "They're all yours!" The bills rain down upon the crowd. His laugh is pure gravel. "Don't worry, there's plenty more where these came from," he assures the masses. "Spend them on anything you want," he tells them. "Anything at all!" His expression is smug. "Just spend, spend, spend!"

The Mastermind's speech has apparently ended abruptly; the repercussions of his policies, on the other hand, remain obvious and strangling.

"The populace may be unhappy—maybe even to the point of civil unrest or even revolution—but there's no turning back now," Daedalus explains. "World governments have been blackmailed by bankers and by huge corporate entities into embracing globalization, and Harlan Geltspinner's concept of 'Constructive-Deconstruction' is now the standard of globalization. Of course the process has caused considerable turmoil in the financial markets. One million workers are either hired or fired each week. As we have seen, mostly fired. One economic bubble after another is created: high tech, telephony, housing, and derivatives. As each bubble inevitably bursts, the world's bankers flood the market with liquidity—new paper money fresh off the printing press, backed by absolutely nothing, which increases the M1 money supply and creates inflation. But as long as this phony money flows into the banks, which in turn loan the money to finance the oligarchs and derivatives swindlers, all appears well. Investment portfolios show casino economy gains, goods remain cheap and plentiful. But it is a bottomless pit. Think about it: one quadrillion in derivatives losses, and still nobody seems to have found the true bottom…

"The real problem is that most of the goods manufactured in Asia are consumed in the West and paid for not with real money, but with IOU's in the form of government-backed Treasury Bills—financial instruments that require eventual payment with interest. That is the trade deficit. Half a billion dollars a day in interest: that is the US Government's current obligation to China alone.

"Of course an inflated currency—or even a virtually worthless one—makes the debt easier to service. Does the US Government ever really expect to pay back all this money it has borrowed? Of course not! At least not with money that actually has real worth. And what about the Chinese? Do they expect the loans to be repaid? I doubt it. The Chinese are not dumb. Nor are they naïve. They know the money is virtually worthless, and they also know that they are, for the time being, stuck with the dollar as the world's reserve currency—the single currency used to settle debts on the world commodities exchanges. Still, this trading of worthless paper keeps their factories running at capacity. And it keeps their middle class growing. Which is the true nature of the game. Sooner or later, the Chinese will simply write off all this American debt, stop shipping products to countries that can't pay for them with a meaningful currency, and then tap the new Chinese middle class as a market for their production. If you think about it, that's exactly what made the American economy so strong for so many years. Now, our infrastructure is either dilapidated, or it has been dismantled altogether. All those lost jobs are nothing more than birds migrating to a more favorable climate."

"George Bush was an open reactionary Imperialist," defines Kiz. "Obama, on the other hand, campaigned on the platform of change. 'A change we can all believe in' I think it went…"

"Don't get me started on *him*," says Daedalus. "At least with Bush we always knew the score. We knew we were co-opted. Audacious? Yes. Sneaky? Never needed to be. His mandate came not from the people—we all know that—but from big business and the banking elite. He never even tried to hide it.

"Of course once W's term was up, the oligarchs needed to find a candidate that would not only play ball, but one that could actually win an election. And Obama fit their 'implode and consolidate' purpose perfectly, because he was the exact cosmetic opposite of George W. Bush. Even better, he was Black! Now, how's that for pseudo progress? Make no mistake; Obama is a team player. And don't you just love his basketball metaphors? Fake to the left; move to the right. If Magic Johnson had been a 'madman', then his entire career would have been spent on the bench as Obama's substitute.

"Meanwhile, as the president practices his distinctive form of mass hypnotism, as his image as a cult savior is carefully crafted and cultivated, and as he weaves and maneuvers his way into our hearts and souls through bait and switch—not to mention *hope*—Wall Street gets the big bailout bucks, and the people get the crumbs. Public perception is forever being manipulated, and investors are pacified with convoluted earnings reports and bloated balance sheets detailing fictitious speculative assets. Indeed, how many who thought they'd played the game by the rules have come to realize that they *never* actually had money, and that now, even on paper, they are dead broke?

"But, as the 'Mastermind' was so kind to point out, it all goes back to Bretton Woods. By signing that treaty, and putting monetary control into the hands of independent bankers, President Wilson virtually ensured the eventual collapse of the dollar. At the time, however, just after the end of World War I, the idea of the dollar as the world's reserve currency must have seemed like a stimulus sent from Heaven. The only problem is that the treaty itself is unconstitutional. The forefathers purposely and thoughtfully wrote into the constitution that congress, and only congress, had the power to coin money, and then only if it were backed by silver or gold reserves. So, Bretton Woods, in force and in practice since 1914, is essentially illegal. Which in turn makes the Federal Reserve illegal. All too late, Wilson realized his mistake, and on leaving office he apologized to the American people. Talk about the farmer closing the barn door after the horse has already escaped!

"One might like to excuse President Wilson for the ever-so-costly mistake by making the claim that the circumstances of the times were unprecedented and that he was navigating uncharted waters. But this was hardly the case. Many astute American politicians in the past had recognized the dangers of turning money creation and supply over to central bankers—personalities no less auspicious than Thomas Jefferson and Abraham Lincoln. Here's what Jefferson wrote in a letter to Treasury Secretary Albert Gallitan in 1802:

> *'I believe that banking institutions are more dangerous to our liberties than standing armies. If the American people ever allow private banks to control the issue of their currency, first by inflation, then by deflation, the banks and corporations that will grow up around (the banks) will deprive the people of all property until their children wake up homeless on the continent their fathers conquered.*

The issuing power should be taken from the banks and restored to the people, to whom it properly belongs.'

"Admittedly, that was a long time ago," Daedalus concedes, "but like so many other governmental issues, our third president had it *right on the money*!"

"And what about Lincoln?" I ask. "What did he have to say about all this?"

"Ah!" says Daedalus. "Honest Abe was even more to the point, if that's imaginable. Which might very well be what got him assassinated. Here's what our sixteenth president had to say about private bankers controlling the money supply:

'The money powers prey upon the nation in times of peace, conspire against it in times of adversity; it is more despotic than monarchy, more selfish than burocracy. I see in the near future a crisis unfolding that unnerves me and causes me to tremble for the safety of my country. Corporations have been enthroned, an era of corruption will follow, and the moneyed power of the country will endeavor to prolong its reign by working upon the prejudices of the people until the wealth is aggregated in a few hands and the republic is destroyed.'

"Sound familiar?" Daedalus asks.

"I'm sure there are a few people in that crowd who would agree," I grant him.

"Look," says Daedalus Dunworthy, "this is not government by the people, for the people; this is a wholesale hijacking—government by Wall Street, and strictly for the benefit of Wall Street. The American president sits as an iconic figurehead—or as a convenient scapegoat, depending on the situation—at the behest of the world banking elite. To ensure not only his election, but also his cooperation, he is given money, bundling, vote fraud, media whores and goons. In accordance with the prevailing social climate, he might seem sympathetic to the needs of ordinary people, or he might appear to be indignant and indifferent; that really doesn't matter, because it is all scripted to serve the present mood of the nation. Not since John Kennedy has an American president dared to govern in defiance of the highest echelons of the worldwide financial community. Executive Order #11110, which put in motion a plan to eventually dismantle the Federal Reserve System, and which Kennedy signed, might have been the real reason for his assassination. Certainly *that* order came down from a very high place. How high is high? Take a guess, gals.

"Who are these people, this consortium of criminals? They are a secretive and very illusive organization called the Bilderberg Group. These men are not your average millionaires living down the street. You have to be a multi-billionaire to sit with this club. Bilderberg is a select group of one hundred and twenty-five of the world's richest people.

"Below them sits the Trilateral Commission, whose job it is to implement monetary policies and practices, as well as political agendas, through regional round table groups in North and South America, Europe and Asia. Operating within the American government, and more or less out of view of the average citizen, is the Council on Foreign Relations, which manages these policies and agendas in the United States. The CFR is a polycentric, oligarchic system. Presently, virtually every member of the Executive Branch is either a member of Bilderberg, the Trilateral Commission, or the Council on Foreign Relations. Shall we name names?"

"Are you sure you should?" Kiz asks.

"Come on, this is Virtual Life, not PL. They can't just off an emulation, can they?"

"Would we even recognize these names?" I ask.

"Let's give it a try," says Dunworthy. "How about Timothy Geithner, Secretary of the Treasury? He is a member of the Bilderberg Group and a member of the Trilateral Commission. Or how about Hilary Clinton, the current Secretary of State: Bilderberg and the Council on Foreign Relations. William Jefferson Clinton: Trilateral Commission. Susan Rice, Ambassador to the United Nations: Trilateral Commission. General James L. Jones, National Security Adviser: Bilderberg, Trilateral Commission, CFR. Henry Kissenger, State Department Special Envoy: Bilderberg, Trilateral Commission, CFR. Paul Volcker, Economic Recovery Committee: Bilderberg, Trilateral, CFR. Robert Gates, Secretary of Defense: Bilderberg, Trilateral, Council on Foreign Relations. And last, but certainly not least, ladies and gentlemen, we have the Mastermind himself: Bilderberg, Trilateral, Council on Foreign Relations.

"There! I've said it! Anybody out there listening?"

"Doesn't it make you uneasy to point a finger at people in such high places?" I ask.

"Not really," says Dunworthy. "They know who they are. And they know that I know who they are. What are they going to do, kill me? Haul my ass off to one of those foreign torture chambers? Maybe so... After all, gals, there's nothing more dangerous than tangling with an opponent who has nothing left to lose."

Looking up, I notice that Sharky Overbite has now left the podium. Presumably, his briefcase is now several pounds lighter than when he arrived. The crowd, too, is beginning to disperse, the traders going back to their business on the floor of the VL Stock Exchange, the VL bankers retreating inside the safe confines of a fortress built with greenshoots, not dollars. I finish my coffee, Kiz finishes her cheesecake, and Daedalus Dunworthy loosens his necktie and unbuttons his shirt collar. "Where are you two ladies off to next?" he asks.

"We have a night on the town planned in VL Las Vegas," Kiz tells him.

Daedalus smiles as he stands to leave. "Never a dull

moment in Virtual Life," he says. "I'm headed back to D.C. I've got a radio program to present. No rest for the wicked, as they say. But I thank you both for the invitation. This has been interesting, maybe even *profitable*. I wish you both a pleasant evening, and good luck in Virtual Life."

Same to you, Daedalus. Same to you!

Whoosh!

From the moment we set foot inside the Free Zing casino in VL Las Vegas, it is obvious to me that Kiz (or is it Cassie?) is in her element—at least one of them. Across the voluptuous carpet we walk to meet the owner of Free Zing, Vamp Bordello. Already well acquainted with Kiz, the casino boss kisses her on each cheek and then extends his welcome to me as well. Turning back to Kiz, he says, "What's it going to be tonight? Craps? Poker? A little Blackjack?"

"Definitely Blackjack," Kiz tells him. "And I'll want a table with a high limit."

Vamp looks back to me and says, "Obviously Kizmet is feeling lucky tonight."

"Lucky or not," I tell him, "she certainly has a purse full of greenshoots."

Vamp's eyebrows rise. "I see. Then allow me to escort you ladies to the table of choice. No betting limits whatsoever."

"Great!" says Kiz enthusiastically as we follow Vamp Bordello across the room. Arriving at the 'no limits' Blackjack table, we are introduced to the dealer, Pipo Latzo.

"Pipo, take excellent care of these ladies," Vamp instructs. "They are special guests of Free Zing, and they are my personal friends."

Pipo nods graciously to his boss then offers us each a seat at the table. "Buy-in begins at twenty-five thousand greenshoots," he tells us.

My emulation's eyes nearly pop out of my head. I whisper in Kiz's ear, "That's way too rich for my blood."

"Don't worry, Fizzy," Kiz informs me in a low voice. "I've got you covered tonight."

"What are you talking about, Kiz? I can't take your money," I tell her.

"What are *you* talking about, Fizzy? I made this money lying around on the beach, while Cassie was with a bunch of Indians sweating her ass off. Take some greenshoots and have a little fun."

"Are you sure?"

Pressing a wad of money into my hand, Kiz instructs me to buy twenty-five thousand greenshoots worth of chips. Reluctantly, I push the money across the table, and Pipo Latzo issues me five tall stacks of chips in exchange. With the transaction completed, my discomfort multiplies. Now, if only Kiz's bankroll will do likewise. But I sense a disaster developing here. I've never been a gambler. So maybe it's not in my nature. Or maybe I'm just chicken.

"Do you do this often?" I ask Kiz.

"I come here now and again," she tells me. "But Cassie has been a regular in Las Vegas for years."

"Really? I would never have guessed," I tell her honestly.

"She started playing the Blackjack tables at the Desert Inn back in the days of the Rat Pack. She was all of twenty-one then, but she had a keen sense of the game (lol)."

"And how is that?" I ask.

Kiz clears her throat and discretely tells me to disable my voice mechanism. Apparently, she wants to chat privately, and out of earshot of the dealer and the other players sitting at the table. Once we have deactivated our voice modules and achieved privacy she types: Cassie holds two graduate degrees: one in Statistical Analysis, and the other in Theoretical Physics. Even as a kid she could cipher complex arithmetic problems instantly in her head.

She also has a more or less photographic memory. Blackjack seemed like a 'simple little game', one that was mathematically possible to beat. With a little help from Professor Hoyle, who wrote the famous book on card counting entitled *Beat The Dealer*, Cassandra was, as they say, off to the races. Over the years she's won hundreds of thousands of dollars in casinos up and down the Strip. Nowadays, they all know (her) in PL Vegas, not to mention her skills, and she's not allowed to play there anymore. Once you get banned from one casino, the word spreads fast. She still knows many of the PL Vegas dealers, and they treat her sort of like a retired pro. It's a mutual respect thing. But, here in VL, Kizmet is free to 'ply my trade'. As you'll soon see, I can count six shoes without a glitch. So what do you say we make a little fun money, Fizzy? Just follow my lead and watch what happens."

(Voice modules back on.)

"Place your bets, ladies and gentlemen," says Pipo Latzo. "Minimum one thousand greenshoots."

One thousand greenshoots! That is roughly equivalent to a month's rent for the Open Books shop. In my head, numbers spin madly, like a digital counter, or like the big sign in Times Square in New York that keeps a running count of the national debt. With a freshly shuffled shoe, Kiz places two chips, the minimum bet, on the table. As instructed, I follow suit. I think about the many donations placed in our container at Open Books—dozens each month just to pay the rent—and I grimace at the high stakes I'm encouraged to wager on this asinine game of chance. Indeed, what might Crystal say about this? I know she would be affronted, not on some immature moralistic level, but at the shear frivolousness of it all. Then again, so am I!

At our table are two other gamblers, Alpha Guardian and Lover Luckless. They seem to be partners, romantically speaking. Lesbians… Why should I care? I don't, really. Pipo Latzo deals out the cards. I know the game of Blackjack, but only the basics. I have no idea concerning its subtleties. Kiz allows me to look over her shoulder. She is smiling the entire time. Meanwhile, my face must surely show the anxiety I'm feeling, the VL gesture bank notwithstanding.

In my hand I'm holding an eight of clubs and a four of diamonds. Kiz (always the lucky one) has drawn two queens. I cannot see what cards Alpha Guardian and Lover Luckless have drawn. Kiz, of course, lays down her cards, indicating that she will stay with her current hand. But with a total of twelve points, I am forced to take another card. I am dealt the ten of hearts, so I bust. One thousand greenshoots (Kiz's beach squatting money) go up in digital smoke. Playing out the hand, Lover Luckless stays pat with a nine and a seven, while Alpha Guardian is holding a pair of eights. When the dealer finally fills out his hand with a total of nineteen, only Kiz has doubled her money, while everyone else has lost his stake. Kiz nudges me with her elbow and says, "Double your bet this time, Fizzy."

"Are you sure?" I ask.

"Trust me," she says.

I lay down two thousand greenshoots. Both Alpha Guardian and Lover Luckless bet the minimum, one thousand. Kiz, on the other hand, lays down five thousand greenshoots.

"All bets final," says Pipo Latzo as he deals the cards.

This time I am dealt a perfect twenty-one, so Pipo Latzo immediately pays me two thousand greenshoots from the bank. Now I am up one thousand greenshoots, which I silently vow I will not gamble away, and which I will use to pay next month's rent on the shop. (Crystal will certainly be happy about that.) Alpha Guardian and Lover Luckless are saddled with miserable hands, and each ends up in a bust. Kiz, on the other hand, is dealt two nines, and elects to split her hand. Pipo Latzo deals a king on top of her first nine, and a queen on top of her second one.

Playing out the house's hand, he is unable to top her twin hands of nineteen points each, so he pays Kiz a cool ten thousand greenshoots. Now, she is up eleven thousand, and she taps her foot upon mine to coax me into another large bet. "How much this time?" I type on private messenger. "Five thousand," she types back. :)

Kiz knows from counting the points of all cards already dealt that the shoe is now rich with ten cards. That makes the odds trend toward the players, rather than towards the house. According to her accounts, her system is well practiced in PL as well as in VL, so who am I to argue? I bet five thousand greenshoots, just as she has instructed, and again I win the hand. Alpha Guardian also wins a thousand greenshoots, but poor Lover Luckless remains true to her emulation's name. Kiz manages to double-down on her hand, and wins another ten thousand greenshoots. I am amazed but still uneasy, because money has never come so easily to me.

"Whatever are we going to do with all this money?" I ask incredulously.

"You'll see," she tells me. "But let's play one more hand."

"I'm game," I tell her.

This time I am dealt two fives. Kiz is dealt two jacks. "Can I split this hand?" I ask the expert.

"You can, but I wouldn't," she advises. Of course she has calculated my odds of winning and found them not to be satisfactory. "Less than fifty-fifty," she tells me.

"I've got a hunch," I say. "I'm going to split my hand."

Kiz shrugs. It's only greenshoots, after all.

The dealer begins to lay down cards as I call for one hit after another. Reaching a point total of sixteen on the first hand, I call for one last card. I am dealt a seven, so I bust. On the second hand, I am first dealt a queen (fifteen), then an ace (sixteen), another ace (seventeen), and then a five—bust. There goes my entire profit, except for the thousand that I put away for shop rent. Easy come; easy go. I guess

I'm just not very lucky at games of chance. Though Kiz has left the table with thirty-two thousand greenshoots profit. Leave it to a pro.

Leaving Free Zing, Kiz's purse now bulging with greenshoots, I tell her that our little gambling junket was great fun but that I probably won't be repeating it anytime soon. Kiz only laughs and tells me that once upon a time she took it all very seriously but now she only plays for fun. "It's no fun losing," I say. "Not in PL or VL." She pats her Gucci bag and says, "That's why I *never* challenge the count!"

As we exit the casino and walk out onto the VL Strip, I am blinded by all the lights, and I can't help wondering if that's how it is with money in general, whether it is made on Wall Street, or on Profit Promenade, or in virtual Las Vegas. Sharky Overbite is tossing it away as if it were beads in the New Orleans Mardi gras parade. Daedalus Dunworthy envisions it as the pivotal instrument to execute some multi-national, Orwellian plot. Kiz Aurora treats it as if it were inconsequential. To my mind, money is only important when it is employed as a tool to achieve something beneficial and of lasting consequence for everyone. Otherwise, whether in PL or in VL, it's only paper.

"Fizzy, do you think you can IM Crystal and have her meet us at Open Books?" Kiz asks me. "I have a little surprise for you both."

"My-o-my! You're just full of surprises today, aren't you?" I tease.

:) types Kiz.

"Let me see," I tell her. "It's already tomorrow morning in Copenhagen, so Sonja is probably up and already at her computer. Let me see if she's online."

I quickly IM Crystal Marbella to see if she can meet us at the shop. She sends back a message that she is already there, and I tell her that Kizmet Aurora and I have been up all night partying, and that we will join her at the shop as fast as we can transfer to Lit-A-Rama.

Whoosh!

Seeing both Kizmet and I dressed up to the tens, Crystal asks, "What in (the world) have you two been up to?"

"Just a little money orgy," I laugh.

Crystal's look is quizzical.

"First, we went to BloomEx to hear a very abbreviated lecture by the emulation of the former Federal Reserve Chairman Harlan Geltspinner," I explain. "Then we had a delightful conversation with the radio personality, Daedalus Dunworthy. After that, we went to VL Las Vegas for a bit of gambling. That was Kiz's idea."

"Hope you didn't get fleeced," says Crystal.

"Oh, that happened quite some time ago," says Kiz. "At least according to Dunworthy."

"A wise man, no doubt," says Crystal.

"We played high stakes Blackjack at Free Zing," I tell Crystal with a blush.

"A couple of high rollers," Crystal observes with no small amount of sarcasm.

"Not me," I tell her. "But you should see Kiz in action."

"Really?" says Crystal feigning genuine interest.

"No, really! She's a real pro. She knows how to count cards, and she won all this money. Thirty-two thousand greenshoots!"

"That's a lot of grass," Crystal allows.

"Which is why I asked Fizzy to make sure you could meet us here," Kiz says to Crystal.

Crystal sits down on one of the easy chairs she made in a VL 'garden'. "I don't follow you, Kiz," she says.

"It's the money!" Kiz proclaims. "I'm giving it to you and to Fizzy."

"For what?" Crystal asks. "What are we supposed to do with thirty-two thousand greenshoots?"

"I want you to use it for the Open Books Project. Or

whatever else you think might be a good cause."

"It's your money, Kiz. You won it fair and square," I remind her. "Well, sort of," I qualify.

"But I don't need it. I have other plans here in VL."

"What plans?" I ask.

"Never mind that now. When it's time, I'll tell you both. The point is that you two will make much better use of this money than I might. Open Books is a terrific concept. And you, Fizzy—I know you'd like to build a Van Gogh REP."

"I don't know, Kizmet?" I tell her. But she pushes her hefty purse into my hands and folds her arms over her inflated chest. On her face is a luminous smile.

"There! That settles that!" she concludes.

"Are you sure about this?" I ask.

"Fizzy, on the very first day we met, as I clumsily dropped into Virtual Life, you told me that people give stuff away all the time in VL. And so it's true. Take the money. Use it for the good of all. It is my gift to you, and to Virtual Life."

"Thank you, Kiz," says Crystal most graciously.

"No kidding. Thanks, Kiz," I echo.

:) means 'you're welcome'.

I must confess that our desert rose now has me wondering about her so-called VL plan. What does that mean? What's she up to? I think she intends to surprise yet again.

2) Art

Crystal Marbella is at my side as I sign the papers to purchase my very own REP with the greenshoots that Kiz won in VL Las Vegas and so generously handed over to us; and while we both know that the creation of a new REP will require vast amounts of my effort and my attention, and as a result I will be spending much less time assisting Crystal with the Open Books Project, she is nevertheless happy for me because she knows that it has been my longtime dream to recreate the life and times of the artist Vincent Van Gogh in Virtual Life.

"Building an entire REP from bare ground up is a huge undertaking, Fizzy? Do you think you're up to it?" Crystal asks.

"Sly Sideways has agreed to help. At least until I master the basics in scripting. If I need more help, there's always VL University. I can learn what I need to know there, *bit by bit*."

"I admire your initiative, Fizzy."

"Thanks, Crystal. I will build it because it *must* be built. I will build it for Vincent. Because he gave everything he had, including his life, trying to find *the high yellow note*."

"I'm going to miss you at Open Books," says Crystal with a bit of sadness in her voice.

"Don't worry, I'll still come around," I assure her.

:) Crystal types.

So, how does one go about recreating a person's life in dot matrix? Especially one as emotionally deep as Vincent Van Gogh. Like any competent biographer, I can accurately document the progression of the events of his life. I can portray his family and his friends; the historical record is at my disposal. I can detail his trials and tribulations: poverty, illness, loneliness and confusion. I can script digital representations of the paintings, and the places he lived and worked, and of his physical features. But how can I possibly portray the spirit that once bestowed such a unique vision and representation of the world in which he lived? Yes, that is the challenge I face. Yet, I know I must try, because not only Vincent, but all artists who strive to represent the human condition—in all its varying hues and textures—deserve such a legacy. I know that if I am successful—even to a degree—then I, too, will become a viable artist. If I fail, then at least I have touched my own brush to the canvas in a genuine and noble attempt to reunite with the spirit of creation itself. And that, my fellow seedlings, is the true purpose of our existence!

I am standing, along with Crystal and Sly Sideways, on the desolate piece of 'ground' on which my Van Gogh REP will (hopefully) soon be situated, a parcel of virtual real estate purchased for greenshoots, terrain lost in time and space (except the matrix on which it is constructed), an island that exists only in the mind surrounded by an ocean whose depths are not plumbed, where the soil is not fertile, nor the water fluid (seedlings can breathe normally even under VL water), yet this ground is my starting point, my basis, my terra firma.

"I know it doesn't look like much now," says Sly the builder, "but once we get the vegetation roughed in, and the streets laid out, and a few buildings erected, your vision will begin to emerge, Fizzy."

"I remember when Lit-A-Rama looked this empty," says Crystal, who has been in VL as long as anybody.

Maybe I'm feeling a bit of buyer's remorse. Or maybe I'm just feeling daunted by the challenge I've undertaken. "You really think so?" I say.

"Don't worry, Fizzy," says Sly. "Together we'll turn this place into a fitting showcase."

"I hope I'm up to it," I tell my friends. "I want to do justice to Vincent's legacy."

"I can't think of a better person for the job," Crystal reassures me.

It has been determined that Sly will be in charge of building out the REP's landscape and (physical) structures, and with Crystal's help I will learn more about scripting at the VL university so I can create not only authentic dioramas, but scrupulous replicas of each and every Van Gogh painting and drawing. I will even recreate, as closely as I can, the artist's correspondence with his brother and benefactor, Theo Vann Gogh, in calligraphy resembling the handwriting of each letter's author. I will study every detail of the artist's life. I will come to understand his triumphs and disappointments, his loves and his loathing, his abject poverty and his illness; I will embrace his passion as if it were my own.

Leaving Sly to begin construction on the REP's visual props, Crystal and I transfer to VL University, where my education in scripting is about to begin. The VL university is not like a traditional school in PL, it is a self-service smorgasbord of information that has been contributed and consolidated by other seedlings and offered free of charge for the benefit of anyone who wishes to access it. (It is a well-documented and well-practiced principle in VL that information is not like other commodities, and therefore not 'saleable'. Rather it is the common practice of seedlings to share information freely, believing that its application is ultimately in the best interest of, and to the benefit of, the VL society at large. I subscribe wholeheartedly to this attitude, and I am grateful to all who have contributed the technical information that I am about to access.) I am no technical wizard. In fact, I sometimes think my literal mind is downright retarded. I never understood Organic Chemistry, or Physics, and I passed high school Geometry only by my teacher's charity. But now I am determined to put my so-called technical learning disability behind me and learn scripting. I suppose a passion to do something one considers worthwhile can break down most walls; so uncertain as I am, I will confront my fear and my reticence, and I will learn what I must to actualize my vision.

Rather than stacks of books, VL University offers row after row of menus. One selects the information he wishes to download from the appropriate menu. Once study is underway, the student practices application not in a traditional science lab, but in a VL 'garden', which is an environment where VL objects are created (scripted). Once the object has been created (and it can be anything from a virtual table and chairs to a new species like a Quinngen), it is then moved from the garden to the cache of the creator. From the seedling's cache it can be placed, using a mathematical grid, within the virtual environment of choice. Sounds easy, but it's not. Scripting is a real challenge for one as technically disadvantaged as me.

Crystal has much more experience at scripting than I do, and she is a patient teacher. Still, I make so many mistakes that sometimes I just want to throw up my hands and quit. Usually Crystal can correct my mistakes with a simple adjustment of the computer code, but sometimes even she does not know how to solve the problems we create. (I often find myself wishing that Kiz, with her facile mathematical skills, were here to help.) Still, no matter how frustrated and distressed we become, someone far more technically inclined always seems to come along to adjust our codes. That's VL for you!

Slowly (and with no small amount of anguish) a replica of Van Gogh's 'Potato Eaters' emerges from the tangled mass of numbers and symbols I have entered on my keyboard. No brush and palette needed, thank you very much! My computer screen is my VL canvass. My fingers are clean, not stained with pigment. What might Vincent think? Am I approaching his *pure yellow note*?

"I think you're getting it, Fizzy" Crystal encourages me.

"I think it lacks dimension," I critique my recreation.

"No, it's good," she confirms.

"I think I'll have another go at it," I finally decide. Because it must be as perfect as digitally possible.

Transferring back to *my* REP, we find that Sly has made considerably more progress on the environment than I have made on the paintings. Of course he has considerable experience in creating such environments, and after trying my hand at scripting I have all the respect in the (virtual) world for his acumen. According to my original plan, he has divided the REP into quadrants representing Vincent's life. The first quadrant has been constructed to look like

Vincent's childhood home in Groot-Zundert in the Netherlands. The second one is reminiscent of the coalmining town of Borinage, Belgium where Vincent worked in abject poverty as a minister to the miners and their families. A third quadrant is evocative of the South of France at Arles and the Asylum in Saint Remy where the artist spent the final years of his life and where so many of his most famous paintings were created. And the fourth quadrant is devoted to a virtual museum—much like the Van Gogh Museum in Amsterdam—where the digital recreations of the paintings that I am producing in the VL 'garden' will eventually be displayed.

"What do think, Fizzy?" Sly asks me.

"Obviously, you've come a long way," I observe.

"Yes, but what do you think?"

I take a moment to assess the terrain. Streets and lanes exist where bare ground once dominated. Trees and shrubbery now lend dimension to what was previously a vast expanse of undeveloped real estate. To accommodate my ultimate purpose, buildings have been erected. Yet, something is wrong. I measure the balance in my mind's eye, and something inside me rebels. "It all looks a bit like California," I tell Sly Sideways the builder.

"Hmmm…"

"I mean, this is supposed to be nineteenth century Holland. And the *Belle Epoch* in the South of France… But it all looks a bit like San Diego."

"What do you mean?" Sly asks.

"You know… Gentrified."

"Really?"

"Well… Yeah!"

"I think Fizzy is envisioning more of a 'period' construction," Crystal helps out.

"Hmmm…" says Sly.

"Yes, that's it!" I confirm. "That's the term."

"I see," says Sly.

"It's not that I don't appreciate all your work, Sly, but

this just isn't right. It must be torn down and rebuilt."

"Well, you're the one paying the bill for the construction. Whatever you say, Fizzy."

With a facile wave of his hand, Sly makes an entire street disappear, buildings and all. Another gesture erases the Mediterranean foliage. Suddenly and decisively, the terrain is restored to its original status.

I decide that a bit of research might be in order, so I conduct a quick search on the Internet for photos and artist's renderings of nineteenth century Holland, especially Groot-Zundert in the Netherlands and Borinage, Belgium. I also download pictures of Arles and Saint Remy and send them to Sly for reference. I watch his emulation as he studies the pictures. "See what I mean?" I ask.

Sly nods as he stashes the pictures in his cache. "I think I get it," he tells me. "Let's see what a second try produces."

"I have the utmost confidence in your abilities," I tell him. "I'll check back in a day or two."

"I should have something by then," he speculates.

"Meanwhile, Crystal and I are headed back to VLU, then to the 'garden'. This scripting language is driving me crazy, and I have to study more, and then experiment. So, if you need me, just IM. You'll find me in either of those two places."

"You're the boss, Fizzy," says Sly as he tips his hardhat.

Back at VLU, I spend no less than six hours studying code. The numbers and symbols mock my ignorance, but I will not give up. I barely notice the passing hours. Crystal comes and goes, checking in with me, measuring my progress, helping whenever she can. Feeling like I've mastered one application or another, I move to the 'garden' to test my newfound knowledge and abilities.

The VL 'garden' is actually like Vincent's wheat field, a vast expanse of topography with an ambiguous vista. A Murder of Crows circles overhead, blackening the sky. A sign? An omen? A warning? I type out numbers and symbols to the fury of flapping wings. Colors emerge at my fingertips, modern-day RBG representations of the pigments employed by the artist more than a hundred years ago: the mysterious indigo and Prussian blue of a swirling sky; the brown earthen pathway lined with a border of verdant green leading into uncertain prospect; the disarming yellow of the living wheat; and the black, black crows swooping in and out of the painter's consciousness.

Aside from the building of the REP and the recreation of the paintings remains the question of who shall portray the artist himself. As I delicately code each color into each virtual canvas, I find myself wondering if a surrogate Vincent will present himself once the REP is finished and accessible. I wonder if perhaps I should advertise in the VL newspapers for a proxy. Or should I assume the role myself through a second emulation? No doubt, the artist himself was a man of extreme complexity, and I find myself wondering whether anyone can actually do justice to the roll. Of course, that is always the problem with resurrection, isn't it?

I search as deeply within myself as I have ever searched, tapping distant and previously unexplored emotions, their source, the myriad possibilities for expression, and the artifacts they produce and leave behind as legacy. I'm searching here for confluence—(Is such unification even possible?). Who am I to think that I, Fizzy Oceans (or Amy Birkenstock), can somehow tap the artistic sensibilities of one such as Vincent Van Gogh? Yet I know I must try, for it is not only my legacy here in VL that hangs in the balance, but a testament to ultimate artistic expression in our PL culture, which by some accounts is disintegrating faster than peeling paint. So I keep crunching numbers and writing code, even as I search for Vincent's *pure yellow note*.

Back at the REP, Sly escorts me to a replica he has created of Vincent's bedroom in Arles. This time he has it perfect. He explains to me that he created the curiously convex room from a digital representation of Van Gogh's painting. Standing at the threshold to the artist's interior, I experience firsthand the texture of the rustic floorboards, the blue, blue walls, the wooden chairs with thatched seats, the rough wooden table upon which a pitcher and washbasin are arranged ever so neatly, a hanging smock, a mirror, the self-portraits, and Vincent's humble single bed with a red blanket and yellow sheets. Dare I enter this room? Tread lightly, I tell myself; this is hallowed ground. Holding my breath, I step tenderly inside the artist's vision—inside his painting. I can't help but wonder: Am I trespassing here, or did the artist create this painting as an invitation into his private world?

Such experiences are unsettling. Never in Vincent's imagination, vibrant and diverse as it surely was, could he have imagined it possible for someone to enter this two-dimensional representation of his private quarters; yet I stand at the center of his revelation, turning round and round in dizzying circles, touching his artifacts, perceiving his symmetry, breathing the very air he once breathed…

We move on to appraise Sly's version of Vincent's studio.

Like the interior of Van Gogh's Groot-Zundert studio, my visceral workplace is filled with empty bird's nests, old mud-stained shoes, broken chairs, fallen limbs, filthy peasant's caps. From every picture, letter, receipt and scrap of hand-written paper, Vincent whispers:

"You cannot be at the pole and the equator at the same time. You must choose your own line..."

To Theo's frustration, Vincent was forever giving away his small stipend to those even less fortunate than himself, if indeed such persons were to be found!

Left alone and misunderstood in Arles by the artist Paul Gaugin, he had preferred oblivion to obscurity and the constant fear of epilepsy, and shot himself point blank in the stomach. Waiting three days to die, he lay back on his bed, bleeding, and smoked his pipe. Fragrant wreaths of tobacco smoke gathered in swirling clouds about his head, and he died as he had wished to die, amidst his own yellow vision.

I leave the studio with flexuous Van Gogh visions freshly imprinted upon my mind: dour and oblique-looking peasants eating potatoes; terrace cafes; landscapes; skeletons; and the red and green and orange portrait of Vincent himself, his ear bandaged and looking quite mad.

Was Vincent really mad? Or was he simply disillusioned? I think the latter. To be sure, he was sick, probably with some form of epilepsy. In Vincent's time they didn't have drugs like Phenobarbital and Valproate to control seizures, so he suffered not only from the effects of the illness, but also the torments of those who did not understand the condition. What must he have thought of himself? He probably believed those who advanced the misconception. He suffered not once, but twice for the same affliction.

Yet Vincent nobly persisted in the quest to portray natural beauty through his artistic passion. Because that is the very nature of art. The painter amplifies and defines the literal world by representing it in symbolic terms. By fusing the capricious element of emotion into the work, he somehow renders his representation to express an even greater unanimity than exists within the inherent. The sum is greater than its parts. And nobody has done that better than Vincent Van Gogh.

Oh fuck! Fuck, fuck, fuck! Amy's lost her job. Just as Fizzy Oceans is hitting her stride, building her very own Van Gogh REP, Amy gets laid off. The doctor told me that because of healthcare reform he just couldn't afford to pay three clerks. Stupid me! I never saw it coming, and I've changed all my spare dollars for greenshoots, and spent most of those on the REP. What am I going to do now? I guess I'll start looking for another job, but finding one could take months. I know people who have been out of work for years now, and some have quit trying altogether. No food needed in VL, but it's another matter in Physical Life. How am I going to pay rent? Without my job, I won't last three months. Shit! Fuck! Goddamn it all!

Deb and Karen took me out for drinks one last time after I was furloughed, and of course they were full of encouragement: "Don't worry, Amy, you'll find another job" and "It's a shitty place to work anyhow, you're the lucky one". But I can tell that they're both scared now, because they know it could just as easily have been one of them to be let go. What are they supposed to say to me? They know it's tough out there; they know it's not going to be easy finding another job. "If there's anything we can do, Amy, you just let us know," Deb said. Which I figure really meant, "Good luck kid; see you in the next life." Of course neither has any idea what I'm up to in VL.

The only upside to losing my PL job is that I get to spend almost all my time in VL now. Both Crystal and Kiz notice that I'm suddenly at my REP during the hours I used to spend billing insurance companies for unneeded procedures. I've not told either of them about losing my PL job because it's not really relevant here in VL, and besides, I neither need nor want sympathy. I'm a big girl, as they say, and I can take care of myself. At least I think I can… At least I've always been able to so far… Under normal circumstances… But what's normal these days in PL? Nothing!

When I'm not in VL at the REP, I'm doing a lot of reading about Vincent. I devour book after book about his life. I read his correspondence with Theo, his brother. I trace his path on a map of Europe I've pinned to my wall. I study his paintings; I construct a timeline of his works. I want everything in the REP to be perfect. Why am I so drawn to this eccentric soul? I guess his paintings and his life move me in a way I cannot articulate. Isn't that what art is supposed to do?

This is what Vincent had to say about it:

> *There may be a great fire in our soul,*
> *yet no one ever comes to warm himself at it,*
> *and the passers-by see only a wisp of smoke*
> *coming through the chimney.*

My ad in the VL newspaper drew many responses, yet I failed to find an applicant I thought worthy to portray Vincent. So the role has fallen upon me to embody the artist. I have created an alternate emulation—one that looks like Vincent's self-portrait painted in 1887 and now on display at the Detroit Institute of Arts. Like all his self-portraits, it shows a dour man, a serious man, perhaps a troubled or tormented man. In this self-portrait, and in others, one senses the artist helplessly searching for himself within his creation. It is because I seem to be able to identify that perspective that I know I am the right player for this persona, and even before I open the REP to others in VL to visit and explore, I walk the various regions alone—in Vincent's shoes, in his ragged clothes and peasant's hat—to experience his world firsthand.

The year is 1879, and Vincent is twenty-six years old. Moving as nimbly as my fingers type commands, he enters the Borinage district. There he determines to enter the Marcasse, one of the deepest and most dangerous coalmines in all Europe, and I direct him into a basket to be lowered deep into the mine. Fifteen hundred feet underground he steps out of the basket and looks up at the shaft's distant opening, no larger than a star in the night sky. Now, I am not only moving Vincent's emulation from point to point, but I feel as though I am breathing the air he once breathed, and feeling the intense claustrophobia he must surely have felt. I feel the tension in his neck, back and torso; I taste the desperate dryness of coal dust. Everyday miners in the Marcasse face poison air, firedamp explosions, water seepage and cave-ins. Wet walls gleam under miners' lights as children of both sexes, some little more than babes, load coal into horse-drawn carts to be shuttled to the main corridor of the mine then lifted to the surface. I feel Vincent's sense of horror in this strange subterranean world.

Vincent, the young parson, has arrived in the Borinage to minister to the miners and their families. In his valise are two suits, gentleman's clothes bought in Amsterdam with money received from his father. He rents a clean room from a baker in which to live. He watches the miners and their humble families with interest and sympathy. They live in huts scattered throughout the woods on the edge of the village—homes without running water or toilets. At night their windows glow from the light of candles. At the entrance of the mine loom tall chimneys and conical mountains of coal—testaments of redundant and dangerous lives led by the miners. He soon gives away his fine suits to one in need. He moves away from the baker's house and takes up residence in a hovel not unlike those in which the miners live. He ceases to wash, and soon his face is as blackened as if he, too, spent his days digging underground. "Why have you given away your clothing?" he is asked by a young woman. "Because I am a friend of the poor," he answers. "Like Jesus…"

Yet, the miners and their families are more than a little uncomfortable with Vincent's devotion. "The parson is no longer normal," they whisper amongst themselves. And it is true! Van Gogh lives more like an animal than like a man. He talks to himself. He prays on bended knees for hours at a time. He eats barely a morsel; his abstinence is notorious. What money he receives he gives away. He says he talks to God. Nobody believes God talks back to him.

This business of portraying another person—a real life individual now dead—is both eerie and exhilarating. I don't know whether or not I like it, but my dedication to this project is documented in code, and there's no turning back now. It is my long felt admiration for this man's particular passion that has led me to create the REP, as well as a profoundly personal search to express something furtively felt within me, something long harbored, something anxious for expression yet fearful of exposure, something disorderly yet divine. I take the next tentative step in Vincent's worn leather shoes.

Unable to relate to his parishioners, Vincent is finally dismissed from his post by the mission sponsors. Officially, they cite his lack of oratory skill, but in reality his behavior is simply too extreme. He moves to the next village where he lives on charity. He sketches the miners, honing his drawing skills. He sleeps outdoors, eats barely anything. Vincent's father suggests having him committed to an insane asylum, but Theo intervenes on his brother's behalf. He begged Theo, the art dealer, to send him prints by Jean-Francis Millet, an artist that drew scenes of peasant life; one he admired above all other artists. "Send me what you can and do not fear for me. If I can only continue to work, it will somehow set me right again," he wrote his brother.

Taking a break from Vincent's life, and from VL too, I (Amy Birkenstock) leave my apartment and trudge through a rainy Seattle morning down to the Pike Place outdoor market to see if I can find some work—even an odd job for a day or two—because I'm really broke now. I can't even afford food, or toiletries, or cigarettes; in fact, I can't even afford to take my clothes to the launderette, so I've been wearing the same jeans and flannel shirt for ten straight days. Thank God my Doc's are sturdy, because I can't afford to take the bus either, so I have to walk the entire way, twenty blocks, more or less. At the market I convince a Chinese fishmonger, Mr. Wang, to let me clean up after he closes his stall. The fish guts and blood make me want to vomit even though my stomach is dead empty. When I finish cleaning his stall he pays me a few bucks so I can buy a burger and fries. Call it good.

Unemployment (and the poverty that results from it) is no fucking fun at all. But hey, real food is expensive these days. Broccoli might as well be made out of gold; cherries out of diamonds. I'm really craving milk; I must be calcium deficient. There are plenty of leftover grunge-hippies here in Seattle, and they'd probably be willing to help out, but they're in the same hard-up circumstance as me, so I don't even bother asking. I make my own way. If Vincent could do it, so can I!

VL is my solace, my oasis, my home away from (home?). After all, everything in VL—except my Van Gogh REP, thanks to Sly Sideways—looks like California, the Golden State. Except California ran out of money back in 2009, and the shine is off that nugget once and for all. Look, it does no good to be bitter. I'm usually not one to complain, either; I just want a good meal once a week, that's all. In VL there is no hunger. That's something—a different kind of nourishment…

Fizzy Oceans is tracking Vincent to the South of France now—all in a few short steps, thanks to my VL REP. I've lent her my trusty Doc's to make the pilgrimage (lol). She is standing in front of Vincent's yellow house in Arles when Paul Gaugin storms out of the door cursing the Dutchman. "That potato-eater just cut off his fucking ear!" Gaugin swears. And he's off to the South Pacific. Just like that!

Shortly, Vincent appears in the street, his severed ear bleeding like a butchered pig. His expression is dazed as he staggers off to present his 'little gift' to the prostitute of his fancy. Oh, what a night!

Look, I've never cut off my ear, so I can't say I know how it feels. But I do know something about sacrifice. It's what you do for love, or passion, or insanity. Or maybe it's what you do when you want to find the *pure yellow note* and you just can't find it. I don't know, but I'm certainly not going to be the one to judge him. He did what he did, and I'm sure he had his reasons. I'm sure it made sense to him as he drew the razor over his skin.

Am I Amy Birkenstock now, or am I Fizzy Oceans? Is Fizzy Oceans that cute little emulation that works like a banshee at Open Books, or has she somehow transformed herself into the artist Vincent Van Gogh? Shit, VL can get to be confusing, can't it? I'm sensing that Fizzy Oceans wants to speak for herself now…

As I work in the VL 'garden' writing code and recreating yet another Van Gogh painting—this time "Vase with Twelve Sunflowers"—it occurs to me that what we create, or more accurately recreate, with our computers is at best a binary representation of our literal world, minus its soul. What Vincent Van Gogh did with tools infinitely more fundamental—a brush, a knife, a board or a bit of canvas, pigments of the primary colors—is quite different indeed. Looking at his paintings, most would agree that the eccentric images—swirling skies ("Wheatfield with Cypresses, c.1889), wavy wheat fields ("Wheatfield Under a Cloudy Sky" c.1890), emaciated jade faces with amethyst lips ("Portrait of Dr. Gachet", c.1890), a humble community of once-proud houses now sagging like melting candle wax ("Houses at Auvers", c.1890), olive trees lined up like soldiers under a blazing Mediterranean sun that shines its light upon the earth in ever-concentric particles ("Olive Trees" c.1890), God's glorious firmament exploding like a Chinese fireworks display at the New Year ("Starry Night" c.1889)—convey not a realistic recreation of the literal world, but a window into the soul of the artist himself. My effort in making this REP is one of re-creation; Vincent's effort, borne of deep humility and lifelong sacrifice, tapped the quintessence of Creation. His unappraised contemporaries failed to recognize his vision, and they scorned him for his eccentricity. In his lifetime he sold but a single painting. Today, of course, his canvases sell for tens of millions of dollars (though you can have a facsimile created by *yours truly* for the very reasonable price of fifteen greenshoots). The song remains the same…

On a final inspection tour of the REP, I tell Sly Sideways what an excellent job he's done in building the virtual environment to my specifications. He's also added a few of his own touches, such as 3D dioramas of *The Red Vineyards at Arles* and *The Café Terrace on the Place du Forum*. We've both done a lot of work to complete the REP, Sly building out the physical representations, and me in the 'garden' replicating the paintings. I gladly pay Sly the six thousand greenshoots I owe for his work, and as a further token of my appreciation I place a digital representation of *Almond Branches in Bloom, San Remy* in his cache. "You don't have to do that, Fizzy," he tells me. But it's my pleasure to give a little tip for a job well done.

So, now it's time to send out invitations to all the seedlings in my database—more than ten thousand people in all. My list of contacts was compiled during the time I worked with Crystal at Open Books. It also includes all those with whom I've interacted as a VL greeter. Such a mailing list might seem extreme if not for mass mailing tools provided by the Farmers at Seedbed Studios.

Meantime, I return to Open Books to see how Crystal is coming along with her latest project, *The Complete and Unabridged Memoirs of Jacques Casanova*. It is an auspicious volume of six books comprising two thousand, five hundred pages, give or take a few. She has been working on the publication ever since I began working on the Van Gogh REP, so we are both feeling a bit exhausted by our respective projects.

"Sometimes I wonder why we do it," Crystal says to me. "Why we work so hard for so little recognition." Her fatalistic mood is a bit uncharacteristic. And probably short-lived as well, I understand.

"We do it to be of use," I tell her. "To make a difference."

"Sometimes I wonder if anybody really cares," she opines.

"Remember all those people who attended the Mark Twain lecture," I remind her.

"Little victories," she admits.

"Exactly!" I affirm.

"Next I suppose you're going to tell me that the reward is in the process, not in the result. And that there's some implicit nobility in sacrifice and commitment."

"Right again," I tell her.

"What would I do without you, Fizzy?" she asks.

"Most of what I know about VL, I learned from you, Crystal."

"I guess we're just twin clowns in this weird and wild circus," she says.

"Speaking of which, I want you at my side at the opening of the Van Gogh REP," I tell her.

"I wouldn't be anywhere else," she says.

"And I want Kizmet there, too."

"I'm sure she'll be there with Hopi bells on." Crystal smiles for the first time during our conversation.

"Get your chin up, girl," I tell her. "Things could be worse."

"How is Amy doing?" Crystal asks Fizzy Oceans. I am surprised by her inquiry, because seldom in the past have we referred to our PL personalities.

"Tough times," Fizzy tells her.

"Can't find a job?" Crystal asks.

"Nothing steady," Fizzy relates.

"Tell her to keep her chin up, too," says Crystal. "I'm sure something will turn up."

"Yeah, I hope so," I tell her a little gravely.

I can't help thinking how ironic it is that here in VL both Crystal and I have far too much work, while over in PL poor Amy Birkenstock can't find enough. All in all, neither gig pays a living wage.

All this I have made without pay. Whether my REP is entertaining or not, enlightening or not, uplifting or not, worthy or not, I humbly present it to all who wish to cross its frontier and experience what it has to offer, or partake in my humble rendition of the passion and the genius and the humility and the tragedy of Vincent Van Gogh. It is my gift to posterity. One more trek through the REP and I am ready to greet my first visitors.

In order to make a final survey of the terrain, I activate Vincent's emulation for the first time. My creation is impeccable, I believe, but have I gathered the courage to finally walk in his shoes? My first steps in this strange body are not unlike those of any other emulation, yet I feel the artist's peculiar presence bearing down on me. From his parents' middle class home in Amsterdam I move to the Borinage in Belgium, then to the parsonage in Etten, England. I visit the Goupil et Cie Gallery in Paris where he worked for a short time as an art dealer with his brother Theo, then the hovel of a home he kept in the Hague with Sein the prostitute and her infant son. Finally, I move on to Arles, France, where Vincent lived for a short time with the artist Paul Gaugin, and where he cut off his ear in a castigatory rage. I also pay a visit to the asylum at St. Remy. In his room I spend a reflective moment peering out his window at the garden where he painted irises and sunflowers. Back in the village of Arles, I set out in my ragged clothes for a day of painting in the countryside, my brushes and pigments stored in a homemade satchel strapped to my back. Under my arm I carry my easel. In my free hand I carry my lunch—a crust of bread, a bottle of milk, nothing more. The children in the streets wait in hiding for me to pass so they can hurl stones at me, knocking my straw farmer's hat off my head. In a wheat field, just beyond the city's border, I paint furiously as a Murder of Crows circles overhead. They call out to me in a language I suddenly understand. Sheathes of wheat dance to the music of the breeze. In my waistband I carry a loaded .22 caliber pistol—a rusting relic of a firearm, really—for a purpose not yet determined.

Once more as the emulation of Fizzy Oceans, I greet Crystal and Kizmet, my two best VL friends, as they transfer into the REP near the museum.

"Oh, Fizzy!" Kiz exclaims. "What a world!"

Crystal, the European, is more demure.

"Let me show you the collection," I offer. Walking through a corner of *my* virtual Amsterdam to reach the museum housing the collection of Van Gogh masterpieces, my friends are wide-eyed and full of compliments.

Once inside, we begin to view the drawings and paintings. Silence marks our collective reverence, and I notice a tear welling in Crystal's eye as she stands before Vincent's portrait of Père Tanguy. I fully understand this wash of sentiment, because I have felt it many times myself. In fact, while I was creating the replicas in the 'garden' I often found myself crying for no apparent reason, and I now understand that such emotion is not abnormal but natural when faced with such unequivocal beauty. It's like staring straight into the face of God. Or suddenly understanding the nature of a universe. Real beauty causes us to release all the false pride and pseudo sophistication we work so hard to maintain in our daily lives. By the time we reach the last painting in the collection, Kiz appears a bit uneasy. She turns to me and asks, "Fizzy, how many invitations did you send out?"

"Uh…" It suddenly occurs to me that we three are alone in the REP. "More than nine thousand, I think," I answer.

"Nine thousand?" she says, incredulous.

"More or less," I confirm.

The number obviously represents a non sequitur in her mind. "Where is everybody?" she says. Her question is not necessarily directed at me but at some nebulous entity.

Crystal looks at me sympathetically but perceptively. Kiz, still the neophyte, is stunned, dumbfounded. I can feel her mind stretching to understand the absence of visitors. Suddenly realizing that I have been ignored, spurned, and summarily dismissed, and that all my sincere and dedicated work may just have been in vain, I am impressed—no, overcome—by a reality even greater than my personal failure, which is the death of beauty itself!

Can such a thing possibly be true? Can a concept or emotion so innate, and so vital to our humanity, actually die? Perhaps the answer to such a question lies in the silence around us as we view these passionate paintings by a master forever in search of recognition, forever in pursuit of expression beyond everyday lexis. The language of the soul, if I am permitted such a cliché. Of course the vocabulary of silence has a meaning too, one that is enveloping and undeniable. And perhaps final.

Sitting together at *The Café Terrace at the Place du Forum*—Sly's 3D re-creation of one of Vincent's most famous paintings—three faithful friends sit together underneath the stars in Arles, France, within the unlikely environment of a masterpiece on canvas, drinking absinthe and waiting for the Renaissance. We think we may be waiting a very long time.

3) Religion

I keep thinking that in the annals of human history a single common thread must surely weave together the fabric of the world's religions. How could it not be so? Yet such a thread is not easily identified—or so it would seem. To find the core of religious belief, we must first cut through the dog pile of dogma and begin by asking the fundamental questions: Who are we? What is our purpose? How long have we been here and how long will we remain? Where are we going? Why do we exist?

Then, of course, the concepts of space and time must be addressed. In effect, we beg to know the nature of our universe, and whether it is finite or infinite? Mankind has been staring at the heavens (for lack of a better focal point, I suppose) and imploring our creator (invisible and presumed though He certainly remains) to give us a sign, or assign us a path, or set down rules, or simply to show Himself. Still, after centuries of seeking we still fumble like blind men in an unfamiliar room, even as we profess our avid beliefs to the point of violence and strong-armed coercion. If only we were committed to the question rather than to its answer, then we might hope to catch a glimpse of the final truth, if indeed such a truth even exists, which is something that I have come to doubt. I think, when all is said and done, relativity rules the day, and Secular Humanism is the one faith—if it is a faith—that actually makes sense.

Most traditional religions take their symbols not from our natural world, but instead evoke them from supernatural deeds—either performed by mortals or by mythical beings. Such symbols serve to strengthen belief and faith, provide cohesion of community, and give comfort in times of trouble and strife. These symbols themselves often become iconic, or objects of worship, supplanting or obscuring altogether the original idea or deity. Such a corruption seems to occur naturally over time, and the original visionary or mystical aspect of the religion becomes mired in ritual. Yet, even as this occurs, a religion gains its greatest following. Apparently, people want easy answers, and they want to be told what to do— especially when it comes to their salvation. A simple set of rules to follow, please; a platitude or two to recite— nothing too complicated; a hierarchy of devotions to perform so the devotee feels a bit less alone in his own mortality. No matter what religion we choose to examine, it is more or less the same story. The faith is born through the vision of an inspired person and gains a following through the dissemination of that person's teachings. Once it has spread sufficiently, politics often enters the mix, which usually precludes a corruption of the original idea. Ritual supplants exaltation, and that which was once profoundly spiritual then assumes an undeniably earthly character. Still, one must wonder—at least I do—whether or not there is a common thread running through all religions that continues to vibrate to the frequency of epiphany, illumination and enlightenment. I honestly want to believe such things are possible. I truly want to believe. Yet, time and again I find my more celestial aspirations grounded by a single concept—one that, to me, seems to define the very nature of our human condition—duality! Whether it is expressed as yin and yang, black and white, light and dark, on and off or good and evil, duality seems to intrude itself upon every aspect of our earthly lives and our universal reality. We cannot escape it. Or at least it would seem so…

So, is duality, or dualism, the chain that shackles us to our earthly existence? Or is it, as Zen Masters assert, the source of an essential tension necessary for the cohesion of a greater whole? And if that's it, then how do we move beyond the yin and the yang to perceive our world from such a causative point of view? Do we immerse ourselves in rituals? Should we attempt to master yoga? Camp out in the dessert for forty days and forty nights? Deny our body food and drink? Spin like a dervish until enlightenment pours over us like morning sunshine? I admit that all this philosophy might be a bit thick for the religious exploration I intend to make here in VL, still it seems to make sense to define the essential questions before trying to find definitive answers, *n'est ce pas*? What I do know for certain is that no matter what our religious persuasion, we're all dying to find out what lies beyond this world. And that all shall make that journey, and enter that realm, alone.

My first destination on my exploration of religion in VL is the Sabarmati Ashram where I have arranged a meeting with the emulation of Mohandas Karamchand

Gandhi. Known during his life in his native country of India as 'Mahatma' or 'Great Soul', Gandhi was the pioneer of *satvagraha*—resistance to tyranny through mass civil disobedience, a philosophy firmly founded upon *ahimsa* or total nonviolence—which led India to independence and inspired movements for civil rights and freedom around the world.

Arriving at Gandhi's private quarters, I see the 'mahatma' seated upon two large pillows, both resting on a bamboo mat that covers a portion of the spotlessly clean, stone floor. In front of him is a small writing table. Under a vaulted ceiling, white washed walls reflect the light from two open windows, and a small fan circulates the humid air coming in from the garden outside. The large room is devoid of furnishings except for a few scrolls offering information to those not initiated in the Hindu faith. As I approach him, he senses my presence and rises to greet me. He is a small man with large hands and feet. His skin is swarthy, his head bald, and his eyes framed by wire-rimmed glasses. Gandhi, the 'mahatma', is dressed all in white, as is his custom. He extends his hand for me to shake, and I lower my eyes in respect and deference as I take his hand in mine.

"Thank you for agreeing to meet with me, sir," I tell him.

"It is my pleasure to be of service," he assures me.

"And a great service you have been to mankind."

"One does what one must do," he says.

"Or in your case, what one must *not* do," I clarify. Of course I am referring to Gandhi's adherence to the principle of non-violence, which ultimately won not only respect for him, but won freedom for an entire nation.

"*Ahimsa*, which is the foundation of my philosophy, is a decree that bars the killing or injuring of all living beings. It is closely connected with the notion that all kinds of violence entail negative consequences. And I am speaking here of karma… And yet, the extent to which the principle

236

of non-violence can and should be applied to different life forms is controversial between various authorities, or movements and currents within the three religions, Hinduism, Buddhism and Jainism, and has been a matter of debate for thousands of years. Though the origins of the concept of *ahimsa* are unknown, the earliest references to it are found in the texts of historic Vedic religion, dating to the eighth century BCE. Here, ahimsa initially relates to 'non-injury' without a moral connotation, but later to non-violence to animals and then, to all beings. In the nineteenth and twentieth centuries, prominent figures of Indian spirituality emphasized the importance of *ahimsa*. I applied *ahimsa* to politics, by my non-violent *satyagrahas*."

"In today's world, religion and politics make very strange bedfellows," I remark to Gandhi, referring to the neo-cons and born-again Christians in America that seem to want to police morality and dictate behavior, and God knows what else. "Of course the authors of the American Constitution foresaw imminent danger in the merging of church and State, and they adamantly discouraged it, even making it illegal in certain circumstances. Yet your experience, Your Excellency, seems to suggest that religion and government are actually inseparable entities in a society."

"Most of the laws that govern a civil society come from the tenets of religious belief. And what is religion if not a manifestation of conscience? This being so, how can religion and government remain separate of one another? If a society were to remain wholly secular, then it would, by definition, have only a relative moral code? We now see this manifestation in Western societies, and I must say, it looks strange indeed to my eyes. And yet... If religion presumes to offer itself as the moral standard of behavior, then it must be true religion. And, by true, I do not mean infallible. Only that it remains committed to the pursuit of truth. Not as we see religion today, all wound up with hyperbole and primed for profit. That is pseudo-religion, and it literally ensures immorality and dissatisfaction and, ultimately, civil unrest."

"Well, you certainly know something about that," I observe.

"Indeed. My life was filled with causes and conflicts. I might have preferred it to be otherwise, but one's destiny is sometimes dictated by exterior events rather than one's private preferences."

"It does seem," I observe, "that certain times are filled with pivotal moments, and that inspirational leaders appear on the scene to direct the course of history, and society, for better or for worse."

"Ah, yes…" Gandhi removes his glasses and wipes the lenses clean with the sleeve of his garment. "So often," he relates, "we become embroiled in issues or causes even before we understand their eventual impact. It simply seems the right thing to do at the moment, and we dive into deep water even before we know how to swim. If we are lucky, our buoyancy keeps us afloat as we struggle. But activism is always tenuous; circumstances can change without warning. Civil disobedience is an edgy game. Dissent is full of critical moments. What will happen, nobody knows. Yet, all the while, decency is our goal, and conscience is our guide. Events move us like pieces on a chessboard. We are destiny's pawns. The years pass by."

"Your life was a long one—"

"Marked by an untimely, and unnatural, death. I can still feel Godse's bullet penetrating my flesh." A flash of pain (or is it one of surprise?) moves over Gandhi's expression as he re-experiences the moment of his death.

"Nevertheless, your accomplishments remain a testament not only to your commitment, but to the principles of non-violence and non-compliance."

Momentarily lost to a desperate memory, or to a wholly unexpected sensation, he recovers his composure and suggests, "Such strategies are unassailable because they confront non-ethical acts with an ethical reaction. It is a non sequitur that the tyrannical objective cannot understand, let alone resist."

"So you see ethics and religion as one and the same…"

"Ethics is the civil by-product of religion."

"And by engaging in ethical acts, one glorifies God?"

Gandhi considers my proposition for a moment before answering: "It glorifies the God in whose image man is cast."

Apparently, the 'mahatma' is saying that God is glorified through the ethical actions of mankind. And that such ethical actions triumph again and again throughout history, because 'good' is actually a real and legitimate cause, and that it somehow enjoys superior standing over 'bad'. Do I believe this? What about the holocaust? What about Tian'anmen Square? Sometimes tyrants do have their way. And civil disobedience doesn't always work out so neat and tidy, that's for sure! "You'd better explain," I tell the 'mahatma'.

"When the Second World War broke out in 1939, I favored offering the British non-violent moral support. Many congressional representatives were deeply offended by Britain's unilateral inclusion of India in the war without the consent of the people, and all members of congress simultaneously resigned in protest. Which caused me to rethink my position: How could India participate in a war that was ostensibly being fought to preserve democracy and freedom when India itself was denied such freedom? The resolution I drafted calling for the British to 'Quit India' drew its efficacy from this essential contradiction.

"Of course some felt that not supporting Britain in its struggle against the Nazis was unethical. Others felt that even more direct action should be taken against the British: How could they oppose Fascism in Europe while practicing it in India? *Quit India* became the most forceful movement in the struggle, with mass arrests and violence on an unprecedented scale. Thousands of freedom fighters were killed or injured by police gunfire, and hundreds of thousands were arrested. I made it clear, along with my supporters, that we would not support the war effort unless India were granted immediate independence. I called on all Indians to maintain discipline and *Karo Ya Maro* ('Do or Die') in the cause of freedom.

"Non-violence and peaceful resistance became our weapons in the struggle against the British for India's freedom. Of course, it was not as simple as that—oh no! In Punjab, the Jallianwala Bagh massacre of civilians by British troops caused deep trauma to our nation, leading to increased public anger and acts of violence. I criticized both the actions of the British Raj and the retaliatory violence of Indians. I authored a sweeping resolution offering condolences to British civilian victims and condemning the riots that, after initial opposition in the party, was accepted following my speech advocating the principle that all violence was evil and could not be justified. But it was after the massacre and subsequent violence that I began to focus on obtaining complete self-government and control of all Indian government institutions as well as individual, spiritual and political independence."

Gandhi puts his arm around my shoulder (it feels light as a feather) and slowly, tenderly leads me outside into the ashram's peaceful garden. Golden sunlight filters through the leafy branches of a eucalyptus tree, and the warmth of the rays caresses my skin. I must admit that I am feeling overwhelmed in the mahatma's presence; he has given me a great deal to think about. Surely each person is influenced by the times in which he lives, and my own destiny—humble though it certainly will be—must also be influenced by the events and circumstances that unfold and govern the issues of the day. Just how I choose to respond to those issues—ethical, political, ecological, economic—will rightly determine my moral rank in society's hierarchy. Will I define those issues clearly, without bias? Or will I be subject to lies and deflection and manipulation and propaganda? Will I uphold fundamental principles, or will I shirk my responsibility out of fear or convenience? Will I stand up not only for myself, but also for the rights of all mankind? Will I have the courage of my convictions? Will I exercise the ability to choose that my Creator gave me? For when all is said and done, perhaps that is the only (religious) question that really matters.

With the help and guidance of biblical scholar Matthew Taylor, I plunge headlong into the virtual world of the ancient Torah. At the foot of the Wailing Wall in virtual Jerusalem, Matthew greets me and asks, "Are you sure you're ready for this, Fizzy?"

What Matthew is referring to is a journey to experience firsthand the events of the Old Testament. "I have to admit," I tell him, "I have a taste for the miraculous. And I've always wondered about the phenomenal stories in the Bible."

Matthew assures me that I will know a new truth about these matters after the VL retro-experience he has arranged for me, because I am to accompany the Israelites on their march into the desert.

OMG! Literally…

One click and I am suddenly inside a humble house made of clay bricks and dried mud. The house is located in the City of Kafr ed-Dawar, where the Jewish slave population is one hundred and twenty thousand. I am with a woman named Deborah, and her daughter Miriam. A rabbi has told us to eat only unleavened bread, and we must drink lots of water, too. We eat by the light of an oil lamp, and our shadows, cast ominously upon rough and colorless stucco, loom large as they foreshadow the exodus that will begin after midnight. Our conversation conducted in breathless whispers: in the wake of nine deadly plagues that have ravaged the land (the Plague of Blood, the Plague of Frogs, the Plague of Lice, the Plague of Flies, the Plague of Livestock Deaths, the Plague of Boils, the Plague of Hail, the Plague of Locusts, the Plague of Darkness) Pharaoh has agreed to allow the entire slave population of Hebrews to leave Egypt, but we all wonder, is it a trap? "Will he have a change of heart once he realizes that all his slaves have gone and that no one is left to build his grand structures? Will Pharaoh's army pursue us? Will they slaughter us like lambs for our insubordination? Or will they stand down and allow us to return to our ancestral home in Canaan?" "How will we survive the desert? Where will we find food and water?" As the bread passes over our lips, our stomach's rumble, our fingers tremble, our teeth chatter. As we drink cupful after cupful of water, our thirst is not slaked. Our skin remains flushed; our throats are parched. We are told we must trust Moshe (he is fully eighty years old, yet still strong) for it is he who will lead the Israelites out of bondage and to the Promised Land. I have my doubts…

As the hour reaches eleven, we hear messengers moving through the streets, going house to house and marking doorways against the tenth and certainly most consequential plague, Death of the Firstborn. This is it! This is the beginning. Generations held in bondage. Our spiritual leader himself the sole survivor of a bygone brutal massacre, an innocent child found amongst the reeds in a basket and reared as an Egyptian Prince by Pharaoh's daughter! Yet, Moshe always knew he was not Egyptian, but a Hebrew; and when he lost his temper and killed an Egyptian guard for beating a Hebrew slave to death, he ran into the desert to escape his fate. There, Yahweh spoke in a thunderous voice to Moshe from a burning bush and told him to return to Egypt and lead His people out of bondage. Was this Yahweh's idea of a joke? Forty years wandering in the Sinai with hardly a drop of water and only manna to eat? Or was it the mass delusion of a captive People with nothing left to lose? Was it the Jewish God's way of delivering His people to the land of milk and honey? Or was it simply the result of a hallucination experienced by Moshe, a man with an iron will and a body far too strong for its years? Whether orchestrated by God, or the fantastic folly of one man with fire in his eyes and steel in his constitution, I realize, from my futuristic point of reference, that this is an event on which two millennia of history will pivot. So I gather my courage and ready myself for the long and arduous journey home.

Silently and steadily, the procession grows in number as we move through the streets. No resistance is offered from Pharaoh's soldiers. We reach the city walls and move into the vast abyss of the desert, a throng of a hundred thousand or more, finally free, finally on our way home, wherever home may be. We walk with our families; we walk with friends. We lead our animals, and we carry what we can upon our backs. We have had no time to bake the bread we will need, so we transport the dough, sour and uncooked. We know our water will not last long, but Moshe entreats us not to worry, that there is water inside the stones. "Water inside the stones? What water, Moshe? A stone is but a stone!" wail the doubters. The prophet taps his staff upon a rock, and a torrent gushes out to quench our thirst—the exigent thirst of a people in bondage for centuries, a people now able to drink freely from God's fountain.

Yet, as the sun rises upon the desert horizon, our travails are only just beginning. A hundred thousand souls cast out of civilization—out of a life of bondage, but one also of relative comfort—and onto a vast and inhospitable desert. We are a people outcast by our own choice. This is the terrain of trial and of time. Time has no end, only the promise of a distant memory. And a leader half our own who carries Yahweh's banner. Feet burn over endless barren ground. This is not the Land of Milk and Honey. This is not the Promised Land. Day after day, week after week, month after month, one encampment after another, a time of trial and of time, a test of endurance, worthiness and desire, a test of ingenuity and faith.

After only a few weeks, the bread we carried with us is gone, and the raw dough is sour and rancid. "Moshe, what shall we eat?" the people ask. They are already weary, exhausted.

"From this moment until we reach the Promised Land, we shall eat only the food that comes from Heaven!" proclaims the prophet.

Next morning, manna arrives after the morning dew has gone.

Manna is white as coriander seed and sweet as honey. Eaten raw, it tastes like sweet wafers; ground and cooked it is like sweetbread. It nourishes the body, but it also nourishes the spirit. Yet we take only what we will use this day, because the manna attracts insects and spoils when not eaten immediately.

How is it possible that this food from God has come to His people in the midst of this hellish place, literally falling from the sky onto this burning desert? And what is its nature? What are its composition and its properties?

For more information, I suspend my virtual 'experience' for a few moments to consult my database in VL. What I find is not only surprising, but also somewhat amusing, if not telling. A number of ethnomycologists, such as R. Gordon Watson, John Marco Allegro and Terence McKenna, have suggested that most characteristics of manna are similar to that of Psilocybe cubensis mushrooms, notorious breeding grounds for insects, and which also decompose rapidly. These peculiar fungi naturally produce a number of molecules that resemble human neurochemicals, and first appear as small fibers that resemble hoarfrost. This speculation (also paralleled in Philip K. Dick's novel, The Transmigration of Timothy Archer, *which Crystal and I republished, posthumously, of course), is supported in a wider cultural context when compared with the praise of Haomain, the Rigveda, Mexican praise of teonanácatl, the peyote sacrament of the Native American Church, and the Holy Ayahuasca used in the ritual of the União do Vegetal and Santo Daime.*

Each day one omer of manna is gathered per family

member, and although some are diligent enough to go into the fields to gather it, like Deborah and Miriam and me, others simply catch it with outstretched hands. It is true that greater amounts of manna are found near the homes of those with a strong belief in Yahweh, while it is found quite far from the homes of those who doubt. In fact, manna is intangible to the Gentiles, as it simply slips from their hands. Yahweh's gift to His people, manna falls in very large quantities each day and is layered out over two thousand cubits square (between fifty and sixty cubits in height); which is enough to nourish the Israelites for two thousand years, as well as be seen from the palaces of every king in the East and the West. *And that's a lotta manna!*

As we approach the Red Sea (or is it the Sea of Reeds?) we learn that Pharaoh has had a change of heart (the final and most devastating plague of all has been wrought upon Egypt by Yahweh) and the Egyptian ruler has sent his armies to recapture the Israelites as slaves. As we travel mostly on foot, and Pharaoh's soldiers pursue us in their horse drawn chariots, we embrace no hope of outpacing them. Indeed, with the sea before us, and with Pharaoh's armies closing from the rear, it would seem that we are pinned down in the desert, where we will either be recaptured or simply slaughtered. Confronting Moshe, many of the Israelites are angry, and suspicious of a deception. "Why has Yahweh led His people into such a threatening position while offering no way to defend His people, or providing no route of escape?" they implore.

Moshe's faith in Yahweh is not shaken.

"The one God, Yahweh by name, has identified the Israelites as His Chosen People, and He will not forsake them!" Moshe thunders.

"Pharaoh's armies are right on our heels," the critics remind their leader.

For a moment only, Moshe seems in a quandary. He looks up, toward Heaven, waiting for Yahweh to either send him inspiration or strike him dead. Either one will do nicely at this precarious moment in time. "Raise your staff before the waters," Yahweh commands Moshe, and the leader of the exodus does as his God bids him.

Miraculously, the sea parts, creating a passageway between two huge walls of water. Looking sternly at those who have lost faith in Yahweh, Moshe proclaims to the Israelites, "We now pass between the swells on our journey home to the land of Canaan. And behold the fate of Pharaoh's soldiers!"

A few of us in close proximity see Moshe shaking his head in consternation. Perhaps he wishes Yahweh would make this journey just a bit shorter, or a bit easier, or that He would at least warn him in advance of some of the more precarious obstacles the Israelites must face. Ah, no such luck, Moshe. As they say on the whiskey commercial: *Just keep walking!*

Through the gorge move one hundred twenty thousand, a three hundred-foot wall of water roaring on either side, women crying and praying for salvation, children clawing their mothers' legs, men beating back imaginary enemies with imaginary swords, animals stinking of fear, lightning crashing overhead, and a relentless wind howling the name of *Yahweh* over and over again.

As Pharaoh's soldiers follow in close pursuit, Moshe presses onward. He knows in every nerve and every fiber of muscle in his lean and hardened body, in every pore, and in tooth and nail, in rash and blister, and in each drop of sweat, that Yahweh is real, and that Yahweh is his master, his God. And that he, Moshe, is God's messenger. He is not only the man of the hour, but he is the man of the Age. His steps are the steps of God. His thoughts are God's thoughts; his purpose is God's purpose. Finally, Yahweh will reign from His throne in Canaan, with the Israelites as His obedient people, forever and ever…

Amen!

As the last of the Israelites emerges from the gulf, the sea folds back upon itself, closing the passageway and drowning every last soldier in Pharaoh's army. Disbelieving pilgrims bow down on bended knee to their all-powerful God, Yahweh, and to his man of the hour, Moshe, son of Amran, descended from the line of Levi. A miracle has occurred. The table has been laid. A place has been prepared for the Israelites—in Heaven and on Earth. The Promised Land cannot be far away now.

As our camp is established at the foot of Mount Sinai—and this is not a camp meant to last a few days, or even a few weeks, but rather months or even years— Moshe is summoned by Yahweh to the top of the mountain to receive God's law. Moshe's solitary communication with Yahweh is well established by now, but even after the miracle delivering the Israelites from Pharaoh's army, many still do not trust Moshe and take every opportunity to discredit him. "Why does God talk only to him?" they ask. "Why will He not speak to Aaron, who is surely a noble man of our people?"

"It is a matter of lineage," answers an old woman who is thought to be very wise.

"And nobility," says another. "Never forget he was raised as royalty!"

"Egyptian royalty, not Hebrew royalty. Do you not remember the difference?"

"Pardon our ignorant ways, but we have never seen the Land of Canaan. A thousand pardons, please!"

"No apologies. We are all ignorant of our true heritage. Not one of us has seen the Promised Land. Perhaps it is only a fantasy. And perhaps Moshe is a fool…"

"Or a crazy man!"

"Would God choose a crazy man for His messenger?" asks a believer.

"Maybe Yahweh is also an imposter. What true God would leave his chosen people stranded in the desert for nearly forty years?"

"An angry God. Or a sadistic one."

"What quarrel has God with our people? We are poor

outcasts."

"But poor no longer. Thanks to Yahweh, who sent us from Egypt with many riches."

"Gold and silver are of little use in a barren desert," one skeptic reminds.

"Perhaps not so useless after all," postures another.

Moshe has been on top of the mountain more than a month. Why is it taking so long? Surely God knows the law He wishes His people to follow. What are they doing up there? Inscribing the commands in stone or something?

Meanwhile, rumors are circulating amongst the Israelites. Whispers at first, and then outright speculation: "Moshe is dead; Yahweh has left us here in the desert to perish." And, "Never shall our people see the Promised Land. We should never have left Egypt. For is it not better to live in comfort as slaves than in austerity as free men?" A statement embossed by the question: "One God? Who ever heard such nonsense? We must return to worshipping Pharaoh's pantheon, and then we will again share in Pharaoh's riches. When can we leave this forsaken desert and return to our lives in Egypt?" Which was qualified by groundless conjecture and an ad hoc decision: "Moshe will never return from the mountaintop, so we must turn to Aaron. He is a wise man, and surely he will know which god we should appeal to for salvation?"

So, in Moshe's absence, Aaron is consulted by the Israelites.

Absolute power corrupts absolutely: we have heard it said so many times that we have come to accept the premise itself as an absolute. But is it true? Because the Israelites maintain little patience with their leader Moshe, or maybe because certain members of society are contrary, or need to cause a little trouble, or are inclined to act out of self interest, Moshe, whatever his reputation and whatever his accomplishments, is marginalized without trial. Aaron is given the keys to the kingdom, windblown and forlorn as it is. Once in power he commands the Israelites to collect all the gold that they've carried out of Egypt—rings and earrings and bracelets, buttons and platters and goblets, which is a sizeable cache because gold as a commodity was plentiful in Egypt, and because Pharaoh, never expecting the Israelites to survive the rigors of the brutal desert, offered no resistance and indeed gave his sovereign encouragement for the Hebrews to take as much gold with them as they desired on their journey. A great smelter is constructed at the center of the encampment, and all the gold collected from the Israelites is melted down and then refashioned into a magnificent idol—a golden calf—to be worshipped on a great altar. An idol to be worshipped in place of Yahweh, the one God of the chosen!

Money is the root of all evil: that's another one we've heard again and again. But should we take it to the bank?

After being away for nearly two months, Moshe finally comes down the mountain. But he looks more like he's been fighting a war than listening to lectures and taking notes in God's classroom. His face is brown as tanned leather; his long white hair is unwashed, matted—a home for lice and insects and God-only-knows-what. His robe is soiled and tattered, his sandals in ruins. Upon his shoulder he carries two stone tablets, and he all but buckles under their weight.

Must be an ominous message chiseled on that stone, I think to myself.

Of course the scene awaiting Moshe upon his arrival at the encampment is nothing less than the most grandiose toga party ever held. (Remember those high school beer keg parties that the jocks always threw when their parents were away for the weekend? Well, that was nothing compared to what poor old Moshe found upon his return from Mount Sinai.) What he sees takes away his breath—Yahweh's too, probably—and infuriates him to the point of losing control. The Israelites have renounced their faith in Yahweh, the one God, and in turn have fashioned an idol out of solid gold—a golden calf—and now they are wildly dancing round and round this burnished feral creature, slobbering drunk, naked, dirty and fornicating openly, singing blasphemies. What has happened in his absence? And what will Yahweh think when He gets wind of this? Moshe is not about to take personal responsibility for such an elemental sin—not after Yahweh has released the Israelites from bondage, taken them as his Chosen People, guided them through the trials of nearly forty years of wondering in the desert, saved them from Pharaoh's armies, and finally given them His law to live by—no small gift, indeed! Yet here they gather to dance around a golden idol—an infraction, though they do not yet know it, of God's most essential law: "*I am the Lord your God, who brought you out of the land of Egypt, out of the house of slavery; Do not have any other gods before me. You shall not make for yourself an idol, whether in the form of anything that is in heaven above, or that is on the earth beneath, or that is in the water under the earth. You shall not bow down to them or worship them; for I the Lord your God am a jealous God, punishing children for the iniquity of parents, to the third and the fourth generation of those who reject me, but showing steadfast love to the thousandth generation of those who love me and keep my commandments.*"

OMG!

Needless to say, Aaron and all his pagan followers are in deep shit. Seeking him out, Moshe asks not a single question, or utters not one reproach, but instead smashes the two stone tablets at the blasphemer's feet, and God's Law lay broken in shards upon the earth.

Chagrinned by Moshe's censure, the Israelites dispense with their idolatry and return to the pious worship of Yahweh. Moshe then goes back up the mountain to see if he might obtain a 'copy' of the original document from God. Of course the outcome of Moshe's journey hangs in the balance, and the Israelites behave themselves scrupulously while he is away.

Luckily, Moshe finds Yahweh at home on top of Mount Sinai when he returns. God is not happy by what has happened but decides to forgive His people anyway (because He actually has no other people to embrace in their place) and He gives Moshe an exact likeness of the original tablets to take back down the mountain to share with the Israelites. Though nobody is really sure—not Moshe, nor any of the Israelites—whether the replacements include the same blessing and power that the original tablets had contained. And I must say that I wonder to this day, three thousand, five hundred years later, if the Jews are still paying for the renunciation.

Back at the modern-day Jerusalem REP, I again meet up with Matthew Taylor. The facilitator of my journey backward in time, he asks, "How was your trip, Fizzy Oceans?"

"Pretty damn interesting," I tell him. "It's one thing to read these ancient stories in archaic language, and an entirely different thing to experience them in the present tense."

"That's VL for you," he assesses matter-of-factly.

"Even so," I observe, "the essence and the power of these events are indisputable."

"And alternative conclusions can be drawn from a retelling, or a reliving, of these events—conclusions relevant in today's, shall we say, more complicated world."

"Do you really think today's situation in the Middle East is more complicated?" I ask.

"Consider this interpretation," he invites.

I take a seat on a bench to listen to his hypothesis.

"Power—and its potential for transformation and compassion—resides at the heart of the story of Exodus. In a dramatic moment, Moses leads the oppressed Jewish people out of slavery in Egypt, only to be halted by the seemingly impenetrable Red Sea. Then, the power: the Red Sea parts, and the Jews walk toward their freedom and self-determination. As autonomous people, the Jews are transformed by this power, and also they are implored to embrace compassion, when God reminds the angels that the Egyptians 'are God's children' too.

"Today, Jews must part a modern Red Sea—the psychosocial fear, anger, and mistrust that divides Palestinians and Israelis—to claim a different kind of freedom, one of communal reconciliation and cooperation for life sustenance.

"If we are to take the parting of the sea as a metaphor in the context of an oppressed people's struggle for freedom, then maybe our inquiry into its applicability to today's challenge could engage the questions of power, transformation, and compassion. What is the power symbolized by the parting of the Red Sea? What does this power make possible?

"Imagine it: The sea stretches in infinity before you. One wave so strong it could pick you up and carry you like a twig to shore. An undertow so powerful it could drag you to the depths, helpless and drowning. Your mortal strength seems powerless against the currents and tides. What force could possibly 'part the sea?' What force could bring about freedom for an oppressed people? What force could facilitate reconciliation in a seemingly 'intractable' conflict? What is that power?

"Many of us are familiar with threat power—it's dramatized in violent Hollywood movies, enacted by armies and police forces, and studied at the military science and political science departments of universities. We are also familiar with exchange power—it resides in our wallets, drives the world's economy, and is studied at economics and business schools. Integrative power, to say the least, is less well understood.

"Could threat power or exchange power 'part the sea'? What power could bring about the kind of reconciliation that would enable long-term healing and cooperation between Israelis and Palestinians? Integrative power is the one at work here—the one we need to harness right now."

"But under current conditions, how could such a philosophy be manifest?" I ask.

"In May of 1893, a young Indian attorney named Mohandas K. Gandhi was ejected from a train in South Africa for one reason: he was not white. Though holding a first-class ticket, the train operators decided he was not fit to occupy a first-class cabin seat, based solely on his skin color. Gandhi made a decision that changed his life, and history. He decided to transmute his anger, remove all hint of vengeance or reprisal, and positively approach this insult as one against all humanity. He concluded that all parties involved were demeaned by this unjust situation. He set out to free oppressed and oppressor alike from the structure of violence. Gandhi converted a negative drive of anger and resentment into a positive drive of universal love and determination for social justice. In the process, he unleashed an indescribable power inside *himself*. This personal *conversion of a negative drive into a positive drive* is precisely what the sea's parting symbolizes—the power unleashed by an individual's spiritual love, a source of limitless strength. This is the greatest power humans have been endowed with. If the sea is a barrier, the parting of the sea can be seen as our personal ability to surmount the most difficult obstacle when we unleash an internal positive drive. Gandhi said of this conversion, 'I have learnt through bitter experience the one supreme lesson to conserve my anger, and as heat conserved is transmuted into energy, even so our anger controlled can be transmuted into a power which can move the world.'

"Integrative Power: 'I do something authentic (from my heart), and in the process, I have faith that we will end up closer in our relations.'

"Gandhi made it his mission in life to right the wrong utilizing integrative power. Thus began a forty-year freedom struggle for Indian civil rights in South Africa and home rule in India. Gandhi's movement involved dialogue, self-sacrifice, constructive work to rebuild India's indigenous economy and cultural civilization, and willingness to nonviolently oppose injustice—always with an eye to an integrative process and outcome. Gandhi's steadfast commitment to right means and right ends, and the ultimate goal of friendship with the oppressors, is reflected by British historian Arnold Toynbee's comment, 'Gandhi made it impossible for us to go on ruling India, but he made it possible to leave with dignity.' Indeed, Gandhi and his followers had done something authentic, and moved closer in relations with the British."

"Yes, I have met Mahatma Gandhi personally," I tell Matthew. "Though even after my experience with the Jews in the desert, I might not have made the connection that you are trying to make."

"The parting of the Red Sea demonstrates what becomes possible when a negative drive is converted to a positive drive. To India's numerous 'realist skeptics', Gandhi's plans to use integrative power to usher out the British as friends seemed about as plausible as parting the Red Sea! To one skeptic who said, 'You know nothing of history; this cannot be done,' Gandhi's response was, 'You know nothing of history. Just because it has never happened does not mean it is not possible.' Of course, now history demonstrates that integrative power can bring about mass social change and freedom for both oppressed and oppressor.

"The main lesson we can derive from the parting of the sea is that the conversion of a negative drive to a positive drive begins *in the individual*. Thus, we who are parties to this conflict—Israelis, Palestinians, the Diaspora—can make *individual* decisions to convert our anger at the injustice we see every day into a positive drive to heal the wounds, love one another, and seek the humanity in each other. We can be angry at the structures that cause pain, but offer love and dignity to the people…

"What if we were to believe that Palestinians and Israelis have been 'chosen' to make peace with each other and to demonstrate to the world the power of love to heal conflict? We can draw upon past real-world examples to envision a radical transformation, both in the *process* and the *outcome*. Gandhi set out to do something so radical that few could even imagine it.

"Just like the skeptics who doubted Gandhi's plans to escort the British out as friends, some might believe Israelis and Palestinians cannot be friends. Israeli/Palestinian communal reconciliation *is* possible, and inevitable when the idea begins to gain traction in the minds of people."

"Thank you, Matthew," I tell him. Not so much for the retro-experience—a real trip though it was—but for his foresight, which we can only hope will soon be regarded as insight.

Shalom…

The PL Garden of Gethsemane at the foot of the Mount of Olives in Jerusalem is a short distance from the Wailing Wall, and my friend Matthew Taylor has directed me to his friend, Sir Harold Smithson, who has consented to be my guide to the fabled events of the Passion as it happened more than two thousand years ago. Sir Harold is waiting for me in the garden as night falls on the evening before the beginning of the Jewish Passover in the year 33 A.D.

"Have no fear, Fizzy Oceans," Sir Harold tells me, "because the players in the drama we are about to watch have no consciousness whatsoever of our presence. They can neither see us nor hear what we say. We are like ghosts in this world. Their drama is an essential one, and they must play their parts in perpetuity."

"Really…"

"Watch and learn," he insists. "Over that hill, the one covered in olive trees, Yeshua is about to enter the garden with his disciples Simon Peter, John and James the Greater. This story is known in Biblical history as the 'Garden of the Agony'."

"Am I really going to see Jesus?" I ask.

"The Lord is entering now," he confirms.

255

Turning toward the hillside stand of olive trees, I see Yeshua emerge from the grove flanked on his left by James and John, and on his right by Simon Peter. At first glimpse of The Son of Man I am dumbstruck by his presence and charisma. He is dressed in a simple white robe with sandals upon his feet, yet an aura of white light seems to engulf him as he walks. Upon his face is the look of inescapable destiny, yet he appears to be calm, if not reconciled. He asks his disciples to grant him privacy, and he moves a stone's throw away from the threesome to talk intimately with his Father. Sir Harold and I follow, careful not to compromise his sanctuary.

"Father," Yeshua prays reverently and humbly, "the spirit is willing, but the flesh is weak. I ask Thee: Remove this cup of wrath from which I am bound to drink." Immediately, the Son of Man collapses over a stone as he receives his Father's answer. "Thy will be done," sobs the Son of Man.

Overhead, the stars swirl against the black backdrop of the desert sky. In the distance, thunder can be heard. Or is it the marching of feet upon hardened earth? Yeshua lifts himself from the rock and again implores his Father to spare him the ordeal that awaits him. Once again, God shows the Son of Man his fate, and sends an angel from Heaven to comfort the lamb in the hour before sacrifice.

"This is heart wrenching," I whisper to Sir Harold.

"This is an eternal struggle," explains my guide, the scholar. "It is the primal conflict experienced by every person who has ever walked in a corporeal body upon the earth. It might seem trite to say it, but we all must eventually face death, and no matter how strong our faith might be in something or someone greater than ourselves, we are all afraid. Yeshua is not immune to the fear of pain and suffering; he is not impervious to anxiety of the unknown. He is first a man; his eternal metaphorical identity is yet to be manifest. This is the inevitable moment of doubt, the urge to cancel at the most critical moment our elemental obligation as human beings."

Who is this person that lived in the ancient land of Palestine and called himself the Son of Man? Why is he willing (albeit somewhat reluctantly) to forfeit his life, to pay the ultimate price for the love of people who do not love him, and to a god he can neither see nor touch nor influence? Is he a martyr? Or is he a fool? Is he a man? Or is he God incarnate?

As Yeshua recovers his composure, the three disciples approach him. James leans close to his ear and informs him, "The others have arrived—all except one: Judas Iscariot." The Lord looks into James's eyes and says, "All is as it *must* be."

The descended angel hovers nearby, but the three disciples seem oblivious to the seraphim. Ever louder grows the thunderous sound of marching feet. The air is thick with moisture. Beads of sweat from the Son of Man's brow hit the ground like droplets of blood that nourish a parched and starving earth. The incessant hissing of a thousand locusts hidden within the leafy trees confuses any attempt at logic and numbs rationality. Faith hangs like a gossamer cloud over the Sea of Galilee. Yeshua lays his tender hand upon John's shoulder and tells him, "Go now and remain with the others until the time comes."

"And what time is that, Master?" John asks.

Yeshua places his finger gently over John's lips. "All your questions will soon be answered," he reassures.

The three disciples leave Yeshua, as he requested, and return to the other eight who are sleeping underneath the olive trees.

As the protective angel evaporates into the dense evening air, we watch as Yeshua again kneels to pray, though this time his prayers are silent ones. As he contemplates his fate and prays to God for his salvation, the moon rises over a nearby hillside, and the lunar light highlights the lines of his solemn face. Here in this garden, the minutes are like hours, the hours like days, and the days as everlasting as eternity. Whatever favor he might enjoy in Heaven, the role he must shortly play here on earth carries with it neither preference nor sympathy. It is the thankless and brutal responsibility of sacrifice, with the finality of the grave its only reward.

At a respectful distance, we follow the rabbi from his sanctuary to the grove where all eleven disciples lay sleeping underneath the olive trees. "Wake up and pray to the Father to deliver you from temptation," he commands his most loyal followers, and all arise to bend their knees as their Master has commanded them.

"None of us would ever betray you, Master," says Simon Peter.

The Lord regards the rock upon which his church shall one day be built. "Before the cock crows, you shall deny me three times," he reveals.

Aghast, the disciples recite in unison, "Never, My Lord!"

Yet even before the declaration has escaped upon the ephemeral breeze, the advance of heavy steps disrupts the fragile tranquility of Gethsemane. Included in the assemblage is a force of policemen from the Sanhedrin, the supreme judicial and ecclesiastical council of Jerusalem, as well as a small detail of Roman soldiers enlisted to carry out the arrest.

"We seek the Nazarene called Yeshua ben Yosef," the leader of the posse announces. The remaining disciple of the Christ, Judas Iscariot, steps out of the horde and approaches the accused. He places a firm kiss upon the rabbi's cheek, the mark of identification.

"As you can plainly see, I am he," says Yeshua.

A Roman soldier steps forward to take the prisoner into custody. Simon Peter reaches for his sword to defend his Master, but a single glance from the Son of Man directs him to replace it in its scabbard. Without protest or resistance, the rabbi is led away to face trial, and the band of disciples scatters to the four corners of the city and beyond.

Even though we cannot be seen, Sir Harold and I follow the arrest detail and the accused at a safe distance to the home of Annas, the powerful father-in-law of Caiaphas, the acting High Priest of the Sanhedrin. It is very late now, but apparently Annas has been waiting for them to bring Yeshua to him for questioning.

As Yeshua stands before the oligarch, Annas tells him, "The disruption you instigated in the Temple with the bankers is quite troubling not only to the Sadducees, but to the Roman authorities as well. It is also troubling to me, personally. And to Caiaphas as well! We in the Sanhedrin are entrusted by our people with keeping the Romans at a respectful distance—at least where it comes to our faith and our territory. Both are in jeopardy. But perhaps the rabbi has too simple a mind to understand such things. And perhaps the *Son of Man* does not know when to hold his tongue."

Yeshua offers no explanation and no apology. Annas grows noticeably more irritated with the situation and with the prisoner. He is not accustomed to dealing so directly with the bucolic masses.

"Yet," he continues, "it would seem that your following grows larger by the day—tradesmen and merchants and farmers, no doubt. Your entry into the city on the Sunday before the Passover feast was quite triumphal, was it not?"

"The multitudes laid palm fronds before him as he entered Jerusalem on the back of an ass, Your Excellency," Annas is told by a man in the arrest detail.

"As it were," says Annas with disgust in his voice.

"He claims to be the Messiah," informs another accuser.

"Which is certainly an act of blasphemy," Annas concludes. "Surely the rabbi is not so simple that he cannot understand the Law of Yahweh!"

"Any child understands God's Law," informs one of the Sanhedrin enforcers.

"As it were," says Annas again. He drinks water from a chalice then turns again to Yeshua. "So… Now I have seen the one who calls himself the Messiah. A man of few words, apparently. At least few in the presence of this council!" Annas steps forward and speaks to Yeshua face to face: "What say you, rabbi? Are you the Messiah sent by God to deliver our people?"

"What I teach, I teach not in private but for all with ears to hear. Perhaps Your Excellency should ask those who hear my words?"

"I have waited my entire life for the Messiah who would come from God to deliver our people from this insipid occupation—a great leader, a soldier, a king!" Annas says not to Yeshua but to the detail. "Yet this dirty, ragged man—certainly not a soldier or like any king I have ever known—presents himself to our people as The One. What am I to think? Indeed, what am I to do?"

"Condemn him, Your Excellency!" calls one of the loyalists. Others voice their agreement.

"Even as I might wish to do as you ask," says Annas, "it is not my place to render judgment on the infidel. Take him to Caiaphas: it is he who is High Priest of the Sanhedrin, and only he can decide the rabbi's guilt or innocence. Leave my house now. And go in the knowledge that you have done your duty!"

Those in the detail closest to Yeshua push him out the door and into the street. They march him back toward the Mount of Olives, where Caiaphas lives in a palatial estate. Arriving at the residence of the High Priest, they are admitted into a courtyard where a quorum of Sanhedrin members has assembled. Shortly, Caiaphas appears, and it is at once obvious that he is expecting the arrest party. Yeshua is again pushed to the fore to face the High Priest of the Sanhedrin.

Caiaphas speaks: "The reason you have been brought here, Yeshua ben Yosef, is because of the disruption you caused in the Temple. Have you no respect for the

Temple, Rabbi?"

"The Temple is the House of the Lord," Yeshua replies.

"Your Excellency, the troublemaker has said publicly that he would destroy the Temple made by men and erect a new Temple made by God three days later," testifies a witness.

The absurdity of the claim brings a sardonic smile to the face of Caiaphas. He walks round and round Yeshua, assessing him from all sides. "Three days only for the destruction and reconstruction of a Temple more than a thousand years in the making," he mocks. "Now that is quite a claim indeed!" The other members of the council laugh out loud at the High Priest's belittlement of the hearsay evidence.

"My body is my only Temple," Yeshua states in response.

"Then you deny your allegiance to the Temple and to Our People, Rabbi?" Caiaphas baits him.

The Nazarene remains silent. His face glows in the light of oil lamps and torches. His expression shows resignation, not tension.

"I am told that you call yourself the King of the Jews," says Caiaphas the inquisitor. "Is this true, Rabbi?"

"It is you who says it," Yeshua replies.

"And that you claim to be God!" Caiaphas accuses.

"I am the Son of Man," the prisoner answers almost inaudibly.

"If you claim to be King of the Jews, then where is your crown?" asks Caiaphas.

Yeshua remains silent.

"King of the Jews... I wonder how our Roman occupiers would feel about such a claim." The members of the Sanhedrin mumble their dismay as Caiaphas continues to question Yeshua. "Neither kindly nor with charity, I suspect," he answers his own rhetorical question.

"This is no god!" shouts another anonymous witness.

"He is but another false messiah, like a hundred others who roam the desert and speak in tongues. He is delusional, a misfit, a danger to Our People!"

"If it is true that you claim to be God, then you have defiled the Law of Moses and committed the worst kind of blasphemy. Do you know the punishment for such a crime, Rabbi?"

Yeshua bows his head. Is he praying silently? Or has he already reconciled himself to the ultimate punishment of stoning? Beads of sweat dampen his brow; his lips are parched; his hand trembles ever so slightly in its binding.

"What witness will step forward to confirm that this man has claimed to be God?" Caiaphas asks.

Strangely, none step forward.

"Come now!" Caiaphas encourages. "Surely one of you has heard the rabbi preach his sermons. Has he claimed to be God, or not?"

No confirmation comes from the assemblage.

"Without corroboration, how am I to convict him then?" Caiaphas asks in frustration.

When no one has a satisfactory answer to his question, Caiaphas proclaims, "I am going to my bed. Take this blasphemer to Pontius Pilate. Maybe he will know what to do with him. Take him at once!"

Pilate is different. He is not a Jew, and he has no axe to grind with Yeshua. In fact, he finds the self-proclaimed king (or was it others who had anointed him as the Messiah?) to be rather comical, a farce. All this talk of Messiahs and Hebrew Kings—it seems only to annoy the governor. "These Jews are a curious tribe," he declares to one of his aids. "They are a people in bondage, yet they remain full of themselves, as if they have a claim on this land, or as if they will be around when the stars fall from the heavens!" He wipes the sleep from his eyes as he assesses the prisoner that has been brought to him by his own people.

"Why have you brought this man before me?" he asks

a member of the Sanhedrin who has accompanied the arrest detail to the governor's headquarters.

"This man is a blasphemer!" the Sadducee replies.

"A blasphemer?" Pilate inquires as he chews a mouthful of savory pie. "But blasphemy is a violation of Hebrew law, not of Roman law. Why has the Sanhedrin not dealt with him according to your laws?"

"He stood before Caiaphas after midnight," the spokesman responds. "The High Priest found him to be most uncooperative, so he told us to bring him to you, Governor."

"I see," says Pilate with mild interest. "And has he committed any other crime?"

"Five days before the Passover, he created a disturbance in the Temple."

"What sort of disturbance?" the governor inquires with a smirk on his face.

"He drove out the money-changers," he is told.

Pilate laughs out loud. "Truly?"

"It is not a laughing matter," replies the Sadducee, irritated with the Roman Governor.

"Nevertheless, these are internal matters not worthy of a hearing by the prelate."

"He says he is King of the Jews," the Sadducee informs trying to evoke a bit more interest from the Roman, if not a rebuke, or better yet, a condemnation.

Pilate looks directly at Yeshua, who has yet to speak a single word in his own defense. "This man says you claim to be a king: is it true?"

"The only kingdom I know is the Kingdom of Heaven," answers Yeshua.

"Do you not acknowledge the divine countenance of the Roman Emperor?" he asks.

Yeshua offers no reply.

"He seems harmless enough to me," Pilate assesses with disinterest.

"Truly, Your Excellency, Yeshua ben Yosef is neither

harmless to our community nor to Rome. He has substantial support among the common people—tradesmen and merchants, beggars and paupers!"

"And you are telling me you fear that the Roman protectorate is in danger from beggars and paupers…"

"This man is not to be underestimated," concludes the Sadducee gravely.

"True or not, Rome is an empire built on laws, and I find no infraction on which to convict this man. He may be a troublemaker, but that is something with which the Sanhedrin must deal. He may be a charlatan, or delusional—like that other one, the Baptist—or maybe he is just a pathetic fool, but none of those conditions—unfortunate though they might be for the one in question—is an infraction of Roman law."

"The Hebrew people demand swift justice, Your Excellency. Even as we speak, they are gathered in the street in great numbers. They call for his crucifixion."

"Since when do the Jews execute their prisoners on the High Holidays?" Pilate asks.

"This is a unique circumstance, Your Excellency," explains the Sadducee. "It is crucial that justice be swift and final."

"But if blasphemy is his offense, then why not stone him according to your laws and be done with him?" Pilate asks.

"The High Priest Caiaphas begs your indulgence in this matter, Prelate," argues the Sadducee.

Again Pilate looks directly at Yeshua. "What do you have to offer in your defense?" he asks. "They claim you call yourself King of the Jews. Are you a king?" he demands.

"It is you who call me king," says Yeshua. "I am the Son of Man."

Supremely irritated, Pilate laments, "Kings dressed in rags! Messiahs! It is all nonsense to me. Tell me directly, Son of Man, are you the Messiah your people are incessantly speaking about?"

"I am…" says Yeshua.

"Then a king should have a crown," proclaims Pilate, and he directs a crown of thorns to be placed on the head of the accused. Once the crown is in place, the prelate smiles and pronounces, "There it is! A crown fit for the King of the Jews!"

"But what of his fate, Prelate?" asks the Sadducee.

"He has committed no crime," Pilate insists. "How can I condemn him for being an insolent idiot?"

"Prelate, go to the window and behold the crowd in the street. Ask them, if you will, what should be done with this blasphemer."

In disgust, Pilate goes to the window and throws open the sash. Just as the Sadducee has described, an angry mob has gathered outside the governor's residence. "I have here the man Yeshua ben Yosef, and he says he is the Son of Man, the Messiah. Is he the one for whom you wait to deliver you from your Roman overlords?"

"No!" screams the mob in unison. "Crucify him, Your Excellency!"

"But he has committed no crime against Rome," Pilate insists.

"His crime is against Yahweh," they proclaim. "He must die!"

"I will give you a choice," says the prelate. "I offer you Yeshua ben Yosef… Or I will give you Barabbas, a known thief. I will spare only one. Which do you choose?"

"Give us Barabbas!" they call out.

"Very well! As you wish, I give you Barabbas!"

Returning to the assemblage, Pilate coughs from the dust that has entered his chambers as a result of the unruly crowd out in the street. "What a stinking, filthy place full of stinking, filthy people," he mutters in disgust, then washes his hands in the clear water of a bathing trough.

So it is done. The Son of Man is found guilty of sedition against Rome and sentenced to death by crucifixion, to be carried out immediately so that the whole ugly business will be finished before the onset of the Jewish Sabbath. The arrest detail disperses, Yeshua is led away by Roman soldiers, and Pilate returns to his breakfast, giving the matter not another thought and wishing only that he were back in Rome, delivered from this squalid society of Jews.

Sir Harold and I are in the street as the Son of Man is brought forth to bear his cross. He has been stripped to the waist and his back shows the bloody marks of nineteen lashes. On his head is the crown of thorns that Pilate ordered made for the King of the Jews.

The street known as the Via Dolorosa is thronged with people ready to follow the condemned man to Gûlgâlta, the Place of the Skull. Some taunt him as he drags the heavy wooden cross along the cobbled street. Others spit at him. Behind him follow three Jewish women, each one weeping openly.

"Daughters of Jerusalem, do not weep for me, but weep for yourselves and for your children. For behold, the days are coming when they will say, 'Blessed are the barren and the wombs that never bore and the breasts that never nursed!' Then they will begin to say to the mountains, 'Fall on us,' and to the hills, 'Cover us.' For if they do these things when the wood is green, what will happen when it is dry?"

The Son of Man stumbles from exhaustion and from the weight of his burden, and a hearty man, Simon of Cyrene, steps forward to bear the cross part of the way to Calvary. The procession continues slowly with Roman soldiers periodically whipping the condemned as they proceed toward a low hillside just outside the city walls. Reaching the mount, the site of countless executions, the crowd disperses, now confident that their bidding will be done by the detail of Roman soldiers enlisted to carry out the sentence. The three women, each one called Mary, watch the horrifying scene from a distance.

Already upon their crosses, two common criminals relive their own agony as nails are driven into Yeshua's hands and feet to secure him to the cross. He is stripped naked, and his clothes are divided among the centurions. As the cross is raised the Son of Man calls out, "Father, forgive them, for they know not what they do."

Quite aware of the identity of the newly condemned man, one of the thieves upon a cross says to Yeshua, "Is what they say about you true, Rabbi? If it is true, save yourself, and save us too."

Yeshua, nearly blind with exhaustion and pain turns to the thief and says, "Truly, I say to you, today you will be in Paradise with me."

And seeing his blessed mother watching from a distance, he proclaims, "Woman, behold, your son!"

As the sun reaches its meridian and the horror continues, the Son of Man, now delirious implores, "*E'li, E'li, la'ma sa bach tha'ni*?" "My God, my God, why have you forsaken me?"

Then, almost replete of breath, he says simply, "I thirst." A Roman centurion offers the dying man sour wine poured over a dried branch, and as he tastes the fruit of the vine gone rancid, the soldier pierces his side with a spear, and liquid pours out of the body of the King of the Jews.

"It is finished," he pronounces, and bows his head.

The three women rush forward, hoping to suspend time, to interrupt the inevitable. Yet they know it is not possible. Their beloved is dying quickly now. The sky darkens, the wind swirls, and a rumbling is heard in the distance.

"Father, into your hands I commit my spirit!"

Then it is finished.

"Surely, this man was the Son of God!" weeps one of the Roman centurions.

Yosef of Arimathea approaches to claim Yeshua's body for burial in a tomb that he has donated, but he is instructed by the Romans to draw back: "Leave him to the bald vultures; it is the way!"

A second rumbling of the earth is heard and felt, and the Romans flee in fear of what they have done. Yosef takes down the body of the crucified rabbi, as the women anoint it with perfumed oil. Yeshua is carried to the tomb, where he is laid to rest. A large stone is placed in front of the sepulcher. It is nearly five o'clock now, and the Passover has begun.

I am shaken, devastated. Sir Harold extends his arm to support me because I can barely stand, and we leave the Place of the Skull and begin walking in the direction of the Temple. Though why we are going anywhere near the Temple I can't say. On the outskirts of the city we pass through farmlands. Coming to a barren tract of land, we see a man hanging from a lone tree in the desert, an array of silver coins scattered on the ground. His blackened tongue protrudes through his cheek; his abdomen has been ripped open and his entrails hang, bloody and gaping, from his body. Already the scavengers have found the corpse.

"Judas?" I say to Sir Harold.

He nods and tells me to look away.

Walking through the city gates, Sir Harold and I are magically transferred (thanks to VL technology) back to modern-day Jerusalem. These days—in PL and in VL, too—the Temple is certainly not what it was in 33 A.D. As history tells us, it was destroyed (for the second time) when the Roman occupation ended, abruptly and violently. Yet the Temple in the heart of Jerusalem remains at the center of the Jewish faith and the Nation of Israel, and it is vital in a different way than it was two thousand years ago. Many in our time decry the policies and actions of Israel as intolerant and inhumane, but that is an argument for a different time and a different venue. What I see here—albeit in VL—is the legacy, or perhaps it is the outcome of the long and colorful history of a culture that has undeniably given the world the foundation on which it still rests to this day. Granted, the Jews have had their ups and downs, and the story of Jesus is just one chapter. Whether one excuses the politically expedient actions of an ancient oligarchy probably depends on your point of view regarding the Christian faith as it has evolved over the centuries. But I know one thing, the drama of the events that I have just experienced firsthand is undeniable and profound. And whether these events actually took place as they are portrayed here in VL, or if something else entirely happened, the story itself has exhibited rather extraordinary staying power. As it should…

But Sir Harold Smithson has his own ideas about all that, as he tells me over coffee at a virtual café in the shadow of the Temple. "Only one question concerning the life and deeds of the man called Jesus 'the Christ' is relevant, and that question concerns authenticity. The means by which we question (or establish) authenticity must be determined by historical documentation, which in this case is somewhat limited. We can rely upon firsthand accounts (authentic or contrived as they may be), or we can base our conclusions on hearsay, which in this case is plentiful. Whatever evidence we have to analyze, we must always differentiate between hardcore physical evidence and mythology.

"Virtually every critical thinker in modern times has abandoned the idea that Jesus of Nazareth was an incarnate manifestation of God Almighty, Creator of the universe and beyond. This abandonment of (faith) is nothing short of progressive western thought at odds with ancient Middle Eastern superstition; and the larger question that arises from this confrontation is whether religion or humanity itself will determine the path of our progress as a race.

"If the mass of historical evidence (or even the lack of it) determines that Jesus was not a manifestation of the God of Everything, then he must assume his rightful place in the pantheon of demigods that populate mythology.

"In the case of Jesus of Nazareth, the sole historical authority is contained within the four Gospels: Mark, Luke, Matthew and John. But the burning historical question remains, Who really wrote these texts? Remember, Mark's Gospel is not titled, "The Gospel *of* Mark" whoever this 'Mark' might have actually been; rather it is entitled, "The Gospel *According to* Mark. It is admittedly a short and simple document. It knows nothing of the Virgin Birth, nothing of the Sermon on the Mount, and it does not record what we have come to call 'The Lord's Prayer'. Historians can find no evidence that this document even existed until 70 AD at the earliest, and it is not discussed in any written reference before the year 160 AD. If the stories it reports were indeed handed down by word of mouth for even seventy years after the death of Jesus, then I think it is safe to assume that they might well have been corrupted or enhanced in the telling. Imagine if we were to try to write an account of Abraham Lincoln's life—or even his last night on earth—without a single written account of the true events of his life. It would be impossible to maintain any degree whatsoever of authenticity. Such is the case in the Gospel *According to* Mark. Yet, there is further historical evidence that the author of this text drew heavily from an even earlier document, one that historians now refer to as the 'Old Mark'. This document has been lost to the Ages. Where did it go? Why was it not preserved by the early Church? Nobody really seems to have an answer to such questions, but what we do know is that the document that has anchored the synoptic Gospels for nearly two thousand years is, in essence a 'copy' and an 'embellishment'.

"Which brings me to the matter of the second and third synoptic Gospels: The Gospel *According to* Luke, and The Gospel *According to* Matthew. Each of these accounts are a bit more detailed than that of Mark, although it is apparent to most scholars that each of the authors drew heavily on Mark's story. In essence, both Gospels, Luke and Matthew, are but enlargements of the Gospel According to Mark. Luke's Gospel is best dated at 110 AD. Mathew's Gospel is dated no earlier that 130 AD. Neither of these books is even mentioned in written history until 190 AD. Obviously, it can be supposed that the hearsay evidence involved in composing both books could be significant, if not overwhelming. In short, both may be rich in mythology, but neither have relevance as historical documents.

"The Gospel According to John is significantly different than the three synoptic gospels. In John's book, ca. 140 to 170 AD, we see a very different Jesus than in the previous three gospels. In fact, John's Jesus seems to behave very differently than the Jesus portrayed by Mark, Luke and Matthew. John's book is derived mostly from Greek philosophy merged with early Christian mysticism, and names Jesus not as a man (The Gospel According to Mark); nor as a demigod (The Gospels According to Luke and to Matthew), but as God Himself!"

"I had no idea you were so anti-Christian," I tell Sir Harold.

"I'm not...necessarily," he says. "For me, the argument—or debate—is a wholly empirical one."

"Then tell me more," I invite the historical scholar.

"The simple fact is this: Whether or not Jesus Christ ever existed is a point open to serious scholarly question. There is just no 'physical' evidence that he did live, so the matter is left to 'faith', which is always blind. Nor is there much evidence that the events described in the four Gospels actually took place. These stories might well be contrivances of writers employing the same techniques that authors today employ: the use of metaphor, and hyperbole, and symbolism, and fantasy!"

"Why was I never told such things in catechism class? Or in school?"

"The perpetration of this myth is very important to

those who benefit most from it in our time," Sir Harold instructs me.

"But what about the Passion we just witnessed? Is it not a worthy story?"

"A worthy story? No doubt it is a worthy story. But nothing more…"

"I don't know, Sir Harold. If what you are saying is true, then the story of Jesus, his crucifixion, his resurrection and his status as the Savior of humanity is perhaps the greatest hoax ever perpetrated on mankind."

"And that, Fizzy Oceans, may be its more lasting legacy…"

"It's not that I'm pleading Christianity's case, Sir Harold. It's just that what you are saying goes against everything I've been told my entire life."

"The Jesus of the Gospels is a combination of impossible elements, Fizzy. If there was a man named Yeshua who lived in Palestine nineteen centuries ago, a man who was loved and admired by the common people, a man who preached as a rabbi in the Temple and who angered the political oligarchs of the time, a man who met a violent death for his deeds as a dissident, then why was not one word written about him and his actions in the time of his life? Or even shortly after his death? No, it is far more likely that the Jesus the world has come to know and worship was an invention of some very creative authors, a church that had its own agenda (mostly economic), and the willingness of people to believe a fantastic (and undocumented) tale to ensure their own salvation. It's easy to sell a martyr, Fizzy. It has happened in every Age, including our own. Once the people of the world have learned that the Christ of the Gospels is but a myth, and that Christianity as we now know it is wholly untrue, then they will (grudgingly) turn their attention from the religious mythology of the past to the vital problems of the present, and begin trying to solve those problems for the betterment of today's society."

"And that, Sir Harold, is called Secular Humanism!"
Touché, Fizzy Oceans!

After many requests, I have finally been given an opportunity to meet with the Dalai Lama to conduct an interview with His Holiness. I must say that I am expecting an encounter far more relaxing than my two previous ones in this ongoing and thorough effort to research and document the world's religions. Because crossing the Sinai Dessert and spending forty years with Moses and the Hebrews (while not aging a day, I might add), and then watching the trial and brutal crucifixion of Jesus, has left me not only emotionally exhausted, but also disenchanted. It is said that the truth shall set one free, but in my case, spying through my proverbial peephole at history, I do not feel any freer; I feel even more alone in a universe that is teaming with other people and rich almost beyond comprehension with their stories and beliefs. Maybe His Holiness can offer me insight—or, if not that, at least a little even-tempered perspective. So off I go!

Whoosh…

Arriving as a novice at the Dharamshala, India residence of Jetsun Jamphel Ngawang Lobsang Yeshe Tenzin Gyatso, the fourteenth Dalai Lama, I am greeted by the emulation of His Holiness, his hands and fingers pressed together in front of his face. He is wearing a red robe with a yellow sash. The room in which we are to meet is neither large nor small. The floor is made of dark hardwood, and a large doorway opens onto a garden in full bloom. On one wall is a sizeable and very ornate altar with a statue of the Buddha in meditation resting upon it. Encircling the head of the icon is an intricate and colorful ceramic aura. The architecture is classical, with pillars and trusses and archways. A single floor-to-ceiling enclosed bookcase contains a collection of ancient artifacts—mostly scrolls. The walls and the ceiling are both painted rosy pink, and a luxurious tapestry hangs from the center of the ceiling. Near the altar is the Dalai Lama's throne, as well as a chair that has obviously been placed there for me.

"It is an honor to finally meet you, Your Holiness," I say with a curtsy.

"I regret that you have had to wait so long for our conversation," he says. "But my position is very demanding. I am head of Tibet's government-in-exile, but of course my spiritual duties and obligations extend far beyond one who is a Head of State. My cause is largely spiritual, you understand."

"I haven't minded waiting," I tell him. "I've used the time to great advantage, and my research is quite far along now."

His Holiness smiles and says, "Yes, I am aware of your recent travels. How very fascinating for you!"

"Fascinating, yes. Though I'm afraid I have reached no conclusion."

"This is not a worry, Fizzy Oceans. Life is a journey, and learning is a process. Conclusions necessarily bring an end to the process of learning, and it is the process itself that has real value."

"Well put, Your Holiness," I concur.

He waves off the compliment as he turns to sit upon his throne. "Just part of my job," he laughs. Then he turns to me and says, "Please take a seat. Make yourself comfortable in my home. May I offer you a cup of tea? It's really very good."

I accept his gesture of hospitality and settle in for what I hope will be a productive interview with this esteemed spiritual leader.

During our initial exchange I ask the Dalai Lama to tell me a little about his personal history and I learn that he was the fifth of seven surviving children to a farming family in the village of Taktster. He was proclaimed the *tulku* or rebirth of the thirteenth Dalai Lama at the age of two. In 1950, the army of the People's Republic of China invaded Tibet. One month later, on November 17, he was enthroned formally as Dalai Lama: at the age of fifteen, he became the region's most important spiritual leader and political ruler.

In 1951, the Chinese military pressured the Dalai Lama to ratify a seventeen-point agreement that permitted the People's Republic of China to take control of Tibet. He fled through the mountains to India soon after the failed uprising in 1959, which effectively ensured the collapse of the Tibetan Resistance Movement.

"The Chinese government regarded me as the symbol of an outmoded theocratic system. Along with eighty thousand others that followed me into exile in India, I have striven all these years to preserve traditional Tibetan education and culture," he relates. His eyes are far away with the memories of now distant events. "You know, we still maintain traditional Tibetan schools here in Dharamshala," he says proudly.

Of course the story of the Dalai Lama is certainly more enigmatic than other Heads of State. The very method by which his selection as the fourteenth Dalai Lama was made is fascinating, and indeed it raises certain questions about the psychic proclivities of Tibetans in general. At any rate, nobleness seems to have run in the Döndrub family.

"I was born into a farming and horse trading family in the small hamlet of Taktster, on the eastern border of the former Tibetan region of Amdo, which was then already incorporated into the Chinese province of Qinghai. I was one of seven children to survive childhood. The eldest was my sister Tsering Dolma, who was eighteen years older than I. My eldest brother, Thupten Jigme Norbu, was recognized at the age of eight as the reincarnation of the high Lama Takster Rinpoche. My sister, Jetsun Pema, who is affiliated with the Tibetan Youth Congress and Tibetan Women's Association, portrayed our mother in the 1997 Hollywood film *Seven Years in Tibet*. Imagine that!" he muses. "My sister is a Hollywood starlet!" He laughs heartily at the absurdity of his own joke. I smile too.

275

"Can you tell me a little about the tradition of the Dalai Lama?" I ask him.

His Holiness settles back in his adorned chair as he relates, "Tibetans traditionally believe Dalai Lamas to be the reincarnation of their predecessors, each of whom is believed to be a human emanation of the bodhisattva Avalokitesvara. A search party was sent to locate the new incarnation when I was about two years old. It is said that, among other omens, the head of the embalmed body of the previous Dalai Lama, at first facing southeast, mysteriously turned to face northeast, indicating the direction in which his successor would be found. The Regent, Reting Rinpoche, shortly afterwards had a vision at the sacred lake of Lhamo La-tso indicating that Amdo was the region in which to search—and specifically a one-story house with distinctive guttering and tiling. After an extensive search, the Thondup house, with its features resembling those in Reting's vision, was finally found.

"And I was presented with various relics, including toys, some of which had belonged to the thirteenth Dalai Lama, and some of which had not. Apparently, I correctly identified all the items owned by the previous Dalai Lama, exclaiming, 'That's mine! That's mine! And that, too, is mine!'

"So, at the age of two, I was recognized formally as the reincarnated Dalai Lama and renamed Jetsun Jamphel Ngawang Lobsang Yeshe Tenzin Gyatso, which means *Holy Lord, Gentle Glory, Compassionate, Defender of the Faith, Ocean of Wisdom.*"

"Sort of like the Queen of England," I observe.

"The position of Dalai Lama is not royalty, you understand," His Holiness informs. "And Her Majesty certainly has more money than a Dalai Lama might require."

"So, what was your childhood like?" I inquire.

"My monastic education commenced at the age of six. My teachers were Yongdzin Ling Rinpoche and Yongdzin

Trijang Rinpoche. At the age of eleven I met the Austrian mountaineer Heinrich Harrer—I spotted him in Lhasa through my telescope! He became one of my tutors. He taught me about the outside world. We remained friends until his death.

"During 1959, at the age of twenty-three, I took the final examination at Lhasa's Jokhang Temple during the annual Monlam, or Prayer Festival. I passed with honors and was awarded the Lharampa degree, the highest-level *geshe* degree, roughly equivalent to a doctorate in Buddhist philosophy."

"Then came all the trouble," I prompted.

His Holiness inhaled deeply, then exhaled. "Yes, the trouble," he confirmed.

"What happened?" I asked.

"Well, it was not a simple matter. You see, the Tibetan Parliament called Chen Xizhang, the acting director of the Mongolian and Tibetan Affairs Commission office in Lhasa, and informed him that the Tibetan Government had decided to expel all Chinese connected with the Guomingdang Government. Fearing that the Chinese might organize protests in the streets of Lhasa, the Kashag imposed a curfew until all the Chinese had left, which they did. At the same time, the Tibetan Government sent a telegram to General Chiang Kai-shek and to President Liu Zongren informing them of the decision. In October 1950, the army of the People's Republic of China entered the country, moving through Tibetan defenses with ease."

"It must have been terrifying," I offer.

"I was a boy of fifteen. I understood many things, but not the type of violence that people often perpetrate on their neighbors. But I was lucky. I had several astute advisers."

"What happened then?" I ask.

"What happened then was that I was assisted by the CIA in leaving the country and re-establishing a government-in-exile here in India. It was the American

Central Intelligence Agency that funded our cause for several decades—one million, seven hundred fifty thousand dollars per year, every year!"

"It must have been nearly impossible to re-establish the Tibetan culture in a new land," I suggest.

"Of course it was difficult," His Holiness tells me, "but don't forget that I was not alone. Nearly eighty thousand Tibetans had followed me to Dharamsala, and we created a Tibetan educational system in order to teach the Tibetan children the traditional language, history, religion and culture. We established the Tibetan Institute for the Performing Arts in 1959, and the Central Institute of Higher Tibetan Studies became the primary university for Tibetans in India. We also founded two hundred monasteries and nunneries. This was our primary way of preserving Tibetan Buddhist teachings and the Tibetan way of life."

"Do you think you will ever return to Tibet?" I ask His Holiness.

A nostalgic smile crosses his lips. "Only if China agrees not to make any precondition for my return," he answers. "Which they have so far refused to do."

For a moment we sit in silence, yet His Holiness seems at peace, content to wait, not needing to fill every empty space. I take a moment to assimilate the history lesson the Dalai Lama has given me. Outside, bluebirds sing and flutter in the trees; thunder rolls through a distant canyon. I right myself on my chair, take a sip of tea, and straighten the hem of my dress. Finally, I ask His Holiness to tell me a bit about his philosophy and his teachings.

"I practice Dzogchen," he tells me. "Dzogchen means 'Great Perfection', and it is the natural condition of the mind. Dzogchen is also a body of teachings and meditations that can be practiced as the most direct path to enlightenment.

"Dzogchen teachings focus on three terms: View, Meditation, and Action. To see the absolute state of our mind is the *View*; the way of stabilizing that View and making it an unbroken experience is *Meditation*; and integrating that View into our daily life is accomplished by *Action*.

"Dzogchen lies at the heart of all things and is nothing less than wisdom's recognition of itself as unbounded wholeness—the incorruptible mind-nature. Such awareness is inherent within all beings, but not to be attainable by thought. It refers to the true primordial state of every individual and not to any transcendent reality.

"Dzogchen is an approach to non-dualism."

"Yet dualism seems to be the undisputable law of the universe," I say.

The Dalai Llama laughs loudly: "The Grand Illusion!" he proclaims.

"Then the universe is really not dualistic in nature?" I waver.

"What do you think, Fizzy Oceans?"

"Everything I have been taught supports the concept of duality. Everything I see, hear, taste, smell and touch seems to reinforce duality. Other religions thrive on duality: good and evil, mostly. We define our space/time continuum in terms of duality: up and down, in and out, before and after. But you say that duality is not the fundamental state of the universe…"

"Even our physicists are coming to understand what those who practice Dzogchen and have achieved enlightenment have understood for centuries. The state that we have called Nirvana, modern-day physicist describe as 'tendencies' or 'relativity'. But it is nothing new. The difference, though, is that a Master of Dzogchen practice lives continually in this state of mind, while our scientists only describe it. Which approach seems better to you, assimilation or approximation?"

"Assimilation means Enlightenment, right?"

"Of course," he counsels.

"I could use a bit of enlightenment," I lament.

"And so it is already within you," he reassures. And suddenly the room is engulfed by an unqualified peacefulness. The Dalai Llama closes his eyes, and for a moment he seems to have fallen asleep. What am I supposed to do now?

I breathe in. I breathe out. I breathe in. Breathe out. In… Out… Okay, I can dig this. We are just sitting here…being. Just…being. It's okay, I tell myself. I have nowhere else I have to go. And His Holiness surely won't sleep forever. He's bound to wake up sooner or later. So I begin to think about what it might be like to see the world in non-dualistic terms. Can I possibly do it? I don't know. This seems like a riddle wrapped up inside an anomaly, encased within a conundrum.

Whoosh…

And suddenly, within this great silence, I think I get it! His Holiness has imparted to me the great secret of the Ages. Except it is no secret at all. On the contrary, it is obvious. It is the simplest thing in the world. I break into a broad smile. I chuckle to myself. I check my pulse. It occurs to me that I will never again be the same as I was before. And at the same time it occurs to me that nothing is different. I wish His Holiness would wake up so I can share my revelation with him, but of course he already knows all about it. He must know…

Abruptly, Dalai Llama's eyes spring wide open, and within his dilated pupils I can see the infinite expanse of space. Stars swirl into galaxies, quasars at the center of each massive galaxy that surround a central, super-massive black hole, each one ten thousand times the size of nothingness. No duality out here. Yet, I AM!

"Well, this has certainly been a pleasant hour," His Holiness tells me as if nothing has happened.

And of course, nothing is exactly what has happened. I get it! Nothing—no thing. I get it!

His Holiness takes a final sip of tea then stands to escort me to the door. I am grinning like a hippie on LSD.

His arm crosses my shoulder, ever so gently. "You must visit me again sometime," he says sincerely.

"Yes, I would like that very much," I tell him. My words are automatic, though, because I am a million miles away. No. Not miles. Not kilometers. Not anything.

"Be well, Fizzy Oceans. Now go in peace and do useful work."

"I try, Your Holiness. I really, really try!"

The Dalai Llama smiles beneficently.

I get it!

I GET IT!

I first became aware of the poet Jalāl ad-Dīn Muhammad Rūmī when I came across one of his poems during a project I was doing for Open Books. Here is the poem:

> *I died as a mineral and became a plant,*
> *I died as plant and rose to animal,*
> *I died as animal and I was Man.*
> *Why should I fear? When was I less by dying?*
> *Yet once more I shall die as Man, to soar*
> *With angels bless'd; but even from angelhood*
> *I must pass on: all except God doth perish.*
> *When I have sacrificed my angel-soul,*
> *I shall become what no mind e'er conceived.*
> *Oh, let me not exist! for Non-existence*
> *Proclaims in organ tones,*
> *To Him we shall return.*

And now I am on my way, courtesy of the ever-efficient Virtual Life transfer system (and here space and time are one and the same), to a personal meeting with the most famous Mawlawïhah Sufi poet of the millennium. Lucky girl I am!

Jalāl ad-Dīn Muhammad Rūmī—or simply Rūmī, as he is now known—meets me in the Anatolian city of Konya, in virtual Turkey. He is elderly but still vivacious. A white linen turban covers his head, but his beard is full and long and white. Over his shoulders he wears a green cape that descends to a hem that encircles his ornate slippers. His loose-fitting shirt is made of linen; his pants are gold satin. His black eyes are gentle; his mannerisms are smooth and subtle. As I approach, he places his right hand over his heart then extends his open palm to me.

We are standing in the courtyard of the Mevlana Museum. In the background is a massive mosque, its minarets rising like needles to pierce the casing of Heaven. This is the world of Allah, and Rūmī is one of His primary messengers.

Sitting upon a Persian carpet, Rūmī invites me to sit opposite him. He crosses his legs, one over the other, and I do likewise. Once we are both comfortable, he relates, "I was born in Persia, now called Iran, in the province of Balkhi. I lived the majority of my life under the Sultanate of Rum, and it was at the Sultan's estate that I produced most of my poetic works. It was my son, Sultan Walad, who founded the Mawlawïyah Sufi Order, which is also known as the Order of the Whirling Dervishes, famous for the Sufi dance known as the sama ceremony."

"I have always been fascinated by the Whirling Dervishes. I think many people are intrigued, but I also think that few understand the purpose of the dance."

"*Samä* represents a mystical journey of spiritual ascent through mind and love to the Perfect One," Rūmī explains. "In this journey, the seeker symbolically turns towards the truth, grows through love, abandons the ego, finds the truth, and arrives at Perfection. The seeker then returns from this spiritual journey with greater maturity, to love and to be of service to the whole of creation without discrimination in regard to belief, race, class, or nationality."

"In western culture, we have come to regard dance as an artistic expression rather than one of prayer or meditation," I offer.

"*Samä* is all of these," he instructs. "After all, art is the one human expression that even attempts to speak the divine language. Poetry, dance, and music offer humans a vehicle by which we can approach God."

"So it is like Eastern meditation," I propose.

"Not exactly," says Rūmī. "Eastern meditation is undertaken for the purpose of emptying one's mind of all worldly thoughts, leaving only the divine to inhabit one's consciousness. *Samä* is different; it is metaphor."

"You mean it's a story?"

"More than a story," he relates. "It is an entire philosophy."

"A philosophy expressed by turning endlessly in circles…"

"Not endlessly, but repeatedly."

"Can you explain the philosophy to me?" I ask.

"I can write it in my poetry," he answers. "And I can also express it in the dance… Can I explain it in words? Let me try.

"The spirit, after devolution from the divine, undergoes an evolutionary process by which it comes nearer and nearer to Godhood. This is not only true for human beings, but for animals and plants, as well as all matter in the universe. Such unidirectional movement is due to the natural urge to evolve and to seek a union with that from which it has emerged—God. Do you understand?"

"On an empirical level, yes," I tell him. "But experientially…"

"Which is why we must dance," he says. He rises from his seat upon an ornate carpet and tells me to do the same. "Perhaps you also need to dance," he says. "The steps are not difficult to master; it is the repetition that produces the desired effect."

"Do you think I can do it?"

"You must try," he implores.

At the center of the vast courtyard outside the museum

and mosque we are joined by other dancers as well as a troupe of musicians playing tambourines, cymbals and wooden drums with natural skins (I had always thought that music—and particularly dancing—was strictly forbidden in Islam, but Rūmī informs me that it is permitted in circumstances when the dancing and the music—always played on 'natural' instruments—is for the glorification of Allah; though to me, this seems like something different, more, as Rūmī told me earlier, like a metaphysical exercise, such as yoga or magick). I am given a flowing white dress to wear, and one of the dancers gives me a crash course in the proper way to whirl.

"What if I get dizzy?" I ask, and they all look at me as if I am crazy. But I always get dizzy when I spin in circles; I thought that was normal.

"Allow yourself to move beyond physical sensation," Rūmī advises.

The musicians begin playing a curious percussive rhythm, and the dancing begins. Round and round I go, ever so slowly at first, then gaining what can only be described as an inborn velocity. To my surprise, the dance becomes effortless; my body feels lighter than air. The more I whirl, the deeper into a trance I fall. I am unraveling everything I thought I knew. I am devolving, revolution-by-revolution, back to my source, my essence. Physical sensation dissipates into the thin Anatolian air; time becomes an asterisk. The cumulative history of the Ages unfolds before me—not only human history, but evolutionary history. I am human, yes, but I am animal too; I am bird and fish and mollusk, I am vegetable and mineral. I am the sun and the sea and the stones. Finally, I am without form altogether: I am pure energy. Is this how God feels, I wonder?

How long I have been dancing, I cannot say. Time has no meaning whatsoever in this state. This is a different dimension altogether. Yet, slowly my momentum slows, and I know instinctively that this is the way of not only the universe we know, but the way of the multi-verse as well. Where am I? Am I still alive? I don't know.

Suddenly I regain physical sensation. I fall to the ground; I open my eyes. The planet is spinning (like a Whirling Dervish), but wasn't that always true? Rūmī is gone. The dancers and the musicians are gone. The museum and the mosque are gone, too. I am back inside my body…at the fish market in downtown Seattle.

4) War

Why do people engage in war? Surely by now they understand the devastation, the suffering and the grief. Often, when it is finally over, hardly anyone can explain what all the fighting was about. Most wars are settled through diplomacy (which ultimately means compromise) rather than by some decisive military victory. The dead are mourned by their loved ones, lines on a map might change by a degree or two, old leaders succumb to new ones, new rules or laws are laid down, and then life goes on more or less as it had prior to the carnage. War has been going on since any human can remember—before Europe went crazy in the first half of the twentieth century, before Napoleon, before feudalism, before the Roman Legions, before Genghis Khan… Why?

I've been thinking a lot about it lately, and I think I know the answer. War is not waged over any single political or religious issue. It is not waged over injustice. Wars are certainly not fought for moral reasons, or even ethical ones. One might make the argument that wars are fought for material gain, and it is true that the winner usually profits handsomely while the loser is left impoverished, but that is not the reason either. The real reason that people fight wars has to do with our evolution: we are descendants of the reptilian species, and the lively and aggressive lizard lives still within our mentality, ever-present and waiting to strike, fearless, stupid, without the capacity to reason. Wars happen when reason (diplomacy) fails. Where does our higher consciousness go? Underground—deep, deep, deep underground. It takes a break, a breather, a masochistic holiday. We stop thinking, stop feeling, and stop listening. Our vision becomes as absolute as kill or be killed, fight or flight. We stop seeing the world in terms of metaphors and symbols; the color spectrum fades leaving only black and white as options. It's the lizard—the infernal lizard—that has left us its legacy. We don't know how to control it—at least not yet—so from time to time we thirst for blood, a taste we find bittersweet.

I have contacted the emulation of Sid Messersmith, the founder of Poraxis Strategies and the creator of *Sid Messersmith's Battleground!* It is a real-time tactics computer game that was released back in 1991 by Electronic Applications and won the 1991 Origins Award for Best Strategy Computer Game of 1991.

The American Civil War application allows the player to control either the Confederate or Union troops during the Battle of Gettysburg. It can be played as a single scenario, or as a campaign of linked scenarios, either recounting the original history or exploring alternate possibilities. I have chosen to experience a historical enactment via Virtual Life, so what I will be watching, in effect, is a simulation within a VL REP, one that mirrors the historical events of July 1, 2, and 3, 1863. Sid has enlisted several well-known expert players to execute the re-enactment of the famous battle.

Rendezvousing in VL, Sid and I take flight and soar high above northern Virginia. It is the last week of June 1863, and it is hot. Very hot! The land beneath us is dry from drought as well as battle-scarred from years of warfare. Confederate troops march in the thousands toward their destiny in Pennsylvania, and as the column presses northward, many soldiers succumb to heat and hunger and dehydration and collapse by the side of the road. Yet the line moves onward to the sound of fife and drums, generals and their adjutants on horseback at the front, caissons following them, then the infantry, and finally the support personnel bringing up the rear.

"In mid-summer of 1863," Sid tells me, "General Lee had determined to move the war northward and establish a stronghold in southern Pennsylvania. His strategy was based on the assumption that if a presence could be established and maintained, then he could eventually attack Philadelphia, or Baltimore, or even Washington, D.C. And if he were able at some point to stage an assault on one or more of these important northern cities, then it might well bring an end to the war, the South, of course, prevailing in their bid for autonomy. So he concentrated his forces—seventy-three thousand strong—and marched them northward into the Shenandoah Valley. "Boots and saddles!" the command went up, and the troops moved out amidst thick clouds of choking dust, from their bivouac in Fredericksburg, Virginia en route to the Keystone State. Of course Lee's vision was tenuous: establishing a stronghold was more easily conceived than achieved, as history now confirms. And what a bloody and heartbreaking bit of history it is!

"Thank God it's in the past," I comment.

"But never out of sight," Sid laments. "Never forget, Fizzy Oceans, that history is alive. In a causative context, it is always in the present tense!"

From above, Sid and I can see the fierce battle at Brandy Station, Virginia, which is an antecedent to Gettysburg itself. The fighting is often hand-to-hand, soldiers from both sides wielding rifles, pistols and sabers. Horses are cut down in mid-gallop by cannon fire; their riders are pitched to the ground, open and vulnerable, the thick white smoke of the exploded ordinance their only cover. The drums of war beat as the men cheer marching comrades on to the charge. Caissons are aimed, loaded and discharged, and the reverberation of exploding shells thunders through the nearby valleys.

As General Lee's infantry secretly marches toward the Shenandoah Valley, the Union Army of the Potomac, commanded by Major General Joseph Hooker, is still encamped in positions taken after the Battle of Chancellorsville. Not until late June did they break camp and set off in pursuit of Lee's army.

In addition to General Hooker's army, we see the veteran Iron Brigade break camp in the west and begin their march towards Gettysburg to rendezvous not only with General Hooker's troops, but also to engage the Confederate army. The weather is inhospitable, the heat and humidity oppressive. It is nearly two o'clock in the afternoon when the brigade finally stops for rest and food. Some of the soldiers strip naked and bathe in an inviting stream, while others sleep in a grove of leafy oak trees. Interrupting their short respite, the bugler summons them to assemble into formation.

It has been determined that a cowardly soldier who has deserted for the fourth time is to be shot, and the men are obliged to watch the execution. The brigade is formed into a hollow, three-sided square. A coffin arrives upon a horse-drawn hearse and is placed on the ground as the prisoner is led to the execution site in the company of the chaplain. Together they kneel to pray.

Taciturn and stoic, Brigadier General Wadsworth rides on horseback into the assembly. He reads the order of execution to the selected twelve riflemen who stand ready to carry out the sentence. One rifle, they know, is loaded with a blank cartridge.

Then the provost rips open the condemned soldier's shirt to expose his chest. He binds the prisoner's arms and ankles then fixes a blindfold over his eyes. General Wadsworth calls "Attention!" and the firing squad aims their rifles. A hat is raised then quickly lowered, and the shots ring out. The condemned man slumps lifeless onto the ground. Later, the entire division is marched past the body as the gravediggers shovel earth over the corpse. The message is unmistakable: deserting one's comrades is *not* an option.

My stomach is in knots. I feel like I might vomit. Sweat covers my brow. My mouth is as dry as the parched landscape. Oxygen has gone out of my lungs and my throat refuses to allow inhalation. "I've never seen a man gunned down like that," I choke.

"I fear you shall soon see much worse," Sid says with reverence and deep regret.

Meanwhile, General Lee's Confederate columns march over the mountains and into the verdant Shenandoah Valley. Not nearly ready to confront a brigade of nearly two thousand Confederate cavalrymen, Colonel Andrew McReynolds commands his wagon train of supplies to evacuate the area under guard of the 1st New York Cavalry.

And as the Confederates chase the Yankees out of the garrisoned towns of Winchester, Martinsburg and Berryville, they receive a warm welcome, as well as gifts of food and drink and clothing, from supportive civilians.

Finally out of Virginia and passing through central Maryland, members of both armies seem stunned by the prosperous agrarian region. Sid and I focus on one particular soldier who is writing a letter as his company enjoys a rest stop.

> "The troops are in a section wholly unacquainted with great bodies of armed men," he writes. "Thickly peopled, highly cultivated, alternating between wood, meadow and field, it rolls in easy undulations, and from its gently rising knolls one scene of rich grandeur appears as the other fades from view. The grasses have been garnered; vast fields of golden grain are ripening; oats and corn are advancing. Over the

succulent meadows and on the green sloping hillsides flocks and herds revel in fattening pasturage. Poultry is plentiful, milk, butter and eggs abundant. The miller has grist to grind, the blacksmith his horses to shoe, the wheelwright his wagons to build. Peace, plenty, thrift, prosperity everywhere abound. Men, maidens, matrons and children gaze in wonderment as the columns hurry through their villages."

Yet, not all the proud and prosperous Maryland farmers are supportive of the rallying troops, Federal or Confederate, as their crops of corn and barley and oats are raided to feed cavalry horses and mules, hay is confiscated, without payment, for bedding, and fence posts are torn down and burned as firewood.

Near the town of York, Pennsylvania, troops forage for supplies and appropriate horses and mules. Mostly, such appropriations are outright thievery, but even when the rebel raiders pay for what they take, they compensate the farmers and shop owners in Confederate money.

We watch from on high as tens of thousands of Confederate troops march across Pennsylvania with the Federal Army of the Potomac in hot pursuit. We watch as the 12th New Hampshire crosses the river into Maryland under copious moonlight. We watch in astonishment as General Jubal A. Early's division routes a hastily aggregated band of Union protectors and occupies the town of Gettysburg, and as Brigadier General John Buford's division of Union cavalry soldiers arrives shortly after Confederate General J. J. Pettigrew's detail has withdrawn from the town and established camp on a western hillside.

As the sky darkens on the evening of June 30, 1863, Ewell's Confederate Second Corps is camped north and northeast of Gettysburg, while Hill's Third Corps has claimed a position along the pike to Chambersburg.

Nearing the city is Longstreet's First Corps, with General Lee close behind.

On the Union side, Buford's cavalry soldiers are stretched in a crescent from west to northeast. A Federal infantry corps is within a day's march of the battlefield. Several cavalry units support the foot soldiers.

The clear night sky is filled with stars, one for each soldier. Which stars shine brightly, and which glow dimmer, portend the future. The sleep of the older, well-seasoned veterans is fitful, while the younger soldiers rest like babies in the arms of their mothers. Messengers ride on horseback behind the lines between friendly encampments to gather intelligence and convey support positions. Commanders sleep not at all as they formulate strategies for the upcoming battle. Will providence be kind to the boy from Georgia? Or will it extinguish his light in a defining moment of passion? Will the soldier from Illinois be decorated as a hero, or will he lose his arm to a well-placed cannon shot? Which cause will fate call noble, and which one will it deny? These soldiers have all seen combat, and all witnessed death. They know one side will prevail, and the other will taste bitter defeat. Some will live; others will die. Each life hangs in the balance tonight. A single shooting star arcs above tomorrow's battlefield, dusting those underneath its path with courage and resolve. Their duty be done, for country and family and friends.

As the dawn breaks on the morning of July 1, 1863, the various commanders fully understand the enormity of the situation. Such a convergence of forces has not occurred before, and it will no doubt have a defining effect on the outcome of the war.

"Every available man is to join the ranks," General Buford instructs Captain Frank Donaldson. "I don't care who he is—cook, wheelwright, blacksmith—all non-combatants are to be forced into the brigade ranks, issued rifles and made to fight. Assemble a detail to bring up the rear, and if any man dares not to fall in step, he is to be shot on the spot. Those are your orders, Captain. Do you understand and accept them?"

"Yes, sir!" Donaldson replies with a salute.

"Then carry them out," says Buford as he turns his back on mercy.

As the troops march to their assigned posts on McPherson's Ridge—not one man daring to step out of alignment—Confederate General Harry Heth's forces stage an attack. Just after eleven o'clock the rebel sharpshooters occupy the Harmon farm. Susan Castle and her fourteen-year-old niece Amelia occupy the house. As the 'Johnnies' crash through the door, the woman and child hide themselves in the cupola. For several hours rebel snipers pick off infantrymen from Colonel Chapman Biddle's brigade and Cooper's artillery battery, both entrenched atop McPherson's Ridge. The woman and girl watch the action from their position of relative safety. Finally, division commander James Wadsworth orders the 80th New York to flush out the Rebels. Captain Ambrose Baldwin draws the duty, and with thirty men manages to retake the farm. Relieved, Susan and Amelia descend from the cupola, but Baldwin knows that even though his troops have retaken the farm, their dominance might well be short lived, so he instructs the women to hide in the cellar. His suspicion proves correct: General Heth soon arrives with two Confederate brigades.

From a cellar window, Susan and Amelia watch as the superior Confederate force advances toward the farm. Having held the position for only an hour, Baldwin orders his soldiers to abandon their position. The women watch in horror as their barn goes up in flames, and moments later they hear the sound of footsteps overhead as the 'Johnnies' first occupy then begin ransacking the house. Rather than be trapped in the cellar, the two women climb the stairs to beg for mercy from the Rebel soldiers. In the parlor they see Confederate soldiers piling their belongings—rugs, furniture, linens, bedding—onto a conflagration of newspapers. "Take whatever you want, but spare this fine house," they beg. Their plea is ignored, so the woman and the girl flee the house and go running through open pastures teeming with enemy combatants. Caught in the crossfire, bullets whiz over their heads as ordinance explodes all around them. Chaos reins as mortal fear powers their legs. Mercifully, a Confederate colonel offers them sanctuary.

It is now past noon, and for the Union army the fighting is not going well. They are out manned and out maneuvered. Reinforcements are coming from the south but General Meade cannot easily locate the forces they are to relieve.

Meanwhile, fierce fighting is underway in the forests and fields near McPherson's Ridge. A young sergeant helps a wounded comrade off the field of battle as Confederate lead flies all about them. A corporal, who takes the wounded man's other arm, quickly assists him but they do not get very far as both are shot dead within seconds of one another. A Minié ball severs the wounded man's foot, and his life's blood pours from the smoking, gaping wound onto the ground where he lay.

"I don't know how much more of this I can watch," I tell Sid. "This is horrendous!"

"Courage, Fizzy Oceans," he bolsters. "Watch and learn…"

Confederate forces are now in hot pursuit of retreating Union troops from the western front on their way to a rallying point on Cemetery Hill. As they enter Gettysburg, bullets fly in every direction, penetrating houses, shops and barns. One of the errant bullets finds an unfortunate civilian as he sits inside his outhouse, and he is killed while relieving himself of his fear. Within minutes streets and sidewalks are strewn with the dead and the wounded from both sides. A once serene and scenic village has become the scene of a hideous nightmare.

Darkness has fallen after the first day of battle and the weary soldiers retreat into the shadows. Relief patrols search for the living among the dead and retrieve the wounded to receive treatment behind the lines. One group of Confederate boys eats dinner from a bagful of candy that was stolen from a Gettysburg store. Sweetness is much appreciated wherever it can be had. The only gunshots heard are from the rifles of soldiers killing badly injured horses.

The Confederates have occupied Gettysburg. Cautious civilians dare not come out of their houses for fear of what the Rebels might do to them. Well aware of the day's battle outcome, the Union High Command debates in earnest whether to go on with the fight or retreat to a safe position. It is determined that they will remain and fight.

Culp's Hill; Little Roundtop; Devil's Den; Plum Run; Houck's Ridge; Cemetery Hill; Stony Hill; Rose Wheatfield: these are the now famous places in which the battle rages. But my shattered attention is focused, for the moment, on Sherfy's peach orchard. The fighting there is particularly intense and brutal, often hand-to-hand. Hundreds of men are killed or wounded in less time than it takes to eat a meal. I hear the roar of artillery, caissons standing side-by-side for a quarter mile along a low stone buttress, firing in rapid succession. Soldiers try to take cover behind overturned wagons, or even behind their fallen mounts, but hiding is not possible as the shells explode, one after another, throughout the orchard. Often one shell will take out ten to twenty men at a time, severed limbs flying through the air and rich red blood gushing out of bodies like water pouring from an abundant fountain. One astonished cavalryman sits astride his horse as the animal is cut in two by a cannonball. Moments later, the rider, too, is dead from a gunshot through his neck.

All the while drummers drum and buglers blow the call to charge. Men rush to duty and death not one-by-one, but in the hundreds. Smoke from the exploded ordinance is as thick as a burning barn filled with hay. Screams of the wounded cut through the battlefield cacophony as swords rip open tender flesh, and as bayonets savagely pierce hardened sinew and wishful dreams for a lavish future. "For Virginia!" calls a Confederate soldier carrying his regiment's colors, but even as the echo from his noble words has not yet faded away upon the wind, the flagstaff is cut in half by a Mimié ball, and the banner falls to the ground where it is stained by earth and by blood. As the color-bearer bends down to retrieve the silken image, his legs are blown out from under him and he falls upon the treasured emblem, dead.

Sid now directs my attention to a skirmish between two soldiers, one Federal and the other Confederate, at Little Roundtop. "A situation that is particularly tragic," he laments. "Two brothers on opposite sides of the conflict meet in battle. Which loyalty shall prevail?"

Jonathan McCormick is ten years older than his brother Matthew. Both were born and raised on their father's fruitful plantation in central Mississippi. At age nineteen, Jonathan went away to attend a prestigious medical school in the North. Upon graduation he became a prominent doctor in Baltimore. When the war broke out, his sympathies were with the North, and particularly with President Lincoln. He enlisted in the 37th Maryland, but instead of an assignment to the medical corps, he chose infantry service.

His younger brother Matthew, now just nineteen, had never left home prior to the war. On the plantation he enjoyed a comfortable lifestyle, attending parties and courting young women. His sympathies were unquestionably with the Old South, and he enlisted to do his duty for the Confederacy and for Jefferson Davis.

Today, at Gettysburg, they encounter one another for the first time in ten years—at the point of a bayonet! "This is for Mr. Lincoln!" screams Matthew as he plunges the blade into his brother's chest. Jonathan's look is incredulous as he recognizes his brother. "Tell mother I am fine," he says breathlessly as he falls at his brother's feet. Matthew is dumbstruck. He has killed his own brother. What cause demands such sin and sacrifice? No redemption is possible for such an act. Removing the bayonet from his brother's body, he turns his gun upon himself. "No!" I scream. But my words are lost in cyber-garble. Matthew pulls the trigger and follows his brother into oblivion.

It is difficult to imagine that the third day of fighting could be as horrific as the first two, but it proves to be even worse. It is only five in the morning, and from high above Cemetery Hill, Sid and I watch as Union artillery is discharged upon Confederate camps. Each volley is like a tremendous crack of thunder that wakes one from the peace of early morning slumber, but unlike simple thunder, these volleys rain down death. The rebels respond with indifference, and soon the shelling abates. Then I see a vehement cloud of smoke curling up from the dark woods on the right, and suddenly the muskets crackle.

Union signal officers are in constant communication with General Howard on Cemetery Hill. Shortly, the batteries open once more. Those on Slocum Hill and near Baltimore Pike follow the signal, and soon every little crest between Slocum's Hill and Cemetery Ridge is belching smoke and thunder.

Still, there is no artillery response from the Confederates. "Are they short of ammunition?" I ask Sid. "Have they failed to bring up all their guns? Have they massed their artillery elsewhere, and only keeping up this furious crash of rifle fire on the right as a blind?" A serious student of this battle, Sid tells me to bide my time and just watch what happens. Opposed as I am to war and violence, I feel like a cadet in the Military Academy.

To the front, Confederate skirmishers and

sharpshooters are still at work picking off Union officers who dare expose themselves. On the right, the Union artillery continues to boom, doubled and redoubled again. Suddenly, amidst the rumble and roar, a cheer is heard, and Confederate troops come charging through the trees. Union gunners measure their response solely by the sound of the spirited voices, then discharge. The line is broken for only a moment or two, and then it is reformed and the charge resumes. The carnage unfolding before us is both sickening and at the same time amazing. "Ride over to General Meade," General Howard instructs one of his aids, "and tell him the fighting on the right seems more terrific than ever and appears to be swinging somewhat toward the center, but that we know little or nothing of how the battle goes, and ask him if he has any orders." A few moments later, the aid returns. "The troops are to stand to arms, and watch the front."

A concentration of Confederate artillery fire meant to silence Union batteries and eliminate resistance from the slope is unleashed, but the Union troops are not unprepared, and a tornado of death sweeps over the fields. After two hours of fierce fighting, the Union defenders still maintain their positions; so the Confederates stand down for the present to reserve both energy and ammunition for the greater battle yet to come.

The final attack comes sooner than expected—and wider, too! Two hundred and fifty rebel cannons unleash their fury on the Union forces, causing mayhem and doom. General Longstreet and General A.P. Hill follow up the artillery attack with thousands in the front line, and countless reserves behind them. Union General Howard issues a command for his men to lie down, and for the batteries of cannon to cease firing. Apparently, the Confederates believe they have silenced the Union troops, and charge. Still, the cannons remain silent, and the infantrymen hold their positions without firing. Not until the Confederate forces are so close as to see the determined expressions on their faces does the entire infantry corps spring up and discharge a rain of steely death. This is face-to-face, fire-in-the-eyes, to the death, cold steel combat.

The final, desperate Confederate charge comes at four o'clock in the afternoon. Gathering all their strength, the Confederates mean to wipe out Union resistance once and for all.

The Rebel line stretches miles to the left, in magnificent array, Picket's division of General Longstreet's corps the strongest of any and at the front. The rebels hold back until they reach the Emmitsburg road, then open fire with ferocity. Again, the Union defenders are ordered to hold their fire. The Rebels—three lines deep—come into point black range. Then, finally, the order is given, and eighteen thousand guns unleash a rush of leaden death. The frontline falters, but a second moves into place. The Union resisters are not up to the assault.

Up to the rifle pits and over the barricades, the momentum of their charge carries them onward. The Union line is pushed behind the big guns as the Confederate attackers bayonet the gunners and raise their flag over the captured artillery. But in their zeal, the Confederates have penetrated to a fatal point, and a storm of grape and canister tears its way from man to man, marking its track with corpses all along their line. "They have exposed themselves to the guns on the western slope of Cemetery Hill," Sid tells me. "And that exposure has sealed their fate!"

Over the fields, the escaped remnants of the charging lines fall back—the battle is over, a fruitless sacrifice.

"OMG!" I say breathlessly to Sid. "I had no idea…"

"Such atrocities are better forgotten, perhaps," he consoles. Then he reconsiders: "No, they should never be forgotten," he says. "Because if we allow ourselves to forget them, we become vulnerable to repeating them. As history has shown…"

"It almost meant the end of America," I observe.

"If it were not for the resolution of President Lincoln, it well might have meant the end," Sid affirms.

"How could they do such a thing?" I ask, bewildered.

"This is what can happen when a culture becomes fractured along ideological lines," he says.

"Do you think it could happen again?" I ask.

"I'm sorry to say, Fizzy Oceans, it *always* happens again."

"Let's get out of here, Sid. I'm feeling sick to my stomach."

"Wait!" Sid implores. "I have something else I want to show you."

"Does it involve guns and cannons and dying people?" I ask wearily.

"It does and it doesn't," he says. "Come along now. And trust me. If you want to really understand war, this is something you *should* see."

Whoosh…

Sid furnishes me with the coordinates to a place in Virtual Philadelphia. The REP into which we transfer was built and is maintained by the U.S. Army.

"In 2008," Sid tells me, "the U.S. Army closed five recruiting centers in Philadelphia and replaced them with this thirteen-million-dollar, fourteen thousand, five hundred square foot Army Experience Center."

What lies before me is similar to any vast gaming parlor, or more specifically the now famous Apple Store, because that is what this placed was partially modeled after. Here kids, thirteen and up, come to play on X-boxes and PC gaming stations, for free. The recruitment officer explains to boys barely out of adolescence, "These are simulated rifles; they are not real rifles." Watching the boys playing at the consoles, I say, 'Thank God for that!' because these boys play the war games with both zeal and cunning. Recruiters circulate among the contestants, giving not only gaming advice, but also less than subtle suggestions that in just a few years they could be experiencing the real thing.

"Have you signed up for one of our tournaments?" asks a recruiter.

"I signed up for two," a young boy answers.

Major Harry X. Dullwit, Jr. explains to us that, "Video games are never going to replicate the real thing. This is just a sampling experience, to pique interest and encourage young men to learn more about what we do."

"These are simulated rifles; they are not real rifles…"

"We have what young Americans want and like," says Captain Jeremy Archer. "They like video games, and that's why we're here."

"Did you sign up for one of our tournaments?"

"These are simulated rifles; they are not real rifles…"

And next to the gaming stations are life-size simulators featuring war machines such as Humvees and helicopters. Private Chuck Norgate says, "I came here to play video games, but after a few days I knew I had to do more than just play games. So I talked with the recruiters and signed up for the Army."

"Have you signed up for one of our tournaments?"

Suddenly, a group of protesters enters the center. With signs held high they chant, "Shame, shame, shame, war is not a game!"

Which I know all-too-well after the past three days at Gettysburg.

Sarah Klein tells us, "My thirteen-year-old boy loves video games, but this is nothing but a recruitment tool used by the military."

"Please push the re-set button."

A moment later security personnel move in and begin arresting the demonstrators.

'Cyber-killing is not child's play!' reads one sign. It is confiscated by the police and immediately crushed.

Says Major Dullwit: "Kids are smart enough to

understand the difference between virtual reality and Iraq."

"Have you signed up for one of our tournaments? Please push the re-set button."

Of course I know very well that the proverbial line between the physical world and the virtual world is a thin one. I'm sure that after spending time in VL, you also know this to be true. My question to Sid is this: "Do these kids *really* know it, too?"

"Please press the re-set button."

The next place Sid has decided I need to see to round out my exploration of war is another cyber-center, this one in the Nevada desert. He furnishes me some highly classified coordinates, and I engage my transfer device.

Whoosh...

At an unnamed flight control center soldiers dressed in battle fatigues enter an air-conditioned computer lab to pilot drone aircraft thousands of miles away. Sid poses the question, "What does it mean, psychologically, to wage war where one side is on a physical battlefield, and the other is on a virtual one?"

On a monitor a drone approaches its target in Iraq, seven thousand, five hundred miles away from where the 'pilot' controls it. A moment later, the target, a single male, is spotted on a rooftop. The 'pilot' has been monitoring his movements from a satellite camera all day, most of which the 'target' has spent on a playground playing soccer with children. But now he has been spotted and isolated on the rooftop. Why is he there? Undetermined. What is he doing? Undetermined. The decision is made. The 'pilot' centers the 'target' in his crosshairs. He counts down, and then squeezes a trigger. An explosion occurs on screen. When the smoke clears, the target is no longer there, nor is the building.

Sid tells me, "The number of drones has multiplied in recent years and the Pentagon is clamoring for more. These planes are extremely precise, as you can see, and there is no cost in human life—at least not on one side…"

"The biggest problem," one of the pilots tells me, "is a feeling of detachment from the aircraft."

What? I can hardly believe what I am hearing.

"It's just a three dimensional problem," he continues.

And I'm worried about sensuality loss in VL?

Says Captain Archer: "We had intel that there was a 'bad guy' riding around on a motorcycle. We located him by virtual reconnaissance, and sure enough, we found him at a meeting of 'bad people'." (I added the single quotes; I thought I'd better tell you that.)

Real live aircraft; real live mission; and real live bombs. Once a drone pilot steps into the GCS, he is then immersed in the theatre (figuratively and literally). Once he deploys his payload, he sees the bomb going into a building, he sees the explosion, but he cannot see the aftermath. *He can never see the aftermath*… At the end of his shift, he leaves the control center and drives his air-conditioned, army-issued car to his suburban home in Las Vegas where he has dinner with his wife (like any other businessman or tradesman) then helps his children with their homework.

All in a day's work…

Crisis… What crisis?

Art, money, religion and war: I have studied each in some detail now, met with brilliant and influential people—even some who actually took part in PL historical events—and what have I learned?

I have come to the conclusion that each of these influential ideas—whether a concept, a discipline, or a commodity, and whether noble or ignoble—is highly political. That's right! Which art is accepted and which is rejected: largely political. Whether money is real (like gold) or fabricated, like the bucks that Sharky Overbite threw into the air that nobody seemed to want anymore, or even like the greenshoots in my VL account, it's value is determined by consent or agreement: politics. Is religion political, too? You bet! It is probably the most political of all, even including war. No doubt Jesus was a pretty righteous dude, but he got the political shaft—big time! (Believe me, the cross was no joke, and we each have to carry it sooner or later.) Gandhi got it in the seat, too. So did the Dalai Llama. And what about war? War is certainly political, though it is seldom fought over ideology; rather it is almost always economic, in one sense or another. Even the first American Civil War was fought largely for economic solvency. Ideas and ideals always masquerade as war's cause, but behind the scenes the politicos pull the strings, and also reap the spoils. In war, greed goes giddy even as the lizard darts its tongue at its prey—all humanity! I wouldn't steer you wrong here: I know these things to be true.

What crisis, you ask? *What crisis?*

Well, let me put it this way: if I can just get up off the concrete and wash all the fish guts away, I'll be fine. We'll all be fine. Just fine!

12
IS THE GLASS HALF EMPTY?
OR IS THE GLASS HALF FULL?

I'VE BEEN THINKING lately about whether I would define myself as an optimist or a pessimist. In PL, I am unemployed, unless you count my gig at the fish market (which is not exactly what I'd call an upwardly mobile position), I live alone and more or less forgotten in a small apartment where I can barely afford the rent, and my family and friends are scattered to the four winds; but in VL, I am a property owner (the Van Gogh REP), a book publisher, and I associate with all sorts of interesting and enlightened characters, both living and dead. So, I guess the answer to my question about optimism or pessimism depends on which world, and also to which personality, I am referring. Admittedly, Amy Birkenstock does not have much to be optimistic about, whereas Fizzy Oceans is sitting on top of the world.

When I ask both Crystal and Kiz the same question, (Are you an optimist, or are you a pessimist?), each has an interesting (and somewhat complex) answer. Crystal relates that Sonja's PL existence is a pretty comfortable one. She is by no means rich, yet she wants for nothing important. She lives in a large apartment in Copenhagen; she has a secure job, plenty of good food to eat, she can visit a doctor whenever she needs one, she has a respectful and loving relationship with her family, a good social life with friends that she sees regularly, and she even takes vacations to Sweden during summer and Switzerland for skiing in winter.

In VL, however, Crystal confesses to being a bit frustrated. Books are very important to her, and she feels disheartened that so few people value the written word as they once did. "Everything worth knowing is written in books," she says. "Whether you're talking about philosophy or physics, ethics or endocrinology; it's all there. Our history as a race, and our legacy as a civilization, is written in the volumes of the Ages." Which is why she remains so dedicated to Open Books and to VL. "Am I an optimist or a pessimist?" she reverberates my original question. "I'd say, over all, I'm an optimist. Yes, I'm an optimist!"

Kizmet's answer is grounded in spiritual rather than in physical terms, true to the character I know in VL. Cassandra lives in a Navajo Hogan in the high desert of Northern Arizona. She works as an administrator at a Navajo school. Her job is both frustrating and satisfying. Most of her friends are Native Americans. She has a sister who is a nun. They rarely speak. Her parents are both dead. She is married but does not live with her husband anymore. She takes part in many Indian ceremonies (particularly Hopi), practices traditional tribal medicine (which in the case of Native Americans means religion), and she eats mostly foods that she grows herself (which in Arizona means corn, beans, squash, chili, tomatoes, hominy and a few roots). She likes to make tortillas on an open fire, Indian sweat lodges, and she also likes to gaze at the stars on clear Arizona nights through a telescope she owns. She goes often to California to swim in the Pacific, and sometimes she goes gambling in Las Vegas. Her clothes are funky-chic, and her skin is brown as wheat toast.

Kizmet, on the other hand, is still new to VL. When I ask whether she has really found herself there, she answers, "I'm not sure if I'll ever really find myself in VL, at least not in the same way that you and Crystal have found yourselves. It's true that I find VL a bit surreal, but that's not an impediment; my physical life is a bit surreal, too. What could be more surreal than the Hopi Snake Dance?" she asks. "What's that?" I want to know. Kiz smiles and says, "I'll tell you about it sometime… *Or maybe I can even take you there courtesy of VL!*" As for whether she considers herself an optimist or a pessimist, Kizmet relates, "I never know what will happen, and I find myself surprised and delighted by life's diversity. But I also find modern life to be a bit tragic. Negligence is a big problem. And greed, too! Most of what we really need is in our midst. Nature is glorious, and She wants to take care of us if we will only allow her to do it. Too often, we think we are smarter than the Natural Order. That's where we get into trouble. Most of us want far too much. We become exploitive, and in so doing, we become destructive. That's why I live with Native Americans, in the desert. Nothing much to exploit there: in Rough Rock, it's all about subsistence. And even that has a much different meaning than it does elsewhere. I have learned how to be in harmony with the earth and the heavens, and I am happy about that. So, I guess you could say that I am pretty pessimistic about how most people live in PL, but I am optimistic because I have found a different way of living. And, a different way of seeing…"

For Sonja, PL is a measured and satisfying existence; whereas Crystal finds VL a bit frustrating. Cassandra has more or less traded a modern PL life for one far more elemental, and she takes comfort in a more spiritual or causal lifestyle; whereas Kizmet looks at VL as another alternate reality, a sandbox in which she sometimes plays and experiments with playmates like Crystal and me.

What do I think? Is the glass half empty? Or is the glass half full? Sometimes I can't even seem to find the glass—that's what I think. Clearly, more research is needed to answer my own inquiry.

(Earth)

So off I go again, this time to Pakistan (will my search ever end?).

In the VL mountain village of Asama Bashir, I meet a woman named Edina Bassan who tells me what she went through in the massive earthquake of 2005.

"At first it was a mild shaking," she relates, "then stones were falling from the sky. I didn't know what to do. I stood in my house, frozen like a statue. Then the ceiling collapsed. My house was leveled, and I was buried underneath the rubble. I could not move. My eyes and ears were so full of dust that I could neither see nor hear. My shoes were torn off my feet, and my clothes were shredded. With only one finger free, I pointed to the daylight. Would I live or die? I did not know, but I begged for help. Allah heard my prayer and saved me. It took the men twelve hours to dig me out me of the rubble."

"Weren't you scared?" I ask.

"My first thought was that we had been bombed. Then I realized it was an earthquake. I became very upset with Allah for making such a horrible thing happen, but then I came to my senses and understood that it was Allah that had allowed me to survive. So I could struggle forward. Praise Allah!"

As we walk through the REP, Edina shows me men making coffins. Though they work day and night, they cannot hope to keep up with the demand as bodies of both young and old are brought in by the truckload.

In another part of what was once a vibrant city, thousands now live in tents. They cook over open fires. Children are malnourished and dehydrated. Some suffer from cholera. Others are simply dazed and uncommunicative. Maybe they are paralyzed from fear, or maybe they are simply so disoriented that nothing makes sense anymore beyond the arms of their mothers. Some have lost everyone, including their mothers.

"After the quake," Edina tells me, "the rains came in torrents. It was monsoon season, but we had no adequate shelter. We had no food (other than what Islamic Relief brought us). We had little water. People fought over what food there was, but the women—especially the older ones—were helpless. When winter came we were still in tents, and we were so cold. Many died of infections and exposure. Some simply gave up. One must always have hope if life is to have any meaning at all. This is the lesson that Allah taught me through this catastrophe."

We walk further, toward the edge of what was once the city of Asama Bashir. It is twilight now, and the horizon glows a particularly rich shade of orange. When I remark to Edina on the beauty of the sunset, she says, "It has been that way ever since the earthquake. Some say it is because of all the dust in the air, but I know it is a representation of the blood that was shed by those we lost in those twenty-eight seconds."

Skip ahead five years and Pakistan is again devastated, this time by floods. The rain began in July, as it usually does when the monsoon comes to the Pakistani regions of Khyber Pakhtunkhwa, Sindh, Punjab and Balochistan. In the wake of the flood, thousands of people have died and over a million homes have been destroyed. More than twenty-one million people were injured or made homeless as a result of the flooding, exceeding the combined total of individuals affected by the 2004 Indian Ocean tsunami, the

2005 Kashmir earthquake and the 2010 Haiti earthquake. Approximately one-fifth of Pakistan's total land area is now underwater.

The flooding is attributed to unprecedented monsoon rains caused by La Niña. In June, the Pakistan Meteorological Department cautioned that urban and flash flooding could occur from July to September in the northern parts of the country. The same department recorded above-average rainfall in the months of July and August 2010, and monitored the flood wave progression. Discharge levels recorded were comparable to those seen during the floods of 1988, 1995, and 1997.

New Scientist Magazine has attributed the cause of this exceptional rainfall to the freezing of the jet stream, a phenomenon that also caused an unprecedented heat wave and wildfires in Russia.

Many towns and villages are not accessible, and communications have been disrupted. In some areas, the water level is five and a half meters high. People wait on rooftops for aid to arrive. The Karakoram Highway, which connects Pakistan with China, is closed after the collapse of a vital bridge. Floodwaters have destroyed much of the health care infrastructure in the worst affected areas, leaving inhabitants especially vulnerable to water-borne disease. In Sindh, the Indus River burst its banks near Sukkur, submerging the village of Mor Khan Jatoi; an absence of law and order allows looters the opportunity to ransack abandoned homes using boats.

I am with a small group of doctors from *Medecins Sans Frintieres* (Doctors Without Borders). Dr. Kristina Nesvig from Norway heads the team. We are traveling south by van to the region of Peshawar. The difficult roads make it a longer and more tiring journey than it should be. It is still the early hours of the morning and were it not for the blasting AC in the car, we would already be under severe stress from the scorching heat. We are traveling to the Village of Tangi, which is sixty kilometers north of

Peshawar. Assessments have already been made and the results, we learn, are not good. People there are waiting for our arrival with great anticipation. They have been told a medical team will arrive soon.

The aftermath of the flood is unbelievable. I see the rooftop of a building just above water level. It appears to have been a hotel, but now it is all but underwater. In other areas, the level of water has receded, leaving nothing intact.

"In this region alone," Kris tells us, "Eleven thousand people are already dead and approximately five million are homeless. People are living in graveyards, or on roadsides—anywhere they can. They have no food, no water, no shelter and no medicines."

Though heartfelt and filled with concern, Dr. Nesvig's words are unnecessary, for all around us the devastation is obvious and far-reaching. People wander, dazed and confused and in muddy clothes, from place to place. Everything they once owned is gone. Water and mud are everywhere, and I wonder how we will ever make it to Tangi.

Yet even as we are all but submerged in Pakistan, I am reminded of the famous poem by Samuel Taylor Coleridge, 'The Ancient Mariner': "Water, water, everywhere, And all the boards did shrink; Water, water, everywhere, Nor any drop to drink." Such irony is not lost on me, and I mentally concoct my own version, equally dire for a different time: "Drowning here in sultry heat, the mortal cry of children's thirst; As fires ravage Russian peat, the Earth I fear is cursed!" Well, no poet am I, that's for sure, but I do know one thing: we as humans proclaim our superiority and our sovereignty over nature, but our proclamation is a hollow one indeed. As I look around it is obvious that in the end it is the Earth, not man, who will have the final word. And much too soon, I fear…

Arriving in Tangi, we are directed to an abandoned building where a makeshift hospital is to be established.

Dr. Nesvig immediately designates one area as a de facto triage center, and then establishes a surgery inside the cleanest area of the building. Patients begin arriving immediately, and I act as a processor. With no medical training whatsoever, it is my job to establish which patients are most in need of care. It is an impossible job, but I persist. The line is endless. As the day wears on I am drenched in sweat. My hair hangs limply over my forehead and my face. When a woman with an infant stands before me, I lead her without pause into Dr. Nesvig's surgery. The eleven-month-old baby boy is limp and unresponsive in his mother's arms. Dr. Nesvig tenderly takes the infant from his forlorn mother and assesses his condition.

The mother tells Dr. Nesvig that her beloved Ali has been in this horrible condition for five days. He cannot swallow, he has severe diarrhea and he is vomiting. Kris's eyes reveal a dire prognosis.

"He is suffering from severe dehydration," Kris tells the mother. "We will send him directly to Dr. Menendez, the pediatrician."

I accompany baby Ali and his mother to a different room in the building where Dr. José Menendez is ministering to more than fifty other children. But baby Ali is given immediate attention, as his condition is deemed critical. He is placed on a fluid drip to hydrate and nourish him. He is also given Kaopectate to stop his diarrhea, and Imodium to stop his dry heaves. Even so, Dr. Menendez assesses his chances for survival at one in five.

On our first day alone at the Tangi Hospital, we see more than two thousand patients. To say that the numbers are overwhelming would be a ridiculous understatement; and while my own impression is no doubt given to hyperbole, I am crushed by the feeling that I am watching not only the tragedy of one village, or one country, but possibly the death of an entire race. My sleep this night is dreamless.

And as the eighteen-hour days drag on, and one humid

misfortune after another passes my station begging for help and refuge, my mind goes numb and my limbs ache, my temples pulse, my feet swell. On which level of Dante's Inferno is this tragedy manifest, I ask myself? Is mercy itself blinded by the intense reflection of an unrelenting sun upon fields and fields of water once grain? Are we as Humans not more than mere clay in the hands of the ephemeral? Need is eternal; work is my salvation.

At Dr. Nesvig's surgery, we receive word from the mother that baby Ali is doing better. He is now conscious and he is able to take water by mouth. "Praise Allah! Praise Allah!" she prays. We, too, praise Allah…

We see a man who has lost his sight, a woman whose lower legs and feet are gangrenous, a ten-year-old child whose tongue is so swollen he cannot eat or drink. Dr. Nesvig stitches a man's scalp back onto his head, then proceeds without a moment's rest to treat a patient whose bowels are enflamed and blocked. We admit a woman who is having a severe diabetic reaction, and another who is in labor. No departments here, no specialists or interns or orderlies. One doctor per one thousand patients, that's the rule at this hospital, and sleep when and where you can.

By the end of the first week, it feels like I have been here a year. By the end of the second week, it feels like a lifetime. More doctors arrive. Food arrives from Islamic Relief. Nothing glorious, of course: bulk grains, canned goods, orange juice. The doctors give away their rations to those more in need. I sometimes forget to eat. I have ceased to feel anything as I watch and administrate the parade of misery.

Then, on the eighth day (or is it the ninth?), I learn that baby Ali has died. Yes, it can even happen in VL. My throat closes and I break into tears. I go running through the village. My hysteria is barely noticed by those whose suffering is paramount to mine. When I reach the water— the blessed, cursed water—I bathe myself in my own grief.

Whoosh…

OMG! I need a break (maybe you do, too). To regain my balance. So I'm meeting Igloo Iceman at Dirty Nellie's Pub. It's nice to be back in a VL REP where buildings aren't falling down and people aren't dying from Cholera. Dirty Nellie's is a sanctuary, just as VL is my personal safe haven. Even before Iggy arrives I order two pints of Guinness. I know it is his preferred brew. As for me, I don't care (because I can't taste it anyway).

To tell the truth, I'm still feeling weak and a bit overwhelmed by what I saw in virtual Pakistan. The devastation and human suffering—whether in VL or in PL—is more than I could have imagined. Seeing babies dying everyday of dehydration and dysentery, and even from diseases that the doctors could not easily identify, has not only taken my (physical) strength, but also exhausted my will. It's going to take me a long time, if ever, to recover fully from what I experienced there.

When Iggy drops into Dirty Nellie's I am very happy to see him. That's the way it is with old friends. And Iggy is one of my oldest and best friends here in VL. We have known one another since the beginning—at least since shortly after I arrived in VL—and we have always felt a unique connection. Not because we are alike (after all, he lives in Greenland on a melting glacier, and I live in Seattle and work at a stinking fish market) but because we see the world in a similar way. And that's what's really important, isn't it?

"You're a sight for sore eyes," I tell him as he maneuvers his giant body into a seat at the table.

"You don't say?" he smiles.

"You have no idea what I've been through during the past forty years…" Of course I'm referring not only to the time I spent in Pakistan but also the time I spent in the Sinai with the Jews, and in the Holy Land with Jesus, not to mention the time I spent in India with Gandhi, and with the Dalai Llama, and in Turkey with the Dervishes; then, of course, there was Gettysburg!

"In VL, time goes by in the wink of an eye," Iggy concedes.

"Or maybe there is no such thing as time," I offer.

"I see you've ordered the Guinness," he says.

"It's on me," I tell him.

"Thanks." He takes a long pull of the black beer then wipes froth from his mouth.

"How's the Ark coming along?" I ask.

"Almost ready," he says.

"So you're really going to do it. You're going to leave Greenland and sail that thing into forever…"

"Sail it right off a cliff, so to speak," he confirms.

"Why not?" I say. "The world is going to hell anyway."

"Or melting away, in my case."

"Right."

As we talk I'm looking at Iggy's hands. They appear rough and calloused. No doubt the result of his carpentry. Similarly, all the muscles of his upper body seem even more developed than when I last saw him. In his eyes I see a far-away look, but of course Greenland is a far-away place, and Iggy has always been a dreamer.

"I got the IMs you sent from the Middle East," he says.

"I had to share what I was going through with someone," I tell him.

"What about Crystal and Kiz? Are they aware of your 'travels'?"

"Yeah, they know all about it."

"Most people I know in VL see it as a 'future' experience," he relates, "but you have taken a step back in time, Fizzy. Don't you think it's a little risky to be walking through history?"

"Mostly, I've just been an observer," I explain. "Just along for the ride, if you know what I mean."

Iggy shrugs as he drains half a glassful of beer. "I can't say that I—or any of us here in VL—actually have a grasp of time anymore. Who's to say what's past, present or future? Not me, that's for sure."

"There are just too many questions in my mind," I try to explain. "Things I just have to find out. Things I feel I have to *know*…"

"Right now, my gig is the *un*known," he admits.

"But here in VL, even the unknown can be experienced."

"If you have the courage…"

"Oh, I've got plenty of that. Too much, probably."

"I know," he says. "I was thinking about inviting you to be First Mate on the Ark."

I smile at the suggestion. "I'm no sailor," I beg off. "I get sea sick in my own bathtub."

"Just a suggestion," he says. "No worries, I have somebody else in mind for the job."

"Anyone I know?" I ask.

"Are you kidding me, Fiz? You know everybody in VL."

"Hardly," I dismiss. "VL is a big place. And getting bigger every day."

"No doubt thanks to enthusiasts like you. And like Crystal…" Iggy finishes off his beer and settles back in his chair. "So, what's next for you?"

"I've got a few more adventures of my own planned before I settle down," I tell him.

"You don't say?"

"I'm just taking a little break to rest up. Then I'm back on the road," I confirm. "I know I still have so much to see, so much to learn…"

"Where to next?" Iggy asks.

"North Africa, I think. I'll keep you posted."

"Please do," he says.

"Then I think I'm off to Iowa," I add.

"Iowa?"

"To research soil contamination," I tell him.

Iggy smiles and shakes his head in wonderment. "You're one of a kind, Fizzy Oceans," he says. "Nothing will stop you here in VL."

I know that Iggy is right; I have a grander purpose to fulfill here in virtual reality. And time grows short…

Note: It's 4:00 a.m. in Seattle and I (Amy Birkenstock) have just finished listening to a radio interview with a guy named Texe Marrs, and he says that the BP oilrig explosion in the Gulf was no accident. (Here we go again; the Mother of all conspiracy theories.) But wait! Maybe this guy, Texe, has a point. He says that the derrick was purposely blown up to keep world oil prices artificially high. Can it be? He says that a month after President Obama took office he ordered laws to be changed to exempt BP from certain environmental regulations. Can it be? He says that in the late thirties oilrigs were purposely blown up and destroyed for all time in Azerbaijan by the then new (Communist) Russian government for the same reason. He also says that the three main entities involved in that drilling venture were the Rockefellers, the Rothschilds and the Nobel family, and that because they knew that development of what was then the world's largest untapped oil reserve would plummet oil prices, they blew the thing to Kingdom Come. And that is what he says happened in the Gulf, too. He says that the oil field underneath the Gulf is the largest known reserve in the world. And that there's plenty more underground beneath the Dakotas and Wyoming and Montana. And if those reserves were developed, the world would be awash in cheap oil. So why would the American government not want to exploit its own reserves? Simple, says Texe Marrs. It's because now that the US has gained control of the Iraqi oil fields (the world's second largest reserve already under development), they want to ensure the price set by the oil cartel because they are shipping the oil (through northern Israeli ports and southern Lebanese ports) to China, a country without any significant oil reserves. So of course they want the price of oil to remain high. And this guy, Texe Marrs, also says that an underwater explosive device—not one like was used in WWII—washed up on the beach in Alabama. Some of the BP clean-up crew found it there, and the area was immediately sealed off by security personnel. Even the TV stations could not gain access to the area to report the incident. But Texe Marrs says he has film of the thing. Imagine that! And now that the rupture has been capped, and the clean-up is nearly done, he says that the chemical used to disperse the sludgy mess, COREXIT, is so toxic that people in the Gulf States are throwing up blood, and all sorts of other unspeakable things… Can it be? He says that in New Orleans it is literally raining oil. Can it be? He has documentation that the levels of toxicity caused by COREXIT are some three thousand to five thousand times the acceptable limit established by the EPA. Can it be? And that the sludge is just sitting at the bottom of the Gulf (along with dead dolphins and whales and fish), and that it is only a matter of time before the current carries it around the tip of Florida and across the northern Atlantic all the way to the fjords of Norway. And God knows, those folks up there like their Halibut!

Whoosh???

My arrival in VL Darfur, Sudan is like touching down on another planet. Or maybe it is similar to landing on the moon, except that there are homeless, starving people everywhere, bombs are going off (or just lying around unexploded), villages have been pillaged and then burned to the ground, most of the men have gone to war, many of the women have been raped, and virtually all the children are sick—especially the babies. The first woman I encounter lives on a bundle of straw—no roof over her head, but she is alive. Her family has perished, she tells me.

By prior arrangement, I am supposed to meet a man called Dr. Deng. But how will I ever locate him? I type his name into my VL search bar, but for some reason the system cannot locate him. But I'm sure he is here somewhere. I ask several people if they know where I might find him, but I am met only with blank stares. Such expressions disarm me, because I know that they are the expression of hope's retreat. I make my way through this camp of refugees living in huts constructed of twigs and mud. Women cook what they have (mostly bulk grains and dried beans—maybe a few onions or other roots) over pitiful open fires. Water is scarce. It never rains in this desert. The current drought has lasted forty years or so, and many believe it will be permanent. The few animals that survive—goats, sheep, chickens and dogs—are little more than skeletons. They are not worth killing for their meat. There aren't even any birds flying overhead.

As for Dr. Deng, perhaps he is nothing more than a figment of my imagination, another merciful archetype in a world totally without mercy. Mother Theresa worked her entire life in such degraded circumstances, and she became a saint. The good doctor, if he even exists, will in all probability have a very different legacy; he will probably be executed by Janjaweed, or by Khartoum backed militias, or by the police, or by some government-sanctioned group of mercenaries. It looks as if I might be on my own here, which is not an encouraging prospect.

Wandering amongst the displaced multitudes, I become lost. Which, in effect, renders me right at home, because here everyone is lost. And here—which indeed is nowhere—they make a home, because their homes have been lost. I am the only white-skinned person in this sea of Black humanity.

As I reach the center of the camp—at least I think it's the center—I suddenly see my contact, Dr. Deng. He is a bald, diminutive man dressed in African clothing. He looks as if he could use a good meal, or even a cool drink of water. He is bent over an ailing child, whose bed is his mother's lap, as he tries to treat some untreatable illness, except he has no equipment other than a stethoscope, nor medicines other than herbal concoctions.

Dr. Deng's effort is noble, no doubt, but probably hopeless. I approach the treatment area and stand outside the circle of friends and family. I wait until he is finished with the child before approaching.

"Dr. Deng?" I inquire.

The doctor turns to me. The appearance of my white skin is apparently startling to him. "You are Miss Fizzy?" he asks.

"Yes," I tell him.

"I have been expecting you," he says calmly.

"I didn't know how to find you," I tell him.

"Everyone here knows how to find me," he says. "I am the only doctor for nearly seven thousand people."

"I can barely believe what I'm seeing," I say breathlessly. "I spent time in Pakistan, after the flood. I was there with a group from Doctors Without Borders. We worked round the clock. That was very bad. But this! This is something else altogether."

"Please," implores Dr. Deng, "don't hyperventilate. I don't even have a paper bag to give you."

"I'm okay," I tell him. "Really…"

"You'll get used to it," he says. "Or you won't…"

"How can such suffering be possible?" I ask Dr. Deng.

The doctor sighs deeply. I can see frustration written all over his face. "Politics," he says. "Stupid, racist politics!"

"I've read up on the political situation," I tell him.

"So you know the western version," he says with a bit of sarcasm in his tone.

"What do you mean?" I ask.

"The story of Darfur is not as simple as they write it in the *New York Times* or the *Guardian* in London. The West has its own interests in Somalia."

"Oil?" I ask.

Folding his arms across his chest, Dr. Deng says, "So you know about that…"

"I've read a little," I tell him.

319

"But it's not that simple—not like it is in Iraq. This conflict goes back hundreds of years. It is basically racial in nature. In the north you have an Arab-Muslim culture, always superior in its views of the southern African Christians. The most recent version of the Pan-Arabic philosophy came directly from Libya. The irony here, though, is that virtually the entire population is a bastard race. That's what happens over centuries. Now, the Arabic nomads want to make slaves of the southern African farmers. The southerners, in the name of the Darfur Liberation Front and the Justice and Equality Movement, have risen in defense of themselves against the Arab-leaning government. The president, Omar el Bashir, countered with a force composed mainly of the official Sudanese military and police, as well as the Janjaweed, a Sudanese militia group recruited mostly from the Arab Abbala tribes of the northern Rizeigat region in Sudan; these tribes are mainly camel-herding nomads. The other combatants are made up of rebel groups, notably the SLM/A and the JEM, recruited primarily from the non-Arab Muslim Fur, Zaghawa, and Masalit ethnic groups."

"So where does the oil come in?"

"Yes, that is interesting. You see, in the western press the Americans in particular, and the Europeans to a lesser extent, are always characterized as the peacemakers, but from the point of view of the Middle Eastern world, they are in fact quite the opposite; they are perceived as conquerors, intervening in Middle Eastern countries with significant oil reserves, and which already have some degree of discord within their cultures. The greater aim of such western powers like America and Britain is seen by Arabs to be a systematic destabilization of governments and cultures, their final aim being to fracture those countries and render them more or less powerless, thereby making it impossible for the people to defend their interests in their own natural resources. When the plan works, the western governments and big multi-national businesses profit handsomely, and to make the booty all the sweeter, they have a native slave class to do much of the so-called heavy lifting. At any rate, countries such as Iraq and Sudan are more or less helpless to this kind of hegemony. These are simple people: nomads and shepherds and farmers. Ignorance and prejudice rules the situation, and the Sudanese people end up fighting one another, while the real culprit, the invisible one, waits to claim the spoils."

"Are you sure about all that?" I ask Dr. Deng.

"I'm just telling you how I see it, and how many in the Middle East see it. Now, I must tend to my next patient. Excuse me, Fizzy Oceans."

Dr. Deng bends to examine yet another child, the next in a never-ending line of innocents. He presses his stethoscope to the child's chest, and he must not like what he hears, because his expression falls as he removes the earpieces from his ears. He brushes flies away for the girl's head. A gust of wind blows sand in everyone's face. Dr. Deng whispers something in the mother's ear, and she immediately takes the child away.

Into the gathering comes an emaciated man, his black skin looking like leather draped over his bones. On his back he carries a heavy burden of sticks and twigs, firewood collected God-knows-where, which he wants to sell for food and water. But there is no water—only dust and misery. He moves along, hoping to find a buyer for his wood.

I have been to refugee camps before, but nothing like this. This is Hell on Earth—or at least Hell in VL. What's the difference? None, I think. Darfur in VL is as distressed as Darfur in PL.

And I am choking… Is it from the dust, or is it from disgust? I don't know, and I don't care. Again, what's the difference? I feel ashamed of the Human Race, of its greed, of its ignorance, of its insensitivity. Maybe we do not deserve to survive as a species. Maybe it would be better if the earth flicked us off its arm as we flick off a mosquito. Maybe She would be happier if dolphins or whales were running the show. I don't know; I just wish for sanity and a bit of compassion. I wish we saw ourselves as a family—the Family of Man. Does that sound hokey to you? Maybe a bit dated or cliché? Again, who cares how it sounds if it would make a difference, if it would alleviate suffering, if it would consign such events as Darfur to the Hell in which they belong, never to occur again? But that's not going to happen, is it? No, there is too much to be gained; and too much to be lost, too. Yet I cannot help but feel that while even one person suffers such indignity, and such misery, that we all suffer a similar fate. Maybe not in PL, or even in VL, but suffer we do the degradation of omission and selfishness. We have lost ourselves, I fear. We are beyond redemption.

One click and I am away from Sudan and in the heart of America's grain belt, western Iowa. I am here to meet my friend Randy Skinner, who has agreed to take me on a tour of his Farm Town REP. Standing amidst the scenic rolling hills planted with tall corn swaying in the summer breeze, I wait for Randy to arrive. Were I in PL, the scene would be a sentient one, even intoxicating; but alas, here in VL it is but a recreation of something that once existed, of something now gone and consigned to memory and to virtual experience, where the senses do not function and the corn itself is food only for nostalgia.

Here comes Randy now, tramping through the eye-high corn under a cerulean sky. His tall muscular body and suntanned face are a sight for my sore eyes. As he emerges from the cornstalks, I see that he is wearing blue dungarees, a plaid shirt and a straw hat. In his hand he holds a pitchfork.

"Hey, Fizzy! Welcome to Iowa!" he drawls.

"Hey, Randy. How's it going?"

"Happy as a pig in shit that you came," he tells me.

"Soo-ey!" I proclaim.

Randy looks me over and quickly determines that my clothes are not appropriate for my visit to Farm Town: "You look like you been through a twister, sister," he says. "Where you been hanging out, Hell's Kitchen?"

"Something like that," I tell him. "Darfur."

"What-fur?" he says.

"Western Somalia."

"I think I have some clothes for you back at the farmhouse. You can clean up there and get changed."

"I'm just glad to be someplace green," I tell him.

As we approach Randy's farmhouse in VL, it looks like a dream from out of the past. Situated in a large clearing with a venerable oak tree shading the entire front yard, the wooden house is substantial and dignified—broad at the shoulders, like its owner. It stands two stories high with the parlor, the kitchen, the dining room and the mudroom located on the ground floor and the bedrooms (each with its own dormer) and bathroom located on the second floor. The entire house is painted white with gray trim around the doors and windows. On the side of the house is a screened-in porch where cool drinks can be enjoyed on summer afternoons, or where Randy can sleep if it is a particularly hot night. The house is an exact replica of the one where he lived as a child. The PL/NL house was built in the 1880s, but it was finally torn down in 1992. "Not that there was anything wrong with it," he tells me, "but Archer Daniels Midland bought the land, and I guess they had no use for the house."

"That's a real shame, Randy," I say.

Randy shrugs. I know he is sad about the loss of his family's farm, and of the home where the Skinners lived for three generations, but he is also resigned to the present day situation. "I'm just glad that VL came along when it did," he says. "When there was still somebody around that remembers how it once was, somebody who actually cares…"

The clothes that Randy provides for me are hardly my usual style, but they seem quite appropriate for farm life. The dungarees fit my ass pretty well, and I've tied the tails of the plaid shirt together underneath my ribcage to form a pretty sexy halter top (not that I'm expecting anything to happen between Randy and me, because as I said a long time ago, I don't do sex in VL anymore). As I come down the stairs from the sewing room to the parlor, Randy greets me with a playful catcall, which I can't help but appreciate considering it's coming from this big, strapping, handsome farm boy. "Mind your manners," I tell him as I swagger my hips and click my tongue.

"So, I suppose you want to see my farm," he says to me.

"You bet," I tell him.

We go outside and climb into Randy's 4X4 Ford pickup. He starts the motor and takes off down a dirt road. On either side of us 'the corn is as high as an elephant's eye'. In the distance I can see grain elevators and a water tower. Nice props...

"I tried to make it exactly as it was," he tells me as we drive. "Exactly as I remember it..."

"When did it all begin to change?" I ask.

"Late seventies and early eighties," he relates. "Mostly, it was caused by politics. Embargos, subsidies, fuel prices, lending practices. You name it. Some folks like to blame Jimmy Carter, but the fix was in way before he came along. And don't forget, he was a farmer himself. Or, at least his folks were farmers... Back in the sixties when I was born—and a long time before that, too—virtually all the land in Iowa was privately held—family farms—some large, others smaller. But when the OPEC fuel embargo happened in the seventies, it kicked off a lot of delinquencies. You see most of these farmers were operating each year on the next year's money, so when the price of fuel skyrocketed, you can just imagine what happened. It kicked off even more borrowing. For machinery, for seeds and chemicals—you name it. So then the government, in its infinite wisdom, makes this treaty with the Russians to ship them millions of tons of wheat, because the Russian farmers weren't doing so well, and the people were facing a pretty hard winter. As usual, things went from bad to worse for the independent farmer. Before long, because of subsidies, it made more sense to plow the land under than to actually grow crops. If you'd driven down Interstate #80 in 1980, you would have seen one field after another plowed under for three hundred miles. And for anybody who was used to seeing Iowa like this—like I've recreated it—it was a shock. Anyway, one by one the independent farmers got into trouble with the banks, and before they really understood what was happening, they were getting foreclosed on and their equipment was being auctioned off. I can remember those auctions; they were not only sad, they were infuriating. Looking back on it, I'm surprised there wasn't some kind of farmer's revolt. But there wasn't, and most went quietly. They lost their farms and went to either Des Moines or Lincoln or even Chicago and got jobs in factories. That's what happened to my papa, except he lasted all of two years in the Berwyn, Illinois factory where they put him to work making air conditioners. I think my papa died of a broken heart. I think a lot of those farmers who lost their farms did…

"Anyway, once the banks had control of the properties, they started selling huge tracts of farmland off to companies like ADM and Heartland. Plenty of others, too. They were all waiting in line to bid on Iowa black dirt. Not just food producers, either. The list of Fortune 500s that now own PL Iowa is a long and auspicious one. Besides ADM, which is the largest property holder in the state, you got companies like Ajinomoto, Cargill, Diamond V Mills, Garst Seed Company, Heartland Pork Enterprises, Hy-Vee, Monsanto, Pioneer Hi-Bred International, and Quaker Oats. Which some might argue was not such a bad thing, since these companies employed some of the farmers that lost their own farms, and also because they had all the latest technology—not to mention all the money they needed for upgrades—and in the end productivity actually went up, at least for a while. Now it is on its way down again. Fact is that collective farming just doesn't work—whether it's a government collective or a corporate one—and some might argue that it's the same anyway. Look what happened in the Soviet Union. The communists took over all the farms and made them collective. For a time, productivity went up. Then it fell off a proverbial cliff. What you had in the end was a whole country full of farmers who couldn't manage to feed the people. There were shortages of virtually everything. That hasn't happened here in the States yet, but mark my words, it will happen sure as we're standing here in VL. But that's not the worst of it…

"The really sad part of all this isn't even the lost way of life. I realize that over time things change. Change is the law of the universe. You ever hear of entropy? No, the saddest part—at least to my mind—is what they did to the soil."

"You mean toxic chemicals," I say.

"Yep. Of course the independent farmers were using pesticides and herbicides and other shit too, but nothing like what happened when the corporations took over management of the land. (Now, ain't that an oxymoron if I ever heard one?) And you can bet your life that if farmers like my papa had known the dangers of those chemicals, they would have stopped using them, pronto! They cared about the land, because it belonged to them. Whatever Carl Bremer and Elmer Sedgwick were doing to the land, the corporations did a thousand times more, you can bet on it. Because they had to maximize short term profits for shareholders, and they didn't care what they did to the ground itself."

"So you're saying that the land has been poisoned," I

extrapolate.

"Yep."

"And the food that's grown on it?"

"I wouldn't eat it. And I wouldn't drink the ground water either. It's not safe anywhere in the Midwest."

"They don't tell us that, Randy."

"They don't tell us a lot of shit, Fizzy."

"Yeah, I've noticed."

"It's pretty much a see-no-evil, hear-no-evil, speak-no-evil situation. But the health effects are certainly not invisible…

"Health consequences from exposure to soil contamination vary greatly depending on pollutant type, pathway of attack and vulnerability of the exposed population. Chronic exposure to chromium, lead and other metals, petroleum, solvents, and many pesticide and herbicide formulations can be carcinogenic; can cause congenital disorders, or other chronic health conditions. Industrial or man-made concentrations of naturally occurring substances, such as nitrate and ammonia associated with livestock manure from agricultural operations, have also been identified as health hazards in soil and groundwater.

"Chronic exposure to benzene at sufficient concentrations is known to be associated with higher incidence of leukemia. Mercury and cyclodienes are known to induce higher incidences of kidney damage, some irreversible. PCBs and cyclodienes are linked to liver toxicity. Organophosphates and carbamates can induce a chain of responses leading to neuromuscular blockage. Many chlorinated solvents induce liver changes, kidney changes and depression of the central nervous system. At sufficient dosages a large number of soil contaminants can cause death by exposure via direct contact, inhalation or ingestion of contaminants in groundwater contaminated through soil."

"You're just full of good news, aren't you?" I observe.

"Hey, Fizzy, don't shoot the messenger," he says.

After riding another ten minutes along an interior gravel road, Randy stops the truck near a barn to show me his hog operation. The barn itself is a majestic sight cast against the rolling fields of corn and the hazy Iowa horizon. In their pen, the pigs conduct their own unique society, which reminds me for the moment of George Orwell's *Animal Farm*, and I wonder if Orwell might not have been on to something. Are the seeds of revolution not sown in sloth?

"Nothing wrong with these porkers," says Randy. "I know. I made them myself."

"Playing God in VL?" I tease.

"You know how it is," he says. "You've got to work with what you have."

"Precisely," I affirm.

After seeing not only the hog operation, but also Randy's personal crop of Iowa Gold (he picks a few buds for us to enjoy later that evening), we return to the house to have dinner. And wouldn't you just know it, a honey-glazed ham is already prepared with all the fixings: creamy mashed potatoes, peas and carrots, vine ripened tomatoes as big as a fist—Randy's fist, not mine—as well as freshly baked dinner rolls dripping with butter churned just this morning. "What a feast!" I proclaim.

"Best ham in the world comes from Iowa," says Randy as he eats voraciously. "At least it used to, anyway…"

After dinner, we do the dishes together: I wash and Randy dries and puts them in the cupboard. Day has turned to dusk (I'm sure Randy has maneuvered the lighting controls in his VL REP for my benefit) and the ambiance is perfect. We take a six-pack of Pabst Blue Ribbon (Randy's choice) out to the screened-in porch and settle onto a rocking love seat. Randy rolls a couple of joints of his homegrown, lights one, takes a pull then passes it to me. I, too, inhale the smoke, and as the high comes on the sounds of the rural night grow sharper, more distinct. The crickets chirp in perfect rhythm with Randy's father's Patti Paige record, which he is playing on the stereo. Over the eastern horizon the moon comes up and casts its gentle light on the feral fields. The cold beer goes down easy on this warm, humid evening, and I lay my head upon Randy's massive shoulder. Ah, sweeter times in America…

Earth—the foundation upon which our existence is built.

(Air)

I have an appointment to meet my good friend Trick Walkman in front of the Open Books shop, and when I transfer to the familiar coordinates he is already waiting for me. In Virtual Life, Trick is a poet; in Physical Life, Trick Walkman is actually Kenneth Rockford, an attorney practicing environmental law in the State of Connecticut.

On first consideration, the idea of an attorney parading around a virtual world as a poet might seem a bit out of character, but once you read Trick's poems, which all deal in some manner with environmental issues of the day, the connection becomes crystal clear. At least that's what Crystal and I thought when we first heard him recite some of his poems at the VBV. In fact, we were so impressed with the poems that we offered to publish them in a book entitled *The Loyal Opponent*, which we eventually did. The cover we chose for the book came from an infrared NASA photo showing the massive ozone hole in the atmosphere above the North Pole. That was how I came to know Trick, and we have been friends ever since.

"Don't you find it curious," I say to him, "that in PL so many people end up doing something other than their most natural or dominant talent in order to make a living? Whereas in VL, everybody is more or less free to follow his passion? "

Trick smiles as he answers, "That's because VL is a silicon based world, whereas PL is carbon based."

"I don't follow you," I tell him.

"In PL, you have a body, which is essentially made up of carbon, hydrogen and oxygen. But take away the water and what you're left with is mostly carbon plus a few trace elements. Now, your body needs food to replenish itself, which is also mainly composed of carbon. We find it difficult to live out in the elements, so we need shelter. With what do we construct our homes? Mainly carbon. In PL, we need to transport ourselves from place to place. What fuel propels our vehicles? Carbon based fuels. See what I mean?"

"Sure. But I don't see where you're going with this line."

"Well, in VL none of that is necessary. VL is a silicon-based world. Our emulations are not self-generated or self-replenishing; they are projections within silicon-based circuits. They don't need food, or shelter. And transportation is merely a matter of rerouting circuits. No petrol needed for that—just a couple of microwatts of power, which can come from any number of naturally occurring circumstances in the physical universe— electromagnetic (or solar), geothermal, gravity (or inertia)—even the nervous energy generated within our PL brains. So it stands to reason that if we are not saddled with the perpetual and rather clumsy burden of carbon maintenance, then we have the time and energy to pursue a different course than we might need to follow in PL."

"Then you think it all comes down to elements…"

"So it would seem," says Trick. "I know that VL does not seem to be physical in the conventional sense, yet it is a sub-dimension within the greater physical universe. It's just a dimension that operates around a different elemental fulcrum."

"I never thought about it that way," I admit. "I just feel

more comfortable in VL than I do in PL. Had it not been for Virtual Life, my existence would have been nothing more than that of a drone."

"Well, Fizzy, you certainly do shine here in VL," says Trick.

And now it is I who is smiling. Or at least the projection of (me) through a silicon microchip…

Of course we are not here to discuss the elemental nature of VL. We can do that any time. And since time does not even exist in the conventional sense here in VL, we probably have hundreds, if not thousands of (years) to figure out what makes this place (tick). Today, however, we are taking a little trip, Trick and I, to…China. That's right! My friend Lili Xu, also an environmental advocate, has agreed to show us some of the less than beneficial side effects of China's economic miracle—namely, the air pollution generated from the tens of thousands of factories that produce the goods that the First World can't seem to live without. It's a big deal, really. Because millions of Chinese are working as many as three hundred sixty days a year, living far away from families that they seldom see, making squat-all for their labor while the owners of the factories rack up millions, or even billions; and besides the human (or is it inhuman?) toll for all this, the atmosphere (and the rivers, too) are being so horribly polluted that they may never recover, even if the mass manufacturing ceased today! It's all pretty hard to imagine, I guess, unless you are living the dream (or horror). I want to see it for myself, and Trick says he wants to see it too. So, off we go to Beijing!

Whoosh…

We meet Lili Xu, a real beauty with jet black hair, Asian facial features and a slim figure, standing in front of a two story-high statue of Chairman Mao, his left arm poised at his side and his right arm extended and pointing (ironically) at a distant belching smokestack. The scene is an obvious non sequitur, and I can't help thinking that if Mao Zedong himself could see what is happening today in China, he would either mount a counter-revolution to the People's Revolution, or kill himself in shame and disgust. Contrary to Mao's unyielding pose, Lili Xu's posture is not like that of the former leader, or even similar to most Western personas; her body language is fluid, without resistance. Yet even as her emulation conveys an attitude of subtlety and tranquility, Lili Xu is all business.

"Welcome to my homeland, Fizzy Oceans. Welcome, Mr. Trick Walkman." Lili Xu bows in respect.

"Thanks for the invitation," I return.

Trick shakes her hand.

The sky overhead is stone gray, almost as if it were dusk; but it is not dusk, it is mid-day, and the effects of China's industrial miracle are at once obvious. Of course I cannot smell anything here in VL, but if I could, I know I would smell the odor of burning sulfur, not to mention other pollutants.

"As you can see," Lili Xu explains, "the air quality in Beijing is deplorable. It is also bad in Shanghai. In fact, sixteen of the world's twenty most polluted cities are in China. One in five urban Chinese breath heavily polluted air. More than a hundred Chinese cities do not meet China's own pollution standards. Everywhere the smell of high-sulfur coal and leaded gasoline permeate the air.

"The smog in Beijing and Shanghai is so bad that airports are periodically shut down due to poor visibility. In Shanghai, you can't see the street from a fifth-floor window. Blue sky is an extremely rare sight. Fresh air tours to the countryside are very popular."

"And all this happened in a period of about twenty years," Trick comments.

"Yes," Lili Xu confirms.

"Hydro-carbons," the environmental poet says repugnantly.

"Coal is the number one source of air pollution,"

explains Lili Xu. "China gets eighty percent of its electricity, and seventy percent its total energy from coal—most of it high-sulfur bituminous. Six million tons are burned everyday to power factories, to heat homes. Heavy traffic and low-grade gasoline have made cars a leading contributor to the air pollution problem."

"An entire nation choking on its success," I comment ironically.

"Sadly, you are correct, Miss Fizzy. But it is not so simple. Our leaders understood that a country as large as ours could not flourish in a post-modern world without industrialization, so they opened the economy to private enterprise. This change in philosophy and practice has brought many good things to China as well."

"I'm sure you are correct, Lili Xu," says Trick. "But you must know that the level of pollution we see here is unsustainable."

"Many here in China—both scientists and members of government—recognize that what you say is true, and they are trying to make a difference. Yet we find ourselves in a Catch-22. A market economy has its own mind and its own momentum, and because policy, no matter how well intentioned it might be, is only implemented after the damage is already done, the pollution just gets worse and worse.

"According to the World Health Organization, only one percent of the China's five hundred and sixty million city dwellers breath air considered safe by European Union standards. Another study done by WHO estimates that the amount of suspended airborne particulates in the air of northern China are almost twenty times what WHO considers safe."

"What is to be done?" I ask Lili Xu.

She turns her palms up and shrugs. "Nothing will be done," she says, "because money has taught the people to love money more than life."

Good-bye China (gasp)! Viva Mexico City (gasp-gasp)!

In just one generation, the air in Mexico City has gone from among the cleanest to among the dirtiest of all large metropolitan cities. Visibility, nearly a hundred kilometers in the 1940s, is now down to about one and a half kilometers. Three snow-capped volcanoes, Popocatepetl, Ixtacihuatl and Paricutin, were once a prominent part of the landscape; now they are rarely visible, and pollutants like nitrogen dioxide regularly exceed international standards. Levels of ozone are twice as high as the maximum allowable limit for one hour per year, but this level occurs in Mexico City several hours per day, every day. A haze hangs over the city most of the time, endangering the health of inhabitants.

Trick and I are here to meet with Pedro Cisneros, who owns an oxygen booth located at a busy intersection in downtown Mexico City. The price for one minute of pure oxygen is one dollar, and Pedro is *never* short of customers.

"Industrial development is a major cause," Pedro tells us. "The population in 1950 was three million; today it is twenty million. And we now have more than three million cars on the streets."

A woman pulling a shopping cart stops at Pedro's booth, pays her money, and enters the chamber. She sits down then crosses herself as she breathes deeply. The oxygen she is breathing inside the booth is like the Holy Spirit filling her with life.

"*Gracias, Señor*," she gasps.

Mexico City is two thousand, two hundred forty meters above sea level. Incomplete fuel combustion and higher emissions of carbon monoxide are the result of lower oxygen content in the atmosphere. Concentrated sunlight produces higher than normal smog levels, which prevents the sun from heating the atmosphere enough to penetrate the inversion layer. Not the best geographical location to build the largest city on earth. Yet, here it is!

"It's not the pollution that kills people," says Pedro,

"but I guess some people die sooner than they would have breathing clean air."

"It's not the gun that kills people," I echo, "but the gaping hole in the body made by the bullet."

Fair enough?

Anyway, it seems as if Pedro's got himself a pretty good business for as far as the eye can see. Which, come to think of it, may not be all that far these days. Especially in Mexico City.

If you were going to visit the most polluted city in America, where would you go? Well, don't buy your ticket for LA or Pittsburgh. Not for Chicago or New York. Not Gary, Indiana or Youngstown, Ohio or Detroit, Michigan. Buy your ticket for Bakersfield. That's right: Bakersfield, California. Care for a little car exhaust with your morning cappuccino?

But how can this be true?

Well, it *is* true; whether or not we want to admit it. Environmental degradation is not only for big cities anymore; it's everywhere. And it seems to have come out of nowhere, while we weren't paying attention. It happened while we were sipping Chardonnay and slurping oysters on the half-shell. Or when we were stuffing our faces with McDonald's hamburgers, of Pizza Hut pizzas, or Pita Pockets. It happened as we drove our cars to the mailbox, or to the swimming pool three blocks away. It happened as we enjoyed the fruits of technology, and Ziploc bags, and disposable diapers.

Sitting at Otto's Patisserie in Bakersfield, Trick and I deplore the fact that we cannot see the mountains that surround the Central Valley.

"Bakersfield is now the American city with the most fine particulate pollution," reads a report from the American Lung Association.

The article serves as documentation for the obvious. I ask our waitress how she feels about Bakersfield's air pollution, and she says, "Smog? What smog?"

Imagine that!

But I don't know why I am surprised. These days, people seem willing to accept most anything if it doesn't affect them directly, or immediately. Where's the foresight? Apparently up in smoke!

Still, this is not a new development; it has been years in the making. The ALA report goes on to say, "The Central Valley, where nearly half the nation's food is grown, has been severely compromised by the overuse of fertilizers and pesticides, not to mention particulates caused by farm equipment."

Half the nation's food… There's the trade-off, I suppose.

"An unsustainable equation of diminishing returns," Trick reminds me.

I read further in the report: "The American Lung Association has found that the lives of six of every ten Americans are now endangered by pollution."

Say no more. I'm outta here!!!

Word has come of the death of Sister Dorothy Stang in the Amazon Rainforest, so I immediately IM Crystal and Kiz with the news. We three have long suspected that the PL identity of our old friend Omar Paquero was none other than Sister Dorothy. I am not only shocked by the news but also concerned for the well being of our friend. Crystal immediately answers my IM: "Where did you hear this news?"

"I read it in the online version of *The Guardian*," I write back.

Next comes a message from Kiz: "Has anybody in VL seen Omar?"

"Not that I know of," I answer her.

"Oh, shit!" writes Kiz.

Even as I exchange instant messages with Crystal and Kiz, I am looking at a picture of Sister Dorothy. In the picture the American-born nun stands amidst the rainforest splendor; she appears to be seventy if she's a day. Her hair is grayish-white and cut short and her face is tanned. She is wearing simple earrings, wire-rimmed glasses and a white t-shirt with the slogan stenciled upon it: "*A Morte da floresta é o fim da nossa vida.*" Which In Portuguese means, "The death of the forest is the end of our life." My question is this: Did Sister Dorothy understand that her unwavering dedication to rainforest ecology and fair land use practices for the peasants of Anapu would lead to her death too?

The unfortunate answer to that question is, probably yes. Certainly there were those in the logging industry who saw her as more than a nuisance and wanted her out of the way. Her commitment to land reform enabling peasants who had never before owned land to engage in sustainable farming—as well as preserve valuable forest against clear-cutting—enraged those who saw the forest not as 'the lungs of the world' but as a fast track to huge profits. Already, twenty percent of the Amazon rainforest has been lost to clear-cutting, and the rate of deforestation promised to increase unless opposing forces were able to impose a moratorium of conscience. It is also unfortunate, as well as ironic, that such movements seem to take time to gain governmental support, and resources that are plundered are impossible to recover. What is happening in the Amazon rainforest is not unlike the range wars that once occurred on the American plains, but the stakes here are much higher. For each and every person on earth, our next breath is at stake.

Then there is the IMF… Who loaned Brazil billions during the recession of 2002, not out of any real sense of charity or good will, but rather to guard its back, and that of the other developed nations on earth—or at least their bankers. Shortsighted and selfish attention to economics once again cost the earth and its peoples an irreplaceable resource—nothing less than the air we breathe. Without the forest to produce oxygen, the atmosphere turns in ever-greater percentage to carbon dioxide, which as far as I know will not sustain animal life.

Sister Dorothy Stang knew all this as far back as the sixties when she first moved to Anapu, Brazil. And it was she who conceived and eventually effected changes in Brazilian law to allow the peasants to acquire two hundred and fifty-acre tracts of land for sustainable agriculture, the plan calling for farming of a mere fifty acres (which was enough for these peasants to earn a reasonable living for the first time in their lives or the lives of their ancestors) while allocating the other two hundred acres for rainforest conservation. All well and good for the peasants, but the program pissed off those in the logging industry big time, and of course a mafia mentality emerged. Killings were common and rampant. And Sister Dorothy was on the hit list. Did she know it? Of course she knew it. When they finally came for her at the Boa Esperanca settlement, she did not flinch. "Are you armed?" her assassins demanded. "Only with my Bible," she answered, and began reading to them from the Beatitudes, "Blessed are the poor in spirit..." As she read, the two gunmen shot her at point blank range in the abdomen. She fell forward into the mud and they shot her again in the back. Finally, they emptied their weapons into her skull.

As Sister Dorothy Stang lay silenced, the rainforest wept for its fallen heroine, and the world gasped for breath. Just as I gasp relating this story to you... And now, it is time for my friends and me to search for our old friend Omar Paquero, if indeed he still walks the terrain of Virtual Life. I wonder if we'll ever find him. I fear something essential has been lost. *Buenas noches, mis amigos. Respira profundamente!*

Air—the medium from which we draw life.

(Fire)

The place is the ancient Roman City of Misenum; the NL date is 24 August, 79 AD; and my host is Pliny the Younger. Pliny is a lawyer and an author; his uncle, Pliny the Elder, was a renouned naturalist of his time, a prolific author, a Roman senator and the commander of a Roman naval fleet. Just prior to the eruption of Mount Vesuvius in NL 79 AD, Pliny the Elder had embarked on a sea crossing to the Italian mainland. Though he was invited, Pliny the Younger chose to remain at his uncle's villa in Misenum, a decision that not only saved his life but haunted him for the rest of his years.

"Your story is one that has survived the Ages," I tell Pliny. "And I will republish your writings, as well as your uncle's, and place them in the Open Books VL vault."

"It is a violent and a tragic tale," he laments. "And I thank you for your archive."

"You saw it happen with your own eyes," I acknowledge. "Only you can tell this tale authentically."

"Yes, I watched thousands die that day, including my beloved uncle," he confirms.

From where we stand at Pliny the Elder's opulent villa in Misenum, we can easily see the Italian mainland across the Bay of Naples. We cannot only see the city of Naples itself but also Mount Vesuvius looming in the background.

"The volcano is a mere eleven miles from Naples, which today is one of the most densely populated cities in Europe," Pliny tells me. "If the mountain were again to explode, as it did that fateful day my uncle set off for Stabiae, then surely hundreds of thousands, if not millions, would die."

"It must have been horrible to watch," I say.

"It rained fire and rock for days," he relates. "The sky turned black as night, and the temperature dropped as if it were winter. And we were powerless to intercede." Pliny gazes into the distance, into history itself, and his emotions are obvious on his face. A tear falls from his eye for the many who died the day fire and poison gas had enveloped all the cities and villages on the skirt of Mount Vesuvius.

"It must have been terrifying," I say.

"Like nothing you can imagine," he tells me. "The fire at the center of the earth is malevolent, merciless and all-consuming. I will share my story with you, Fizzy Oceans, so that you might warn those living in PL who scoff at the idea of another eruption of Vesuvio!"

Pliny and I sit upon a low garden wall where we can plainly see the site of the historical disaster.

"The day began as any other," he relates, "except that my uncle, who was a well respected naturalist, statesman and soldier, had left from Misenum for the mainland with a detail of friends and sailors. Then, in the afternoon, Mount Vesuvius erupted violently and without warning. So it is for my dear uncle, Pliny the Elder, that I give this account of the circumstances of his death, and of the deaths of the good citizens of Pompeii, Herculeneum and Stabiae.

"My uncle perished in a devastation of the loveliest of lands, in a memorable disaster shared by peoples and cities, but this will be a kind of eternal life for him. Although he wrote a great number of enduring works, the imperishable nature of *your* writings will add a great deal to his memory and legacy. Happy are they, in my opinion, to whom it is given either to do something worth writing about, or to write something worth reading; most happy, of course, those who do both. With his own books and *yours*, my uncle will be counted among the latter. It is therefore with great pleasure that I take up, or rather take upon myself, the task to which you entreat me.

"He was at Misenum (where we stand today in Virtual Life, whereas on that fateful day we moved in the light and grace of Natural Life) in his capacity as commander of the fleet on the 24th of August, 79 AD, when between two and three in the afternoon my mother drew his attention to a cloud of unusual size and appearance. He had had a sunbath, then a cold bath, and was reclining after dinner with his books. He called for his shoes and climbed up to where he could get the best view of the phenomenon. The cloud was rising from a mountain—at such a distance we couldn't tell which, but afterwards learned that it was Vesuvius. I can best describe its shape by likening it to a pine tree. The cloud rose into the sky on a very long 'trunk' from which spread some 'branches'. I imagined that it had been raised by a sudden blast, which then weakened, leaving the cloud unsupported so that its own weight caused it to spread sideways. Some of the cloud was white; in other parts there were dark patches of dirt and ash. The sight of it made the scientist in my uncle determined to see it from closer at hand.

"He ordered a boat made ready. He offered me the opportunity of going along, but I preferred to study—he himself happened to have given me a writing exercise. As he was leaving the house he was brought a letter from Tascius' wife Rectina, who was terrified by the looming danger. Her villa lay at the foot of Vesuvius, and there was no way out except by boat. She begged him to get her out. He changed his plans. The expedition that started out as a quest for knowledge now called for courage. He launched the quadriremes and embarked himself, a source of aid for more people than just Rectina, for that delightful shore was a populous one. He hurried to a place from which others were fleeing, and held his course directly into danger. Was he afraid? It seems not, as he kept continuous observation of the various movements and shapes of the evil cloud, dictating what he saw.

"Ash was falling onto the ships now, darker and denser the closer they went. Now it was bits of pumice, and rocks that were blackened and burned and shattered by the fire. Now the sea is shoal; debris from the mountain blocks the shore. He paused a moment, wondering whether to turn back as the helmsman urged him. "Fortune helps the brave," he said. "Head for Pomponianus!"

At Stabiae, on the other side of the bay formed by the gradually curving shore, Pomponianus had loaded up his ships even before the danger arrived, though it was visible and indeed extremely close, once it intensified. He planned to put out as soon as the contrary wind let up. That very wind carried my uncle right in, and he embraced the frightened man and gave him comfort and courage. In order to lessen the other's fear by showing his own unconcern, he asked to be taken to the baths. He bathed and dined, carefree, or at least appearing so (which is equally impressive). Meanwhile, broad sheets of flame were lighting up many parts of Vesuvius; their light and brightness were all the more vivid for the darkness of night. To alleviate people's fears my uncle claimed that the flames came from the deserted homes of farmers who had left in a panic with the hearth fires still alight. Then he rested, and gave every indication of actually sleeping; people who passed by his door heard his snores, which were rather resonant since he was a heavy man. The ground outside his room rose so high with the mixture of ash and stones that if he had spent any more time there, escape would have been impossible. He got up and came out, restoring himself to Pomponianus and the others who had been unable to sleep. They discussed what to do, whether to remain under cover or to try the open air. The buildings were being rocked by a series of strong tremors, and appeared to have come loose from their foundations and to be sliding this way and that. Outside, however, there was danger from the rocks that were coming down, light and fire-consumed as these bits of pumice were. Weighing the relative dangers, they chose the outdoors; in my uncle's case it was a rational decision; others just chose the alternative that frightened them the least.

"They tied pillows on top of their heads as protection against the shower of rock. It was daylight now elsewhere in the world, but there the darkness was darker and thicker than any night. But they had torches and other lights. They decided to go down to the shore, to see from close up if anything was possible by sea. But it remained as rough as before. Resting in the shade of a sail, he drank once or twice from the cold water he had asked for. Then came the smell of sulfur, announcing the flames, and the flames themselves, sending others into flight. Supported by two slaves he stood up then immediately collapsed. As I understand it, the dust-laden air obstructed his breathing; and his innards, which had never been strong, and often blocked or upset, simply shut down. When daylight came again two days after he died, his body was found untouched, unharmed. He looked more asleep than dead.

"Meanwhile at Misenum, my mother and I—oh, but this has nothing to do with history, and you asked only for information about his death, so I'll stop here then... But I will say one more thing; namely, that I have written out everything that I did and heard at the time while memories were still fresh. You will use the important bits, for it is one thing to write a letter, another to write history; one thing to write to a friend, another to write for posterity."

I am inclined to thank Pliny the Younger for his detailed account of the destruction of Pompeii, Herculeneum and Stabiae, but before I can utter a single word, the ground beneath us begins to tremble and shake (we are at the convergence of two tectonic plates), and by a means which I have never before encountered, and one that I am at a loss to explain, we are suddenly transported from Virtual Life into another dimension altogether— Future Life.

Whoosh...

"What's this? What's going on? Where are we?" I ask in alarm.

"Oh, no!" Pliny exclaims. "It's happening again!"

"You mean..."

"Yes, it's Vesuvius!"

"What should we do?"

343

Pliny shakes his head in resignation. "There is nothing we *can* do, except watch the horror unfold," he says.

Within minutes we see a towering cloud of smoke and ash rising into the sky. Lightning flashes over the distant mountain. Thunder rolls over the landscape and out to sea. The light of day turns gradually into the black of night. We are safe here at Misenum, but the basin in which the City of Naples sits is directly in the path of destruction. For more than a million inhabitants there is no escape.

As time moves forward, or in reverse, or inside out, it becomes apparent to me that Pliny and I are experiencing an event not particular only to NL, but that we exist, as it were, in several dimensions at once—NL (or Natural Life) the source from which Vesuvius draws its strength and power; PL (or physical Life) where the doomed residents of Naples and its surrounding megalopolis will suffer their fate; VL (or Virtual Life) where we are able to create and recreate at will our visions and alternate realities; and finally FL (or Future Life) an existence that supersedes all three previous worlds, and where emulations are our primary vehicles, and from where we can experience multiple realities and/or existences.

Fire—the force from which cataclysmic change emanates.

(Water)

High in the Andes Mountains, glaciers feeding Lake Titicaca, the water source for La Paz, Bolivia (population 2,350,000), have receded by ninety-five percent; the massive lake has all but gone dry, and the people of La Paz are feeling a little dehydrated.

It's no joke! In PL, we need water. Our bodies are mainly composed of it. Without water, we die. Plain and simple. But here in La Paz, they've all but run out of this vital life resource. People are leaving in droves. But some cannot leave. They are crushingly poor, and moving somewhere else is simply out of the question. So they take whatever water they can get and conserve it. They have become experts in recycling earth's most elemental liquid.

Here, recycling mostly means multiple use. Water used for bathing is collected and used to water gardens; water used for cooking vegetables becomes the stock of tomorrow's soup; toilets are flushed only after several uses. Drinking water has become a commodity valued more than gold. And it's not going to get any easier for these people. Not ever…

To compound the problem of volume, the water in the world's highest lake has been shamelessly polluted with the garbage of the very people who depend on it for sustenance. Apu Qullana Auki, the god who (according to local legend) created the universe, also created Lake Titicaca by means of the Great Flood. Talk about irony…

I have to admit that high in the Andes at twelve thousand, five hundred feet, I'm feeling a little parched. What to do?

"*Buenos dias, Señorita!*"

The voice I hear from behind me is a familiar one. I turn round to see…

OMG! It's Omar Paquero!

"Omar! I thought you were dead," I say, exuberant in the fact that my supposition is obviously in error.

"*No, no estoy muerto. Bolivia es mi patria.*"

"But everybody thought that in PL you were Sister Dorothy…"

"*Una mujer noble. Su muerte es una pérdida para la humanidad.*"

"Hmmm..." Then maybe in PL, Omar really is a ten-year-old kid from Bolivia. Or maybe he is someone else altogether...

"*Puedo ofrecerle un vaso de agua de mi cantina?*"

Now that's an offer I'm not going to pass up. I take a

long drink from Omar's canteen. No longer parched, I ask, "What's the deal here?"

"*No hay agua más limpia.*"

"How will the people of La Paz go on living?" I ask.

Omar only shrugs, and I can't help wondering how Cateret Rose, soaked to the proverbial gills, is faring on her Pacific island home. I wonder if she's still there. Or if she has left. Or drowned…

"And what about you, Omar? Do you have enough water? What is to be done?"

Omar lowers the brim of his hat to almost cover his eyes as he ponders my question. "*Qué es bedone? Cuando la situación se vuelve crítica, hacemos otra inundación.*"

"Can you do that?" I ask incredulously.

"*Tal vez... Posiblemente...*"

Nobody's talking. That's right, nobody's talking about what happened in the Gulf of Mexico after the BP oil platform exploded, spilling millions of gallons of oil into the water, and after the so-called clean-up.

Apparently Texe Marrs, the guy I heard late one night on a talk radio show, was right. The toxins from the oil spill itself, but more so from the chemical dispersants, have killed virtually all marine life in the Gulf. It is now a dead sea, and we're not talking Jordan here!

What's more, nobody's talking about the resultant human migration. The Gulf states have now lost more than a million people, and they are likely to lose millions more. Some have left because their livelihood was destroyed, and others have left for fear of poisoning. Some who remain will eventually die prematurely of cancer or other diseases due to their exposure to toxins; others who do leave will die prematurely for the same reason.

It has now been determined—but nobody's talking about it—that it is raining Corexit three hundred miles inland in Louisiana, Alabama, Mississippi and Florida. Even Texas, the great oil producing state, is not totally spared. Dolphins, sharks, shrimp; marlins, sailfish, snapper: marine creatures of every variety—gone.

So I guess that frees the area for more drilling... Right?

More drilling, that is, if cartels demand it... If the crude really does run low some time in the PL twenty-second century. Ha! I wonder if we'll even be around in PL by the year 2100. Some in VL don't think so. Cousteau doesn't think so—at least not as we are today. Iggy is building an Ark. Cateret Rose is probably swimming for her life. Omar is handing out drinks from his canteen. We can't drink oil, you know. Or can we?

Meanwhile, the moon rules the tides. Water from the Gulf is moving inexorably northward along the Atlantic Conveyor, and it's carrying with it...you-know-what. In PL Norway, they're bracing themselves for impact. Hey! Look! There's water in the oil! So... How to separate the black gold from the H2O. There must be a chemical. What d'ya think?

What I think is that we'd all better pack our bags. Just like the millions of scared people leaving the Gulf States. All aboard the VL express! Got to cut and run. It's always sunny in VL (Hey! That's a lie!), and transportation is corbon free (and that's not a lie). Yep, there's water in the oil—their oil—and you can be sure that separation will be accomplished one way or another. That's my bet, anyway. So I'll be taking my chances elsewhere, where the sun always shines (Ha!) and the water is crystal clear.

Water—the medium from which our diversity comes.

PART IV
A CHICKEN IS ONE EGG'S WAY
OF BECOMING OTHER EGGS

13
LEGACY
(OR WELCOME TO FUTURE LIFE)

KIZ AND I are at Samantha's Music Bar because we are hoping to meet up with Filo Farmer (aka Theo Ola, founder and CEO of Seedbed Studios and Virtual Life). I've heard he hangs out here sometimes, so Kiz and I have taken seats at a corner table and we're trying to look inconspicuous. We sip our drinks—mine a glowing red concoction, hers a blue one—and try to act cool and detached. Though if truth were told, I've not felt detached since the first day I signed on to Virtual Life.

I know the odds of finding Filo here are a thousand to one, yet it's common knowledge in VL that his emulation turns up here from time to time, and that he's really a nice guy, and quite approachable, too. So, why not try? I'd love to talk to him—EM-to-EM—about Virtual Life, and about PL, too. I have a gazillion questions I'd like to ask him, and I know he'd have insights and visions I've never even thought about. Am I overestimating his contribution to modern culture through technology? Maybe… But for me, meeting Theo would be like meeting Socrates, or Galileo, or Thomas Edison.

Whether by chance or by coincidence, or by deep longing, or simply by blind luck, our purpose for being at Samantha's Music Bar is realized when Mr. Virtual Life himself saunters into the saloon for a drink. How do we know it is Theo, the Creator? Buy his emulation's legendary appearance, of course. Tall and lean, and wearing chaps and a cowboy hat over blonde uncombed hair, his handlebar moustache half-covering a thin-lipped, precocious smile, there is no mistaking him. Meeting the Creator is, by all accounts, the chance of a *Virtual Lifetime*. But is God really supposed to look like Billy the Kid?

Theo's story in PL is no secret to anyone involved in Virtual Life. He was born in San Bernardino: shy as a kid, his family moved around a lot; he spent much of his time alone in his room; he was a nerdy, creative kid, a C student with a preoccupation for 'inventions'. He spent his adolescence not playing sports or pursuing girls, but surfing the Internet. At the age of twenty-five, he founded Seedbed Studios, which embarked upon the creation of Virtual Life. Starting with only a few simulators, he grew his newly made 'world' into a virtual community approximately ten times the geographical size of the Silicon Valley (where Seedbed Studios is actually located) which is now powered by forty thousand simulators hosting four hundred terra-bytes. In essence, Theo has created a flea market reality in which many of us now live and communicate, work and build and love, and yes, even sometimes where we die.

Once Filo Farmer has greeted the staff, ordered his drink, and settled himself at one of the tables, I gather my courage and approach him. "Hi, Filo," I say.

"Hello, Fizzy Oceans." He knows my name from my ID banner.

"My friend Kizmet Aurora and I were hoping to find you here. Would you mind if we join you?"

"Pretty ladies are always welcome in my 'world', he quips.

I motion for Kiz to bring the drinks, and we join Filo at his table. "Filo Farmer, this is Kizmet Aurora; Kiz, Filo Farmer, Mr. Virtual Life."

Filo stands and shakes hands with each of us. "The pleasure is mine," he says.

We take seats at the table and endure a moment of awkward silence (it's not every day you meet a god).

"I've wanted to meet you for a very long time," I tell him.

"Then I'm glad the opportunity has finally 'materialized'," he laughs.

"All kidding aside," I say, "I have some important questions to ask you." I pause a moment. "And a favor to ask as well. Or maybe it's actually a suggestion…"

"Tell me, Fizzy, what's on your mind?"

"VL, of course. I mean the nature of it. You know what I mean."

"I could give you my standard interview description," he offers.

"That might do for a start."

"Okay, here goes. I started with a couple of essential questions: Is it possible to digitize a person, a human being? And if so, is it feasible—or even possible—to create a matrix, or meta-verse in which digitized people can interact? Each question, I found, led to an answer. The concept of emergence… Bit by bit, the digital atomics were created. One mega-watt runs the entire Virtual Life structure.

"Originally I thought VL would be a world full of nameless entities, but the opposite has come to pass. Because VL's development is left to the seedlings, the greater setting has developed as those in VL project their thoughts and intentions and fantasies into the matrix. Virtual Life has become a world of vision and inspiration. What we build here in VL is the algorithmic expression of our dreams…"

"Thanks for the media blurb, Filo, but I already know all that."

"Some do and some don't," he relates.

"What I'm really interested in is the convergence of PL and VL. And what comes next…"

"Why don't you elaborate a bit?" Filo invites.

"In PL, my life isn't so great. I used to work as a medical billing clerk (ho-hum), but when the big economic meltdown came, I lost my job. Now I work in a fish market mopping up fish guts. Most of the time I'm dead broke (although I always manage to pay my IP bill). I don't have many friends—I guess I'm not that attractive to most people; constantly smelling of dead fish is a pretty big turn-off, obviously…

"But my life here in VL is quite different. It's made all the difference in the 'world' (lol)! Especially since I became a VL greeter. I've met some really great people here in VL (I nod at Kiz), and I've really 'bloomed' like a flower. So I totally get the Seedbed Studios bit, and the seedlings, and all the rest. Those are pretty great metaphors, Filo. But you probably planned all that in advance. Whatever…

"Anyway, I've really found myself here in VL. I help a woman named Crystal Marbella with her publishing project, Open Books. We are trying to republish as much of the 'world's' great literature online as we possibly can. For a time when… Well, I'm getting to all that. Bear with me."

"Of course I will," says Filo. As he takes a sip of his drink and assesses me over the rim of his glass, I can tell I've captured his interest.

"And that's not all. Besides being a VL greeter, and helping out at Open Books, I've created my own REP to dramatize the life of Vincent Van Gogh and to display his life's work. And I've also been doing a bit of traveling, you know?"

"What sort of traveling?" Filo asks.

"Well, here in VL—but not really. You see I've been visiting some of the more 'realistic' REPS—places like virtual Pakistan, and virtual Bolivia. Places where PL is in serious peril, you know?"

"I know that some seedlings have recreated some of the not-so-nice places and events that exist in PL…"

"Right! Have you ever been to the Big Easy?"

"Not here in VL," he admits.

"They also call it 'The City That Care Forgot'. And with good reason! Hurricane Katrina is perpetually going on there in real time—or in VL 'real' time at least. The Cateret Islands in the South Pacific are in the midst of sinking—both in PL and here in VL, too. If you visit the VL Amazon Rain Forest, you get the PL picture of the devastation pretty well. The air in China is a mess, not to mention chemical pollution in the water system. My friend Randy, who is also a 'farmer' in Iowa, says the ground there is contaminated beyond repair with pesticides and herbicides and other shit. Lately, I've been monitoring the oil spill off the Gulf Coast, and it looks like not only the marine life there will be totally destroyed, but over time as many as thirty million people might suffer physical consequences from the various dispersants that were used, many eventually dying from exposure to Corexit and other toxins. My VL friend Igloo Iceman, who lives in PL Greenland, has told me all about the melting glaciers and the rising water. He's even building an Ark, though I'm not sure whether that's in PL or in VL. Whatever…

"I get the picture," says Filo.

"And I've had other experiences as well. I spent an evening with Jacques Cousteau—or at least with his EM (Is there really any difference?). And the picture that he paints of the PL aquatic environment is grim to say the least. I also had a chat with radio talk show host Daedalus Dunworthy, and together we watched Harlan Geltspinner (aka Sharky Overbite) speaking at the BloomEx mall and giddily laughing as he threw dollars up into the air as if they were worthless pieces of paper, which in my personal PL life I guess they are! I've met Gandhi, the Dalai Llama, accompanied Moses on his pilgrimage through the desert, stood by at the trial and the Crucifixion of Jesus and watched the Battle of Gettysburg. PL can be a pretty scary place, Filo."

"But it's altogether different here in VL," he says.

"It sure is!" Kiz interjects.

"All for the better, I'm convinced," I say.

"It is what we make it," Filo reminds us.

Our waitress waltzes over in her cute mini, winks at Filo, and asks if we'd all like another drink. We all nod that we would, and Filo says, "This one's on me; VL is awash in greenshoots these days."

"Glad to hear at least one economy is not in the tank," I tell him.

Filo smiles and repeats, "It is what we make it."

As we sip our drinks I'm trying to figure out just how to approach the dénouement of my VL story, how to tie it all together, and how to make my 'suggestion' to Filo Farmer (aka Theo Ola), the Creator, the facilitator, the god of VL). If I hesitate, it might just be curtains for us all. And I've got an idea—a really good idea—one that just might save our civilization from extinction. I decide that I have to trust my instincts, my intelligence and my vision. Filo will understand. He has to understand! Dive off the platform, Fizzy, straight into the deep end of the pool. It's sink or swim, girl!

"So this is what I think we've got to do," I begin. Then I qualify, "Or rather what you've got to do, Filo… I mean Theo…"

The Creator nods for me to continue.

"Virtual Life is certainly everything you say it is," I recap. "But at least in my mind it is something more as well. It is an archive, so to speak. It is a record of our culture, of our very civilization, with all its triumphs and all its disasters. You're absolutely right, Filo: It is what we make it. And what we are making here in VL is not only a manifestation of our dreams and aspirations—though we are certainly doing that, and one can only hope we do a better job of it this time than we did in PL—but it's also a legacy of sorts of who we are, and maybe even what we once were, in PL. If I don't miss my guess, Dr. Adler is right when he says we're going to need a guidebook pretty soon, because we will not only be creating an alternate world, but our primary one. See what I mean?"

"Yes, I see where you're going," he says.

"So I think it's absolutely essential that VL be protected against PL catastrophes. We can't have all this washed away—*whoosh*!"

"What do you suggest, Fizzy?" he asks.

"A vault in PL," I tell him.

"A vault?"

"Yes, an underground vault to protect the mainframes, to safeguard all the data. If the bomb goes off, or the planet decides to rebel in some way, then VL will be intact."

"But if PL is destroyed, as you and others suggest it might be, and somehow the mainframes and all the data survive, how would the emulations reanimate without their PL counterparts?"

"I guess that's your challenge to figure out; I'm no technical wizard. But I know one thing: I feel alive here in VL, even more alive than I feel in PL, and that has to account for something. There's more here, Filo, than even you imagine."

"I think you're talking about FL, Fizzy. Future Life."

"Maybe I am. But FL has to start sometime…"

"VL is not FL," he corrects.

"But it could be," I assert. "Maybe it has to be."

"I don't know how that would work," Filo confesses. "What you're really talking about here is the chicken or egg conundrum: which came first?"

"Look," I argue, "I don't know shit about chickens, or

eggs for that matter, but I do know that PL and VL converge, so why not VL and FL? Surely it must be possible…"

Filo raises his eyebrows. Obviously I have presented him with a challenge. At least I think he understands how critical it might be to protect VL.

"A time capsule: that's what you are suggesting," he says.

"More!" I tell him.

"Yes, more than a record. A blueprint for a new start."

"Exactly!" I confirm.

"Isn't she just wonderful?" says Kiz with a smile.

"I think I'm going to offer her a job at Seedbed," says Filo. "In the think tank!"

"I accept!" I joke.

"Look, I know you've got something here. But even if I can figure out how to do it—to save and protect everything—you do realize that some things will be lost."

"We've got to do what we can," I emphasize. "I think the time might be short."

"You're right, Fizzy Oceans! I'll get our team working on it right away."

"I knew you would understand, Filo," I say with relief.

He nods his head, obviously already cogitating on the problem at hand. "Thank you for your insight and your vision," he tells me.

I am flattered; I activate my blush response. "Let me know if there's anything I can do to help," I tell him.

"You're already doing it," he encourages.

Yes, I AM!

14
THE VELVET UNDERGROUND

KIZMET has created her own REP. Apparently she bought the 'real estate' with greenshoots won at the blackjack tables in virtual Vegas, and undertook the construction of the REP without telling Crystal or me a thing about it. The REP is an exact recreation of the Hopi Pueblo at Old Oraibi, and Kiz has invited Crystal and me to a ceremony to initiate it.

At least that's what we think it's all about...

Crystal and I arrive, a bit disoriented, at the newly created REP under a scorching desert sun. The rust-colored adobe pueblos just ahead offset the cloudless turquoise sky. The vista from Third Mesa, where the pueblo has existed since 1609, is expansive and inspiring. The distant San Francisco peaks rise off the desert floor and hover over the horizon like ships at sea. In the dusty central plaza the entire Hopi Nation has gathered, and nearly all are dressed as kachinas, symbolic manifestations of Hopi gods and spirit manifestations.

"This is paganism to the tens," I tell Crystal. Not being

familiar with pre-Caucasian America, Sonja doesn't know what to make of this spectacle, but the look on Crystal's face tells me that she is fascinated nonetheless. I *am* American (at least Amy is), but in all my life I have never seen anything like this. And not only are the Hopi dressed as fierce warriors, or sacred animals, or benevolent caretakers of the earth, but Kiz is also wearing a vibrant Native American costume—the 'Corn Woman'. I'm wondering just what she's got up her colorfully embroidered sleeve…

Since Kizmet will be participating directly in the ceremony we are here to observe, she has asked her old friend, the esteemed American writer Frank Waters, to show us around and give us an orientation of the Hopi community and of Hopi customs. In the literature of the American Southwest, Frank Waters is nothing short of an icon. Author of such titles as *The Book of the Hopi*, *Pumpkin Seed Point* and *The Man Who Killed the Deer* (I have read all these books and others), this dean of American letters and Indian lore is purportedly the only White man ever to be allowed by the Hopi into a kiva, their place of high worship. In PL, I know that Waters has been dead for more than a decade; but in VL he is alive and well. For Crystal's benefit, I access the Wikipedia page about Waters and place it in her cache to read for reference.

"Frank Waters was born on July 25, 1902, in Colorado Springs, Colorado to May Ione Dozier Waters and Frank Jonathon Waters. His father, who was part Cheyenne, was a key influence in Water's interest in the Native American experience. Frank Jonathon Waters took his son on trips to the Navajo Reservation in New Mexico in 1911, described by Frank in his book *The Colorado.*

Waters continued his education at Colorado

College in Colorado Springs. He studied engineering but left school before receiving a degree. Between 1925 and 1935, he worked on his first novel, *Fever Pitch* (1930) and a series of autobiographical novels beginning with *The Wild Earth's Nobility* (1935). In 1936, he moved to Taos, New Mexico where he completed a biography of W.S. Stratton, *Midas of the Rockies*. Waters' masterpiece, *The Man Who Killed the Deer*, was published in 1942.

In 1947, Waters purchased property at nearby Arroyo Seco, New Mexico, and married Jane Somervell. He served as editor-in-chief of Taos's bilingual newspaper, *El Crepusculo* from 1949-1951, and as a reviewer for the Saturday Review of Literature from 1950-1956.

In 1953, Waters was awarded the Taos Artists Award for Notable Achievement in the Art of Writing. Waters also held positions as information consultant for Los Alamos Scientific Laboratory, New Mexico, and for the City of Las Vegas, Nevada, (1952-1956). He held a variety of other jobs, including writer-in-residence, Colorado State University, Fort Collins (1966); and director, New Mexico Arts Commission, Santa Fe, New Mexico, (1966-68). On December 23, 1979, Waters married Barbara Hayes. He continued to write and make public appearances. He and his wife lived alternately in Arroyo Seco and Tucson, Arizona. Frank Waters died at his home in Arroyo Seco on June 3, 1995."

"It is a great honor to meet you, Mr. Waters," I tell him as he approaches us.

"Welcome to Hopiland," he says as he shakes both our

hands. "And you can call me Frank."

In her VL invitation, Kiz has cited the words of the Hopi Elder, Grandfather David. I show the invitation to Frank, and he reads the words of the Hopi Elder aloud:

"'You have been telling the people that this is the Eleventh Hour, but now you must go back and tell the people that this is *the* Hour. And there are things to be considered...

'Where are you living? What are you doing? What are your relationships. Are you in the right alignment? Where is your water? Know your garden. It is time to speak your Truth. Create your community. Be good to each other. And do not look outside yourself for the leader. This could be a good time!

'There is a river flowing now very fast. It is so great and swift that there are those who will be afraid. They will try to hold on to the shore. They will feel they are torn apart and will suffer greatly.

'Know the river has its destination. We must let go of the shore, push off into the middle of the river, keep our eyes open, and our heads above water. I say, see who is in there with you and celebrate! At this time in history, we are to take nothing personally, least of all ourselves. For the moment that we do, our spiritual journey comes to a halt.

'The time for the lone wolf is over. Gather yourselves! Banish the word struggle from your attitude and your vocabulary. All that we do now must be done in a sacred manner, and in celebration. We are the ones we've been waiting for.'"

My unspoken question: Are these lines merely the ravings of a senile old man, or does this one hundred and fourteen-year-old Indian actually know something that we don't?

As Frank directs us to a ladder leading onto the rooftop of one of the pueblo buildings, the drama of the event unfolding before us becomes apparent. Thousands of Indians, their faces and bodies painted, and dressed in garish costumes and fearsome headdresses, prepare to dance a dance prescribed by their ancestors, the ancient Aztecs, a thousand years ago. Both Crystal and I are stunned speechless by the spectacle, so Frank fills in a few details about the Hopi.

"Oraibi was actually founded sometime before the year 1100, which makes it the oldest continually inhabited settlements in North America," he tells us. "But Old Oraibi remained unknown to European explorers until about 1540 when Spanish explorer Don Pedro de Tovar (who was part of the Coronado expedition) encountered the Hopi while searching for the legendary Seven Cities of Cibola, or the Lost Seven Cities of Gold.

"The Hopi are the most mystical of Native American people, and while they welcome visitors to the village, they remain secretive about their culture and their beliefs."

"But you were able to penetrate their culture," I observe.

"Only to a point," Frank explains. "It's true that I was told things and shown things—the sacred Hopi tablet, for instance, foretelling the return of the *Pahana*, the long lost White Brother. The tablet that I saw is a grayish marble with rosy highlights, broken away at its top. (Marble, you understand, is found nowhere in the vicinity of Northern Arizona.) The Hopi say that though he has been gone a long, long time on a mission to the east, he will return again, and at his coming the wicked will be destroyed and a new age of peace, the Fifth World, will begin. It is foretold that he will bring with him the missing part of the sacred stone, the other half of which is now in the possession of the Fire Clan. It is also said that he will come wearing red."

I look over at Frank, and he is dressed all in red. (Gulp!)

"Do you have the broken piece of the stone?" I ask.

Waters' limpid blue eyes gaze upon the distant horizon, their color a reflection of the infinite sky. "Is the Fifth World a real place?" he asks rhetorically. "Or is it merely a manifestation of hope and superstition?"

I guess I have my answer.

Just what Kiz has cooked up here, and what Crystal and I have gotten ourselves into, we shall know within the hour. Meanwhile, Frank continues to tell us about these enigmatic Indians. Both Crystal and I now want to learn as much as we can, because if we are also to be thrust into this so-called Fifth World, like it or not, a little orientation might serve us well.

"The legend of the *Pahana* is intimately connected with the ancient Aztec story of Quetzacoatl, the horned or plumed serpent," Frank continues. "Both cultures draw vast amounts of their mythology from the Mayan civilization, and in fact, the Hopi concept of time is Mayan in origin. And the Mayan calendar is more accurate than the Roman one."

"Doesn't the Mayan calendar end on the winter solstice of the Roman year 2012?" Crystal asks.

I swallow hard at her observation. Remember, I tell myself, this is VL, not… But of course by now I know that reality is not grounded in one dimension.

Frank then brings us back to the present moment: "Hopi legend tells that what we know as the current earth is the Fourth World—what you call PL, I believe. The story essentially says that in each of the previous worlds, the people, though originally happy, eventually became irreverent and lived contrary to the laws of nature—what you call NL, right? They fought one another and would not live in harmony. Spider Woman then led the righteous into the next world—a higher world. Physical changes occurred in the people themselves, and in the environment of the next world. In some stories, these former worlds were then destroyed along with their iniquitous inhabitants, whereas in others the good people were simply led away from the chaos that had been created as a result of their own actions.

"Two main versions exist as to the Hopi's emergence

into the present Fourth World. The more prevalent is that Spider Woman caused a hollow reed to grow into the sky, and it emerged in the Fourth World at the *sipapu*. The people then climbed up the reed into this world, emerging from the earth's naval. The location of the *sipapu* is said to be the Grand Canyon."

As Frank's voice falls, the rise of a drumbeat replaces his tutorial. Thousands of Hopi dressed as various kachina spirits representing the forces of nature: rain, stars, animals—even watermelon—move to the center of the plaza to begin the dance. As the beating of the drums grows louder, a dozen young men dressed only in loincloths dance into the center of the plaza with live rattlesnakes in their mouths. They dance round and round the central kiva before another group approaches to take the writing serpents from the clenched jaws of the dancers. Not a single dancer has been bitten, nor have the handlers. Once relieved of their burden, the young men enter the kiva, and they do not come out. The rattlesnakes are then released into the desert to return to their habitat in the center of the earth.

The drumbeat grows louder as more dancers join the rhythmic ritual. A chant rises up from others still waiting to join the procession, and together the beating drums and chanting voices call to a force not known by White men. Over the distant peaks of the San Francisco Mountains, thunderheads emerge, layer upon blackening layer, toward the heavens. The beat goes on. The dance continues. And the consuming power of a feverish trance envelopes the entire mesa.

One by one, each dancer kneels down before the priest that guards the entrance to the kiva, and one after another each is blessed then disappears inside the circular temple. Down the ladder they climb, but none re-emerge.

"What's inside the kiva?" Crystal asks Frank.

"Not much of anything," he tells her. "Just a deep hole at the center—*sipapu!*"

At that moment, I spy Kiz in the line of dancers. I almost don't recognize her because she is wearing the costume of the Corn Woman kachina. I want to call out to her, ask her what she thinks she's doing, and tell her not to go inside the kiva. But the drums and the chanting are far too loud for me to be heard. And now, the clouds are gathering overhead—big, dark ominous clouds, the kind that can unleash a torrent, a deluge, a FLOOD!

Whoosh...

Just as Kiz reaches the priest for a blessing, she looks for a nanosecond (or is it for eternity?) at me and at Crystal. The look in her eye is filled with fire. Her body shakes in a trance that is at once haunting and commanding. Don't do it! I want to shout. Don't go in there! But my voice is frozen in the desert heat. My body is numb with the impending finality of the event. I look to Frank for help, but Frank is gone.

Perhaps to deliver the missing part of the stone tablet...

Suddenly, there is a flash of lightning followed by a tremendous crack of thunder. The skies open and the rain comes pouring down in sheets. The Hopi dancers turn their heads in unison towards the sky, and their faces are pelted with raindrops. Is this the end of the Fourth World? Are my relationships right? Is my garden tended? Where is Grandfather David? Has he already entered the kiva and descended through *sipapu* into the Fifth incarnation? Should Crystal and I join the dance? Or is there still time?

Having received the blessing of the Hopi priest, Kizmet turns her back and heads for the kiva ladder. "She's going to go in there," I say to Crystal in desperation, "and there's nothing I can do to stop her."

Step by deliberate step, my friend Kizmet Aurora (Cassandra Stephens) disappears into the kiva, and I know I will never see her again.

15
SMOKE ON THE WATER

WINTER IS COMING IN SEATTLE. I can always tell, because clear blue skies give way to an overcast dome, and a procession of rainy days that lasts until spring always follows. It has been raining for three straight weeks now, except it is only June.

Seattle Harbor is up eighteen inches and is still rising. Mr. Wang at the fish market says it's an omen. I am inclined to agree. I know what I saw when the rains came at Old Oraibi. The village at the top of Third Mesa is now an island. If downtown Seattle floods, Mr. Wang will probably close his stall and maybe even go home to his wife in China. What would Amy do for a job then?

Sonja says that Tivoli Gardens in Copenhagen is flooded, too. People all over Europe are beginning to panic. In Holland, the dikes are under stress and in danger of failing. Several Greek islands have already disappeared. Liverpool is being battered by huge waves, and the coast of Normandy is suffering severe erosion.

Here in America, New Orleans is a vast sewer

system…again. Manhattan is at times a canal city, like Venice used to be… Virginia Beach is long gone. In Florida, the Everglades are coming back to life. Strangely, nobody is even talking about evacuations. In fact, no one in government is saying jack shit. It's like the whole world is holding its breath. Waiting for what? Nobody knows.

…A comet to come and smash into earth and create a nuclear winter lasting a thousand years or more… Another Great Flood… A nuclear accident that will make Chernobyl look like the first sneeze of the cold season… On the radio I hear that a three thousand mile ribbon of the Atlantic Ocean stretching from Florida almost to Norway is on fire.

So we haven't been spending nearly as much time in VL lately. The situation as it is developing in PL seems to be commanding everybody's attention, and that's understandable. I haven't heard from Iggy for a while, nor have I seen Omar or the Quinngen. But I did get a PM from Filo the other day telling me that the 'Virtual Life Security Plan' is underway and will soon be completed. That's good news, I guess. But if everything goes *whoosh*, then it's not going to matter anyhow, because without PL people to operate computers, VL will be a static world. Unless Theo Ola has managed to figure out something that he's not sharing with me…

And Sonja has begun sending me (Amy Birkenstock) emails, which is uncharacteristic to say the least. In the past, though Crystal and I have been best friends in VL for more than two years now, Sonja has always kept her PL business to herself. The emails are highly personal and quite reflective in tone. Something's up with my friend; something's rotten in the State of Denmark, I fear. I don't know how to respond to her melancholic mood. And mine is not much better.

Lately, my life as a VL greeter has been a whirlwind, because thousands of new people are signing on every day. I suppose it's because of all the bad news in PL. For example, just since yesterday I've been subjected to social chaos in Bangalore, erosion of the Queensland coastline in Australia, the devastating agricultural effects of a late May freeze in southern Florida, noxious gas coming from Mount Fuji in Japan (nobody seems to know exactly what it is; or at least if they do, they're not saying), and the sudden widening of the San Andreas Fault in California. Not to mention the ridiculous ads which have suddenly surfaced on TV, and on the Internet as well. How about a mid-winter golfing vacation in the Scottish Highlands? Or skiing in Honduras? (Iggy might like that.) Or, if you just can't get away right now, be sure to get your disaster survival kit from Wal-Mart, just $99.99! I mean you can only stand to watch so much destruction before you have to do something positive.

Crystal is doing double duty, too. She had never worked as a VL greeter in the past, but most who are highly experienced in Virtual Life are taking their turn. It's the least we can do. In a way, it's like processing refugees. Most of the new seedlings are not only uncertain and disoriented, but scared as well. I get the feeling that they are not here in VL as a first choice, but rather as a last chance. I hope they can adjust.

On a more positive note, I received a PM yesterday from Igloo Iceman asking me to meet him at one o'clock today at Dirty Nellie's Pub. "I have something important to tell you" the note said. So I'm taking some time off from my duties to see my old friend the iceman. I wonder what he's up to…

It's a typical day in VL—sunny, warm, birds singing in the trees. As I once said, every day in VL is like living in California—or at least what California once was. When I arrive at Dirty Nellie's, Iggy is already sitting on the patio drinking a beer, so I take a seat at the table. When the waitress comes, I order a cup of tea (my drink of choice lately). "What brings you out of the mountains?" I say. "Need a bit of warm air?"

367

"You've got to be kidding," he smirks. He rolls up his sleeve to show me his tan line.

"Who would have thought?" I say.

"The truth is, Fiz, I'm under water up there," he says as he swallows half a mug of beer.

"It's that bad?" I ask.

"First it was just the bottom floor of my house, so I moved to the second floor. But now the second floor is submerged as well. So I guess I'm homeless."

"Do you need a place to crash?" I offer.

"Thanks," he says, smiling. "But that's not why I asked you to meet me here today."

"Really," I insist. "You can stay at my place for as long as you need to. It's not like I take up all the space."

"No, I'm staying on the boat now. It's finished, you know."

"I knew you were making fast progress," I say. "When did you finish?"

"Only last week," he tells me.

"So, what are your plans?" I ask.

"Well," he says, "I'm ready to launch."

"No kidding," I say. "Well, watch out for icebergs…"

"Very funny, Fizzy Oceans!" he laughs. "And I would steer clear, if there were any left. But the truth is that the Bearing Straight is ice-free for the first time in recorded history. So I shouldn't have any problem navigating."

"Are you sailing alone, Igloo?" I ask.

"As a matter of fact, I'm not. Do you remember the last time we talked—right here, I think it was—and I asked you to sign on as my First Mate?"

"Sure, I remember," I tell him.

"You begged off for your own reasons," he recalls. "Might have been the mistake of your life…"

I shrug. "We all place our bets and take our chances," I say.

"Don't get me wrong," says Igloo. "I have no hard feelings. Besides, it's all worked out for the better. I found my First Mate after all." Smiling broadly, he holds up his hand to show me a wedding ring on his finger.

"Iggy! Who's the lucky girl?"

"I think you know her," he says.

"Really? Who is she?"

"I married Cateret Rose," he says with a shy (and slightly sly) smile.

"No kidding, Iceman! Congratulations to you both!"

"Not the most likely match one might imagine," he muses. "I mean a Greenland Viking hermit and a Pacific Islander? Go figure…"

"That's VL for you," I observe.

"I guess…"

"So, Rose is your First Mate. Are you taking anyone else along for the ride?"

"Just the two of us on this voyage," he confirms. "Adam and Eve searching for the garden. You suppose we'll find it?"

"Sure… You'll find it if you search long enough."

"Well, one thing is certain," he says. "There's no going back for either of us."

A sad and repetitive reality in PL these days…

"There's just one thing I don't understand," I tell Iggy. "I mean I probably should understand, but it's never really been clear to me."

"What's that?" he asks.

"Are you launching the Ark in PL, or are you launching it in VL?" I question.

"Honest answer," says Iggy, "is that I really don't know anymore. The lines have blurred. Know what I mean, Fiz?"

"Sure," I say. "I mean, I think it's that way for some of us." Then, "I guess it's supposed to be that way."

"Part of the Grand Plan, you mean?" he asks.

"Oh, I don't know if there's any Grand Plan, Iggy. I think we just make it up as we go along."

"Kind of sad, don't you think?"

"No, choice is not sad. Nor is serendipity… Look at you and Rose!"

"You've got a point there," he says. Then he smiles. Igloo Iceman is in love.

"Anyway, Iggy, I'm glad you brought me here today, even if it is to say good-bye."

"Do you really think this is good-bye, Fizzy?" he asks.

"In some ways… And for some things… It's okay, Ig."

"Yeah, I guess there's a whole new world out there waiting to be discovered," he postures.

"If we're lucky," I say.

If we're lucky…

Omar Paquero is really Theo Ola! Crystal writes in an IM.

What do you mean, 'really'? I write back.

Oh yeah, she types. :)

I have to admit that as PL collapses I'm wondering what will become of all these EMs. It's not like we can move about, or talk to one another, or do stuff without our PL bodies in front of our PCs. And if Crystal is right (though just where she comes by her information, I don't know) that Omar is 'really' Theo Ola walking through VL as an alternate emulation, then I really have to wonder what our chances might be of survival should PL go down the drain, *whoosh*.

My real fear, my utmost terror, is that I will have to say good-bye to Crystal, too. And to my Virtual Life! Some people in PL still call Physical Life 'real' life. Not me. My virtual life is my *real* life. This is where my friends are, where my life has real meaning. Crystal is my best friend, of course. She is the best friend I've ever had, the best friend anyone could ever hope to meet. Saying good-bye to Crystal would be like tearing out my own heart. I can't even bear the thought of it. Yet, I am saying good-bye to so many here in VL. Why? Because PL is failing—it's so obvious now—and because we just don't know what comes next. Or if anything comes next… I guess that depends on Theo. Or on Omar (God help us!), if Crystal is right...

But Sonja keeps writing me emails (as Sonja) telling me how bad things are becoming in Copenhagen. Streets are flooded, shops are closed, and even the toilets are backing up. It sounds dire, but it's not all that much better here in Seattle. Seawater (or salt water; I don't know if it comes from the sea) now comes out of my tap. The lower areas of the city never drain. The streetlights have been out since I can't remember when, and gas now costs more than two hundred fifty dollars per gallon!

Most people seldom go out of their houses. It's dangerous out there! The streets are virtually empty. The fish market has no customers because it has no fish. Mr. Wang said he was sorry to have to lay me off, but I knew it was coming. I'm still getting by, but for the life of me, I don't know how.

So maybe it's just a matter of time... Until the lights go out for good and we're sitting in the cold, cold darkness with our thumbs up our ass, and tears in our eyes, and wondering why we waited so long to see the 'forest for the trees'. Christ, it's not like the information we needed to save PL wasn't out there. It was! All along! No, this cannot be part of some Grand Plan. Not this!

And have you heard about the black cloud that has now covered all of Florida and blocked out the sun? Sunshine State no more! They say it's because the ocean is on fire—well, copy this, it's not the ocean that's on fire, it's the oil slick on top of the water that's burning!

But don't cry for me Argentina. Before the water reaches my eyes, I will be gone, safe and sound in Virtual Life, maybe at Dirty Nellie's, or at Quinn Town, or at my Van Gogh REP showing visitors Vincent's paintings, or at Open Books helping Crystal publish *Paradise Lost* (because I know she'll be in VL too). Or maybe I'll be writing my own VL memoir (lol)—who knows? Amidst all the devastation, and all the chaos, and all the tragedy, and all the tears, and all the prayers, I do know this: it is now certain—and perhaps always was inevitable—that PL is kaput, doomed, done for, finished, history.

Whoosh...

16
SINCE YOU DECIDED TO DROP BY…

WELCOME TO VIRTUAL LIFE!

Although I have to tell you, it's not all that I envisioned it to be. And there are so many things I still don't understand. Primarily, how is it that we (the EMs) don't need somebody behind a PC to move about, to interact, to create, and to pose questions? In short, how is it that we can function without our PL counterparts?

That's right: PL is no more; at least not in the present tense. Sure, I have memories of PL, but I can't really gain a sense of Amy's existence. I think she is not there anymore. Nor can I gain any sense whatsoever of Sonja, or Cassandra. Back in PL, even when I was not in close proximity with another person, I could still somehow sense his presence—at least it seemed that way. In PL, I guess sensuality actually went beyond the physical senses, which I probably already knew, but I still have no idea how that might have worked. Somebody a lot smarter than I might have a theory about that.

As for VL, I remember the good old days when all the

emulations were still connected to PL people. I'm as guilty as anybody who spent considerable time in VL, in that we made fun, or even belittled PL existence. We saw PL as a very literal world, one divested of meaningful metaphors and sophisticated symbols, a world caught up in materialism (PL certainly was the ultimate material world), one seriously lacking creativity (in the most essential sense of the word). In short, PL was all about acquisition, which was accomplished with money. How the money was obtained grew less and less important because it became a goal unto itself. Intrinsic value actually vanished. Imagine that! In VL, materialism was never a problem, because it was a non-material world. No actual land, or houses, or shops, or cars, or clothes, or books ever existed. What did exist in VL were symbolic representations of objects. And sure, we had money in VL, just as we do here in FL, but in both VL and in FL money is more or less a joke. Of course some people acquire loads of greenshoots— millions even! Perhaps they produced some 'commodity' that they could sell; or maybe they won the money in Virtual Vegas, like Kiz did; or maybe they got it playing the BloomEx market. But however they acquired it, chances are that they probably gave it away at first opportunity to somebody who had little or none, so that the person with less could use it to actualize some vision or project he had in mind. That's because in both VL and FL money is not the end game. Here the real currency is, and always has been, the currency of ideas.

In all fairness, though, PL was a world based on the carbon atom (just as Trick Walkman once articulated to me), whereas both VL and FL are based on the silicon atom. What does that mean? It means that PL was composed of organic compounds; VL did not, and FL does not depend on those compounds. In VL and FL our world, and everything in it including the 'people' are pixilated images projected through silicon chips. We don't need food, or water, or protein to survive. We might partake of such things symbolically, but they are merely references to our past lives in PL and NL. What I'm saying is that nothing in FL is 'real' in the PL sense. That wasn't wholly true in VL, because in VL we were still connected to our PL counterparts. In FL, that connection has been severed except for the odd memories we experience, and I must admit that even those are fading. I guess that happens with the passing of time. How much time, you ask? Beats me! Here in FL, time does not exist—at least not in the PL sense. Maybe that is because we do not experience physical degeneration—death. So our vision of self becomes rather infinite. That is unless something unforeseen might occur, as it did in PL. *Whoosh* was no joke when it actually came down.

But I have to tell you, also, that it's pretty lonely here in Future Life, which is why I say that it's not all that I expected it to be. You know how it is: EVERYBODY EXPECTS THE FUTURE TO BE GREAT. Why? Because it's supposed to be great, and because we want it to be great, and because we need it to be great to get us out of the messes we create, and because time moving forward is supposed to equal progress, which is supposed to be great, isn't it? Let me tell you this: time moving forward is not necessarily progress; it can also be a regression. That's basically what happened in PL. People understood how to move forward in PL; that wasn't the problem. The shit hit the fan when progress was confused with control, and with acquisition, which seems to come with control. At least that's how some of us saw it in PL. In VL, we learned it could be different. VL taught us that materialism was a game not worth playing. In VL, as I've said time and again, there were no 'real' materials, only representations of materials. We came to understand that materials were nothing more than the manifestations of ideas, and in VL we were able to manifest ideas at the drop of a hat. No impediments, so to speak. That's true here in FL, too. In fact, FL looks a lot like VL. They cross over, just as PL crossed over into VL. But crossover is not always natural—or at least it's not complete—not for everyone in every degree at the same rate of assimilation. No, it happens differently for different people. And that's natural, I guess. I mean, some people move from the literal world(s) into the metaphorical and symbolic world(s) kicking and screaming all the way. But if they want to survive the proverbial Flood, they move, inch by grudging inch, until they get it, until they finally come to understand that the material universe is a whole lot less 'real' than they might have thought, and that it is essentially composed of the projections of what is real: ideas. That's it! That's metaphor; that's symbolism! How else can I describe it?

Still, I tend to long for the VL days when Crystal and I were feverishly trying to republish the world's great literature, and when I was recreating the world and works of Vincent Van Gogh, and when we could all go to the VBV to hear lectures presented by the emulations of PL's visionaries, and when Igloo Iceman would come into VL via Broadband from his home in Greenland to update us on the melting glaciers, or when we'd run into Omar Paquero in Quinn Town and he would greet us comically in Spanish: "*Buenos dias, señoritas!*" I miss being able to transfer in the blink of an eye to the VL recreations of PL places: of course those REPS still exist here in FL, but somehow their vitality is gone along with PL. But what I miss most of all is my VL friends. You see, I'm here in FL (and I don't really know how I got here), but my friends— Crystal and Kizmet and Omar and Iggy and everybody else—are not here. At least I've not found them yet. What might have happened to them when PL collapsed? Did they not flee into VL as the waters rose? Or as volcanoes erupted, and fire moved over the landscape? Or as the parched earth sucked the fluidity right out of humanity? Or as the air became thick with soot and hydrocarbons and choked every living thing in PL? In essence, why did I survive the cataclysm and not them? Why me? Is there something essential that I'm not getting?

Another question: How is it that the emulations here in Future Life seem not to need their PL counterparts? As I said, I think Amy Birkenstock is dead (grieve now for Amy). In fact, I think everybody that ever existed in PL is now dead. And that's a pity! But what's the deal? How is it that we exist without them? What did Theo Ola manage to do before the end came for Physical Life? I'd like to know, because maybe knowing what he did would give me some understanding about why I survived (Did I actually survive?) and why I can't find any of the VL EMs I once knew and loved. As I said, Future Life is not all I thought it would be: it's a bit lonely here.

But since you decided to drop by, and since I just happen to be here, let me welcome you to Future Life. It's not all bad, you know…

"*Buenos dias*, Fizzy Oceans!"

OMG! It's Omar Paquero!

"Where did you come from?" I ask incredulously.

"Same place as you, I suspect," he says.

"Whatever… I'm just glad to finally run into somebody I knew from VL. Have you seen anybody else? I mean the old gang?"

"No," he says. "This is a new world."

"No kidding… Hey, Omar, just before PL went *whoosh*, I got an email from Crystal claiming that she'd found out that you are actually the emulation of Theo Ola. Is that true?"

"I am Omar Paquero. You are Fizzy Oceans. I have always been Omar. You have always been Fizzy. We will always be Omar and Fizzy."

"Yeah, and a Quinngen will always be a Quinngen…"

"*Si*…"

"It's just that sometimes people embody more than one EM, you know?"

"*Si*…"

"And I just thought that if you actually were Theo Ola—"

"I fear that Theo Ola is dead," says Omar.

"Hmmm… I never thought of that. Is that really possible?" I ask.

"I'm sure of it, Fizzy Oceans. Theo is dead."

"Just like Amy Birkenstock is dead," I admit.

"*Si…*" Omar lowers his head and scratches at the ground with his shoe. "But I think I might have seen Filo Farmer here in FL. *Si*, I'm sure of it! If I see him again, would you like me to tell him you're looking for him?"

"Filo Farmer? Oh, please yes, Omar!"

"If I run into him, I'll tell him to IM you."

"Yes, thank you. It's been great seeing you again, Omar."

"You too, Fizzy Oceans. Keep in touch."

"Yes, I will. I will!"

"*Buenos dias, señorita!*"

"*Bien venidos*, Omar Paquero!"

What a relief! Seeing Omar I mean… It's good to know that someone besides me has made it through from VL to Future Life. I mean it's good to know that it's possible… But of course it's possible, because I'm here! Wherever here might be…

Nevertheless, if Omar is here, others must be here too. It stands to reason. And my sense of reason seems to be intact. If Omar is correct, then Filo Farmer is also here. I really hope I run into Filo, because he might have answers to some of my BIG questions, unless, like me, his memories of Theo Ola are fading fast. Then I might never know…

What is it I want to know? Oh, yeah… I want to know why it is that the emulations here in Future Life don't need their PL counterparts. Still, I wonder if knowing the answer to that question is really so important. The longer I'm here, the less relevant it seems. Am I just forgetting who I really am? Or who I once was? Do we really have to navigate whatever existence seems real at the time in total blindness?

Maybe...

And maybe not! Maybe it's possible to live in all worlds at the same time, in full consciousness, and in full appreciation. What a concept! I'll have to give that one some thought...

I have to admit, I can't help returning time and again to all the old REPS where Crystal and Kiz and I used to hang out in VL. I could say that I don't know what I'm searching for in those all but abandoned places, but that would be a lie. What I'm searching for is a link with my past, even if it is a fairly recent past. I cannot return to PL, that's gone now. Nor would I want to if I could. I am a child of a transitional Age, of course. I may have been born into PL, but my true nature, and my talents, and even my revelation was revealed and came to fruition in Virtual Life. That's just the way it happened.

Stepping into Quinn Town I am reminded of the cave where Crystal and I often went to discuss our deepest emotional longings, as well as the very nature of our existence. That cave was certainly my VL womb. The fire inside is still burning, though here in FL nobody seems to be feeding or tending it. To me, that seems a shame, a matter of neglect. Abandonment is NOT an option. Yet it's almost as if the light of regeneration is being ignored, or at least neglected. I toss another log onto the fire then stir the ashes. A tear comes to my eye.

Then, outside, I hear a familiar sound (Jeff Beck blues riff). OMG! It must be Tooltech, the Quinngen! And his partner in crime, Ego Ectoplasm!

I leave the cave and look out across Sugarland. There they are, all right: the funny little kid that never talks and his invented sidekick with a generator for a back.

"Hey you guys!" I call to them.

"It's Fizzy Oceans," I hear Tooltech say to Ego as they approach.

I hop over sugary stepping-stones to meet them. As I arrive, Tooltech plays a blues fanfare on his Les Paul Jr.

"Am I ever glad to see you guys!" I say breathlessly.

"Hello, Fizzy Oceans," says the Quinngen.

"I've been here in FL for I don't know how long," I tell them. "I've been looking for everybody we knew in VL, but I was beginning to think that I was the only one that crossed over."

"No, we're here," says Tooltech.

"So I see. Have you seen anybody else? Crystal? Kizmet? Igloo Iceman?"

"No," says Tooltech.

"I don't know how I got here," I tell them.

Tooltech laughs like a child. "That's easy," he says.

"Then tell me, please," I implore him.

"Adaptability, that's it!"

"What do you mean?" I ask.

"Moving from one world to another one, or from one universe to another, adaptability is what's important. That's why Ego (aka AQ) made me as I am—for adaptability. You know, a Quinngen is always a Quinngen, and will always…"

"…be a Quinngen," I finish.

"A Quinngen is totally adaptable. Just like you, Fizzy Oceans."

"Like me?" (Eric Clapton blues riff played on Les Paul Jr.) "But I'm not even sure that I like it here. Or that I want to stay… I miss VL, don't you?"

"Moving from one universe to another ain't easy, girlie," says Tooltech. "Unless, of course, you are a…"

"…Quinngen," I finish again.

Tooltech laughs and gives me a Mustardseeds t-shirt. Then he plays a B.B. King riff on his guitar. Ego and Tooltech move off to do their business, whatever that might be, and I am again left alone.

Where might I go in this all-too-familiar yet wholly strange world called Future Life? I have the same facility to move from REP to REP that I had in VL, yet time and again, once I arrive at a familiar destination, I find that it not only looks a little odd, but that I am alone. Something's got to give here…

Finally, the IM comes from Filo Farmer. Happy to see that you've made it to FL, it says. When and where shall we meet?

Immediately I reply: Your EM will be a sight for sore eyes. Meet me at Open Books, asap.

How about right now?

:) I type.

I arrive first in front of the Open Books shop. But it's not like it was in VL. For one thing, all the lights are turned off and the door is locked. For another, Crystal is not there. Nor has she been there for some time. That's obvious because the greenshoots have not been collected from the donations box in front of the shop. I sit down on the steps to wait for Filo to arrive. The street is deserted; there's not a soul around.

At last Filo comes walking round the corner. Even though we only met once, somehow he seems like a long lost cousin. I greet him with a tender kiss on the cheek.

"I have a few questions to ask you," I tell him.

"In light of our one and only conversation, I'm sure you do," he says. "I'm happy to tell you whatever I can, Fizzy."

"Can you tell me where all my friends are?" I ask.

Filo sighs: "Not specifically, I'm afraid. But they might be on their way. It's hard to say. I know the transference is not yet complete. And it takes some longer than others, you know."

"I suspected that," I tell him.

"It's a whole new world, after all…"

"Right," I confirm. "But how did you do it, Filo?"

381

"How did I do what?" he asks, truly puzzled.

"How did you save us?"

"I was not the one who saved us," he says.

"Of course it was you," I maintain. "Who else had the vision? Or the power?"

"I'm not God, Fizzy. More like a low level beaurocrat. I think you're referring to Theo, not me."

"One and the same, I thought."

"Not exactly, though we were intimately connected," he explains. "Let's take a little walk together, and I'll tell you what I know. And what I don't…"

Filo and I walk first along the sea near the lighthouse where Crystal and I used to go for privacy, then up a trail leading to Grove Press Square. Mostly we are quiet, but he does have some important information for me.

"Just as it is for you and Amy, it is for me and Theo. I know you're feeling a bit lost without Amy. I'm feeling the same about losing Theo. FL may not be everything we hoped for, but we've got to make the best of it. We've got to enliven it, just as we did in VL. You told me that you thought it was important that we continue, and as I remember, you were pretty worried about PL. Rightly so, as it turned out. Theo heard what you were saying. He heard everything, you know. After all, VL is (was) *his* world; he invented it. He oversaw everything that went on. He even participated, through me and through other EMs."

"You mean Omar Paquero?" I ask.

"Omar and others," he says.

"Crafty, wasn't he?"

"Theo was brilliant. There's no doubt about that. But Theo is now dead. And there's no doubt about that either."

"But you're still here," I maintain.

"It's not the same as it was in VL," he tells me. "Here, I'm just like you, Fizzy. But I do know what happened at Seedbed Studios at the very end of PL."

"Do tell!" I implore.

"I relayed everything you said to me to Theo. He was very impressed—so much so that he got on the project right away. And it's a good thing he didn't wait, because as we both know, PL came down faster than anyone ever expected."

"*Whoosh*!" I exclaim.

"Precisely! But by then Theo already had the mainframes protected. They are encased in titanium vaults and buried seven stories underground out in the Mojave Desert. I don't even know the precise location. And I suspect that if I don't know where they are buried, neither does anyone else who has managed to bridge into FL. It may remain a mystery for centuries, or eons, or even forever!"

"Imagine that!" I gush.

"So that is why we are here in FL. It's all because of your foresight! You recognized how late it actually was in PL. And you spoke out. Theo heard you and he acted according to your wishes. That's about all I know."

"That's really amazing, Filo. But there's still one thing I don't understand."

"What's that?" he asks.

"Where is the power source?"

"Ah!" he says. "That is the really interesting part…"

"No shit, Sherlock."

We sit on a bench in front of the Writer's Pen Café. Nobody else is around. We are 'virtually' alone in Future Life talking about the demise of a universe.

"Finding the power to run the mainframes was not the issue," Filo explains. "In fact, they take minimal power to operate, and there is enough electricity out there—from the sun, the wind, and even emanating from the soil—to run those mainframes virtually forever. The bigger challenge, as I understand it, was how to re-animate the emulations that managed to bridge from VL into FL. Because of course in VL we had our PL counterparts…

All of whom had unlimited access to the PL power grid…
But once PL collapsed, and the power grid with it… Well,
I'm sure you see the problem.

"Theo and the engineers at Seedbed knew that we—the
EMs—would be on our own, not to mention dead as
anybody unfortunate enough to remain in PL at the end.
What they knew they had to do at Seedbed—and certainly
they understood that the time was growing short—was to
find the life source itself. So the engineers turned to the
one place on Earth where they might find the answer to
life's very essence, and they were in luck, because even
though it never became widely known to the general
public, the scientists working with the Large Hadron
Collider in Geneva, the largest and highest-energy particle
accelerator ever created in PL, had already addressed some
of the most fundamental questions of physics and nature.

"In March 2010, the first planned collisions took place
between two 3.5 TeV beams, which set a new world record
for the highest-energy man-made particle collisions. They
did indeed find the so-called God particle."

"You mean…"

"As it turns out, it was right in front of them (us) all the
time. But in light of everything we know now, that makes
perfect sense, doesn't it?"

"So you're saying we now know how to create life?"

"Not me. And not anyone in FL, I suspect. The
knowledge was gained in PL, and then lost almost as soon
as it became known. Ironic, don't you think? But we are
the beneficiaries. We 'live' here in FL. We are no longer
organic, so we no longer must depend on PL. We still can't
experience sensuality—that is the price of our loss, and of
our continuance. And like it was in VL, we still can't
procreate. But we are *alive!*"

"But I don't really feel alive," I tell him. "Not fully
alive…"

"Something we'll all have to work on," Filo concludes.
"But look on the bright side, Fizzy. We are the lucky

twelve million who survived the end of the world as we knew it!"

I guess he's right about that. But I sure wish I had a little help here. Does anybody know where I can find an FL greeter?

Visiting the old REPS is pretty depressing because, invariably, nobody's there. It's sort of like going back to a city you once knew and loved, except while you were away a neutron bomb went off leaving all the structures in perfect condition but vaporizing all the people.

Nevertheless, I decide to pay one more visit to Kiz's Hopiland REP, her recreation of Third Mesa in northern Arizona where the Hopi lived and waited for the end of the Fourth World and the beginning of the Fifth World. How prophetic were they? They not only saw it coming down in the present tense, but knew about it centuries ago. The Great White god had finally returned, bringing with him the missing part of their sacred tablet, and as a race they were certainly ready for what came next. That Frank Waters had turned out to be the one for whom the Hopi were waiting was ironic, to say the least. That Kizmet Aurora (aka Cassandra Stephens) had chosen to go down into that hole in the ground with them defied all reason—at least my sense of reason. Where she ended up is anybody's guess.

All that aside, I really like it here in Hopiland. Though it is silent now, the vista is expansive. Cylindrical red rocks stand like sentries against time itself. If I squint, I can almost see the Spanish soldiers marching on the settlement; I can see the ceremonial dances held each summer to welcome the kachinas back from their six-month sojourn at the San Francisco Peaks; and I can see the Hopi Elders convened in the kiva, divining the future and planning their escape into the Fifth World. Somehow Kiz had managed to include something of each dimension here: NL, PL, VL, FL (where I'm standing), and something else as well… Could it be that I sense something of the so-called Fifth World? Who knows? I may never know.

As I prepare to transfer away from the REP (where I might be going next I have no idea), I feel compelled to turn my attention to the kiva where thousands of Indians, as well as Kizmet and Frank Waters too, had disappeared during the VL ceremony just prior to the big meltdown in PL. Am I simply waxing nostalgic, or do I actually sense activity in the kiva? I move from my perch atop one of the pueblos to take a closer look. Then I hear it: chanting! Without warning, the first of the Hopi emerges from the *sipapu*, then another, and another, and still another. As each emerges, he kneels down upon the ground and offers his thanks. For he knows he has now emerged into the Fifth World. It is a new existence, a new life.

One by one, the Indians climb from the bowels of the earth into a promised world. At the center of the plaza they gather to wait for their brethren. I continue to watch the reunion, unnoticed. Finally, when all seven thousand members of the ancient tribe are gathered in the plaza, the final two pilgrims emerge from the womb: Frank Waters and Kizmet Aurora.

For the first time since I entered FL, I am overwhelmed with joy, because not only will I be reunited with my dear friend Kizmet, but I now know that another reunion is imminent—one with Crystal Marbella, my friend, collaborator, confidant and soul mate. I know I must return immediately to Open Books, because that is where I will find her.

On first glance of the OB shop I know that my instinct was correct. The lights have been turned on and I can see Crystal inside the shop working away as if nothing had gone wrong, as if nothing at all had happened. As I walk in through the open doorway, no words are necessary—only hugs and kisses. Lots of hugs and lots of kisses! There's no point in recounting what happened in PL. It was bad; what else needs be said? And we both know that, strictly speaking, we are no longer in VL. This is Future Life, a new world with new rules—and a few of the old ones too! Somehow we have both managed to survive.

"I missed you so much," I tell her as we embrace. I start to weep, and Crystal weeps too.

"I know," she says. "I would have been here sooner, but I lost my way."

"It's okay," I say. "You're here now."

"Yes, we're both here now. And I guess here and now is all there really is anyhow."

"So, what are we supposed to do?" I ask Crystal.

"I suppose we resume exactly where we left off," she says. "We move fearlessly into the future, with all our doubts, and our insecurities, and our misperceptions, and our neuroses, and our ignorance."

"Don't forget our passions!" I add.

"Those too," she confirms.

"Yes, we must try," I agree. "We must try to become better people, to show greater sympathy for our fellow (human) beings. We must evolve (though I think a Higher Power already has that one all worked out for us). And we must have faith, not only in ourselves, but in our world(s). We must be willing to embrace new realities, and even new universes, because I suspect a new one is born every single day, if not moment-to-moment. Yes, wherever we find ourselves, we have to keep trying. Really, what else is there to do?"

"I think you've got it, Fizzy," says Crystal as she begins to sweep the detritus of two former worlds out of the Open Books shop. "Got any ideas for our next project?"

"Only one," I tell her.

"What's that?" she asks with a knowing smile.

"We've got to get started documenting VL," I say.

"Because you just never know what might come next."

"Right you are!" Crystal proclaims. "We'll get on it first thing tomorrow."

And we both laugh at her ever-so-slight procrastination, because we know that time is on our side, and that today (and everyday) is ours.

So, my dear friends, that's about it. Thanks for listening to my story, and I'll see you all in ML—Meta Life. (Don't worry, it's not an insurance company; I promise.)

Until then,

Love to All,

Fizzy Oceans (lol)

ACKNOWLEDGEMENTS

In Chapter 4, profile of Burning Man® derived from http://en.wikipedia.org/wiki/Burning_Man.

In Chapter 6, profile, history and quotes from Mark Twain derived from http://www.twainquotes.com/quotesatoz.html and http://en.wikipedia.org/wiki/Mark_Twain.

In Chapter 7, profile and history of Dion Fortune (Violet Mary Firth) derived from http://en.wikipedia.org/wiki/Dion_Fortune, http://www.innerlight.org.uk/dion/DionFort.html, http://www.themystica.com/mystica/articles/f/fortune_dion.html and http://www.answers.com/topic/dion-fortune as well as from the books *Spiritualism and Occultism* by Dion Fortune, *Psychic Self-Help* by Dion Fortune and *The Mystical Qabala* by Dion Fortune.

In Chapter 8, history and observations concerning the Cateret Islands derived from http://transcripts.cnn.com/TRANSCRIPTS/0912/20/se.

01.html. Profile and history of Bibliotheca Alexandria derived from http://www.helleniccomserve.com/revivalofbibliotheca.html. Profile and history of Ancient Babylon derived from http://en.wikipedia.org/wiki/Hanging_Gardens_of_Babylon, http://en.wikipedia.org/wiki/Babylon, http://en.wikipedia.org/wiki/Code_of_Hammurabi and http://en.wikipedia.org/wiki/Babylonian_law. History of the Seven Wonders of the Ancient World quoted and derived from http://en.wikipedia.org/wiki/Seven_Wonders_of_the_Ancient_World. Profile and history of Saddam Hussein quoted from http://en.wikipedia.org/wiki/Saddam_Hussein.

In Chapter 9, profile of Jacques Ives Cousteau derived from *The Human, the Orchid, and the Octopus: Exploring and Conserving Our Natural World* by Jacques Cousteau and Susan Schiefelbein, Bloomsbury USA (October 30, 2007).

In Chapter 10, the comments of C. Ray Nagin, Mayor of New Orleans, quoted from *"When the Levees Broke: A Requiem in Four Acts"*: A Film in Four Acts by Spike Lee, HBO Productions, 2006

In Chapter 11, Matthew Taylor's comments extracted from "Parting Today's Red Sea: Integrative Power, Transformation, and Compassion in the Israeli/Palestinian Conflict" by Matthew Taylor, used with permission from the author.

ABOUT THE AUTHOR

David A. Ross was born January 6, 1953 in Chicago, Illinois. He attended William Rainy Harper College for three semesters before dropping out. After being excused from military service on a physical deferment, he moved to a remote area of northern Idaho, where he lived a subsistence lifestyle in a rustic log cabin without plumbing or electricity for more than a year. Returning to Chicago, he worked for Follett Publishers for a short time before relocating to Denver, Colorado. There he taught music for twenty-five years, wrote three unpublished novels, and worked as an associate editor for *Southwest Art Magazine* before moving first to Arizona then to New Mexico.

From 1987 through 2000, he engaged in a series of twelve extended trips to Europe, as well as several to the South Pacific. In 2001, he relocated permanently to Greece where he currently lives with his wife, author Kelly Huddleston, and works as an author, editor and Internet developer. *The Virtual Life of Fizzy Oceans* is his sixth published novel. Also to his credit is *Sacrifice and the Sweet Life*, a collection of short stories and poetry, and *Good Morning Corfu: Living Abroad Against All Odds*, a memoir.

David A. Ross

www.ingramcontent.com/pod-product-compliance
Lightning Source LLC
Chambersburg PA
CBHW060811030726
47503CB00002B/442